高等学校英语专业系列教材
Textbook Series for Tertiary English Majors

高 等 学 校 英 语 专 业 系 列 教 材　求知 STEM
Textbook Series for Tertiary English Majors

总 主 编　石 坚

副总主编　黄国文　陈建平　张绍杰　蒋洪新

编委单位（排名不分先后）

广东外语外贸大学	华南农业大学
广西大学	陕西师范大学
云南大学	武汉大学
中山大学	贵州大学
中南大学	贵州师范大学
四川大学	重庆大学
东北师范大学	重庆邮电大学
西安外国语大学	湖南师范大学
西安交通大学	……
华中师范大学	

策　　划　张鸽盛　饶邦华　周小群

高等学校英语专业系列教材
Textbook Series for Tertiary English Majors

STEM 求知

总 主 编：石 坚
副总主编：黄国文 陈建平 张绍杰 蒋洪新

文学研究方法

A

Approaches to the Study of Literature

＋ 骆 洪 编著

重庆大学出版社

内容提要

本教材介绍文学研究的基本方法,重点放在英美文学作品的阅读与分析之上,强调以文本细读为核心,综合实践文学阅读的不同层面,涉及小说、诗歌和戏剧三个文类。提倡在文本细读的基础上,尝试对作品进行"体验""阐释"和"评价",结合文学的基本要素对作品进行研究分析。本教材以"方法"为主,在选用文学作品时仍以英美文学名篇为主,所选作品的语言和内容具有代表性,有的还具有较强的时代感,且难易适中。本教材主要针对英语专业的本科生,也可以作为英语专业研究生或广大英美文学爱好者的参考读本。

图书在版编目(CIP)数据

文学研究方法/骆洪编著.--重庆:重庆大学出版社,2018.10

求知高等学校英语专业系列教材

ISBN 978-7-5689-1251-8

Ⅰ.①文…　Ⅱ.①骆…　Ⅲ.①英国文学—文学研究—高等学校—教材②文学研究—美国—高等学校—教材

Ⅳ.①I561.06②I712.06

中国版本图书馆 CIP 数据核字(2018)第 157237 号

文学研究方法

骆　洪　编著

责任编辑:陈　亮　　版式设计:杨　琪

责任校对:邬小梅　　责任印制:赵　晟

*

重庆大学出版社出版发行

出版人:易树平

社址:重庆市沙坪坝区大学城西路 21 号

邮编:401331

电话:(023) 88617190　88617185(中小学)

传真:(023) 88617186　88617166

网址:http://www.cqup.com.cn

邮箱:fxk@ cqup.com.cn(营销中心)

全国新华书店经销

重庆市正前方彩色印刷有限公司印刷

*

开本:787mm×1092mm　1/16　印张:16　字数:379 千

2018 年 10 月第 1 版　　2018 年 10 月第 1 次印刷

ISBN 978-7-5689-1251-8　定价:49.00 元

总　序

进入 21 世纪,高等教育呈现快速扩展的趋势。我国高等教育从外延式发展过渡到内涵式发展后,"质量"已成为教育改革与发展的关键词。由国务院颁布的《国家中长期教育改革和发展规划纲要(2010—2020)》(以下简称《纲要》)明确要求狠抓本科教育人才培养存在的主要问题,厘清高等教育人才培养目标、理念、社会需求,制订本科教学培养模式、教学内容和方法、质量保障与评估机制,切实提高人才培养的质量。我国英语专业在过去的数十年中经过几代人的努力,取得了显著的成绩和长足的发展。特别是近年来随着经济社会的快速发展和对外交流活动的增多,"一带一路"倡议的提出和"讲好中国故事"的需要,英语专业的学科地位也随之大大提升,其规模目前发展得十分庞大。英语专业虽然经历了一个"跨越式""超常规"的发展历程,但规模化发展带来的培养质量下滑、专业建设和人才需求出现矛盾、毕业生就业面临巨大挑战等严峻的现实表明,英语专业的教育、教学与育人又到了一个不得不改的关键时刻。

《纲要》在强调狠抓培养质量的同时,也提出了培养"具有国际视野、通晓国际规则、能参与国际事务和国际竞争"人才的战略方针。基于这样的战略需求,外语专业教学指导委员会明确提出了人才"多元培养,分类卓越"的理念。基于这样的理念,即将颁布的《英语专业本科教学质量国家标准》(以下简称《国标》)对英语专业本科的现有课程设置提出新的改革思路:英语专业课程体系包括公共课程、专业核心课程、专业方向课程、实践环节和毕业论文(设计)五个部分;逐步压缩英语技能课程,用"内容依托式"课程替代传统的英语技能课程,系统建设语言学、文学、文化、国别研究等方面的专业课程。

自 2001 年开始,在重庆大学出版社的大力支持下,我们成立了由华中、华南、西南和西北以及东北地区的知名专家、学者和教学一线教师组成的"求知高等学校英语专业系列教材"编写组,以《高等学校英语专业英语教学大纲》为依据,将社会的需求与培养外语人才的全面发展紧密结合,注重英语作为一门专业的学科系统性和科学性,注重英语教学和习得的方法与规律,培养学生能力和育人并举,突出特色和系列教材的内在逻辑关系,反映了当时教学改革的新理念并具有前瞻性,建立了与英语专业课程配套的新教材体系。"求知高等学校英语专业系列教材"经历了 10 余年教学实践的锤炼,通过不断的修订来契合教学的发展变化,在教材的整体性和开放性、学生基本技能和实际应用能力的培养、学生的人文素质和跨文化意识的培养三方面有所突破。对于这套系列教材的开发建设工作,我们一直在探讨新的教学理念、模式,探索英语专业人才培养的新路子。今天,我们以《国标》为依据,回顾我们过去十多年在教学改革上所做的努力,我们欣慰地看到我们的方向是契合英语专业学科定位和发展的。随着《国标》指导思想的明确,为了适应英语专业学科课程设置的进一步调整,我们对"求知高等学校英语专业系列教材"进行了新一轮的建设工作。

全新的系列教材力求在以下方面有所创新：

第一，围绕听、说、读、写、译五种能力的培养来构建教材体系。在教材内容的总体设置上，颠覆以往"以课程定教材"的观念，不再让教材受制于刻板的课程设置体系，而是引入Program理念，根据《国标》中对学生的能力要求，针对某方面的具体能力编写对应的系列教材。读写和听说系列不再按照难度区分混合编排题材，而是依据文体或专业性质的自然划分，分门别类地专册呈现，便于教师在教学中根据实际需要搭配组合使用。例如，阅读教材分为小说类、散文类、新闻类等；口语教材分为基本表述、演讲、辩论等，并专题成册。

第二，将五种能力的提升融入人文素养的综合提升之中。坚持英语专业教育的人文本位，强调文化熏陶。在跨学科新专业不断涌现的背景下，盲目追求为每种新专业都专门编写一套教材，费时费力。最佳的做法是坚持英语专业核心教材的人文性，培养学生优秀的语言文化素养，并在此基础上依照专业要求填补相关知识上的空缺，形成新的教材配比模式和体系。

第三，以"3E"作为衡量教材质量的标准。教材的编写上，体现Engaging, Enabling, Enlightening的"3E"功能，强调教材的人文性与语言文化综合能力的培养，淡化技能解说。

第四，加入"微课""翻转课堂"等元素，便于课堂互动的开展。创新板块、活动的设计，相对减少灌输式的lecture，增加学生参与的seminar。

我们希望通过对这套系列教材的全新修订和建设，落实《国标》精神，继续推动高等学校英语专业教学改革，为提高英语专业人才的培养质量探索新的实践方法，为英语专业的学生拓展求知的新空间。

"求知高等学校英语专业系列教材"编委会
2017 年 6 月

前 言

众所周知,文学阅读与读者的情感和思想紧密相连,阅读需要读者的积极参与。在阅读过程中,读者往往会将其情感反应与生活经历结合起来,对文学的内容与形式进行思考与评价。读者还会结合文本中的具体事例,对体现文本诸要素的内容做出反应,进行阐释和评价。文学阅读就是读者与作品、作家互动的过程,而读者与文本及其作者的互动也具有相应的特征。本教材旨在对文学研究的基本方法进行介绍,重点放在英美文学作品的阅读与分析之上,强调以文本细读为核心,综合实践文学阅读的不同层面,涉及小说、诗歌和戏剧三个文类。

本教材的编写深受罗伯特·狄亚尼《文学:小说、诗歌、剧本的研读》(Robert DiYanni. *Literature*:*Reading Fiction*,*Poetry*,*and Drama*[M]. Compact Edition. Boston:McGraw-Hill Companies,Inc.,2000.)一书的启发。本教材的总体设计框架借鉴该书关于文学作品阅读的3个基本步骤或3种基本方法,即"体验""阐释"和"评价"。这3个步骤是文学作品阅读最基本的方法。"体验"指的是读者对作品作出的情感反应,更多的是主观印象(即"我的感受"或作品"对我的影响"、让"我展开什么样的联想"等,涉及个人或与他人共享的经验);"阐释"指对作品进行知性思维与分析,主要针对作品的意义而言(即作品"表达什么样的意义"和"为什么是这样的意义"等,而作品的意义既是文本蕴含的信息又是读者解读的结果);"评价"主要涉及对作品作出的价值判断(读者结合自己的社会、伦理、文化等方面的价值观对作品的内容,尤其是其中所涉的价值观作出评价)。值得注意的是,在实际阅读和分析的过程中,这3个步骤看似相互区别但实则紧密联系,而且发生的顺序也并非是固定的,"体验"的同时也在"阐释","阐释"免不了作出"评价"。

同时,为更好地理解作品,做到合理的阐释与评价,读者必须深入了解文学的基本要素及其特征。具体言之,对不同文类(小说、诗歌、戏剧)的基本要素进行分析和探讨也是文学研究的重要方法之一。本教材在介绍文学研究的总体方法("三步骤")的同时,也重点探讨和分析不同文类的基本要素,如小说的情节、人物、背景、视点、主题和语言风格等,诗歌的用语、意象、句法、结构、语气、语调、韵律和主题等,戏剧的对话、场景、情节、人物、舞台指示和主题等。

作为英语专业文学研究的基础教材,为了便于学生更好地了解不同部分的内容,掌握基本的研究分析方法,本教材各部分末尾均附有相应的思考练习题。这样编排旨在启发学生对所学的内容进行思考,进一步加深对所学内容的印象。鉴于各种考虑,本教材没有提供相应的"参考答案",而且这些思考题也很难直接从教材中找到全部答案。不过,各部分所探讨和分析的内容可以作为答题的重要参考。与此同时,学习者也需要做进一步的资料查询和阅读分析,研读更多的资料之后将"答案"整理成文。这样或许会更有利于激发学习者的积极性,使其主动参与到相应的文学作品阅读活动之中,学会并掌握好基本的文学写作方法。

本教材主要分为四部分:第一部分介绍文学的基本内涵和文学的类别、阅读文学作品的乐趣、文学研究的基本方法("体验""阐释"和"评价")、文学作品的主题分析等;第二部分为小说研究,涉及小说的内涵和分类、小说的"体验""阐释"和"评价"、小说基本要素的分析;第三部分为诗歌研究,涉及诗歌的内涵和分类、诗歌的"体验""阐释"和"评价"、诗歌基本要素的分析;第四部分为戏剧研究,涉及戏剧的内涵和分类、戏剧的"体验""阐释"和"评价"、戏剧基本要素的分析。各个部分相互之间有一定的独立性,但同时又是有机联系的,共同构成本教材的整体全貌。

本教材主要针对英语专业的本科生,也可以作为英语专业研究生或广大英美文学爱好者的参考读本。

由于编著者水平有限,书中难免有不尽如人意之处,敬请广大读者批评指正。

骆　洪

2017 年 10 月 15 日

Contents

Introduction   **1**

    What Is Literature? / 1

    Types of Literature / 2

    The Pleasure of Reading Literature / 3

    The Basic Approaches to the Study of Literature / 12

    Understanding the Theme of Literary Works / 14

Part 1   Fiction

Chapter 1   **An Overview**   **18**

Chapter 2   **Types of Fiction**   **19**

    Short Fiction and Long Fiction / 19

    The Short Novel / 24

Chapter 3   **Reading Stories: the Basic Approaches**   **27**

Chapter 4   **Elements of Fiction**   **43**

    Plot / 54

    Character / 66

    Point of View / 67

    Setting / 74

    Language and Style / 84

    Imagery / 101

    Symbol and Irony / 103

    Allegory / 106

    Theme / 109

Part 2   Poetry

Chapter 5   **An Overview**   **124**

Chapter 6   **Types of Poetry**   **128**

Narrative Poetry / 128

Lyric Poetry / 129

Chapter 7   **Reading Poetry: the Basic Approaches**   **138**

Chapter 8   **Elements of Poetry**   **146**

Voice: Speaker and Tone / 146

Word Choice (Diction) / 152

Word Order / 155

Imagery / 158

Figures of Speech / 160

Symbolism / 165

Allegory / 167

Sound / 170

Form / 178

Theme / 186

Part 3   Drama

Chapter 9   **An Overview**   **194**

Chapter 10   **Types of Drama**   **195**

Tragedy / 195

Comedy / 197

Chapter 11   **Reading Drama: the Basic Approaches**   **199**

Chapter 12   **Elements of Drama**   **221**

Plot / 221

Character / 223

Staging / 227

Theme / 230

References   **243**

后记   **245**

Introduction

People read literature for different purposes: for fun, amusement or entertainment, for wisdom, or for academic research. For literature majors or scholars, literature may mean mostly academic work. They may go into literary history, literary works, writers, or theories for academic purposes (reading and writing about literature). The study of literature thus becomes an integral part of their academic activities. In this sense students are encouraged and expected to have certain systematic practices and strict training so as to improve their skills in this domain. To begin with, it is thus important for students to have some knowledge of literature and to become familiar with the practical approaches of its analysis. Finally, it should also be acknowledged that the study of literature, even for academic progress, can be a highly enjoyable and rewarding endeavor.

■ What Is Literature?

Literature, in its broadest sense, is any single body of written works considered an art form, or any single piece of writing assumed to have artistic value. In this sense, literature refers to all written narratives to be read.

> … Literature is the body of works of art produced in linguistic media, and that this body is to be defined in terms of the possession of certain artistic values (Stecker 1996, 681−694).

In contemporary interpretation, literature may also include texts that are spoken or sung, which is known as oral literature. Additionally, some non-written verbal art forms are also considered to be literature such as electronic literature that has appeared with technological development.

> Literature is a set of texts (a general term for objects made of words, no matter what their format) whose purpose includes, but extends beyond, communication, in which the language itself is as much a part of the end product as is the content. Those texts might include everything from lyric poetry to feature films and television series that use language not only in the typed screenplays but also in the spoken performances of script and body language and in the relationship between the words and screen images (Kusch 2016, 3−4).

Many scholars throughout history have attempted to define literature and their ideas can be summarized as:

> literature is imitation; literature is function; literature is an expression of emotion; or literature is literature (Liu 2009, 1).

Definitions of literature have also changed over time and the definition itself has a strong cultural note. Many of the definitions attach great importance to the conventions of the earlier time, while others allude to the popular and ethnic genres. Such attempts at defining literature never end.

In short, there are many perspectives to considering literature. The value judgment of literature involves interpretation or highlighting of "high quality or distinctive works" in the fine writing tradition. The formalist definition of literature attaches great importance to the poetic effects of literature that distinguish it from ordinary speech or other kinds of writing.

According to Kirszner & Mandell (1997), in literary creation, writers attempt to express their personal ideas to their readers. Though writers of literature may often take advantage of facts such as historical documents, newspaper reports, life events or daily happenings, their overarching aim is to present a unique view of the experience, of what happened, what is happening and what will happen. They often take creative liberty with dates, characters, events, dialogue and more to shape their narratives. Certainly what is written means more than just the facts. The author uses his or her literary work to achieve certain ends, to praise or belittle, to defend or attack, to enlighten or blindfold, or to persuade or dissuade.

Literature is imaginative. Writers use verbal images and associative references to create a world of imagination. Most importantly, they exploit the rich connotations of words and images to create a literary text that is full of possibilities and interpretation.

Questions for Reflection

1. There have been various attempts to define literature. Please illustrate.
2. The concept of literature has changed over time. How so?
3. What are the problems in the value judgment of literature?
4. What are the problems in the formalist definition of literature?
5. As proposed by different scholars, "literature is imitation; literature is function; literature is an expression of emotion; or literature is literature (Liu 2009, 1)".

   How do you understand these statements?

■ Types of Literature

Literature can be classified according to whether it is fiction or non-fiction, poetry or prose. It can be further distinguished according to major forms such as the novel, short story or drama; and works are often categorized according to historical periods or their adherence to certain aesthetic features or expectations, i.e. genre. The nature of genre may differ somehow from culture to culture despite the shared similarities. However, for the sake of study and discussion, literature is divided into three genres: fiction, poetry, and drama. Generally, literature has similar effects on readers. It helps the readers to understand the experiences of themselves and others, too.

Questions for Reflection

1. How would you explain the statement that the nature of literary genres varies from culture to culture?
2. Please illustrate how the narrative organization may vary from culture to culture.
3. In what way can literature have similar effects on readers despite cultural backgrounds?

The Pleasure of Reading Literature

Reading literature can be of great fun for people of all ages and all walks of life collectively love literature, especially stories. Reading literature involves thought and feeling and encourages readers to value their own emotional beliefs and to reflect on their life experiences. Literature is usually taken as a reflection of the world and an extension of the possibilities of life. Moreover, the language of literature is deeply fascinating because of the ways writers manipulate words to bring surprise and merriment to their readers. Reading literature is a deeply emotional and intellectual exercise that brings great joy to many.

The Pleasure of Reading Fiction

Reading stories brings readers pleasure, entertainment, and enlightenment. Stories introduce readers to imaginative worlds and help readers understand more about themselves and about life.

Readers enjoy the pleasures of being surprised by a turn of events, satisfied when their expectations are met, and disturbed or confused when they are not. Good stories involve readers emotionally in the lives of the characters. As readers empathize the protagonist or antagonist, they begin to understand more about the worlds that are portrayed, and about the characters' behavior and speech.

Stories entertain and also instruct, showing meaning about the world that the readers had not known before. Take for example "The Buffoon and the Countryman" from *Aesop's Fables*. The story brings readers entertainment and moral instructions.

The Buffoon and the Countryman

A rich nobleman once opened the theaters without charge to the people, and gave a public notice that he would handsomely reward any person who invented a new amusement for the occasion.

Various public performers contended for the prize. Among them came a Buffoon well known among the populace for his jokes, and said that he had a kind of entertainment which had never been brought out on any stage before. This report being spread about made a great stir, and the theater was crowded in every part. The Buffoon appeared alone upon the platform, without any apparatus or confederates, and the very sense of expectation caused an intense silence. He suddenly bent his head towards his bosom and imitated the squeaking of a little pig so admirably with his voice that the audience declared he had a porker under his cloak, and demanded that it should be shaken out. When that was done and nothing was found, they cheered the actor, and loaded him with the loudest applause.

A Countryman in the crowd, observing all that has passed, said, "So help me, Hercules, he shall not beat me at that trick!" and at once proclaimed that he would do the same thing on the next day, though in a much more natural way.

On the morrow a still larger crowd assembled in the theater, but now partiality for their favorite actor very generally prevailed, and the audience came rather to ridicule the Countryman than to see the spectacle. Both of the performers appeared on the stage. The Buffoon grunted and squeaked away first, and obtained, as on the preceding day, the applause and cheers of the spectators. Next the Countryman commenced, and pretending that he concealed a little pig beneath his clothes (which in truth he did, but not suspected by the audience) contrived to take hold of and to pull his ear causing the pig to squeak. The Crowd, however, cried out with one consent that the Buffoon had given a far more exact imitation, and clamored for the Countryman to be kicked out of the theater.

On this the rustic produced the little pig from his cloak and showed by the most positive proof the greatness of their mistake. "Look here," he said, "this shows what sort of judges you are."

The story is enjoyable in both the reading and telling, and readers or listeners can easily remember it, or perhaps the point, and they can learn the moral of it: Men often applaud an imitation and hiss the real thing. Thus the story also makes instruction, or teaching, its primary purpose. It is didactic.

Quite often, stories do not show their point or theme clearly though they do have one(s). In this sense, making clear of the theme can also be a pleasure in reading stories. Take the following story for example.

Learning to Be Silent

The pupils of the Tendai School used to study meditation before Zen entered Japan. Four of them who were intimate friends promised one another to observe seven days of silence.

On the first day all were silent. Their meditation had begun auspiciously, but when night came and the oil lamps were growing dim one of the pupils could not help exclaiming to a servant: "Fix those lamps."

The second pupil was surprised to hear the first one talk. "We are not supposed to say a word," he remarked.

"You two are stupid. Why did you talk?" asked the third.

"I am the only one who has not talked," concluded the fourth pupil.

(DiYanni 2000, 3)

At the first glance the theme of "Learning to Be Silent" is not certain. There may be different interpretations, a promise unfulfilled, self-control, the hardship of meditation, human conceit, or poor wiseacres. However, it is precisely the ambiguity of the story's theme which can make the tale so enjoyable. Moreover, the vivid dialogue is also a way to produce a pleasing experience for the readers.

Reading stories enables readers to enter into a different imaginative world, which is not only of great fun but also a way to expand the sight.

The Pleasure of Reading Poetry

Poetry often brings pleasure to readers through its sound, meaning, images, symbols, speech, and feeling. Poetry best embodies the idea that form carries meaning and that sound clarifies sense. The pleasure that comes from reading poetry can be intellectual in terms of witty words and syntactic structures which connote thought-provoking ideas, can be emotional as to how it evokes sorrow or pity, fear or joy, and can even be physical in the ways it seems to stimulate one's senses of touch, taste, smell, sight, and hearing. Engaged in such a multidimensional experience, readers will thus become more perceptive to the imaginative experiences of the poetic worlds.

Dust of Snow

—Robert Frost (1874−1963)

> The way a crow
> Shook down on me
> The dust of snow
> From a hemlock tree
>
> Has given my heart
> A change of mood
> And saved some part
> Of a day I had rued.

The pleasure in reading this poem comes firstly from its brevity. The poem is actually a single sentence that speaks to the senses at different levels, which also touches on the relationship between man and nature. It connotes that nature can help (re-)adjust one's mood, from downcast to cheerfulness. This may account for people's love of returning to nature. Additionally, the sound effects of the poem from its rhythm and rhyme give readers enjoyment as well.

Poetry also produces pleasures in the way it engages with the relationship between man and man, and man and society as suggested in the poem "We Real Cool" (1960) by Gwendolyn Brooks.

We Real Cool

—Gwendolyn Brooks (1917−2000)

> *The Pool Players.*
> *Seven at the Golden Shovel.*

We real cool. We

Left school. We

Lurk late. We

Strike straight. We

Sing sin. We

Thin gin. We

Jazz June. We

Die soon.

Like "Dust of Snow", "We Real Cool" fascinates the readers by its brevity. "We Real Cool" portrays the young black Americans living in a world where racial discrimination prevails and the poem connotes their sense of life, their social surroundings and their future. Moreover, the poem is musical in its construction. It is very expressive and forceful in terms of monosyllabic words, enjambment and rhyme. The application of these figures of speech such as alliteration, irony, pun, and apostrophe also adds strength to the poetic effect.

On a whole, besides the thematic idea(s), poetry is also to interest and enlighten people through the connotations of its words, its expressive qualities of sound and rhythm, and its special manipulation of syntax. Poetry is a complex art teeming with implications.

The Pleasure of Reading Drama

Drama is an active art form made to be performed on the stage. Drama has representational and mimetic characteristics in that it imitates or represents the world, and life and experiences of people. If literature means imitation, drama as one of the literary genres is actually a more direct form of imitation. It is featured through the immediacy of imitation. The speech and action of the characters help to reproduce human life and experiences through their dialogues and movements, along with the effects of audio and visual displays. Drama best embodies the features of imaginative literature through expected performance that enlivens the past, present, and future. While reading drama, readers seem to watch things happening before their eyes and they may become totally involved in the scene as if they were part of the actual performance. They are tempted to participate in the action on the (imaginative) stage and may laugh, cry, be astonished and feel regret along with the theatrical development. They associate their feelings and experiences with the dramatic situations. The whole process brings with it entertainment and inspiration.

Take for example the selected section of *A Raisin in the Sun* (1958) by Lorraine Hansberry, a well-known African American woman playwright.

A Raisin in the Sun

—Lorraine Hansberry (1930−1965)

Scene Three

Time: Saturday, moving day, one week later.

Before the curtain rises, RUTH's *voice, a strident, dramatic church alto, cuts through the silence.*

It is, in the darkness, a triumphant surge, a penetrating statement of expectation: "Oh, Lord, I don't feel no ways tired! Children, oh, glory hallelujah!"

As the curtain rises we see that RUTH is alone in the living room, finishing up the family's packing. It is moving day. She is nailing crates and trying cartons. BENEATHA enters, carrying a guitar case, and watches her exuberant sister-in-law.

RUTH: Hey!

BENEATHA (*Putting away the case*): Hi.

…

RUTH (*Looking up at her and smiling*): You and your brother seem to have that as a philosophy of life. Lord, that man—done changed so 'round here. You know—you know what we did last night? Me and Walter Lee?

BENEATHA: What?

RUTH (*Smiling to herself*): We went to the movies. (*Looking at BENEAHA to see as if she understands.*) We went to the movies. You know the last time me and Walter went to the movies together?

BENEATHA: No.

RUTH: Me neither. That's how long it been. (*Smiling again.*) But we went last night. The picture wasn't much good, but that didn't seem to matter. We went—and we held hands.

BENEATHA: Oh, Lord!

RUTH: We held hands—and you know what?

BENEATHA: What?

RUTH: When we come out of the show it was late and dark and all the stores and things was closed up… and it was kind of chilly and there wasn't many people on the streets… and we was still holding hands, me and Walter.

BENEATHA: You're killing me.

(*Walter enters with a large package. His happiness is deep in him; he cannot keep still with his newfound exuberance. He is singing and wiggling and snapping his fingers. He puts his package in a corner and puts a phonograph record, which he has brought in with him, on the record player. As the music, soulful and sensuous, comes up he dances over to RUTH and tries to get her to dance with him. She gives in at last to his raunchiness and in a fit of giggling allows herself to be drawn into his mood. They dip and she melts into his arms in a classic, body-melding "slow drag".*)

BENEATHA (*Regarding them a long time as they dance, then drawing in her breath for a deeply exaggerated comment which she does not particularly mean*): Talk about—olddddddddd-fashioneddddddd—Negroes!

WALTER (*Stopping momentarily*): What kind of negroes? (*He says this in fun. He is not angry with her today, nor with anyone. He starts to dance with his wife again.*)

BENEATHA: Old-fashioned.

WALTER (*As he dances with RUTH*): You know, when these New Negroes have their convention—(*Pointing at his sister.*) that is going to be the chairman of the Committee on Unending Agitation. (*He goes on dancing, then stops.*) Race, race, race! … Girl, I do believe you are the first person in the history of the entire human race to successfully brainwash yourself. (*BENEAHTA breaks up and he goes on dancing. He stops again, enjoying his tease.*) Damn, even the N double ACP takes a holiday sometimes! (*BENEATHA and RUTH laugh. He dances with RUTH some more and starts to laugh and stops and pantomimes someone over an operating table.*) I can just see that chick someday looking down at some poor cat on an operating table and before she starts to slice him, she says… (*Pulling his sleeves back maliciously.*) "By the way, what are your views on civil rights down there? …"

(*He laughs at her again and starts to dance happily. The Bell sounds.*)

BENEATHA: Sticks and stones may break my bones but… words will never hurt me!

(*BENEATHA goes to the door and opens it as WALTER and RUTH go on with the clowning. BENEATHA is somewhat surprised to see a quiet-looking middle-aged white man in a business suit holding his hat and a briefcase in his hand and consulting a small piece of paper.*)

MAN: Uh—how do you do, miss. I am looking for a Mrs.—(*He looks at the slip of paper.*) Mrs. Lena Younger? (*He stops short, stuck dump at the sight of the oblivious WALTER and RUTH.*)

BENEATHA (*Smoothing her hair with slight embarrassment*): Oh—yes, that's my mother. Excuse me (*She closes the door and turns to quiet the other two.*) Ruth! Brother! (*Enunciating precisely but soundlessly: " There's a white man at the door!" They stop dancing, RUTH cuts off the phonograph, BENEATHA opens the door. The man casts a curious quick glance at all of them.*) Uh—come in please.

MAN (*Coming in*): Thank you.

BENEATHA: My mother isn't here just now. Is it business?

MAN: Yes… well, of a sort.

WALTER (*Freely, the Man of the House*): Have a seat. I'm Mrs. Younger's son. Look after most of her business matters.

(*RUTH and BENEATHA exchanged amused glances.*)

MAN (*Regarding WALTER, and sitting*): Well—My name is Karl Lindner…

WALTER (*Stretching out his hand*): Walter Younger. This is my wife—(*RUTH nods politely.*)—and my sister.

LINDNER: How do you do.

WALTER (*Amiably, as he sits himself easily on a chair, leaning forward on his knees with interest and looking expectantly into the newcomer's face*): What can we do for you, Mr. Lindner!

LINDNER (*Some minor shuffling of the hat and briefcase on his knee*): Well—I am a representative of the Clybourne Park Improvement Association—

WALTER (*Pointing*): Why don't you sit your things on the floor?

LINDNER: Oh—yes. Thank you. (*He slides the briefcase and hat under the chair.*) And as

I was saying—I am from the Clybourne Park Improvement Association and we have had it brought to our attention at the last meeting that you people or at least your mother has bought a piece of residential property at—(He *digs for the slip of paper again.*)—four o six Clybourne Street...

WALTE: That's right. Care for something to drink? Ruth, get Mr. Lindner a beer.

LINDNER (*Upset for some reason*): Oh—no, really. I mean thank you very much, but no thank you.

RUTH (*Innocently*): Some coffee?

LINDNER: Thank you, nothing at all.

(*BENEATHA is watching at the man carefully.*)

LINDNER: Well, I don't know how much you folks know about our organization. (*He is a gentle man; thoughtful and somewhat labored in his manner.*) It is one these community organizations set up to look after—oh, you know, things like block upkeep and special projects and we also have what we call our new neighbors Orientation Committee...

NENEATHA (*Drily*): Yes—and what do they do?

LINDNER (*Turning a little to her and then returning the main force to WALTER*): Well— it's what you might call a sort of welcoming committee, I guess. I mean they, we—I'm the chairman of the committee—go around and see the new people who move into the new neighborhood and give them the lowdown on the way we do things out in Clybourne Park.

BENEATHA (*With appreciation of the two meanings, which escape RUTH and WALTER*): Un-huh.

LINDNER: And we also have the category of what the association calls—(*He looks elsewhere.*)—uh—special community problems...

BENEATHA Yes—and what are some of those?

WALTER: Girl, let the man talk.

LINDNER (*With understated relief*): Thank you. I would sort of like to explain this thing in my own way. I mean I want to explain to you in a certain way.

WALTER: Go ahead.

LINDNER: Yes. Well, I'm going to try to get right to the point. I'm sure we'll appreciate that in the long run.

BENEATHA: Yes.

WALTER: Be still now!

LINDNER: Well—

RUTH (*Still innocently*): Would you like another chair—you don't look comfortable.

LINDNER (*More frustrated than annoyed*): No, thank you very much. Please well—to get right to the point I—(*A great breath, and he is off at last.*) I am sure you people must be aware of some of the incidents which have happened in various parts of the city when colored people have moved into certain areas—(*BENEATHA exhales heavily and starts tossing a piece of fruit up and down in the air.*) Well—because we have what we think is going to be a unique type of organization in American community life—not only do we deplore that kind of thing—but we are trying to do something about it. (*BENEATHA stops tossing and turns with a new and quizzical interest to the man.*) We feel—(*Gaining confidence in his mission because of interest in the faces of the people he is talking to.*) We feel that most of the trouble in this world, when you come right down to it—(*He hits his knee for emphasis.*)—most of the trouble exists because people just don't sit down and talk to each other.

RUTH (*Nodding as she might in church, pleased with the remark*): You can say that again, mister.

LINDNER (*More encouraged by such affirmation*): That we don't try hard enough in this world to understand the other fellow's problem. The other guy's point of view.

RURH: Now that's right.

(*BENEATHA and WALTER merely watch and listen with genuine interest.*)

LINDNER: Yes—that's the way we feel out in Clybourne Park. And that's why I was elected to come here this afternoon and talk to you people. Friendly like, you know, the way people should talk to each other and see if we couldn't find some way to work this thing out. As I say, the whole business is a matter of caring about the other fellow. Anybody can see that you are a nice family of folks, hard working and honest I'm sure. (*BENEATHA frowns slightly, quizzically, her head tilted regarding him.*) Today everybody knows what it means to be on the outside of something. And of course, there is always somebody who is out to take advantage of people who don't always understand.

WALTER: What do you mean?

LINDNER: Well—You see our community is made up of people who've worked hard as the dickens for years to build up that little community. They're not rich and fancy people; just hard-working, honest people who don't really have much but those little homes and a dream of the kind of community they want to raise their children in. Now, I don't say we are perfect and there is a lot of wrong in some of the things they want. But you've got to admit that a man, right or wrong, has the right to want to have the neighborhood he lives in a certain kind of way. And at the moment the overwhelming majority of our people out there feel that people get along better, take more of a common interest in the life of the community, when they share a common background. I want you to believe me when I tell you that race prejudice simply doesn't enter into it. It is a matter of the people of Clybourne Park believing, rightly or wrongly, as I say, that for the happiness of all concerned that our Negro families are happier when they live in their own communities.

BENEATHA (*With a grand and bitter gesture*): This, friends, is the Welcoming Committee!

WALTER (*Dumbfounded, looking at LINDNER*): Is this what you came marching all the way over here to tell us?

LINDNER: Well, now we've been having a fine conversation. I hope you'll hear me all the way through.

WALTER (*Tightly*): Go ahead, man.

LINDNER: You see—in the face of all the things I have said, we are prepared to make your family a very generous offer…

BENEATHA: Thirty pieces and not a coin less!

WALTER: Yeah?

LINDNER (*Putting on his glasses and drawing a form out of the briefcase*): Our association is prepared, through the collective effort of our people, to buy the house from you at a financial gain to your family.

RUTH: Lord have mercy, ain't this the living gall!

WALTER: All right, you through?

LINDNER: Well, I want to give you the exact terms of the financial arrangement—

WALTER: We don't want to hear no exact terms of no arrangements. I want to know if you got any more to tell us 'bout getting together?

LINDNER (*Taking off his glasses*): Well—I don't suppose that you feel…

WALTER Never mind how I feel—you got any more to say 'bout how people ought to sit down and talk to each other? … Get out of my house, man.

(*He turns his back and walks to the door.*)

LINDNER (*Looking around at the hostile faces and reaching and assembling his hat and briefcase*): Well—I don't understand why you people are going to gain by moving into a neighborhood where you aren't wanted and where some elements—well—people can get awful worked up when they feel that their whole way of life and everything they've ever worked for is threatened.

WALTER: Get out.

LINDNER (*At the door, holding a small card*): Well—I'm sorry it went like this.

WALTER: Get out.

LINDNER (*Almost sadly regarding WALTER*): You just can't force people to change their hearts, son.

(*He turns and puts his card on a table and exits. WLATER pushes the door to with stinging hatred, and stands looking at it. RUTH just sits and NENEATHA just stands. They say nothing. MAMA and TRAVIS enter.*)

A play can be an immediate imitation and reflection of reality. This selected part of the play reflects the life of African American people who are pursuing the American Dream or African American Dream in their efforts to establish themselves in the white community while they still harbor their African Americanness. The action of the play took place in a poor African American community in Chicago probably around 1958 when the Civil Rights Movement had just begun.

In the beginning, the readers (or audience) are involved in the happy atmosphere of the Youngers' house with light-hearted smiles, music and dance, and witty remarks. They can feel African American people's expectations of the new time in the rise of the Civil Rights Movement. "*It is in the darkness, a triumphant surge, a penetrating statement of expectation…*" (Stage directions at the very beginning of Scene Three). African Americans hope to enjoy equal rights with their white neighbors. In the play, the Youngers, an African American family, bought a house in the white community nearby and they were preparing to move. However, to own property in the white community was extremely difficult for people of color in the mid-20th century. Predictably they encounter resistance from their white neighbors. Lindner is the representative of the white community sent to persuade the Youngers to abandon their moving plan. "... for the happiness of all concerned that our Negro families are happier when they live in their own communities," says he. At this, the readers will feel annoyed or upset by this injustice.

Moreover, a deeper understanding of the play brings great enjoyment to its readers. Readers or audience respond inevitably along with the development of the play. The pleasure of reading the selection also comes from the dialogue and interactions between the characters (Lindner on one side and Walter, Beneatha and Ruth on the other). Readers experience the funny, ironical but serious situation. Lindner's affected, ambivalent, roundabout, and disguised speech sheds light on his hypocritical character as well as the racial phobia of the white neighborhood and the severe reality facing African Americans.

■ The Basic Approaches to the Study of Literature

The approaches to the study of literature in this textbook touch on three basic aspects of literary analysis: experiencing, interpreting and evaluating, in reference to DiYanni's *Literature*: *Reading Fiction*, *Poetry*, *and Drama* (2000). They are "basic" and "practical" forms in contrast to other more theoretical approaches. As proposed by DiYanni, the approach to reading, understanding and appreciating literature involves three aspects:

> Experiencing and responding to literary works; interpreting literary works; and evaluating works of literature by considering the values they express (DiYanni 2000, 7).

At the very beginning, readers read a literary work subjectively, associating personal or shared experiences with the reading. Experiencing is a subjective, emotional and impressionistic process. For example,

> a poem may provoke our thinking, evoke a memory, [and] elicit a strong emotional response. A short story may arouse our curiosity about what will happen, engage our feelings for its characters, [and] stimulate our thought about why things happen as they do. A play may move us to laughter or tears, [and] may prompt us to link its dialogue and action with our lives (DiYanni 2000, 7).

Readers then move beyond the subjective and emotional steps to other practices. Readers may want to interpret the literary work, or to make sense of it, particularly the implied meanings. Interpretation involves intellectual and analytical thinking.

> Our interpretation of literature provides an intellectual counterpart to our emotional experience. When we interpret literary works we concern ourselves less with how they affect us

and more with what they mean. Interpretation, in short, aims at understanding; it relies on our intellectual comprehension and rational understanding rather than on our emotional response (DiYanni 2000, 8).

Interpretation means to determine its possible meaning. It is an interaction between the reader and the text.

> Meaning is created partly by what is supplied by a work (the information that enables a reader to follow the plot of a story, the action of a play, or the development of a poem) and partly by what is supplied by the reader (Kirszner & Mandell 1997, 8).

The work may convey the writer's social, political and cultural values and the reader's response may also involve his or her value orientations. These values may converge or separate. In other words, the meaning of a work may be different to different people in terms of their age, race, gender, class, political inclination, religious orientation, or experiences. That's why people often say that a work has more than one meaning.

To interpret a literary work or to better understand it requires a good knowledge of the basic elements and characteristics of literature which is often divided into three genres of fiction (story), poetry and drama.

> In reading fiction, for example, we rely on analysis of such elements as plot, character, setting, and point of view. In interpreting poems, we analyze their diction, imagery, syntax, and structure to get at meaning. In viewing or reading plays we focus on dialogue, setting, plot, and character (DiYanni 2000, 8).

Still, to make sense of a literary work, often considerations of the basic elements are not enough. Readers may also make judgments on it. After they respond to it, and get meaning out of or make sense of a literary work, they will inevitably begin to evaluate it, assessing "its quality and value, and the cultural, social and moral values" (DiYanni 2000, 8) displayed in it. In other words, the evaluation of literature involves an assessment of aesthetic distinction along with a consideration of a work's social, moral, and cultural values. Or to evaluate a literary work means to make a judgment about it considering its individual elements, thinking about how various elements function individually within a work. These elements are the choices of the writers. Readers may often pay attention to the major ones, those that play a major role in determining their responses to the work.

To sum up, the experience of literature concerns the readers' impressions of a work, especially their subjective impressions and emotional responses; the interpretation of literature touches on intellectual and analytical thinking; and the evaluation of literature involves an assessment of aesthetic distinction along with a consideration of a work's social, moral, and cultural values. Evaluation is a comprehensive and complex process.

Meanwhile, it should be noted that these three steps are closely related to each other. Readers deal with certain literary works in terms of experiencing, interpreting and evaluating, with consideration to the traditional elements of literature. Of course, when they read the works, they do not necessarily follow the exact order from one step to the other. Rather they may do it based on what interests them the most or quite often they read the text in different approaches simultaneously. Moreover, interpretation and evaluation of a piece can never end for readers may change their minds along with views on it over time.

Questions for Reflection

Experiencing

1. Read a literary work more than one time and compare the initial experience with that from the re-reading.
2. Read a literary work and explain how it relates to your situation.

Interpreting

1. Analyze the use of figurative language in a literary work. Please illustrate with examples and comment on their effects.
2. Explain the theme of a literary work and support your argument with sufficient evidence from the text.

Evaluating

1. In evaluating a literary work, how are the elements of it interconnected with each other to achieve a shared goal?
2. Along with your evaluation of a literary work, do you think that the work strengthens or undermines your interpretation?
3. Is the evaluation intellectually challenging? How?
4. Does the evaluation give you pleasures accordingly? How?

■ Understanding the Theme of Literary Works

Whatever the genres or approaches, the theme of a literary work always arouses the attention and interest on the part of the readership.

The theme of a literary work refers to its central or dominant idea manifested via the manipulation of details, the intentional use of specific words or syntactic forms, or the reactions of characters, the tone of the speakers, or the action of actors/actresses. The theme is often expressed in a hidden way though sometimes it is conveyed explicitly. Many literary works have more than one theme. For example, Walt Whitman's *Leaves of Grass* praises nature and the human individual role in it while also stressing the role of the mind or spirit. Other themes are also found in it such as exploration and celebration of Whitman's own self, his individuality and personality. Deeper analysis of *Leaves of Grass* also reveals the themes of glorification of American democracy and the American nation, as well as reflections on birth, death, and rebirth. Another example of a work with multiple themes is Mark Twain's *The Adventures of Huckleberry Finn* which contains the following themes simultaneously:

> that an individual's innate sense of right or wrong is superior to society's artificial or sometimes unnatural values; [...] that Mark Twain criticizes the racism and religious hypocrisy that pervaded the towns along the Mississippi (Kirszner & Mandell 1997, 3).

The play *A Raisin in the Sun* (1958) by Lorraine Hansberry has two primary or dominant themes: the identification of African American in early period of the Civil Rights Movement, and the pursuit of the American Dream.

Some themes have even become universal because they appear again and again in different literary works despite differences in the time and place the works were written and the subjects that these works describe. Common universal themes are:

> A character's loss of innocence; the conflict between an individual's values and the values of society; the individual's quest for spiritual enlightenment; the *carpe diem* ("seize the day"); the making of the artist; the nostalgia for a vanished past; the disillusionment of adulthood; the pain of love; the struggle of women for equality; the conflicts between parents and children; the clash between civilization and the wilderness; the evils of unchecked ambition; the inevitability of fate; the impact of the past on the present; the conflict between human beings and machines; and the tensions between the ideal and the actual realms of experience (Kirszner & Mandell 1997, 3–4).

In American literature, themes occurring constantly are found as follows:

> the loss of innocence, rite of passage, childhood epiphanies, and the ability (or inability) to form relationships (Kirszner & Mandell 1997, 4).

Of course, there are more than just these themes. Many American themes also involve race, gender and class in modern time. Writers of different cultural backgrounds will also often develop themes that reflect their unique experiences and perspectives.

Part 1

Fiction

✑ Chapter 1 ✑
An Overview

A narrative tells a story which is generally taken, in the literary sense, as a tale. The story is told in a way commonly accepted in terms of order and logic. In other words, something happens in a place at a particular moment or things happen in different places at the same or different time. And the happening is told or retold in a way that may be well accepted by people of the similar customs or cultural background. Further, the way of story telling has much in common across peoples in the world. It seems that people are born with the genius of story telling. Whenever they hear a story, they seem to be able to retell it, though they may possibly make some changes, intentionally or unintentionally. In this sense, exaggeration, omission, addition, and/or reorganization are the norm. In doing so, they "fictionalize a narrative to a desired effect" (Kirszner & Mandell 1997, 38). What ordinary people have done for a millennium is informal and personal but the way we are naturally inclined to make up a story shares much in common with those of the professional literary writers. Fictionalization is an integral part of human life and fiction is found to be entertaining, instructive, enlightening, or inspiring.

Generally, fiction refers to "narrative writing drawn from the imagination of the author rather than [completely] from history or fact. [Fiction] is most frequently associated with novels and short stories" (Holman & Harmon 1986, 202). Though some fictions portray real people and actual events, such as historical fiction or autobiographical fiction, "the way the characters interact and how the plot unfolds are the author's invention" (Kirszner & Mandell 1997, 38).

Questions for Reflection

1. Despite the fact that fiction is not entirely real, why do people often ascribe a certain type of truth to it?
2. How much do you know about legal fiction and science fiction?

∂ Chapter 2 ℬ
Types of Fiction

▪ Short Fiction and Long Fiction

Fiction can refer to any story that is produced out of imagination but in this textbook the introduction is restricted merely to literary fiction which includes short stories, novellas and novels. Fiction can be classified as short fiction and long fiction. Usually the classification in this sense comes out in terms of the length of the story. It is often easy to see a story more than 50,000 words (like Joseph Conrad's "Heart of Darkness") as a long fiction but it is sometimes not so easy to distinguish a short story from a short novel or a novella. A long fiction is usually taken as a novel which, besides the greater length, has more complex plots and structures, concerns more events, and involves more and varied characters. Both types of these fictional works produce the effects in ways that are both similar and different. In other words, they exist in their own ways and they are equally effective socially and culturally. As a result, for the sake of limited space, discussions of fiction in this book, despite a quick touch on novella or even longer novels, are restricted primarily to short stories.

Short fiction has different varieties, such as parables, modern realistic short stories, as well as fairy tales, mystery stories, science fiction stories, and popular romance. Here introduction is given to the more popular types like the early forms (parable, fable and tale), the short story, the nonrealistic story, and the short novel. A parable is

> a brief story that teaches a lesson, often as a religious or spiritual nature… [and] fables are brief stories that point to a moral. The moral of the fable is stated explicitly, whereas the moral of the parable is implied (DiYanni 2000, 38).

Moreover, fables have animals as characters to shed light on human nature, especially human failings, while parables are stories about everyday life, usually with a religious and spiritual bent. In this sense, fables are satirical and parables are instructive and serious. These are the general distinctions but there are exceptions too. For example, George Orwell's *Animal Farmland* (1984) has the features of fables and parables simultaneously.

Questions for Reflection

Read the following stories and answer the questions.

(1)

The Prodigal Son

A certain man had two sons: and the younger of them said to his father, "Father, give me the portion of goods that falleth to me." And he divided unto them his living. And not many days after, the younger son gathered all together, and took his journey into a far country, and there wasted his substance with riotous living. And when he had spent all, there arose a mighty famine in that land, and he began to be in want. And he went and joined himself to a citizen of that country, and he sent him into his fields to feed swine. And he would fain have filled his belly with the husks that the swine did eat: and no man gave unto him. And when he came to himself, he said, "How many hired servants of my father's have bread enough and to spare, and I perish with hunger? I will arise and go to my father, and will say unto him, 'Father, I have sinned against heaven, and before thee. And am no more worthy to be called thy son: make me as one of thy hired servants.'" And he arose, and came to his father. But when he was yet a great way off, his father saw him, and had compassion, and ran, and fell on his neck, and kissed him. And the son said unto him, "Father, I have sinned against heaven, and in thy sight, and am no more worthy to be called thy son." But the father said to his servants, "Bring forth the best robe, and put it on him, and put a ring on his hand, and shoes on his feet. And bring hither the fatted calf, and kill it, and let us eat, and be merry. For this my son was dead, and is alive again; he was lost, and is found." And they began to be merry. Now his elder son was in the field, and as he came and drew nigh to the house, he heard music and dancing. And he called one of the servants, and asked what these things meant. And he said unto him, "Thy brother is come, and thy father hath killed the fatted calf, because he hath received him safe and sound." And he was angry, and would not go in: therefore came his father out, and entreated him. And he answering said to his father, "Lo, these many years do I serve thee, neither transgressed I at any time thy commandment, and yet thou never gavest me a kid, that I might make merry with my friends: but as soon as this thy son was come, which hath devoured thy living with harlots, thou hast killed for him the fatted calf." And he said unto him, "Son, thou art ever with me, and all that I have is thine. It was meet that we should make merry, and be glad: for this thy brother was dead, and is alive again: and was lost, and is found."

(DiYanni 2000, 21−22)

Questions

1. Is "The Prodigal Son" a parable? Why?
2. Do you have such kind of stories in your culture? Explain in detail.

(2)

The Ass and His Masters

An ass, belonging to an herb-seller who gave him too little food and too much work, made a petition to Jupiter to be released from his present service and provided with another master.

Jupiter, after warning him that he would repent his request, caused him to be sold to a tile-maker. Shortly afterwards, finding that he had heavier loads to carry and harder work in the brick-field, he petitioned for another change of master. Jupiter, telling him that it would be the last time that he could grant his request, ordained that he be sold to a tanner. The Ass found that he had fallen into worse hands, and noting his master's occupation, said, groaning: "It would have been better for me to have been either starved by the one, or to have been overworked by the other of my former masters, than to have been bought by my present owner, who will even after I am dead tan my hide, and make me useful to him."

Moral lesson: He that finds discontentment in one place is not likely to find happiness in another.

(Aesop's Fables)

Questions

1. Do you agree with the moral lesson given at the end of the story? Why?
2. Can you find another moral lesson from the story?

Besides the parable and the fable, a tale is not necessarily meant to instruct. Quite often it is simply another form of fiction from early times.

A tale is a story that narrates strange or fabulous happenings in a direct manner, without detailed descriptions of character. A tale does not necessarily point to a moral as a fable or a parable does, but it is almost as generalized in its depiction of character and setting (DiYanni 2000, 39).

Most people read a tale for its action and show their emotions at its outcome rather than try to find some moral generalizations contained in it. Nevertheless, many readers will like to infer, from their own perspective, some morals from the descriptions.

Questions for Reflection

Read the following story and answer the questions.

The Widow of Ephesus

Once upon a time there was a certain married woman in the city of Ephesus whose fidelity to her husband was so famous that the women from all the neighboring towns and villages used to troop into Ephesus merely to stare at this prodigy. It happened, however, that her husband one day died. Finding the normal custom of following the cortege with hair unbound and beating her breast in public quite inadequate to express her grief, the lady insisted on following the corpse right into the tomb, an underground vault of the Greek type, and there set herself to guard the body, weeping and wailing night and day. Although in her extremes of grief she was clearly courting death from starvation, her parents were utterly unable to persuade her to leave, and even the magistrates, after one last supreme attempt, were rebuffed and driven away. In short, all Ephesus had gone into mourning for this extraordinary woman, all the more since the lady was now passing her fifth consecutive day without once tasting food. Beside the failing woman sat her devoted maid, sharing her mistress's grief and relighting the lamp whenever it flickered out. The whole city could speak, in fact, of nothing else: here at last, all classes alike agreed, was the one true example of conjugal fidelity and love.

In the meantime, however, the governor of the province gave orders that several thieves should be crucified in a spot close by the vault where the lady was mourning her dead husband's corpse. So, on the following night, the soldier who had been assigned to keep watch on the crosses so that nobody could remove the thieves' bodies for burial suddenly noticed a light blazing among the tombs and heard the sounds of groaning. And prompted by a natural human curiosity to know who or what was making those sounds, he descended into vault.

But at the sight of a strikingly beautiful woman, he stopped short in terror, thinking he must be seeing some ghostly apparition out of hell. Then, observing the corpse and seeing the tears on the lady's face and the scratches her fingernails had gashed in her cheeks, he realized what it was: a widow, in inconsolable grief. Promptly fetching his little supper back down to the tomb, he implored the lady not to persist in her sorrow or break her heart with useless mourning. All men alike, he reminded her, have the same end; the same resting place awaits us all. He used, in short, all those platitudes we use to comfort the suffering and bring them back to life. His consolations, being unwelcome, only exasperated the widow more; more violently than ever she beat her breast, and tearing out her hair by the roots, scattered it over the dead man's body. Undismayed, the soldier repeated his arguments and pressed her to take some food, until the little maid, quite overcome by the smell of the wine, succumbed and stretched out her hand to her tempter. Then, restored by the food and wine, she began herself to assail her mistress's obstinate refusal.

"How will it help you," she asked the lady, "if you faint from hunger? Why should you bury yourself alive, and go down to death before the Fates have called you? What does Vergil say? —

> Do you suppose the shades and ashes of the dead are by such sorrow touched?

No, begin your life afresh. Shake off these woman's scruples; enjoy the light while you can. Look at that corpse of your poor husband: doesn't it tell you more eloquently than any words that you should live?"

None of us, of course, really dislikes being told that we must eat, that life is to be lived. And the lady was no exception. Weakened by her long days of fasting, her resistance crumbled at last, and she ate the food the soldier offered her as hungrily as the little maid had eaten earlier.

Well, you know what temptations are normally aroused in a man on a full stomach. So the soldier, mustering all those blandishments by means of which he had persuaded the lady to live, now laid determined siege to her virtue. And chaste though she was, the lady found him singularly attractive and his arguments persuasive. As for the maid, she did all she could to help the soldier's cause, repeating like a refrain the appropriate line of Vergil:

> If love is pleasing, lady, yield yourself to love.

To make the matter short, the lady's body soon gave up the struggle; she yielded and our happy warrior enjoyed a total triumph on both counts. That very night their marriage was consummated, and they slept together the second and the third night too, carefully shutting the door of the tomb so that any passing friend or stranger would have thought the lady of famous chastity had at last expired over her dead husband's body.

As you can perhaps imagine, our soldier was a very happy man, utterly delighted with his lady's ample beauty and that special charm that a secret love confers. Every night, as soon as the sun had set, he bought what few provisions his slender pay permitted and smuggled them down to the tomb. One night, however, the parents of one of the crucified thieves, noticing that the watch was being badly kept, took advantage of our hero's absence to remove their son's body and bury it. The next morning, of course, the soldier was horror-struck to discover one of the bodies missing from its cross, and ran to tell his mistress of the horrible punishment which awaited him for neglecting his duty. In the circumstances, he told her, he would not wait to be tried and sentenced, but would punish himself then and there with his own sword. All he asked of her was that she make room for another corpse and allow the same gloomy tomb to enclose husband and lover together.

Our lady's heart, however, was no less tender than pure. "God forbid," she cried, "that I should have to see at one and the same time the dead bodies of the only two men I have ever loved. No, better far, I say, to hang the dead than kill the living." With these words, she gave orders that her husband's body should be taken from its bier and strung up on the empty cross. The soldier followed this good advice, and the next morning the whole city wondered by what miracle the dead man had climbed up on the cross.

(DiYanni 2000, 39−41)

Questions

1. How do you respond to "The Widow of Ephesus"? Do you pay attention to a moral or its action? Why?
2. What is the pleasure in reading this tale?
3. What kind of action in the tale that attracts your attention the most?
4. Is there a moral in the story?

The short story, as a form of short fiction, owes much to the oral story-telling tradition and novel writing. It began to develop rapidly since its appearance. The 19th century witnessed the prosperity of short story. Since the 20th century, though revolutionized in forms and medium, it has been popular too. Particularly after World War II, short fiction enjoyed prosperity in the United States as well as in United Kingdom and Canada. Nowadays, short story still remains one of the important literary forms.

Stories are seen roughly in two forms, factual stories and fictional stories. Sometimes the two forms are intermingled as found in some modern narratives. In this book, short story generally refers to fictional ones.

A short story is

> a relatively brief fictional narrative in prose ... It has a definite formal development, a firmness in construction ... It finds its unity in many things other than plot—although it often finds it there—in effect, in theme, in character, in tone, in mood, even on occasion, in style (Holman & Harmon 1986, 469).

The short story is generally featured by "realism or a detailed representation of everyday life, typically the lives and experiences familiar to middle-class individuals" (DiYanni 2000, 42). Compared to early forms of short fiction, like parables, fables, and tales which "tend to summarize action, to tell what happens in a general overview of the action" (DiYanni 2000, 42), the modern short fiction enjoys a realistic flavor,

> [reveals character] in moments of action, and in exchanges of dialogue detailed enough to represent the surface of life, [... and] has traditionally been more concerned with the revelation of character through flashes of insight and shocks of recognition (DiYanni 2000, 42).

What's more, the modern realistic short story has such characteristics as follows:

1. Its plot is based on probability, illustrating a sequence of causally related incidents.
2. Its characters are recognizably human, and they are motivated by identifiable social and psychological forces.
3. Its time and place are clearly established, with realistic rather than fantastic settings.
4. Its elements—plot, character, setting, style, point of view, irony, symbol and theme— work toward a single effect, unifying the story (DiYanni 2000, 42).

Some short stories have combined the realistic features with nonrealistic elements, involving the supernatural events, legendary materials, and magic phenomena. Examples are seen in I. B. Singer's "Gimpel the Fool," in Leslie Marmon Silko's "Yellow Woman," and in Gabriel Garcia Marquez's "A Very Old Man with Enormous Wings." These stories may appear mysterious or enigmatic in that the conventions of realism in the mind of the readers do not work or the stories do not correspond well to the readers' expectations as usual.

■ The Short Novel

The short novel is often called a novella. The term "novella" usually reminds readers of the early tales of Italian and French writers, such as the *Decaneron* of Boccaccio and the *Heptameron* of Marguerite of Valois. Many English writers have also adopted this form of writing from which the term novel evolved. The novella has exerted great formative influences on the English novel (Holman & Harmon 1986, 341).

As the name suggests, short novel has the characteristics of both short story and novel. The short novel or novella is longer than a short story but shorter than a novel. It has more conflicts than a short story but fewer conflicts than a novel. A novella frequently deals with personal and emotional development. It is featured by "a consistency of style and focus and a concentration and compression of effect" (DiYanni 2000, 43). Modern examples of novella are found in Joseph Conrad's *Heart of Darkness* (1899), James Joyce's *The Dead* (1914), Nella Larsen's *Quicksand* (1928) and *Passing* (1929), George Orwell's *Animal Farmland* (1945), and Ernest Hemingway's *The Old Man and the Sea* (1952), to name a few.

A novel generally refers to any lengthy fictional prose narrative. In practice, however, it is used, in a narrower sense, to refer to

> narratives in which the representations of character occurs either in a static condition or in the process of development as the result of events or actions (Holman & Harmon 1986, 335).

There are some differences between a short story and a novel. Generally, a short story

> tends to reveal character through a series of action or ordeals, the purpose of the story being accomplished when the reader comes to know what the true nature of a character (or sometimes a situation) is... On the other hand, the novel tends to show character developing as a result of actions and under the impact of events (Holman & Harmon 1986, 469).

Moreover, a short story involves "one unified episode or a sequence of related events" (Charters 1999, 3) while a novel which is often more complex, may not follow such a unity. Further, a short story

> begins close to or at the height of action and develops one character in depth... showing his or her responses to events (Kirszner & Mandell 1997, 40).

It often deals with a single incident. The character usually undergoes an epiphany, or

> a moment of illumination in which something hidden or not understood becomes immediately clear (Kirszner & Mandell 1997, 40).

For example, the chief character in James Joyce's "Araby" or the protagonist in O'Henry's "The Cop and the Anthem" undergo a sort of epiphany.

Many short stories may also concentrate on more than one character, and they may experience epiphanies too though at times the epiphany can be different from one character to another. For example, in Alice Walker's "Everyday Use for Your Grandmamma," both Mama and Maggie, the younger daughter, have undergone an epiphany. Mama's appears evident while Maggie's is not so clear.

Fiction, short or long, is meant to entertain or interest, and quite often it is also able to instruct, enlighten, and persuade. It is used as a means for people to express their ideas about the reality, themselves and their relationship with the world at large.

People read stories for pleasure, entertainment and enlightenment. They enter into the imaginative worlds of stories to become fascinated by the power of creation. Stories help people understand more about themselves and about the world.

In this textbook, discussions of short stories are focused on because of limited space, but the basic approaches to the study of short stories can also be applied, to a large extent, to the analysis of long stories or novels.

♂ Chapter 3 ♀
Reading Stories: the Basic Approaches

Reading stories usually involves the processes of experiencing, interpreting and evaluating. In other words:

(1) we take in its surface features, and form impressions of character and action; (2) we observe details, make connections among them, and draw inferences and conclusions from those connections; (3) we evaluate the story, measuring its moral, political, and cultural values against our own (DiYanni 2000, 22).

These processes are illustrated in terms of the following small story about a soldier.

While the bombardment was knocking the trench to pieces at Fossalta, he lay very flat and sweated and prayed, "Oh jesus christ get me out of here. Dear jesus please get me out. Christ please please please christ. If you'll only keep me from getting killed I'll do anything you say. I believe in you and I'll tell every one in the world that you are the only one that matters. Please please dear jesus." The shelling moved further up the line. We went to work on the trench and in the morning the sun came up and the day was hot and muggy and cheerful and quiet. The next night back at Mestre he did not tell the girl he went upstairs with at the Villa Rossa about Jesus. And he never told anybody.

—from Chapter VII, *In Our Time* (1925) by Ernest Hemingway
(DiYanni 2000, 8)

Experiencing

Experiencing fiction touches on a reader's subjective, emotional, and impressionistic response and reaction to the story. It involves the feelings, attitudes, and beliefs of the readers regarding the character, action, and plot. Readers bring their personal experiences to the story and are affected by what happens in the story.

In the soldier's story, the words like "bombardment," "knocking," "trench," "shelling," and "killed" show that it is a scene in a battle field and "he" is a soldier in action. From his reaction and behavior, readers immediately feel, in connection with their own experiences, that the soldier is not a soldier at all. He is timid, coward, and irresponsible. Moreover, he tells a lie, and he does not keep his promise. He takes on a negative image. Some readers may feel surprised at the soldier's action and some may even be angry at him. They may curse the man, "You timid coward!" "What a shame!" The readers may further blame the soldier for taking advantage of God whom he seems to have forgotten in peace time. What's more, some readers may also despise him for visiting a prostitute.

Interpreting

Interpretation means to make sense of the story and give it an objective consideration. Rather than an emotional response as in experiencing, interpreting is an intellectual, analytical, and rational process. Put simply, interpretation asks questions like what the story *means* or *suggests* rather than how it directly affects the readers. Interpreting generally involves the actions of observing, connecting, inferring, and concluding. The four interpretive actions are mutually related and dependent.

So what does the soldier's story mean? What does it suggest? The text does not state directly the authorial orientation (or the writer's standpoint) and the narrator's voice sounds nearly neutral and objective. However, a closer reading of the text reveals that this description of a soldier's experience has some implications about the subjects of war, love affairs, and religion. By establishing connections among the details and making inferences, the readers may reach their own conclusions from their own perspectives.

The fight is fierce, and "the bombardment was knocking the trench to pieces." The soldier hides in the trench, "sweated and prayed," so as not to be killed. He prays, "oh jesus christ get me out of here." He makes a promise too. "If you'll only keep me from getting killed I'll do anything you say." This is not a promise at all but a bargain with God. Later he does not keep the promise. "[He] did not tell the girl... about Jesus. And he never told anybody."

The story reveals the human weakness and moral vulnerability in time of great danger or death. It also deconstructs the sacredness of Christianity and the divinity of God. The soldier survives the bombardment more because of luck than God's intervention. It shows that Christianity seemed to be less important at the time when the event took place, possibly in the early 20th century.

Evaluating

To evaluate a story usually involves two aspects. One is the assessment of its literary quality, and the other is the consideration of, or judgment on, the cultural, social, and moral values displayed or implied in the text.

Considering the literary quality, this story, though very short, is quite effective and successful in accomplishing its intentions. The small piece is first featured by brevity, and it is devoid of redundancy. The pace of narration is well disposed and the readers are able to seize the narrative structure. Moreover, the tone of narration is neutral and objective. The narrator does not intervene to give moral judgment or remarks. All the events are presented to the readers who may make inferences or draw conclusions by themselves. A well-designed story allows readers to be entertained with reading the story and provoked by what the text has to say in terms of the values. This story of the soldier is rich in cultural commutations and moral implications.

The image of a soldier is generally that of a hero. That is what a reader may expect given the traditional conventions of soldiery. The soldier in the story is however a coward whose behavior and action have proved his cowardice. He does not do his duty as a soldier. Moreover, he professes to believe in Christianity but his words and action betray him. He is not pious. Thirdly, he appears corrupt for he solicits prostitutes (as implied in "the girl he went upstairs with at the Villa Rossa"). Though the story touches on a "loving affair," it is an illicit love between man and woman.

In view of religion, readers, if they are devout Christians or pious religious followers, may condemn the soldier's blasphemous behavior and his bargain with God. Or if readers do not believe in religion, they may not take seriously the praying or just find it easy or amusing.

In terms of morality, readers may have different moral standards based on their cultural upbringings. The soldier's whoring may be considered corrupt, illicit, or morally degenerated in some cultures while in other cultures, it might be tolerable or even accepted. The readers' evaluation of prostitution is affected by the moralities popular in their cultures.

As for value, the apparent neutral and objective tone of narration is itself an attitudinal orientation or affective disposition. Though the story is devoid of evident evaluation by the narrator, the detachment and even indifference of tone in narration as well as the description imply the cruelty of war and the distortion of humanity.

One more point goes to the subject of sexual identity. It seems that the text demonstrates a tendency of male-centeredness. In the story, the man (the soldier) is depicted in detail. His thinking, his words, his behavior, and his state of mind are all presented as much as possible. The narration is focused on man. In the story there is a woman ("the girl") but she remains just a foil, a marginal figure for the man's sake. Nothing is reveled about her thoughts or feelings (about the man, about the war or something else). If one makes the point that women are far from the madding war, it is just an irony here. There is a notable absence of women and their perspectives in this story.

Experiencing, interpreting and evaluating altogether help with a more comprehensive and thorough understanding of a literary text. Certainly, the three processes do not take place independently. Rather they are interrelated and they happen simultaneously. One step of the process corresponds to and relies on the others. Meanwhile, the readers respond to, make sense of, or give evaluations on a story in different ways. Readers at different stages of life may also do these in different ways due to the influences from personal experiences, social attitudes, religious beliefs, and cultural dispositions. The readers' reading level also plays an important part in the reading of stories.

Questions for Reflection

Read the following stories and answer the questions. You must provide enough evidence from the text to support your answers.

(1)

The Ones Who Walk Away from Omelas (1976)

—Ursula K. Le Guin (1929-)

[1] With a clamor of bells that set the swallows soaring, the Festival of Summer came to the city Omelas, bright-towered by the sea. The rigging of the boats in harbor sparkled with flags. In

the streets between houses with red roofs and painted walls, between old moss-grown gardens and under avenues of trees, past great parks and public buildings, processions moved. Some were decorous: old people in long stiff robes of mauve and grey, grave master workmen, quiet, merry women carrying their babies and chatting as they walked. In other streets the music beat faster, a shimmering of gong and tambourine, and the people went dancing, the procession was a dance. Children dodged in and out, their high calls rising like the swallows' crossing flights over the music and the singing. All the processions wound towards the north side of the city, where on the great water-meadow called the Green Fields boys and girls, naked in the bright air, with mud-stained feet and ankles and long, lithe arms, exercised their restive horses before the race. The horses wore no gear at all but a halter without bit. Their manes were braided with streamers of silver, gold, and green. They flared their nostrils and pranced and boasted to one another; they were vastly excited, the horse being the only animal who has adopted our ceremonies as his own. Far off to the north and west the mountains stood up half encircling Omelas on her bay. The air of morning was so clear that the snow still crowning the Eighteen Peaks burned with white-gold fire across the miles of sunlit air, under the dark blue of the sky. There was just enough wind to make the banners that marked the racecourse snap and flutter now and then. In the silence of the broad green meadows one could hear the music winding through the city streets, farther and nearer and ever approaching, a cheerful faint sweetness of the air that from time to time trembled and gathered together and broke out into the great joyous clanging of the bells.

[2] Joyous! How is one to tell about joy? How describe the citizens of Omelas?

[3] They were not simple folk, you see, though they were happy. But we do not say the words of cheer much any more. All smiles have become archaic. Given a description such as this one tends to make certain assumptions. Given a description such as this one tends to look next for the King, mounted on a splendid stallion and surrounded by his noble knights, or perhaps in a golden litter borne by great-muscled slaves. But there was no king. They did not use swords, or keep slaves. They were not barbarians. I do not know the rules and laws of their society, but I suspect that they were singularly few. As they did without monarchy and slavery, so they also got on without the stock exchange, the advertisement, the secret police, and the bomb. Yet I repeat that these were not simple folk, not dulcet shepherds, noble savages, bland utopians. They were not less complex than us. The trouble is that we have a bad habit, encouraged by pedants and sophisticates, of considering happiness as something rather stupid. Only pain is intellectual, only evil interesting. This is the treason of the artist: a refusal to admit the banality of evil and the terrible boredom of pain. If you can't lick 'em, join 'em. If it hurts, repeat it. But to praise despair is to condemn delight, to embrace violence is to lose hold of everything else. We have almost lost hold; we can no longer describe a happy man, nor make any celebration of joy. How can I tell you about the people of Omelas? They were not naive and happy children—though their children were, in fact, happy. They were mature, intelligent, passionate adults whose lives were not wretched? O miracle! But I wish I could describe it better. I wish I could convince you. Omelas sounds in my words like a city

in a fairy tale, long ago and far away, once upon a time. Perhaps it would be best if you imagined it as your own fancy bids, assuming it will rise to the occasion, for certainly I cannot suit you all. For instance, how about technology? I think that there would be no cars or helicopters in and above the streets; this follows from the fact that the people of Omelas are happy people. Happiness is based on a just discrimination of what is necessary, what is neither necessary nor destructive, and what is destructive. In the middle category, however—that of the unnecessary but undestructive, that of comfort, luxury, exuberance, etc.—they could perfectly well have central heating, subway trains, washing machines, and all kinds of marvelous devices not yet invented here, floating light-sources, fuelless power, a cure for the common cold. Or they could have none of that: it doesn't matter. As you like it. I incline to think that people from towns up and down the coast have been coming in to Omelas during the last days before the Festival on very fast little trains and double-decked trams and that of the train station of Omelas is actually the handsomest building in town, though plainer than the magnificent Farmers' market. But even granted trains, I fear that Omelas so far strikes some of you a goody-goody. Smiles, bells, parades, horses, bleh. If so, please add an orgy. If any orgy would help, don't hesitate... One thing I know there is none of in Omelas is guilt. But what else should there be? I thought at first there were no drugs, but that is puritanical. For those who like it, the faint insistent sweetness of *drooz* may perfume the ways of the city, *drooz* which first brings a great lightness and brilliance to the mind and limbs, and then after some hours a dreamy languor, and wonderful visions at last of the very arcane and inmost secrets of the Universe, as well as exciting the pleasure of sex beyond all belief; and it is not habit-forming. For more modest tastes I think there ought to be beer. What else, what else belongs in the joyous city? The sense of victory, surely, the celebration of courage. But as we did without clergy, let us do without soldiers. The joy built upon successful slaughter is not the right kind of joy; it will not do; it is fearful and it is trivial. A boundless and generous contentment, a magnanimous triumph felt not against some outer enemy but in communion with the finest and fairest in the souls of all men everywhere and the splendor of the world's summer: this is what swells the hearts of the people of Omelas, and the victory they celebrate is that of life. I really don't think many of them need to take *drooz*.

[4] Most of the processions have reached the Green Fields by now. A marvelous smell of cooking goes forth from the red and blue tents of the provisioners. The faces of small children are amiably sticky; in the benign grey beard of a man a couple of crumbs of rich pastry are entangled. The youths and girls have mounted their horses and are beginning to group around the starting line of the course. An old woman, small, fat, and laughing, is passing out flowers from a basket, and tall young men wear her flowers in their shining hair. A child of nine or ten sits at the edge of the crowd, alone, playing on a wooden flute. People pause to listen, and they smile, but they do not speak to him, for he never ceases playing and never sees them, his dark eyes wholly rapt in the sweet, thin magic of the tune.

[5] He finishes, and slowly lowers his hands holding the wooden flute.

[6] As if that little private silence were the signal, all at once a trumpet sounds from the

pavilion near the starting line: imperious, melancholy, piercing. The horses rear on their slender legs, and some of them neigh in answer. Sober-faced, the young riders stroke the horses' necks and soothe them, whispering, "Quiet, quiet, there my beauty, my hope..." They begin to form in rank along the starting line. The crowds along the racecourse are like a field of grass and flowers in the wind. The Festival of Summer has begun.

[7] Do you believe? Do you accept the festival, the city, the joy? No? Then let me describe one more thing.

[8] In a basement under one of the beautiful public buildings of Omelas, or perhaps in the cellar of one of its spacious private homes, there is a room. It has one locked door, and no window. A little light seeps in dustily between cracks in the boards, secondhand from a cobwebbed window somewhere across the cellar. In one corner of the little room a couple of mops, with stiff, clotted, foul-smelling heads, stand near a rusty bucket. The floor is dirt, a little damp to the touch, as cellar dirt usually is. The room is about three paces long and two wide: a mere broom closet or disused tool room. In the room a child is sitting. It could be a boy or a girl. It looks about six, but actually is nearly ten. It is feeble-minded. Perhaps it was born defective, or perhaps it has become imbecile through fear, malnutrition, and neglect. It picks its nose and occasionally fumbles vaguely with its toes or genitals, as it sits hunched in the corner farthest from the bucket and the two mops. It is afraid of the mops. It finds them horrible. It shuts its eyes, but it knows the mops are still standing there; and the door is locked; and nobody will come. The door is always locked; and nobody ever comes, except that sometimes—the child has no understanding of time or interval—sometimes the door rattles terribly and opens, and a person, or several people, are there. One of them may come in and kick the child to make it stand up. The others never come close, but peer in at it with frightened, disgusted eyes. The food bowl and the water jug are hastily filled, the door is locked, the eyes disappear. The people at the door never say anything, but the child, who has not always lived in the tool room, and can remember sunlight and its mother's voice, sometimes speaks. "I will be good," it says. "Please let me out. I will be good!" They never answer. The child used to scream for help at night, and cry a good deal, but now it only makes a kind of whining, "eh-haa, eh-haa," and it speaks less and less often. It is so thin there are no calves to its legs; its belly protrudes; it lives on a half-bowl of corn meal and grease a day. It is naked. Its buttocks and thighs are a mass of festered sores, as it sits in its own excrement continually.

[9] They all know it is there, all the people of Omelas. Some of them have come to see it; others are content merely to know it is there. They all know that it has to be there. Some of them understand why, and some do not, but they all understand that their happiness, the beauty of their city, the tenderness of their friendships, the health of their children, the wisdom of their scholars, the skill of their makers, even the abundance of their harvest and the kindly weathers of their skies, depend wholly on this child's abominable misery.

[10] This is usually explained to children when they are between eight and twelve, whenever they seem capable of understanding; and most of those who come to see the child are

young people, though often enough an adult comes, or comes back, to see the child. No matter how well the matter has been explained to them, these young spectators are always shocked and sickened at the sight. They feel disgust, which they had thought themselves superior to. They feel anger, outrage, impotence, despite all the explanations. They would like to do something for the child. But there is nothing they can do. If the child were brought up into the sunlight out of the vile place, if it were cleaned and fed and comforted, that would be a good thing, indeed; but if it were done, in that day and hour all the prosperity and beauty and delight of Omelas would wither and be destroyed. Those are the terms. To exchange all the goodness and grace of every life in Omelas for that single, small improvement; to throw away the happiness of thousands for the chance of the happiness of one: that would be to let guilt within the walls indeed.

[11] The terms are strict and absolute; there may not even be a kind word spoken to the child.

[12] Often the young people go home in tears, or in a tearless rage, when they have seen the child and faced this terrible paradox. They may brood over it for weeks or years. But as time goes on they begin to realize that even if the child could be released, it would not get much good of its freedom: a little vague pleasure of warmth and food, no doubt, but little more. It is too degraded and imbecile to know any real joy. It has been afraid too long ever to be free of fear. Its habits are too uncouth for it to respond to humane treatment. Indeed, after so long it would probably be wretched without walls about it to protect it, and darkness for its eyes, and its own excrement to sit in. Their tears at the bitter injustice dry when they begin to perceive the terrible justice of reality, and to accept it. Yet it is their tears and anger, the trying of their generosity and the acceptance of their helplessness, which are perhaps the true source of the splendor of their lives. Theirs is no vapid, irresponsible happiness. They know that they, like the child, are not free. They know compassion. It is the existence of the child, and their knowledge of its existence, that makes possible the nobility of their architecture, the poignancy of their music, the profundity of their science. It is because of the child that they are so gentle with children. They know that if the wretched one were not there sniveling in the dark, the other one, the flute-player, could make no joyful music as the young riders line up in their beauty for the race in the sunlight of the first morning of summer.

[13] Now do you believe in them? Are they not more credible? But there is one more thing to tell, and this is quite incredible.

[14] At times one of the adolescent girls or boys who go to see the child does not go home to weep or rage, does not, in fact, go home at all. Sometimes also a man or woman much older falls silent for a day or two, and then leaves home. These people go out into the street, and walk down the street alone. They keep walking, and walk straight out of the city of Omelas, through the beautiful gates. They keep walking across the farmlands of Omelas. Each one goes alone, youth or girl, man or woman. Night falls; the traveler must pass down village streets, between the houses with yellow-lit windows, and on out into the darkness of the fields. Each alone, they go

west or north, towards the mountains. They go on. They leave Omelas, they walk ahead into the darkness, and they do not come back. The place they go towards is a place even less imaginable to most of us than the city of happiness. I cannot describe it at all. It is possible that it does not exist. But they seem to know where they are going, the ones who walk away from Omelas.

Questions

The Experience of Fiction

1. How do you react to the story, "The Ones Who Walk Away from Omelas"?
2. What feelings does the story evoke?
3. Do you feel sorry for the kid in the basement? Did you feel anger or resentment at other people's behavior? Why?
4. Do your feelings about any of the characters change during the course of your reading or afterward? Why?
5. How does the story reflect what you have observed of human relations in a society?

The Interpretation of Fiction

1. What sense do you make of the story? What does it suggest? Why so?
2. What details attract your attention? How the details connect with each other?
3. How do the characters interact? What does their interaction imply?
4. How did the people of Omelas react to the misery of the kid in the basement?
5. What is the narrator's attitude toward the people who feed the kid in the basement of Omelas?
6. What general idea about happiness does the story convey?

Evaluation of Fiction

1. Whose values does the story seem to endorse? Whose values are criticized? Why?
2. Do you find the story meaningful? Can you relate it in any significant way to your own life?
3. Do you think it is a good story, a successful example of philosophical fiction? Why?
4. To what extent do the values of the Omelas citizens reflect or depart from today's cultural values?
5. How are the values of the Omelas citizens measured against your own?
6. Do you find the language or structure of the story admirable? Why?
7. What functions do the short paragraphs have?

(2)

Everyday Use

for Your Grandmamma (1973)

—Alice Walker (1944 —)

[1] I will wait for her in the yard that Maggie and I made so clean and wavy yesterday afternoon. A yard like this is more comfortable than most people know. It is not just a yard. It is

like an extended living room. When the hard clay is swept clean as a floor and the fine sand around the edges lined with tiny, irregular grooves, anyone can come and sit and look up into the elm tree and wait for the breezes that never come inside the house.

[2] Maggie will be nervous until after her sister goes: she will stand hopelessly in corners, homely and ashamed of the burn scars down her arms and legs, eying her sister with a mixture of envy and awe. She thinks her sister has held life always in the palm of one hand, that "no" is a word the world never learned to say to her.

[3] You've no doubt seen those TV shows where the child who has "made it" is confronted, as a surprise, by her own mother and father, tottering in weakly from backstage. (A Pleasant surprise, of course: What would they do if parent and child came on the show only to curse out and insult each other?) On TV mother and child embrace and smile into each other's face. Sometimes the mother and father weep, the child wraps them in her arms and leans across the table to tell how she would not have made it without their help. I have seen these programs.

[4] Sometimes I dream a dream in which Dee and I are suddenly brought together on a TV program of this sort. Out of a dark and soft-seated limousine I am ushered into a bright room filled with many people. There I meet a smiling, gray, sporty man like Johnny Carson who shakes my hand and tells me what a fine girl I have. Then we are on the stage and Dee is embracing me with tears in her eyes. She pins on my dress a large orchid, even though she has told me once that she thinks orchids are tacky flowers.

[5] In real life I am a large, big-boned woman with rough, man-working hands. In the winter I wear flannel nightgowns to bed and overalls during the day. I can kill and clean a hog as mercilessly as a man. My fat keeps me hot in zero weather. I can work outside all day, breaking ice to get water for washing; I can eat pork liver cooked over the open tire minutes after it comes steaming from the hog. One winter I knocked a bull calf straight in the brain between the eyes with a sledge hammer and had the meat hung up to chill before nightfall. But of course all this does not show on television. I am the way my daughter would want me to be: a hundred pounds lighter, my skin like an uncooked barley pancake. My hair glistens in the hot bright lights. Johnny Carson has much to do to keep up with my quick and witty tongue.

[6] But that is a mistake. I know even before I wake up. Who ever knew a Johnson with a quick tongue? Who can even imagine me looking a strange white man in the eye? It seems to me I have talked to them always with one foot raised in flight, with my head turned in whichever way is farthest from them. Dee, though. She would always look anyone in the eye. Hesitation was no part of her nature.

[7] "How do I look, Mama?" Maggie says, showing just enough of her thin body enveloped in pink skirt and red blouse for me to know she's there, almost hidden by the door.

[8] "Come out into the yard," I say.

[9] Have you ever seen a lame animal, perhaps a dog run over by some careless person rich enough to own a car, sidle up to someone who is ignorant enough to be kind of him? That is the

way my Maggie walks. She has been like this, chin on chest, eyes on ground, feet in shuffle, ever since the fire that burned the other house to the ground.

[10] Dee is lighter than Maggie, with nicer hair and a fuller figure. She's a woman now, though sometimes I forget. How long ago was it that the other house burned? Ten, twelve years? Sometimes I can still hear the flames and feel Maggie's arms sticking to me, her hair smoking and her dress falling off her in little black papery flakes. Her eyes seemed stretched open, blazed open by the flames reflected in them. And Dee. I see her standing off under the sweet gum tree she used to dig gum out of; a look at concentration on her face as she watched the last dingy gray board of the house fall in toward the red-hot brick chimney. "Why don't you do a dance around the ashes?" I'd wanted to ask her. She had hated the house that much.

[11] I used to think she hated Maggie, too. But that was before we raised the money, the church and me, to send her to Augusta to school. She used to read to us without pity, forcing words, lies, other folks' habits, whole lives upon us two, sitting trapped and ignorant underneath her voice. She washed us in a river of make-believe, burned us with a lot of knowledge we didn't necessarily need to know. Pressed us to her with the serious way she read, to shove us away at just the moment, like dimwits, we seemed about to understand.

[12] Dee wanted nice things. A yellow organdy dress to wear to her graduation from high school; black pumps to match a green suit she'd made from an old suit somebody gave me. She was determined to stare down any disaster in her efforts. Her eyelids would not flicker for minutes at a time. Often I fought off the temptation to shake her. At sixteen she had a style of her own, and knew what style was.

[13] I never had an education myself. After second grade the school was closed down. Don't ask me why in 1927 the colored asked fewer questions than they do now. Sometimes Maggie reads to me. She stumbles along good-naturedly but can't see well. She knows she is not bright. Like good looks and money, quickness passed her by. She will marry John Thomas (who has mossy teeth in an earnest face) and then I'll be free to sit here and I guess just sing church songs to myself. Although I never was a good singer. Never could carry a tune. I was always better at a man's job. I used to love to milk till I was hooked in the side in '49. Cows are soothing and slow and don't bother you, unless you try to milk them the wrong way.

[14] I have deliberately turned my back on the house. It is three rooms, just like the one that burned, except the roof is tin; they don't make shingle roofs any more. There are no real windows, just some holes cut in the sides, like the portholes in a ship, but not round and not square, with rawhide holding the shutters up on the outside. This house is in a pasture, too, like the other one. No doubt when Dee sees it she will want to tear it down. She wrote me once that no matter where we "choose" to live, she will manage to come see us. But she will never bring her friends. Maggie and I thought about this and Maggie asked me, "Mama, when did Dee ever have any friends?"

[15] She had a few. Furtive boys in pink shirts hanging about on washday after school.

Nervous girls who never laughed. Impressed with her they worshiped the well-turned phrase, the cute shape, the scalding humor that erupted like bubbles in lye. She read to them.

[16] When she was courting Jimmy T she didn't have much time to pay to us, but turned all her faultfinding power on him. He flew to marry a cheap city girl from a family of ignorant flashy people. She hardly had time to recompose herself.

[17] When she comes I will meet—but there they are!

[18] Maggie attempts to make a dash for the house, in her shuffling way, but I stay her with my hand. "Come back here," I say. And she stops and tries to dig a well in the sand with her toe.

[19] It is hard to see them clearly through the strong sun. But even the first glimpse of leg out of the car tells me it is Dee. Her feet were always neat-looking, as it God himself had shaped them with a certain style. From the other side of the car comes a short, stocky man. Hair is all over his head a foot long and hanging from his chin like a kinky mule tail. I hear Maggie suck in her breath. "Uhnnnh," is what it sounds like. Like when you see the wriggling end of a snake just in front of your toot on the road. "Uhnnnh."

[20] Dee next. A dress down to the ground, in this hot weather. A dress so loud it hurts my eyes. There are yellows and oranges enough to throw back the light of the sun. I feel my whole face warming from the heat waves it throws out. Earrings gold, too, and hanging down to her shoulders. Bracelets dangling and making noises when she moves her arm up to shake the folds of the dress out of her armpits. The dress is loose and flows, and as she walks closer, I like it. I hear Maggie go "Uhnnnh" again. It is her sister's hair. It stands straight up like the wool on a sheep. It is black as night and around the edges are two long pigtails that rope about like small lizards disappearing behind her ears.

[21] "Wa-su-zo-Tean-o!" she says, coming on in that gliding way the dress makes her move. The short stocky fellow with the hair to his navel is all grinning and he follows up with "Asalamalakim, my mother and sister!" He moves to hug Maggie but she falls back, right up against the back of my chair. I feel her trembling there and when I look up I see the perspiration falling off her chin.

[22] "Don't get up," says Dee. Since I am stout it takes something of a push. You can see me trying to move a second or two before I make it. She turns, showing white heels through her sandals, and goes back to the car. Out she peeks next with a Polaroid. She stoops down quickly and lines up picture after picture of me sitting there in front of the house with Maggie cowering behind me. She never takes a shot without making sure the house is included. When a cow comes nibbling around the edge of the yard she snaps it and me and Maggie and the house. Then she puts the Polaroid in the back seat of the car, and comes up and kisses me on the forehead.

[23] Meanwhile Asalamalakim is going through motions with Maggie's hand. Maggie's hand is as limp as a fish, and probably as cold, despite the sweat, and she keeps trying to pull it back. It looks like Asalamalakim wants to shake hands but wants to do it fancy. Or maybe he doesn't know how people shake hands. Anyhow, he soon gives up on Maggie.

[24] "Well," I say. "Dee."

[25] "No, Mama," she says. "Not 'Dee', Wangero Leewanika Kemanjo!"

[26] "What happened to 'Dee'?" I wanted to know.

[27] "She's dead," Wangero said. "I couldn't bear it any longer, being named after the people who oppress me."

[28] "You know as well as me you was named after your aunt Dicie," I said. Dicie is my sister. She named Dee. We called her "Big Dee" after Dee was born.

[29] "But who was she named after?" asked Wangero.

[30] "I guess after Grandma Dee," I said.

[31] "And who was she named after?" asked Wangero.

[32] "Her mother," I said, and saw Wangero was getting tired. "That's about as far back as I can trace it," I said.

[33] Though, in fact, I probably could have carried it back beyond the Civil War through the branches.

[34] "Well," said Asalamalakim, "there you are."

[35] "Uhnnnh," I heard Maggie say.

[36] "There I was not," I said, before 'Dicie' cropped up in our family, so why should I try to trace it that far back?"

[37] He just stood there grinning, looking down on me like somebody inspecting a Model A car. Every once in a while he and Wangero sent eye signals over my head.

[38] "How do you pronounce this name?" I asked.

[39] "You don't have to call me by it if you don't want to," said Wangero.

[40] "Why shouldn't I?" I asked. "If that's what you want us to call you, we'll call you."

[41] "I know it might sound awkward at first," said Wangero.

[42] "I'll get used to it," I said. "Ream it out again."

[43] Well, soon we got the name out of the way. Asalamalakim had a name twice as long and three times as hard. After I tripped over it two or three times he told me to just call him Hakim-a-barber. I wanted to ask him was he a barber, but I didn't really think he was, so I don't ask.

[44] "You must belong to those beet-cattle peoples down the road," I said. They said "Asalamalakim" when they met you too, but they didn't shake hands. Always too busy: feeding the cattle, fixing the fences, putting up salt-lick shelters, throwing down hay. When the white folks poisoned some of the herd the men stayed up all night with rifles in their hands. I walked a mile and a half just to see the sight.

[45] Hakim-a-barber said, "I accept some of their doctrines, but farming and raising cattle is not my style." (They didn't tell me, and I didn't ask, whether Wangero (Dee) had really gone and married him.)

[46] We sat down to eat and right away he said he didn't eat collards and pork was unclean.

Wangero, though, went on through the chitlins and corn bread, the greens and everything else. She talked a blue streak over the sweet potatoes. Everything delighted her. Even the fact that we still used the benches her daddy made for the table when we couldn't afford to buy chairs.

[47] "Oh, Mama!" she cried. Then turned to Hakim-a-barber. "I never knew how lovely these benches are. You can feel the rump prints," she said, running her hands underneath her and along the bench. Then she gave a sigh and her hand closed over Grandma Dee's butter dish. "That's it!" she said. "I knew there was something I wanted to ask you if I could have." She jumped up from the table and went over in the corner where the churn stood, the milk in it clabber by now. She looked at the churn and looked at it.

[48] "This churn top is what I need," she said. "Didn't Uncle Buddy whittle it out of a tree you all used to have?"

[49] "Yes," I said.

[50] "Uh huh, " she said happily. "And I want the dasher, too."

[51] "Uncle Buddy whittle that, too?" asked the barber.

[52] Dee (Wangero) looked up at me.

[53] "Aunt Dee's first husband whittled the dash," said Maggie so low you almost couldn't hear her. "His name was Henry, but they called him Stash."

[54] "Maggie's brain is like an elephant," Wangero said, laughing. "I can use the churn top as a center piece for the alcove table," she said, sliding a plate over the churn, "and I'll think of something artistic to do with the dasher."

[55] When she finished wrapping the dasher the handle stuck out. I took it for a moment in my hands. You didn't even have to look close to see where hands pushing the dasher up and down to make butter had left a kind of sink in the wood. In fact, there were a lot of small sinks; you could see where thumbs and fingers had sunk into the wood. It was beautiful light yellow wood, from a tree that grew in the yard where Big Dee and Stash had lived.

[56] After dinner Dee (Wangero) went to the trunk at the foot of my bed and started rifling through it. Maggie hung back in the kitchen over the dishpan. Out came Wangero with two quilts. They had been pieced by Grandma Dee and then Big Dee and me had hung them on the quilt frames on the front porch and quilted them. One was in the Lone Star pattern. The other was Walk Around the Mountain. In both of them were scraps of dresses Grandma Dee had worn fifty and more years ago. Bit sand pieces of Grandpa Jarrell's Paisley shirts. And one teeny faded blue piece, about the size of a penny matchbox, that was from Great Grandpa Ezra's uniform that he wore in the Civil War.

[57] "Mama," Wangero said sweet as a bird. "Can I have these old quilts?"

[58] I heard something fall in the kitchen, and a minute later the kitchen door slammed.

[59] "Why don't you take one or two of the others?" I asked. "These old things was just done by me and Big Dee from some tops your grandma pieced before she died."

[60] "No," said Wangero. "I don't want those. They are stitched around the borders by

machine."

[61] "That'll make them last better," I said.

[62] "That's not the point," said Wanglero. "These are all pieces of dresses Grandma used to wear. She did all this stitching by hand. Imagine!" She held the quilts securely in her arms, stroking them.

[63] "Some of the pieces, like those lavender ones, come from old clothes her mother handed down to her," I said, moving up to touch the quilts. Dee (Wangero) moved back just enough so that I couldn't reach the quilts. They already belonged to her. "Imagine!" She breathed again, clutching them closely to her bosom.

[64] "The truth is," I said, "I promised to give them quilts to Maggie, for when she marries John Thomas."

[65] She gasped like a bee had stung her.

[66] "Maggie can't appreciate these quilts!" she said. "She'd probably be backward enough to put them to everyday use."

[67] "I reckon she would," I said. "God knows I been savage 'em for long enough with nobody using 'em. I hope she will! "I didn't want to bring up how I had offered Dee (Wangero) a quilt when she went away to college. Then she had told me they were old-fashioned, out of style.

[68] "But they're priceless!" she was saying now, furiously; for she has a temper. "Maggie would put them on the bed and in five years they'd be in rags. Less than that!" "She can always make some more," I said. "Maggie knows how to quilt."

[69] Dee (Wangero) looked at me with hatred. "You just will not understand. The point is these quilts, these quilts!"

[70] "Well," I said, stumped. "What would you do with them?"

[71] "Hang them," she said. As it that was the only thing you could do with quilts.

[72] Maggie by now was standing in the door. I could almost hear the sound her feet made as they scraped over each other.

[73] "She can have them, Mama," she said like somebody used to never winning anything, or having anything reserved for her. "I can 'member Grandma Dee without the quilts."

[74] I looked at her hard. She had filled her bottom lip with checkerberry snuff and it gave her face a kind of dopey, hangdog look. It was Grandma Dee and Big Dee who taught her how to quilt herself. She stood there with her scarred hands hidden in the folds of her skirt. She looked at her sister with something like fear but she wasn't mad at her. This was Maggie's portion. This was the way she knew God to work.

[75] When I looked at her like that something hit me in the top of my head and ran down to the soles of my feet. Just like when I'm in church and the spirit of God touches me and I get happy and shout. I did something I never had done before: hugged Maggie to me, then dragged her on into the room, snatched the quilts out of Miss Wangero's hands and dumped them into

Maggie's lap. Maggie just sat there on my bed with her mouth open.

[76] "Take one or two of the others," I said to Dee.

[77] But she turned without a word and went out to Hakim-a-barber.

[78] "You just don't understand," she said, as Maggie and I came out to the car.

[79] "What don't I understand?" I wanted to know.

[80] "Your heritage," she said. And then she turned to Maggie, kissed her, and said, "You ought to try to make something of yourself, too, Maggie. It's really a new day for us. But from the way you and Mama still live you'd never know it."

[81] She put on some sunglasses that hid everything above the tip of her nose and her chin.

[82] Maggie smiled; maybe at the sunglasses. But a real smile, not scared. After we watched the car dust settle I asked Maggie to bring me a dip of snuff. And then the two of us sat there just enjoying, until it was time to go in the house and go to bed.

Questions

The Experience of Fiction

1. Describe your experience in reading "Everyday Use for Your Grandmamma." Does the story surprise or entertain you? Why?

2. What is your response to Mama's change near the end of the story?

3. What is your reaction to the attitude of Dee toward Mama and Maggie, and to that of Mama and Maggie toward Dee?

4. Did Maggie change too? In what way?

5. Did your feelings about Maggie and Dee change in the course of reading? How?

The Interpretation of Fiction

1. Characterize Mama's style of telling the story. What do you learn about her from the kind of language she uses?

2. Characterize the three people of the Johnson family: Mrs. Johnson (Mama), Dee, and Maggie.

3. What role does the minor character Asalamalakim play? Is the character dependable? Why?

4. What is the narrator's attitude toward white people in general?

5. What are the attitudes of Mama towards her two daughters? What do her attitudes suggest considering their cultural heritage?

6. Did Mama have a kind of epiphany? Where in the story did it happen?

7. What does the dialogue at the end of the story (Paras. 78−82) suggest? What does Maggie's reaction imply?

"You just don't understand," she said, as Maggie and I came out to the car.

"What don't I understand?" I wanted to know.

"Your heritage," she said. And then she turned to Maggie, kissed her, and said, "You ought to try to make something of yourself, too, Maggie. It's really a new day for us. But from the way you and Mama still live you'd never know it."

She put on some sunglasses that hid everything above the tip of her nose and her chin.

Maggie smiled; maybe at the sunglasses. But a real mile, not scared. After we watched the car dust settle I asked Maggie to bring me a dip of snuff. And then the two of us sat there just enjoying, until it was time to go in the house and go to bed.

8. What idea about the marriage of Dee and Asalamalakim does the story convey?

The Evaluation of Fiction

1. Whose values does the story seem to endorse? Whose values are criticized? Please explain in detail.

2. What social values influence your reading of the story? How?

3. What values underlie the characters' treatment of the quilt?

4. Do you find the story meaningful? In what way?

5. Do you think "Everyday Use for Your Grandmamma" is a successful example of modern short story? Why?

6. Does the African American vernacular English strengthen or undermine the telling of the story? Why or why not?

7. In what way is the aesthetical significance of the story well manifested?

8. Do you find anything in "Everyday Use for Your Grandmamma" to admire considering its language or structure?

As emphasized before, the three steps of the reading process are interrelated and they may occur simultaneously despite the separated discussions in the above for the sake of study. Moreover, personal and cultural differences may give rise to different responses, interpretations and evaluations.

Literature study is a comprehensive practice and it involves more than the three steps. Moreover, to better understand a story, short or long, it is necessary and inevitable to include the elements of fiction.

✎ Chapter 4 ✎
Elements of Fiction

To understand fiction well, it is important to have a good knowledge of the techniques which concern the basic elements of characteristics such as plot, character, point of view, setting, style and language, symbol, irony, and theme. These elements of fiction are interconnected and they work together to express the feeling and embody the meaning in the story. In this sense, the discussion of one element will inevitably touch on other elements and, most importantly, on the story as a whole. The short story "A Good Man Is Hard to Find" (1955) by Flannery O'Connor (1925–1964) can be taken as an example to analyze a story considering the elements of fiction.

A Good Man Is Hard to Find

—Flannery O'Connor (1925–1964)

The dragon is by the side of the road, watching those who pass. Beware lest he devour you. We go to the Father of Souls, but it is necessary to pass by the dragon.

St. Cyril of Jerusalem

[1] The grandmother didn't want to go to Florida. She wanted to visit some of her connections in east Tennessee and she was seizing at every chance to change Bailey's mind. Bailey was the son she lived with, her only boy. He was sitting on the edge of his chair at the table, bent over the orange sports section of the Journal. "Now look here, Bailey," she said, "see here, read this," and she stood with one hand on her thin hip and the other rattling the newspaper at his bald head. "Here this fellow that calls himself The Misfit is aloose from the Federal Pen and headed toward Florida and you read here what it says he did to these people. Just you read it. I wouldn't take my children in any direction with a criminal like that aloose in it. I couldn't answer to my conscience if I did."

[2] Bailey didn't look up from his reading so she wheeled around then and faced the children's mother, a young woman in slacks, whose face was as broad and innocent as a cabbage and was tied around with a green head-kerchief that had two points on the top like rabbit's ears. She was sitting on the sofa, feeding the baby his apricots out of a jar. "The children have been to Florida before," the old lady said. "You all ought to take them somewhere else for a change so they would see different parts of the world and be broad. They never have been to east Tennessee."

[3] The children's mother didn't seem to hear her but the eight-year-old boy, John Wesley, a stocky child with glasses, said, "If you don't want to go to Florida, why dontcha stay at home?" He and the little girl, June Star, were reading the funny papers on the floor.

[4] "She wouldn't stay at home to be queen for a day," June Star said without raising her yellow head.

[5] "Yes and what would you do if this fellow, The Misfit, caught you?" the grandmother asked.

[6] "I'd smack his face," John Wesley said.

[7] "She wouldn't stay at home for a million bucks," June Star said. "Afraid she'd miss something. She has to go everywhere we go."

[8] "All right, Miss," the grandmother said. "Just remember that the next time you want me to curl your hair."

[9] June Star said her hair was naturally curly.

[10] The next morning the grandmother was the first one in the car, ready to go. She had her big black valise that looked like the head of a hippopotamus in one corner, and underneath it she was hiding a basket with Pitty Sing, the cat, in it. She didn't intend for the cat to be left alone in the house for three days because he would miss her too much and she was afraid he might brush against one of the gas burners and accidentally asphyxiate himself. Her son, Bailey, didn't like to arrive at a motel with a cat.

[11] She sat in the middle of the back seat with John Wesley and June Star on either side of her. Bailey and the children's mother and the baby sat in front and they left Atlanta at eight forty-five with the mileage on the car at 55,890. The grandmother wrote this down because she thought it would be interesting to say how many miles they had been when they got back. It took them twenty minutes to reach the outskirts of the city.

[12] The old lady settled herself comfortably, removing her white cotton gloves and putting them up with her purse on the shelf in front of the back window. The children's mother still had on slacks and still had her head tied up in a green kerchief, but the grandmother had on a navy blue straw sailor hat with a bunch of white violets on the brim and a navy blue dress with a small white dot in the print. Her collars and cuffs were white organdy trimmed with lace and at her neckline she had pinned a purple spray of cloth violets containing a sachet. In case of an accident, anyone seeing her dead on the highway would know at once that she was a lady.

[13] She said she thought it was going to be a good day for driving, neither too hot nor too cold, and she cautioned Bailey that the speed limit was fifty-five miles an hour and that the patrolmen hid themselves behind billboards and small clumps of trees and sped out after you before you had a chance to slow down. She pointed out interesting details of the scenery: Stone Mountain; the blue granite that in some places came up to both sides of the highway; the brilliant red clay banks slightly streaked with purple; and the various crops that made rows of green lacework on the ground. The trees were full of silver-white sunlight and the meanest of them sparkled. The children were reading comic magazines and their mother had gone back to sleep.

[14] "Let's go through Georgia fast so we won't have to look at it much," John Wesley said.

[15] "If I were a little boy," said the grandmother, "I wouldn't talk about my native state that way. Tennessee has the mountains and Georgia has the hills."

[16] "Tennessee is just a hillbilly dumping ground," John Wesley said, "and Georgia is a lousy state too."

[17] "You said it," June Star said.

[18] "In my time," said the grandmother, folding her thin veined fingers, "children were more respectful of their native states and their parents and everything else. People did right then. Oh look at the cute little pickaninny!" she said and pointed to a Negro child standing in the door of a shack. "Wouldn't that make a picture, now?" she asked and they all turned and looked at the little Negro out of the back window. He waved.

[19] "He didn't have any britches on," June Star said.

[20] "He probably didn't have any," the grandmother explained. "Little niggers in the country don't have things like we do. If I could paint, I'd paint that picture," she said.

[21] The children exchanged comic books.

[22] The grandmother offered to hold the baby and the children's mother passed him over the front seat to her. She set him on her knee and bounced him and told him about the things they were passing. She rolled her eyes and screwed up her mouth and stuck her leathery thin face into his smooth bland one. Occasionally he gave her a faraway smile. They passed a large cotton field with five or six graves fenced in the middle of it, like a small island. "Look at the graveyard!" the grandmother said, pointing it out. "That was the old family burying ground. That belonged to the plantation."

[23] "Where's the plantation?" John Wesley asked.

[24] "Gone with the Wind," said the grandmother. "Ha. Ha."

[25] When the children finished all the comic books they had brought, they opened the lunch and ate it. The grandmother ate a peanut butter sandwich and an olive and would not let the children throw the box and the paper napkins out the window. When there was nothing else to do they played a game by choosing a cloud and making the other two guess what shape it suggested. John Wesley took one the shape of a cow and June Star guessed a cow and John Wesley said, no, an automobile, and June Star said he didn't play fair, and they began to slap each other over the grandmother.

[26] The grandmother said she would tell them a story if they would keep quiet. When she told a story, she rolled her eyes and waved her head and was very dramatic. She said once when she was a maiden lady she had been courted by a Mr. Edgar Atkins Teagarden from Jasper, Georgia. She said he was a very good-looking man and a gentleman and that he brought her a watermelon every Saturday afternoon with his initials cut in it, E. A. T. Well, one Saturday, she said, Mr. Teagarden brought the watermelon and there was nobody at home and he left it on the front porch and returned in his buggy to Jasper, but she never got the watermelon, she said, because a nigger boy ate it when he saw the initials, E. A. T.! This story tickled John Wesley's funny bone and he giggled and giggled but June Star didn't think it was any good. She said she wouldn't marry a man that just brought her a watermelon on Saturday. The grandmother said she would have done well to marry Mr. Teagarden because he was a gentleman and had bought Coca-Cola stock when it first came out and that he had died only a few years ago, a very wealthy man.

[27] They stopped at The Tower for barbecued sandwiches. The Tower was a part stucco and part wood filling station and dance hall set in a clearing outside of Timothy. A fat man named Red Sammy Butts ran it and there were signs stuck here and there on the building and for miles up and down the highway saying, TRY RED SAMMY'S FAMOUS BARBECUE.

NONE LIKE FAMOUS RED SAMMY'S! RED SAM! THE FAT BOY WITH THE HAPPY LAUGH! A VETERAN! RED SAMMY'S YOUR MAN!

[28] Red Sammy was lying on the bare ground outside The Tower with his head under a truck while a gray monkey about a foot high, chained to a small chinaberry tree, chattered nearby. The monkey sprang back into the tree and got on the highest limb as soon as he saw the children jump out of the car and run toward him.

[29] Inside, The Tower was a long dark room with a counter at one end and tables at the other and dancing space in the middle. They all sat down at a board table next to the nickelodeon and Red Sam's wife, a tall burnt-brown woman with hair and eyes lighter than her skin, came and took their order. The children's mother put a dime in the machine and played "The Tennessee Waltz," and the grandmother said that tune always made her want to dance. She asked Bailey if he would like to dance but he only glared at her. He didn't have a naturally sunny disposition like she did and trips made him nervous. The grandmother's brown eyes were very bright. She swayed her head from side to side and pretended she was dancing in her chair. June Star said play something she could tap to so the children's mother put in another dime and played a fast number and June Star stepped out onto the dance floor and did her tap routine.

[30] "Ain't she cute?" Red Sam's wife said, leaning over the counter. "Would you like to come be my little girl?"

[31] "No I certainly wouldn't," June Star said. "I wouldn't live in a broken-down place like this for a million bucks!" and she ran back to the table.

[32] "Ain't she cute?" the woman repeated, stretching her mouth politely.

[33] "Aren't you ashamed?" hissed the grandmother.

[34] Red Sam came in and told his wife to quit lounging on the counter and hurry up with these people's order. His khaki trousers reached just to his hip bones and his stomach hung over them like a sack of meal swaying under his shirt. He came over and sat down at a table nearby and let out a combination sigh and yodel. "You can't win," he said. "You can't win," and he wiped his sweating red face off with a gray handkerchief. "These days you don't know who to trust," he said. "Ain't that the truth?"

[35] "People are certainly not nice like they used to be," said the grandmother.

[36] "Two fellers come in here last week," Red Sammy said, "driving a Chrysler. It was an old beat-up car but it was a good one and these boys looked all right to me. Said they worked at the mill and you know I let them fellers charge the gas they bought? Now why did I do that?"

[37] "Because you're a good man!" the grandmother said at once.

[38] "Yes'm, I suppose so," Red Sam said as if he were struck with this answer.

[39] His wife brought the orders, carrying the five plates all at once without a tray, two in each hand and one balanced on her arm. "It isn't a soul in this green world of God's that you can trust," she said. "And I don't count nobody out of that, not nobody," she repeated, looking at Red Sammy.

[40] "Did you read about that criminal, The Misfit, that's escaped?" asked the grandmother.

[41] "I wouldn't be a bit surprised if he didn't attact this place right here," said the woman. "If he hears about it being here, I wouldn't be none surprised to see him. If he hears it's

two cent in the cash register, I wouldn't be a tall surprised if he…"

[42] "That'll do," Red Sam said. "Go bring these people their Co'-Colas," and the woman went off to get the rest of the order.

[43] "A good man is hard to find," Red Sammy said. "Everything is getting terrible. I remember the day you could go off and leave your screen door unlatched. Not no more."

[44] He and the grandmother discussed better times. The old lady said that in her opinion Europe was entirely to blame for the way things were now. She said the way Europe acted you would think we were made of money and Red Sam said it was no use talking about it, she was exactly right. The children ran outside into the white sunlight and looked at the monkey in the lacy chinaberry tree. He was busy catching fleas on himself and biting each one carefully between his teeth as if it were a delicacy.

[45] They drove off again into the hot afternoon. The grandmother took cat naps and woke up every few minutes with her own snoring. Outside of Toombsboro she woke up and recalled an old plantation that she had visited in this neighborhood once when she was a young lady. She said the house had six white columns across the front and that there was an avenue of oaks leading up to it and two little wooden trellis arbors on either side in front where you sat down with your suitor after a stroll in the garden. She recalled exactly which road to turn off to get to it. She knew that Bailey would not be willing to lose any time looking at an old house, but the more she talked about it, the more she wanted to see it once again and find out if the little twin arbors were still standing. "There was a secret panel in this house," she said craftily, not telling the truth but wishing that she were, "and the story went that all the family silver was hidden in it when Sherman came through but it was never found…"

[46] "Hey!" John Wesley said. "Let's go see it! We'll find it! We'll poke all the woodwork and find it! Who lives there? Where do you turn off at? Hey Pop, can't we turn off there?"

[47] "We never have seen a house with a secret panel!" June Star shrieked. "Let's go to the house with the secret panel! Hey Pop, can't we go see the house with the secret panel!"

[48] "It's not far from here, I know," the grandmother said. "It wouldn't take over twenty minutes."

[49] Bailey was looking straight ahead. His jaw was as rigid as a horseshoe. "No," he said.

[50] The children began to yell and scream that they wanted to see the house with the secret panel. John Wesley kicked the back of the front seat and June Star hung over her mother's shoulder and whined desperately into her ear that they never had any fun even on their vacation, that they could never do what THEY wanted to do. The baby began to scream and John Wesley kicked the back of the seat so hard that his father could feel the blows in his kidney.

[51] "All right!" he shouted and drew the car to a stop at the side of the road. "Will you all shut up? Will you all just shut up for one second? If you don't shut up, we won't go anywhere."

[52] "It would be very educational for them," the grandmother murmured.

[53] "All right," Bailey said, "but get this: this is the only time we're going to stop for anything like this. This is the one and only time."

[54] "The dirt road that you have to turn down is about a mile back," the grandmother directed. "I marked it when we passed."

[55] "A dirt road," Bailey groaned.

[56] After they had turned around and were headed toward the dirt road, the grandmother recalled other points about the house, the beautiful glass over the front doorway and the candle-lamp in the hall. John Wesley said that the secret panel was probably in the fireplace.

[57] "You can't go inside this house," Bailey said. "You don't know who lives there." "While you all talk to the people in front, I'll run around behind and get in a window," John Wesley suggested.

[58] "We'll all stay in the car," his mother said.

[59] They turned onto the dirt road and the car raced roughly along in a swirl of pink dust. The grandmother recalled the times when there were no paved roads and thirty miles was a day's journey. The dirt road was hilly and there were sudden washes in it and sharp curves on dangerous embankments. All at once they would be on a hill, looking down over the blue tops of trees for miles around, then the next minute, they would be in a red depression with the dust-coated trees looking down on them.

[60] "This place had better turn up in a minute," Bailey said, "or I'm going to turn around."

[61] The road looked as if no one had traveled on it in months.

[62] "It's not much farther," the grandmother said and just as she said it, a horrible thought came to her. The thought was so embarrassing that she turned red in the face and her eyes dilated and her feet jumped up, upsetting her valise in the corner. The instant the valise moved, the newspaper top she had over the basket under it rose with a snarl and Pitty Sing, the cat, sprang onto Bailey's shoulder.

[63] The children were thrown to the floor and their mother, clutching the baby, was thrown out the door onto the ground; the old lady was thrown into the front seat. The car turned over once and landed right-side-up in a gulch off the side of the road. Bailey remained in the driver's seat with the cat—gray-striped with a broad white face and an orange nose—clinging to his neck like a caterpillar.

[64] As soon as the children saw they could move their arms and legs, they scrambled out of the car, shouting, "We've had an ACCIDENT!" The grandmother was curled up under the dashboard, hoping she was injured so that Bailey's wrath would not come down on her all at once. The horrible thought she had had before the accident was that the house she had remembered so vividly was not in Georgia but in Tennessee.

[65] Bailey removed the cat from his neck with both hands and flung it out the window against the side of a pine tree. Then he got out of the car and started looking for the children's mother. She was sitting against the side of the red gutted ditch, holding the screaming baby, but she only had a cut down her face and a broken shoulder. "We've had an ACCIDENT!" the children screamed in a frenzy of delight.

[66] "But nobody's killed," June Star said with disappointment as the grandmother limped out of the car, her hat still pinned to her head but the broken front brim standing up at a jaunty angle and the violet spray hanging off the side. They all sat down in the ditch, except the children, to recover from the shock. They were all shaking.

[67] "Maybe a car will come along," said the children's mother hoarsely.

[68] "I believe I have injured an organ," said the grandmother, pressing her side, but no one answered her. Bailey's teeth were clattering. He had on a yellow sport shirt with bright blue parrots designed in it and his face was as yellow as the shirt. The grandmother decided that she would not mention that the house was in Tennessee.

[69] The road was about ten feet above and they could see only the tops of the trees on the other side of it. Behind the ditch they were sitting in there were more woods, tall and dark and deep. In a few minutes they saw a car some distance away on top of a hill, coming slowly as if the occupants were watching them. The grandmother stood up and waved both arms dramatically to attract their attention. The car continued to come on slowly, disappeared around a bend and appeared again, moving even slower, on top of the hill they had gone over. It was a big black battered hearse-like automobile. There were three men in it.

[70] It came to a stop just over them and for some minutes, the driver looked down with a steady expressionless gaze to where they were sitting, and didn't speak. Then he turned his head and muttered something to the other two and they got out. One was a fat boy in black trousers and a red sweat shirt with a silver stallion embossed on the front of it. He moved around on the right side of them and stood staring, his mouth partly open in a kind of loose grin. The other had on khaki pants and a blue striped coat and a gray hat pulled down very low, hiding most of his face. He came around slowly on the left side. Neither spoke.

[71] The driver got out of the car and stood by the side of it, looking down at them. He was an older man than the other two. His hair was just beginning to gray and he wore silver-rimmed spectacles that gave him a scholarly look. He had a long creased face and didn't have on any shirt or undershirt. He had on blue jeans that were too tight for him and was holding a black hat and a gun. The two boys also had guns.

[72] "We've had an ACCIDENT!" the children screamed.

[73] The grandmother had the peculiar feeling that the bespectacled man was someone she knew. His face was as familiar to her as if she had known him all her life but she could not recall who he was. He moved away from the car and began to come down the embankment, placing his feet carefully so that he wouldn't slip. He had on tan and white shoes and no socks, and his ankles were red and thin. "Good afternoon," he said. "I see you all had you a little spill."

[74] "We turned over twice!" said the grandmother.

[75] "Oncet," he corrected. "We seen it happen. Try their car and see will it run, Hiram," he said quietly to the boy with the gray hat.

[76] "What you got that gun for?" John Wesley asked. "Whatcha gonna do with that gun?"

[77] "Lady," the man said to the children's mother, "would you mind calling them children to sit down by you? Children make me nervous. I want all you all to sit down right together there where you're at."

[78] "What are you telling US what to do for?" June Star asked.

[79] Behind them the line of woods gaped like a dark open mouth. "Come here," said their mother.

[80] "Look here now," Bailey began suddenly, "we're in a predicament! We're in..."

[81] The grandmother shrieked. She scrambled to her feet and stood staring. "You're The Misfit!" she said. "I recognized you at once!"

[82] "Yes'm," the man said, smiling slightly as if he were pleased in spite of himself to be known, "but it would have been better for all of you, lady, if you hadn't of reckernized me."

[83] Bailey turned his head sharply and said something to his mother that shocked even the children. The old lady began to cry and The Misfit reddened.

[84] "Lady," he said, "don't you get upset. Sometimes a man says things he don't mean. I don't reckon he meant to talk to you that away."

[85] "You wouldn't shoot a lady, would you?" the grandmother said and removed a clean handkerchief from her cuff and began to slap at her eyes with it.

[86] The Misfit pointed the toe of his shoe into the ground and made a little hole and then covered it up again. "I would hate to have to," he said.

[87] "Listen," the grandmother almost screamed, "I know you're a good man. You don't look a bit like you have common blood. I know you must come from nice people!"

[88] "Yes mam," he said, "finest people in the world." When he smiled he showed a row of strong white teeth. "God never made a finer woman than my mother and my daddy's heart was pure gold," he said. The boy with the red sweat shirt had come around behind them and was standing with his gun at his hip. The Misfit squatted down on the ground. "Watch them children, Bobby Lee," he said. "You know they make me nervous." He looked at the six of them huddled together in front of him and he seemed to be embarrassed as if he couldn't think of anything to say. "Ain't a cloud in the sky," he remarked, looking up at it. "Don't see no sun but don't see no cloud neither."

[89] "Yes, it's a beautiful day," said the grandmother. "Listen," she said, "you shouldn't call yourself The Misfit because I know you're a good man at heart. I can just look at you and tell."

[90] "Hush!" Bailey yelled. "Hush! Everybody shut up and let me handle this!" He was squatting in the position of a runner about to sprint forward but he didn't move.

[91] "I pre-chate that, lady," The Misfit said and drew a little circle in the ground with the butt of his gun.

[92] "It'll take a half a hour to fix this here car," Hiram called, looking over the raised hood of it.

[93] "Well, first you and Bobby Lee get him and that little boy to step over yonder with you," The Misfit said, pointing to Bailey and John Wesley. "The boys want to ast you something," he said to Bailey. "Would you mind stepping back in the woods there with them?"

[94] "Listen," Bailey began, "we're in a terrible predicament! Nobody realizes what this is," and his voice cracked. His eyes were as blue and intense as the parrots in his shirt and he remained perfectly still.

[95] The grandmother reached up to adjust her hat brim as if she were going to the woods with him but it came off in her hand. She stood staring at it and after a second she let it fall on the ground. Hiram pulled Bailey up by the arm as if he were assisting an old man. John Wesley caught hold of his father's hand and Bobby Lee followed. They went off toward the woods and just as they reached the dark edge, Bailey turned and supporting himself against a gray naked pine trunk, he shouted, "I'll be back in a minute, Mamma, wait on me!"

[96] "Come back this instant!" his mother shrilled but they all disappeared into the woods.

[97] "Bailey Boy!" the grandmother called in a tragic voice but she found she was looking at The Misfit squatting on the ground in front of her. "I just know you're a good man," she said desperately. "You're not a bit common!"

[98] "Nome, I ain't a good man," The Misfit said after a second as if he had considered her statement carefully, "but I ain't the worst in the world neither. My daddy said I was a different breed of dog from my brothers and sisters. 'You know,' Daddy said, 'it's some that can live their whole life out without asking about it and it's others has to know why it is, and this boy is one of the latters. He's going to be into everything!'" He put on his black hat and looked up suddenly and then away deep into the woods as if he were embarrassed again. "I'm sorry I don't have on a shirt before you ladies," he said, hunching his shoulders slightly. "We buried our clothes that we had on when we escaped and we're just making do until we can get better. We borrowed these from some folks we met," he explained.

[99] "That's perfectly all right," the grandmother said. "Maybe Bailey has an extra shirt in his suitcase."

[100] "I'll look and see terrectly," The Misfit said.

[101] "Where are they taking him?" the children's mother screamed.

[102] "Daddy was a card himself," The Misfit said. "You couldn't put anything over on him. He never got in trouble with the Authorities though. Just had the knack of handling them."

[103] "You could be honest too if you'd only try," said the grandmother. "Think how wonderful it would be to settle down and live a comfortable life and not have to think about somebody chasing you all the time."

[104] The Misfit kept scratching in the ground with the butt of his gun as if he were thinking about it. "Yes'm, somebody is always after you," he murmured.

[105] The grandmother noticed how thin his shoulder blades were just behind his hat because she was standing up looking down on him. "Do you ever pray?" she asked.

[106] He shook his head. All she saw was the black hat wiggle between his shoulder blades. "Nome," he said.

[107] There was a pistol shot from the woods, followed closely by another. Then silence. The old lady's head jerked around. She could hear the wind move through the tree tops like a long satisfied insuck of breath. "Bailey Boy!" she called.

[108] "I was a gospel singer for a while," The Misfit said. "I been most everything. Been in the arm service, both land and sea, at home and abroad, been twict married, been an undertaker, been with the railroads, plowed Mother Earth, been in a tornado, seen a man burnt alive oncet," and he looked up at the children's mother and the little girl who were sitting close together, their faces white and their eyes glassy; "I even seen a woman flogged," he said.

[109] "Pray, pray," the grandmother began, "pray, pray…"

[110] "I never was a bad boy that I remember of," The Misfit said in an almost dreamy voice, "but somewheres along the line I done something wrong and got sent to the penitentiary. I was buried alive," and he looked up and held her attention to him by a steady stare.

[111]"That's when you should have started to pray," she said. "What did you do to get

sent to the penitentiary that first time?"

[112] "Turn to the right, it was a wall," The Misfit said, looking up again at the cloudless sky. "Turn to the left, it was a wall. Look up it was a ceiling, look down it was a floor. I forget what I done, lady. I set there and set there, trying to remember what it was I done and I ain't recalled it to this day. Oncet in a while, I would think it was coming to me, but it never come."

[113] "Maybe they put you in by mistake." the old lady said vaguely.

[114] "Nome," he said. "It wasn't no mistake. They had the papers on me."

[115] "You must have stolen something," she said.

[116] The Misfit sneered slightly. "Nobody had nothing I wanted," he said. "It was a head-doctor at the penitentiary said what I had done was kill my daddy but I known that for a lie. My daddy died in nineteen ought nineteen of the epidemic flu and I never had a thing to do with it. He was buried in the Mount Hopewell Baptist churchyard and you can go there and see for yourself."

[117] "If you would pray," the old lady said, "Jesus would help you."

[118] "That's right," The Misfit said.

[119] "Well then, why don't you pray?" she asked trembling with delight suddenly.

[120] "I don't want no hep," he said. "I'm doing all right by myself."

[121] Bobby Lee and Hiram came ambling back from the woods. Bobby Lee was dragging a yellow shirt with bright blue parrots in it.

[122] "Thow me that shirt, Bobby Lee," The Misfit said. The shirt came flying at him and landed on his shoulder and he put it on. The grandmother couldn't name what the shirt reminded her of. "No, lady," The Misfit said while he was buttoning it up, "I found out the crime don't matter. You can do one thing or you can do another, kill a man or take a tire off his car, because sooner or later you're going to forget what it was you done and just be punished for it."

[123] The children's mother had begun to make heaving noises as if she couldn't get her breath. "Lady," he asked, "would you and that little girl like to step off yonder with Bobby Lee and Hiram and join your husband?"

[124] "Yes, thank you," the mother said faintly. Her left arm dangled helplessly and she was holding the baby, who had gone to sleep, in the other. "Hep that lady up, Hiram," The Misfit said as she struggled to climb out of the ditch, "and Bobby Lee, you hold onto that little girl's hand."

[125] "I don't want to hold hands with him," June Star said. "He reminds me of a pig."

[126] The fat boy blushed and laughed and caught her by the arm and pulled her off into the woods after Hiram and her mother.

[127] Alone with The Misfit, the grandmother found that she had lost her voice. There was not a cloud in the sky nor any sun. There was nothing around her but woods. She wanted to tell him that he must pray. She opened and closed her mouth several times before anything came out. Finally she found herself saying, "Jesus. Jesus," meaning, Jesus will help you, but the way she was saying it, it sounded as if she might be cursing.

[128] "Yes'm," The Misfit said as if he agreed. "Jesus thow everything off balance. It was

the same case with Him as with me except He hadn't committed any crime and they could prove I had committed one because they had the papers on me. Of course," he said, "they never shown me my papers. That's why I sign myself now. I said long ago, you get you a signature and sign everything you do and keep a copy of it. Then you'll know what you done and you can hold up the crime to the punishment and see do they match and in the end you'll have something to prove you ain't been treated right. I call myself The Misfit," he said, "because I can't make what all I done wrong fit what all I gone through in punishment."

[129] There was a piercing scream from the woods, followed closely by a pistol report. "Does it seem right to you, lady, that one is punished a heap and another ain't punished at all?"

[130] "Jesus!" the old lady cried. "You've got good blood! I know you wouldn't shoot a lady! I know you come from nice people! Pray! Jesus, you ought not to shoot a lady. I'll give you all the money I've got!"

[131] "Lady," The Misfit said, looking beyond her far into the woods, "there never was a body that give the undertaker a tip."

[132] There were two more pistol reports and the grandmother raised her head like a parched old turkey hen crying for water and called, "Bailey Boy, Bailey Boy!" as if her heart would break.

[133] "Jesus was the only One that ever raised the dead," The Misfit continued, "and He shouldn't have done it. He thown everything off balance. If He did what He said, then it's nothing for you to do but thow away everything and follow Him, and if He didn't, then it's nothing for you to do but enjoy the few minutes you got left the best way you can—by killing somebody or burning down his house or doing some other meanness to him. No pleasure but meanness," he said and his voice had become almost a snarl.

[134] "Maybe He didn't raise the dead," the old lady mumbled, not knowing what she was saying and feeling so dizzy that she sank down in the ditch with her legs twisted under her.

[135] "I wasn't there so I can't say He didn't," The Misfit said. "I wisht I had of been there," he said, hitting the ground with his fist. "It ain't right I wasn't there because if I had of been there I would of known. Listen lady," he said in a high voice, "if I had of been there I would of known and I wouldn't be like I am now." His voice seemed about to crack and the grandmother's head cleared for an instant. She saw the man's face twisted close to her own as if he were going to cry and she murmured, "Why you're one of my babies. You're one of my own children!" She reached out and touched him on the shoulder. The Misfit sprang back as if a snake had bitten him and shot her three times through the chest. Then he put his gun down on the ground and took off his glasses and began to clean them.

[136] Hiram and Bobby Lee returned from the woods and stood over the ditch, looking down at the grandmother who half sat and half lay in a puddle of blood with her legs crossed under her like a child's and her face smiling up at the cloudless sky.

[137] Without his glasses, The Misfit's eyes were red-rimmed and pale and defenseless-looking. "Take her off and thow her where you thown the others," he said, picking up the cat that was rubbing itself against his leg.

[138] "She was a talker, wasn't she?" Bobby Lee said, sliding down the ditch with a yodel.

[139] "She would of been a good woman," The Misfit said, "if it had been somebody there to shoot her every minute of her life."

[140] "Some fun!" Bobby Lee said.

[141] "Shut up, Bobby Lee," The Misfit said. "It's no real pleasure in life."

(Charters 1999, 631−642)

Questions for Reflection

1. Read the story "A Good Man Is Hard to Find" and write an outline of it.
2. Make some comments on the story's plot, characterization, point of view, setting, style and language, symbol, irony, and theme.

 ## Plot

> It's a truism that there are only two basic plots in fiction:
> one, somebody takes a trip; two, a stranger comes to town.
> —Lee Smith, New York Times Book Review
> (Kirszner & Mandell 2006, 82)

Plot is "the action element in fiction, the arrangement of events that make up a story" (DiYanni 2000, 44), or plot is

> the sequence of events in a story and their reaction to one another as they develop and usually resolve a conflict (Charters 1999, 939).

Events do not make a plot. The plot lies in the relations among events. Plot can be described as "an intellectual formulation about the relations among the incidents of a drama or a narrative" (Holman & Harmon 1986, 378). A plot is artificial while an event, natural. It is a plot that turns the disorder into order.

The plot of a story develops in a time frame, coherent or seemingly incoherent. The events are interrelated by causation (why something happens). In other words, plot involves what happens and why so, and it is

> shaped by causal connections—historical, social, and personal—by interaction between characters, and by the juxtaposition of events (Kirszner & Mandell 2006, 83).

Moreover, plot does not always develop in a chronological order, and it often unfolds via inner coherence "in terms of the depth of human nature" (Charters 1999, 939). Quite often, the plot goes on with flashback, flashforward, or foreshadowing.

A story, short or long, is the choice of the writer. A short story usually works with an episode or plot while a long story, more than one episode or plot. Short stories are considered static while long ones, dynamic.

Usually stories that are static, where little change occurs, are relatively short (as Grace Paley's "A Conversation with My Father") while more dynamic actions, covering a longer time and involving the characters' change from one state to another, are longer (as Leo Tolstoy's "The Death of Ivan Ilych") (Charters 1999, 940).

Stories embody certain narrative strategies. A story can be rendered short or a single event can be turned into a longer one for the sake of its dramatic effect.

Considering plot, characters and actions and their relations are of key importance. The function of plot is "to translate character into action" (Holman & Harmon 1986, 378). The relationship is found in the fact that characters perform actions and it involves conflict between opposing forces, physical or spiritual.

Without conflict, without opposition, plot does not exist... This opposition knits one incident to another and dictates the causal pattern that develops the struggle. This struggle between the forces, moreover, comes to a head in some one incident—the crisis that forms the turning point of the story and usually marks the moment of the greatest suspense. In this climatic episode, the rising action comes to a termination and the falling action begins; and as a result of this incident some denouement or catastrophe is bound to follow (Holman & Harmon 1986, 379).

In terms of the plot (of most short stories), there are generally four parts, exposition or introduction, the rising action, the climax and the falling action.

The first part of the plot introduces characters, scene, time, and situation; the second part is called *the rising action*, the dramatization of events that complicate the situation and gradually intensify the conflict; the third [comes] a further development of the rising action which takes the reader to the *climax* of the plot or *turning point* of the story, its emotional high point; and the fourth [is] *the falling action*, where the problem or conflict presented in the earlier sections proceeds toward resolution (Charters 1999, 940—941).

Considering the plot of "A Good Man Is Hard to Find," the exposition introduces the characters (the Grandma and other family members, and The Misfit, a runaway criminal), the time (to go on a vacation), the place (the family house in the rural south), and the (possible disastrous) situation. The family is planning a trip and the grandma tries to persuade the family to go to East Tennessee rather than Florida. A criminal called The Misfit is "aloose from the Federal Pen and headed toward Florida" (Para. 1) and he seems to loom ahead as a forbidding doom for the family.

The rising action or the dramatization of events of the story comes along with the car accident. The family is trapped in a dangerous situation which gradually intensifies the conflict (survival from the car accident and the encounter with the gang of The Misfit). Despite the car accident, the family survives. But danger still seems to loom ahead for the grandma has made a mistake, having taken the family to a wrong place, which implies something bad will happen. The Misfit's arrival seems to make the situation worse and the grandma's recognition of this runaway complicates the situation. Suspense builds up. Will they survive again?

Then comes the climax of the plot or turning point of the story, the grandmother's religious persuasion of The Misfit and her appearance of grace. She is left alone (temporarily) after the death of other family members one by one. She seems to have undergone epiphany and appears to be graceful. In the second part of the story, after she recognizes The Misfit and is brought face to face with the gang of escaped convicts, the grandma seems to have become another person. She experiences an epiphany. In other words, she has gone through a sudden radical change of character. She is no longer the silly, fussy, selfish old lady but becomes a pious Christian, believing that God will help and save anybody, even the criminal. She tries to influence The Misfit with religion, encouraging him to "pray" (Paras. 109, 111, 130) and convincing him that "If you would pray, Jesus would help you" (Para. 117). When The Misfit challenges the traditional authority of God by saying that "Jesus thow everything off balance" (Para. 128), the grandma persists in inspiring him with Christian beliefs, just like an evangelist disseminating the gospel of God. Finally she reaches out to embrace The Misfit, saying "Why you're one of my babies. You're one of my children" (Para. 135). At this moment, she seems to become the incarnation of God, showing love to the sinned human as well. She appears to ignore the dangerous situation and goes on bravely with her sacred task to bring back the lamb that has gone astray.

Here again there is a suspense (regarding life or death). What will happen?

Now begins the falling action where the conflict goes toward resolution. The grandma is shot and disposed of cruelly as shown in The Misfit's words: "Take her off and thow her where you thown the others" (Para. 137). Though she is killed eventually, she seems to be redeemed after she fails to redeem The Misfit.

Questions for Reflection

Read the following story and answer the questions.

Young Goodman Brown (1835)

—Nathaniel Hawthorne (1804–1864)

Young Goodman Brown came forth at sunset, into the street at Salem Village, but put his head back, after crossing the threshold, to exchange a parting kiss with his young wife. And Faith, as the wife was aptly named, thrust her own pretty head into the street, letting the wind play with the pink ribbons of her cap while she called to Goodman Brown.

"Dearest heart," whispered she, softly and rather sadly, when her lips were close to his ear, "prithee, put off your journey until sunrise, and sleep in your own bed tonight. A lone woman is troubled with such dreams and such thoughts that she's afeard of herself sometimes. Pray, tarry with me this night, dear husband, of all nights in the year!"

"My love and my Faith," replied young Goodman Brown, "of all nights in the year, this one night must I tarry away from thee. My journey, as thou callest it, forth and back again, must needs be done 'twixt now and sunrise. What, my sweet, pretty wife, dost thou doubt me already, and we but three months married!"

"Then God bless you!" said Faith with the pink ribbons, "and may you find all well, when you come back."

"Amen!" cried Goodman Brown. "Say thy prayers, dear Faith, and go to bed at dusk, and no harm will come to thee."

So they parted; and the young man pursued his way until, being about to turn the corner by the meeting-house, he looked back and saw the head of Faith still peeping after him with a melancholy air, in spite of her pink ribbons.

"Poor little Faith!" thought he, for his heart smote him. "What a wretch am I, to leave her on such an errand! She talks of dreams, too. Methought as she spoke, there was trouble in her face, as if a dream had warned her what work is to be done tonight. But no, no! 't would kill her to think it. Well, she's a blessed angel on earth; and after this one night I'll cling to her skirts and follow her to heaven."

With this excellent resolve for the future, Goodman Brown felt himself justified in making more haste on his present evil purpose. He had taken a dreary road, darkened by all the gloomiest trees of the forest, which barely stood aside to let the narrow path creep through, and closed immediately behind. It was all as lonely as could be; and there is this peculiarity in such a solitude, that the traveller knows not who may be concealed by the innumerable trunks and the thick boughs overhead; so that, with lonely footsteps he may yet be passing through an unseen multitude.

"There may be a devilish Indian behind every tree," said Goodman Brown to himself; and he glanced fearfully behind him, as he added, "What if the devil himself should be at my very elbow!"

His head being turned back, he passed a crook of the road, and looking forward again, beheld the figure of a man, in grave and decent attire, seated at the foot of an old tree. He arose at Goodman Brown's approach and walked onward, side by side with him.

"You are late, Goodman Brown," said he. "The clock of the Old South was striking, as I came through Boston; and that is full fifteen minutes agone."

"Faith kept me back a while," replied the young man, with a tremor in his voice, caused by the sudden appearance of his companion, though not wholly unexpected.

It was now deep dusk in the forest, and deepest in that part of it where these two were journeying. As nearly as could be discerned, the second traveller was about fifty years old, apparently in the same rank of life as Goodman Brown, and bearing a considerable resemblance to him, though perhaps more in expression than features. Still they might have been taken for father and son. And yet, though the elder person was as simply clad as the younger, and as simple in manner too, he had an indescribable air of one who knew the world, and who would not have felt abashed at the governor's dinner table, or in King William's court, were it possible that his affairs should call him thither. But the only thing about him that could be fixed upon as remarkable was his staff, which bore the likeness of a great black snake, so curiously wrought that it might almost be seen to twist and wriggle itself like a living serpent. This, of course, must have been an ocular deception, assisted by the uncertain light.

"Come, Goodman Brown," cried his fellow-traveller, "this is a dull pace for the beginning of a journey. Take my staff, if you are so soon weary."

"Friend," said the other, exchanging his slow pace for a full stop, "having kept covenant by meeting thee here, it is my purpose now to return whence I came. I have scruples touching the matter thou wot'st of."

"Sayest thou so?" replied he of the serpent, smiling apart. "Let us walk on, nevertheless, reasoning as we go; and if I convince thee not thou shalt turn back. We are but a little way in the forest yet."

"Too far! too far!" exclaimed the goodman, unconsciously resuming his walk. "My father never went into the woods on such an errand, nor his father before him. We have been a race of honest men and good Christians since the days of the martyrs; and shall I be the first of the name of Brown that ever took this path and kept—"

"Such company, thou wouldst say," observed the elder person, interpreting his pause. "Well said, Goodman Brown! I have been as well acquainted with your family as with ever a one among the Puritans; and that's no trifle to say. I helped your grandfather, the constable, when he lashed the Quaker woman so smartly through the streets of Salem; And it was I that brought your father a pitch-pine knot, kindled at my own hearth, to set fire to an Indian village, in King Philip's war. They were my good friends, both; and many a pleasant walk have we had along this path, and returned merrily after midnight. I would fain be friends with you for their sake."

"If it be as thou sayest," replied Goodman Brown, "I marvel they never spoke of these matters; or, verily, I marvel not, seeing that the least rumor of the sort would have driven them from New England. We are a people of prayer, and good works to boot, and abide no such wickedness."

"Wickedness or not," said the traveller with the twisted staff, "I have a very general acquaintance here in New England. The deacons of many a church have drunk the communion wine with me; the selectmen of divers towns make me their chairman; and a majority of the Great and General Court are firm supporters of my interest. The governor and I, too—But these are state secrets."

"Can this be so!" cried Goodman Brown, with a stare of amazement at his undisturbed companion. "Howbeit, I have nothing to do with the governor and council; they have their own ways, and are no rule for a simple husbandman like me. But, were I to go on with thee, how should I meet the eye of that good old man, our minister, at Salem Village? Oh, his voice would make me tremble both Sabbath-day and lecture-day."

Thus far the elder traveller had listened with due gravity, but now burst into a fit of irrepressible mirth, shaking himself so violently that his snake-like staff actually seemed to wriggle in sympathy.

"Ha! Ha! Ha!" shouted he again and again; then composing himself, "Well, go on, Goodman Brown, go on; but, prithee, don't kill me with laughing!"

"Well, then, to end the matter at once," said Goodman Brown, considerably nettled, "there is my wife, Faith. It would break her dear little heart; and I'd rather break my own."

"Nay, if that be the case," answered the other, "then go thy ways, Goodman Brown. I would not for twenty old women like the one hobbling before us that Faith should come to any harm."

As he spoke, he pointed his staff at a female figure on the path, in whom Goodman Brown recognized a very pious and exemplary dame, who had taught him his catechism in youth, and was still his moral and spiritual adviser, jointly with the minister and Deacon Gookin.

"A marvel, truly, that Goody Cloyse should be so far in the wilderness at nightfall," said he. "But with your leave, friend, I shall take a cut through the woods until we have left this Christian woman behind. Being a stranger to you, she might ask whom I was consorting with, and whither I was going."

"Be it so," said his fellow-traveller. "Betake you the woods, and let me keep the path."

Accordingly the young man turned aside, but took care to watch his companion, who advanced softly along the road until he had come within a staff's length of the old dame. She, meanwhile, was making the best of her way, with singular speed for so aged a woman, and mumbling some indistinct words, a prayer, doubtless, as she went. The traveller put forth his staff and touched her withered neck with what seemed the serpent's tail.

"The devil!" screamed the pious old lady.

"Then Goody Cloyse knows her old friend?" observed the traveller, confronting her, and leaning on his writhing stick.

"Ah, forsooth, and is it your worship indeed?" cried the good dame. "Yea, truly is it, and in the very image of my old gossip, Goodman Brown, the grandfather of the silly fellow that now is. But, would your worship believe it? My broomstick hath strangely disappeared, stolen, as I suspect, by that unhanged witch, Goody Cory, and that, too, when I was all anointed with the juice of smallage, and cinque-foil, and wolf's bane—"

"Mingled with fine wheat and the fat of a new-born babe," said the shape of old Goodman Brown.

"Ah, your worship knows the recipe," cried the old lady, cackling aloud. "So, as I was saying, being all ready for the meeting, and no horse to ride on, I made up my mind to foot it; for they tell me there is a nice young man to be taken into communion tonight. But now your good worship will lend me your arm, and we shall be there in a twinkling."

"That can hardly be," answered her friend. "I may not spare you my arm, Goody Cloyse;

but here is my staff, if you will."

So saying, he threw it down at her feet, where, perhaps, it assumed life, being one of the rods which its owner had formerly lent to the Egyptian magi. Of this fact, however, Goodman Brown could not take cognizance. He had cast up his eyes in astonishment, and looking down again, beheld neither Goody Cloyse nor the serpentine staff, but this fellow-traveller alone, who waited for him as calmly as if nothing had happened.

"That old woman taught me my catechism," said the young man; and there was a world of meaning in this simple comment.

They continued to walk onward, while the elder traveller exhorted his companion to make good speed and persevere in the path, discoursing so aptly, that his arguments seemed rather to spring up in the bosom of his auditor than to be suggested by himself. As they went, he plucked a branch of maple, to serve for a walking-stick, and began to strip it of the twigs and little boughs, which were wet with evening dew. The moment his fingers touched them, they became strangely withered and dried up as with a week's sunshine. Thus the pair proceeded, at a good free pace, until suddenly, in a gloomy hollow of the road, Goodman Brown sat himself down on the stump of a tree and refused to go any farther.

"Friend," said he, stubbornly, "my mind is made up. Not another step will I budge on this errand. What if a wretched old woman do choose to go to the devil, when I thought she was going to heaven! Is that any reason why I should quit my dear Faith and go after her?"

"You will think better of this by and by," said his acquaintance, composedly. "Sit here and rest yourself a while; and when you feel like moving again, there is my staff to help you along."

Without more words, he threw his companion the maple stick, and was as speedily out of sight as if he had vanished into the deepening gloom. The young man sat a few moments by the roadside, applauding himself greatly, and thinking with how clear a conscience he should meet the minister in his morning walk, nor shrink from the eye of good old Deacon Gookin. And what calm sleep would be his that very night, which was to have been spent so wickedly, but purely and sweetly now, in the arms of Faith! Amidst these pleasant and praiseworthy meditations, Goodman Brown heard the tramp of horses along the road, and deemed it advisable to conceal himself within the verge of the forest, conscious of the guilty purpose that had brought him thither, though now so happily turned from it.

On came the hoof-tramps and the voices of the riders, two grave old voices, conversing soberly as they drew near. These mingled sounds appeared to pass along the road, within a few yards of the young man's hiding-place; but owing, doubtless, to the depth of the gloom at that particular spot, neither the travellers nor their steeds were visible. Though their figures brushed the small boughs by the wayside, it could not be seen that they intercepted, even for a moment, the faint gleam from the strip of bright sky, athwart which they must have passed. Goodman Brown alternately crouched and stood on tiptoe, pulling aside the branches and thrusting forth his head as far as he durst, without discerning so much as a shadow. It vexed him the more, because he could have sworn, were such a thing possible, that he recognized the voices of the minister and Deacon Gookin, jogging along quietly, as they were wont to do, when bound to some ordination or ecclesiastical council. While yet within hearing, one of the riders stopped to pluck a switch.

"Of the two, reverend sir," said the voice like the deacon's, "I had rather miss an ordination dinner than to-night's meeting. They tell me that some of our community are to be here from Falmouth and beyond, and others from Connecticut and Rhode Island; besides several of the Indian powwows, who, after their fashion, know almost as much deviltry as the best of us. Moreover, there is a goodly young woman to be taken into communion."

"Mighty well, Deacon Gookin!" replied the solemn old tones of the minister. "Spur up, or we shall be late. Nothing can be done, you know, until I get on the ground."

The hoofs clattered again, and the voices, talking so strangely in the empty air, passed on through the forest, where no church had ever been gathered or solitary Christian prayed. Whither, then, could these holy men be journeying, so deep into the heathen wilderness? Young Goodman Brown caught hold of a tree for support, being ready to sink down on the ground, faint and over-burdened with the heavy sickness of his heart. He looked up to the sky, doubting whether there really was a Heaven above him. Yet there was the blue arch, and the stars brightening in it.

"With heaven above and Faith below, I will yet stand firm against the devil!" cried Goodman Brown.

While he still gazed upward, into the deep arch of the firmament, and had lifted his hands to pray, a cloud, though no wind was stirring, hurried across the zenith and hid the brightening stars. The blue sky was still visible, except directly overhead, where this black mass of cloud was sweeping swiftly northward. Aloft in the air, as if from the depths of the cloud, came a confused and doubtful sound of voices. Once the listener fancied that he could distinguish the accents of townspeople of his own, men and women, both pious and ungodly, many of whom he had met at the communion-table, and had seen others rioting at the tavern. The next moment, so indistinct were the sounds, he doubted whether he had heard aught but the murmur of the old forest, whispering without a wind. Then came a stronger swell of those familiar tones, heard daily in the sunshine, at Salem Village, but never until now from a cloud of night. There was one voice, of a young woman, uttering lamentations, yet with an uncertain sorrow, and entreating for some favor, which, perhaps, it would grieve her to obtain; and all the unseen multitude, both saints and sinners, seemed to encourage her onward.

"Faith!" shouted Goodman Brown, in a voice of agony and desperation; and the echoes of the forest mocked him, crying, "Faith! Faith!" as if bewildered wretches were seeking her all through the wilderness.

The cry of grief, rage, and terror was yet piercing the night, when the unhappy husband held his breath for a response. There was a scream, drowned immediately in a louder murmur of voices, fading into far-off laughter, as the dark cloud swept away, leaving the clear and silent sky above Goodman Brown. But something fluttered lightly down through the air, and caught on the branch of a tree. The young man seized it and beheld a pink ribbon.

"My Faith is gone!" cried he, after one stupefied moment. "There is no good on earth, and sin is but a name. Come, devil; for to thee is this world given."

And maddened with despair, so that he laughed loud and long, did Goodman Brown grasp his staff and set forth again, at such a rate, that he seemed to fly along the forest path, rather than to walk or run. The road grew wilder and drearier and more faintly traced, and vanished at length, leaving him in the heart of the dark wilderness, still rushing onward with the instinct that guides mortal man to evil. The whole forest was peopled with frightful sounds: the creaking of the trees, the howling of wild beasts, and the yell of Indians; while sometimes the wind tolled like a distant church bell, and sometimes gave a broad roar around the traveller, as if all Nature were laughing him to scorn. But he was himself the chief horror of the scene, and shrank not from its other horrors.

"Ha! Ha! Ha!" roared Goodman Brown when the wind laughed at him.

"Let us hear which will laugh loudest. Think not to frighten me with your deviltry. Come witch, come wizard, come Indian powwow, come devil himself! and here comes Goodman Brown. You may as well fear him as he fear you."

In truth, all through the haunted forest there could be nothing more frightful than the figure of Goodman Brown. On he flew, among the black pines, brandishing his staff with frenzied gestures, now giving vent to an inspiration of horrid blasphemy, and now shouting forth such laughter, as set all the echoes of the forest laughing like demons around him. The fiend in his own shape is less hideous, than when he rages in the breast of man. Thus sped the demoniac on his course, until, quivering among the trees, he saw a red light before him, as when the felled trunks and branches of a clearing have been set on fire, and throw up their lurid blaze against the sky, at the hour of midnight. He paused, in a lull of the tempest that had driven him onward, and heard the swell of what seemed a hymn, rolling solemnly from a distance with the weight of many voices. He knew the tune; it was a familiar one in the choir of the village meeting-house. The verse died heavily away, and was lengthened by a chorus, not of human voices, but of all the sounds of the benighted wilderness pealing in awful harmony together. Goodman Brown cried out, and his cry was lost to his own ear, by its unison with the cry of the desert.

In the interval of silence he stole forward until the light glared full upon his eyes. At one extremity of an open space, hemmed in by the dark wall of the forest, arose a rock, bearing some rude, natural resemblance either to an altar or a pulpit, and surrounded by four blazing pines, their tops aflame, their stems untouched, like candles at an evening meeting. The mass of foliage that had overgrown the summit of the rock was all on fire, blazing high into the night and fitfully illuminating the whole field. Each pendent twig and leafy festoon was in a blaze. As the red light arose and fell, a numerous congregation alternately shone forth, then disappeared in shadow, and again grew, as it were, out of the darkness, peopling the heart of the solitary woods at once.

"A grave and dark-clad company," quoth Goodman Brown.

In truth they were such. Among them, quivering to-and-fro, between gloom and splendor, appeared faces that would be seen, next day, at the council-board of the province, and others which, Sabbath after Sabbath, looked devoutly heavenward, and benignantly over the crowded pews, from the holiest pulpits in the land. Some affirm that the lady of the governor was there. At least there were high dames well known to her, and wives of honored husbands, and widows a great multitude, and ancient maidens, all of excellent repute, and fair young girls, who trembled lest their mothers should espy them. Either the sudden gleams of light, flashing over the obscure field bedazzled Goodman Brown, or he recognized a score of the church members of Salem Village famous for their especial sanctity. Good old Deacon Gookin had arrived, and waited at the skirts of that venerable saint, his revered pastor. But, irreverently consorting with these grave, reputable, and pious people, these elders of the church, these chaste dames and dewy virgins, there were men of dissolute lives and women of spotted fame, wretches given over to all mean and filthy vice, and suspected even of horrid crimes. It was strange to see that the good shrank not from the wicked, nor were the sinners abashed by the saints. Scattered, also, among their pale-faced enemies, were the Indian priests, or powwows, who had often scared their native forest with more hideous incantations than any known to English witchcraft.

"But, where is Faith?" thought Goodman Brown; and, as hope came into his heart, he trembled.

Another verse of the hymn arose, a slow and mournful strain, such as the pious love, but joined to words which expressed all that our nature can conceive of sin, and darkly hinted at far more. Unfathomable to mere mortals is the lore of fiends. Verse after verse was sung, and still the chorus of the desert swelled between, like the deepest tone of a mighty organ; and with the final peal of that dreadful anthem there came a sound, as if the roaring wind, the rushing streams, the howling beasts, and every other voice of the unconverted wilderness were mingling and according with the voice of guilty man in homage to the prince of all. The four blazing pines threw up a loftier flame, and obscurely discovered shapes and visages of horror on the smoke-wreaths, above the impious assembly. At the same moment the fire on the rock shot redly forth and formed a glowing arch above its base, where now appeared a figure. With reverence be it spoken, the figure bore no slight similitude, both in garb and manner, to some grave divine of the New England churches.

"Bring forth the converts!" cried a voice that echoed through the field and rolled into the forest.

At the word, Goodman Brown stepped forth from the shadow of the trees and approached the congregation, with whom he felt a loathful brotherhood by the sympathy of all that was wicked in his heart. He could have well-nigh sworn, that the shape of his own dead father beckoned him to advance, looking downward from a smoke wreath, while a woman, with dim features of despair, threw out her hand to warn him back. Was it his mother? But he had no power to retreat one step, nor to resist, even in thought, when the minister and good old Deacon

Gookin seized his arms and led him to the blazing rock. Thither came also the slender form of a veiled female, led between Goody Cloyse, that pious teacher of the catechism, and Martha Carrier, who had received the devil's promise to be queen of hell. A rampant hag was she. And there stood the proselytes, beneath the canopy of fire.

"Welcome, my children," said the dark figure, "to the communion of your race. Ye have found thus young your nature and your destiny. My children, look behind you!"

They turned; and flashing forth, as it were, in a sheet of flame, the fiend worshippers were seen; the smile of welcome gleamed darkly on every visage.

"There," resumed the sable form, "are all whom ye have reverenced from youth. Ye deemed them holier than yourselves, and shrank from your own sin, contrasting it with their lives of righteousness and prayerful aspirations heavenward. Yet here are they all in my worshipping assembly. This night it shall be granted you to know their secret deeds: how hoary-bearded elders of the church have whispered wanton words to the young maids of their households; how many a woman, eager for widows' weeds, has given her husband a drink at bedtime, and let him sleep his last sleep in her bosom; how beardless youths have made haste to inherit their fathers' wealth; and how fair damsels—blush not, sweet ones—have dug little graves in the garden, and bidden me, the sole guest, to an infant's funeral. By the sympathy of your human hearts for sin ye shall scent out all the places—whether in church, bedchamber, street, field, or forest—where crime has been committed, and shall exult to behold the whole earth one stain of guilt, one mighty blood spot. Far more than this. It shall be yours to penetrate, in every bosom, the deep mystery of sin, the fountain of all wicked arts, and which inexhaustibly supplies more evil impulses than human power—than my power at its utmost—can make manifest in deeds. And now, my children, look upon each other."

They did so; and, by the blaze of the hell-kindled torches, the wretched man beheld his Faith, and the wife her husband, trembling before that unhallowed altar.

"Lo, there ye stand, my children," said the figure, in a deep and solemn tone, almost sad with its despairing awfulness, as if his once angelic nature could yet mourn for our miserable race. "Depending upon one another's hearts, ye had still hoped that virtue were not all a dream. Now are ye undeceived. Evil is the nature of mankind. Evil must be your only happiness. Welcome again, my children, to the communion of your race."

"Welcome," repeated the fiend worshippers, in one cry of despair and triumph.

And there they stood, the only pair, as it seemed, who were yet hesitating on the verge of wickedness in this dark world. A basin was hollowed, naturally, in the rock. Did it contain water, reddened by the lurid light? Or was it blood? Or, perchance, a liquid flame? Herein did the shape of evil dip his hand and prepare to lay the mark of baptism upon their foreheads, that they might be partakers of the mystery of sin, more conscious of the secret guilt of others, both in deed and thought, than they could now be of their own. The husband cast one look at his pale wife, and Faith at him. What polluted wretches would the next glance show them to each other, shuddering alike at what they disclosed and what they saw!

"Faith! Faith!" cried the husband, "look up to heaven, and resist the wicked one."

Whether Faith obeyed he knew not. Hardly had he spoken, when he found himself amid calm night and solitude, listening to a roar of the wind which died heavily away through the forest. He staggered against the rock, and felt it chill and damp, while a hanging twig, that had been all on fire, besprinkled his cheek with the coldest dew.

The next morning young Goodman Brown came slowly into the street of Salem Village, staring around him like a bewildered man. The good old minister was taking a walk along the graveyard to get an appetite for breakfast and meditate his sermon, and bestowed a blessing, as he passed, on Goodman Brown. He shrank from the venerable saint as if to avoid an anathema. Old Deacon Gookin was at domestic worship, and the holy words of his prayer were heard through the open window. "What God doth the wizard pray to?" quoth Goodman Brown. Goody Cloyse, that excellent old Christian, stood in the early sunshine at her own lattice, catechizing a little girl who had brought her a pint of morning's milk. Goodman Brown snatched away the child as from the grasp of the fiend himself. Turning the corner by the meetinghouse, he spied the head of Faith, with the pink ribbons, gazing anxiously forth, and bursting into such joy at sight of him that she skipped along the street and almost kissed her husband before the whole village. But Goodman Brown looked sternly and sadly into her face, and passed on without a greeting.

Had Goodman Brown fallen asleep in the forest and only dreamed a wild dream of a witch-meeting?

Be it so, if you will; but, alas! It was a dream of evil omen for young Goodman Brown. A stern, a sad, a darkly meditative, a distrustful, if not a desperate man did he become from the night of that fearful dream. On the Sabbath day, when the congregation were singing a holy psalm, he could not listen, because an anthem of sin rushed loudly upon his ear and drowned all the blessed strain. When the minister spoke from the pulpit with power and fervid eloquence, and, with his hand on the open *Bible*, of the sacred truths of our religion, and of saint-like lives and triumphant deaths, and of future bliss or misery unutterable, then did Goodman Brown turn pale, dreading lest the roof should thunder down upon the grey blasphemer and his hearers. Often, awaking suddenly at midnight, he shrank from the bosom of Faith; and at morning or eventide, when the family knelt down at prayer, he scowled and muttered to himself, and gazed sternly at his wife, and turned away. And when he had lived long, and was borne to his grave, a hoary corpse, followed by Faith, an aged woman, and children and grandchildren, a goodly procession, besides neighbors not a few, they carved no hopeful verse upon his tombstone, for his dying hour was gloom.

Questions

1. Considering the exposition of the plot, how does the story introduce characters, scene, time, and situation?

2. What is the rising action? Please illustrate in terms of "Young Goodman Brown."

3. What is the climax and when is the climax of the story?

4. What is the falling action? Please illustrate in terms of "Young Goodman Brown."

5. Comment on the ending of "Young Goodman Brown."

6. How does the plot work in terms of "Young Goodman Brown" and other short stories?

■ Character

Characters make the author do what they want him do.
—Martha Foley, Best American Short Stories (Foreword)
(Kirszner and Mandell 2006, 121)

The action of the plot is performed by the *characters* in the story, the people or personified figures (objects or animals) that make something happen or produce an effect. However, when characters are mentioned, they are usually referred to as people. A character is a fictional representation of a person and characterization is the way writers develop subjects and show the readers their traits (Kriszner & Mandell 2006, 121). In other words:

[Character] is a brief sketch of a personage who typifies some definite quality. The person is described not as an individualized personality but as an example of some vice or virtue or type, such as a busybody, a glutton, a fop, a bumpkin, a garrulous old man, a happy milkmaid, etc.... In fiction (the drama, the novel, the short story, and the narrative form), the author reveals the characters of imaginary persons. The creation of these characters so that they exist for the reader as lifelike is called characterization (Holman & Harmon 1986, 81).

Generally there are some fundamental ways of characterization in fiction,

the explicit presentation by the author of the character through a direct exposition; the presentation of the character in action; and the representation from within a character, ... of the impact of actions and emotions on the character's inner self ... (Holman & Harmon 1986, 81)

It is worth noting that, despite the "explicit" presentation or "direct" exposition, the character may not always be introduced at the very beginning of the story but quite often being made known gradually throughout the story as a whole. Characters are illustrated by action. When characters are presented through action or from within themselves, the narrator usually makes no comment. Whatever methods, it is expected or even believed that the readers can get to know, from their reading experiences, the traits of the character.

Characterization suggests life as viewed by the storytellers. Usually a first-person narration or the presence of an omniscient author involves the explicit method as applied in *David Copperfield*

(1850) by Charles Dickens or in *Tom Jones* (1749) by Henry Fielding.

Besides the basic methods of characterization in fiction, the authors may focus solely on a dominant trait of personality or on a very small group of features while they may disregard other traits the character has. This leads to the creation of a two-dimensional character or a flat figure in E. M. Foster's terms. But quite often, the authors may present a complex character with multiplied personality traits, which is a three-dimensional character or a round character by E. M. Foster. Generally, the major characters or the protagonists in fiction are round characters while the minor ones, flat characters.

Characters can also be classified as dynamic or static ones.

> A static character is one who changes little at all. Things happen to such a character without things happening within... A dynamic character, on the other hand, is one who is modified by actions and experiences, and one objective of the work in which the character appears is to reveal the consequences of these questions (Holman & Harmon 1986, 81).

For example, in Mark Twain's *The Adventures of Huckleberry Finn*, Huckle Finn is both round and dynamic because he has a multifaceted personality as presented in the story and he undergoes changes. Jim is both flat and static in that he changes little.

Questions for Reflection

1. How are the characters in a story to be understood?
2. Make comments on Nathaniel Hawthorne's method of characterization in terms of "Young Goodman Brown."
3. Discuss the personality of Mrs. Johnson (Mama) in Alice Walker's "Everyday Use for Your Grandmamma."
4. How much do you know about characters considered to be round or flat, and dynamic or static?

■ Point of View

> In dealing with point of view the [writer] must always deal with the individual work: which particular character shall tell this particular story, or part of a story, with what precise degree of reliability, privilege, freedom to comment, and so on...
> —Wayne C. Booth, "Distance and Point of View"
> (Kirszner & Mandell 2006, 222)

Point of view means the author's choice of a narrator for the story, and it is "the vantage point from which events are presented" (Kirszner & Mandell 2006, 222). This choice of vantage point decides the development of plot and influences the style and theme of the fiction.

The most frequently used ways of telling stories are seen in two major categories:

First-person narration (narrator apparently a participant in the story)

a. A major character

b. A minor character

Third-person narration (narrator a nonparticipant in the story)

a. Omniscient—seeing into the minds of all characters

b. Limited omniscient—seeing into one or, infrequently, two characters' minds

c. Objective—seeing into none of the characters' minds.

(Charters 1999, 945)

However, from time to time, a second-person point of view is also applied by some writers. It means the use of the imperative mood and the second-person pronouns as well as its variant. In other words, a second-person narration is told through the use of "you." Typical examples are found in the short fictions of Lorrie Moore and Junot Diaz and in Jay McInerney's *Bright Lights*, *Big City* (1984). Here are some paragraphs quoted from Jay McInerney's *Bright Lights*, *Big City* which is narrated mostly from a second-person point of view.

"'Things happen, people change,' is what Amanda said. For her that covered it. You wanted an explanation, and ending that would assign blame and dish up justice. You considered violence and you considered reconciliation. But what you are left with is a premonition of the way your life will fade behind you, like a book you have read too quickly, leaving a dwindling trail of images and emotions, until all you can remember is a name."

…

"You keep thinking that with practice you will eventually get the knack of enjoying superficial encounters, that you will stop looking for the universal solvent, stop grieving. You will learn to compound happiness out of small increments of mindless pleasure."

…

"The candor was infectious. It spread back to the beginning of your life. You tried to tell her, as well as you could, what it was like being you. You described the feeling you'd always had of being misplaced, of always standing to one side of yourself, of watching yourself in the world even as you were being in the world, and wondering if this was how everyone felt. That you always believed that other people had a clearer idea of what they were doing, and didn't worry quite so much about why."

…

"Your head is pounding with voices of confession and revelation. You followed the rails of white powder across the mirror in pursuit of a point of convergence where everything was cross-referenced according to a master code. For a second, you felt terrific. You were coming to grips. Then the coke ran out; as you hoovered the last line, you saw yourself hideously close-up with a rolled twenty sticking out of your nose. The goal is receding. Whatever it was. You can't get everything straight in one night."

First-person narrators are characters who, to tell the story, use "I" when the narrator is the protagonist or a major character (e.g. the boy in "Araby" in *The Dubliners* by James Joyce) or "we" when the narrator is a minor character, an onlooker (e.g. the narrator in "A Rose for Emily" by William Faulkner) who describes events experienced or related by other characters.

A first-person narrator sounds more familiar and closer to the readership and its narration easily involves the feeling of the readers. Besides, it

> simplifies a writer's task of selecting details... [and its] restricted view can create irony—a discrepancy between what is said and what readers believe to be true (Kirszner & Mandell 2006, 223).

Examples of a first-person narrator are shown in the following selections.

First-person Point of View (Child)

"I like the woods," I thought. "They're big and scary. I wonder if they are the same woods that are behind my house. They go on for miles. They're bigger than I could walk in a day, or a week even." It was neat to think that while we were driving into the woods people were going to bed in other countries.

When I woke up this morning, I couldn't wait to go hunting. My mother was cooking the breakfast, but all I could think of was, "When will he come?" and "Won't he even come?" Finally I heard a car honk. "That will be Charlie Spoon," my father said. I think he called him "Charlie Spoon" because he thought Charlie was shaped like a big spoon (Kirszner & Mandell 2006, 228).

First-person Point of View (Adult)

"They are always the same woods," I thought sleepily as we drove through the early morning darkness—deep and immense, covered with yesterday's snowfall, which had frozen overnight. "They're the same woods that lie behind my house, and they stretch all the way to here," I thought. I knew that they stretched for miles and miles, longer than I could walk in a day, or even in a week but that they were still the same woods. Knowing that this made me feel good: I thought it was like thinking of God; it was like thinking of the space between that place and the moon; it was like thinking of the foreign countries from my geography book where even then, I knew, people were going to bed, while we—my father and I and Charlie Spoon and Mac, Charlie's eleven-year-old son—were driving deeper into the Pennsylvania countryside, to go hunting.

We had risen before dawn. My mother, who was yarning and not trying to hide her sleepiness, cooked us eggs and French toast. My father smoked a cigarette and flickered ashes into his saucer while I listened, wondering, "Why doesn't he come?" and "Won't he ever come?" until at last a car pulled into our driveway and honked. "That will be Charlie Spoon," my father said. He always said "Charlie Spoon," even though his real name was Spreun, because Charlie was, in a sense, shaped like a spoon, with a large head and a narrow waist and chest (Kirszner & Mandell 2006, 229).

In a third-person, the narrator is not a character in the story. This kind of narration can be divided into three categories, omniscient narrator, limited omniscient narrator and objective narrator.

Most third-person narrators are omniscient. They appear to be all-knowing and go freely from one character's mind to another. Such narrators seem to take on the features of maturity, dependability and mental stability in contrast with the seemingly naive, dishonest and changeable first-person narrators. The third-person narrators are not characters in the story so that the omniscient ones are able to present a more comprehensive vision of things going on and figures involved. They may convey their attitudes toward the subject matters by means of some linguistic devices concerning diction, sentence, and figurative expressions. For example, the omniscient narrator in Nadine Gordimer's "Once upon a Time" takes advantage of well-chosen words or phrases, sentence structure, repetition, and exaggeration to show her distaste for the scene she depicts:

> In a house, in a suburb, in a city, there were a man and his wife who loved each other very much and were living happily ever after. They had a little boy, and they loved him very much. They had a cat and a dog that the little boy loved very much. They had a car and caravan trailer for holidays, and a swimming pool which was fenced so that the little boy and his playmates would not fall in and drown. They had a housemaid who was absolutely trustworthy and an itinerant gardener who highly recommended by the neighbors. For when they began to live happily ever after they were warned, by that wise old witch, the husband's mother, not to take anyone off the street (Kirszner & Mandell 2006, 225–226).

Sometimes, the omniscient narrator in some stories alternates from the third-person point of view to the first-person perspective, speaking like the author directly to the readers. It seems that such narrators are eager to express their ideas on behalf of the author. Henry Fielding's *Tom Jones* contains some passages of such kind of narration. Le Guin's "The Ones Who Walk Away from Omelas" has both a third-person narrator and a first-person one. This kind of narration highlights the tone and theme of the story.

Some third-person narrators have limited omniscience and they concentrate on merely the experiences of a single character. That is to say,

> events are limited to one character's perspective, and nothing is revealed that the characters does not see, hear, feel, or think (Kirszner & Mandell 2006, 226).

In the following example selected from the story of "Teenage Wasteland" by Anne Tyler, the limited omniscient narrator tells the story from the perspective of a single character, Daisy:

> Daisy and Matt sat silent, shocked. Matt rubbed his forehead with his fingertips. Imagine, Daisy thought, how they must look to Mr. Lanham: an overweight housewife in a cotton dress and a too-tall, too-thin insurance agent in a baggy, frayed suit. Failures, both of them—the kind of people who are always hurrying to catch up, missing the point of things that everyone else grasps at once. She wished she'd worn nylons instead of knee socks (Kirszner & Mandell 2006, 227).

Here the limited omniscient narration drives at home the impression that they are on-lookers, observing Daisy and Matt and interpreting the couple's inner thoughts. This perspective connotes a sense of objectivity and detachment.

Objective narration involves a detached point of view of the characters and the plot. In other words, the narrator sounds objective and its narrative tone seems to be free from bias and self-interest. In the story, there are no comments of the narrator or the reflection of the characters. The narrator uses merely "the facts" in telling the story. He or she simply recounts the events as they happen. Hemingway's "Hills Like White Elephants" is such an example in which the objective narration is applied. In this case, the readers have to read between the lines to figure out the characters' feelings and reflections. Objective narration helps to present events and actions vividly and meanwhile also leaving the scene a "blank" for the readers to "fill in."

In O'Connor's "A Good Man Is Hard to Find," the two characters, Grandma and The Misfit, are presented to readers objectively by the narrator who inserts no comments. The narrator merely gives detailed presentations of their dialogues and actions, leaving the judgment of the two characters for the readership. In Kate Chopin's "The Story of an Hour," the narrator appears to be an objective and detached observer who merely provides details on the feelings and thoughts of the heroine Mrs. Malland.

To be clear, "objective" narration alludes to a matter of degree. That is to say, despite the "objective" narration, or the apparent absence of the narrator's comments, the absence itself points to an attitude too. Indifference and silence speak themselves. Readers can figure out the intention, the attitude, or the feeling of the narrator via this indifference in narration. Take for example Tim O'Brien's "The Things They Carried."

"First Lieutenant Jimmy Cross carried letters from a girl named Martha, a junior at Mount Sebastian College in New Jersey. They were not love letters, but Lieutenant Cross was hoping, so he kept them folded in plastic at the bottom of his rucksack...

The things they carried were largely determined by necessity. Among the necessities or near necessities were P-38 can openers, pocket knives, heat tabs, wrist watches, dog tags, mosquito repellant, chewing gum, candy, cigarettes, salt tablets, packets of Kool-Aid, lighters, matches, sewing kits, Military Payment Certificates, C rations, and two or three canteens of water. Together these items weighed between fifteen and twenty pounds, depending upon a man's habits or rate of metabolism... By necessity, and because it was SOP, they all carried steel helmets that weighed five pounds including the liner and camouflage cove. They carried standard fatigue jackets and trousers. Very few carried underwear. On their feet they carried jungle boots—2.1 pounds—and Dave carried three pairs of socks and a can of... Until he was shot, Ted Lavender carried six or seven ounces of premium dope, which for him was a necessity. Mitchell Sanders, the RTO, carried condoms. Norman carried...Rat Kiley carried comic books...

What they carried was partly a function of rank, partly of field specialty.

As a first lieutenant and platoon leader, Jimmy Cross carried a compass, maps, code books, binoculars... In addition, Dobbins carried between ten and fifteen pounds of ammunition draped in belt across his chest and shoulders...

In addition to the three standard weapon—the M-60, M-16, and M-79—they carried whatever presented itself, or whatever seemed appropriate as a means of killing or staying alive... Some carried CS or tear gas grenades. Some carried white phosphorous grenade. They carried all they could bear, and then some, including a silent awe for the terrible power of the things they carried...

What they carried varied by mission...

If a mission seemed especially hazardous, or if it involved a place they knew to be bad, they carried everything they could...

The things they carried were determined to some extent by superstition. Lieutenant Cross carried his good-luck pebble. Dave Jensen carried a rabbit's foot. Norman Bowker, otherwise a very gentle person, carried a thumb that had been presented to him as a gift by Mitchell Sanders...

They carried USO stationery and pencils and pens... Often they carried each other, the wounded or weak. They carried infections. They carried chess sets, basketballs, Vietnam-English Dictionaries, insignia of rank, Bronze Stars and Purple Hearts, plastic cards imprinted with the Code of Conduct. They carried diseases, among them malaria and dysentery. They carried lice and ringworm and leeches and paddy algae and various rots and molds. They carried the land itself—Vietnam, the place, the soil—a powdery orange-red dust that covered their boots and fatigues and faces. They carried the sky. The whole atmosphere, they carried it, the humidity, the monsoons, the stink of fungus and decay, all of it, they carried gravity. They moved like mules... They carried their own lives...

They carried all the emotional baggage of men who might die. Grief, terror, love, longing... They carried shameful memories. They carried the common secret of cowardice barely restrained, the instinct to run or freeze or hide, and in many respects this was the heaviest burden of all, for it could never be put down, it required perfect balance and perfect posture. They carried their reputations. They carried the soldier's greatest fear, which was the fear of blushing. Men killed, and died, because they were embarrassed not to...

(Charters 1999, 605-616)

From the lists of things the soldiers carried, the tone of the story can be felt and the alleged detachment in narration actually reveals the attitude of the narrator, sorrow, and regret for the soldiers involved in the (Vietnam) war.

The story's list of "things they carried" extends to the burden of memory and desire and confusion and grief. It's the weight of America's involvement in the war (Mason 1994, 829).

The matter-of-fact details in the description of the things the soldiers carry grip the hearts of the readers. The recounting of the details gives away the narrator who is in fact making comments in a hidden way and it best embodies the narrator's attitudinal inclination. The narrator actually announces silently the real terror of war.

In many stories, however, writers may use a mixed approach to narrative perspective so that in both short and long stories the first-person and third-person narrators are seen to achieve some ideal effects. For example, in the third paragraph of "The Ones Who Walk Away from Omelas" (1976) by Ursula K. Le Guin (1929—), "they" and "I" / "we" are both used to start the narration.

> They were not simple folk, you see, though they were happy. But we do not say the words of cheer much any more. All smiles have become archaic. Given a description such as this one tends to make certain assumptions. Given a description such as this one tends to look next for the King, mounted on a splendid stallion and surrounded by his noble knights, or perhaps in a golden litter borne by great-muscled slaves. But there was no king. They did not use swords, or keep slaves. They were not barbarians. I do not know the rules and laws of their society, but I suspect that they were singularly few. (Para. 3)

Sometimes, a third-person narration mixes with a second-person one as in this part of the story "The Things They Carried."

> Before Lavender died there were seventeen men in the platoon, and whoever drew the number seventeen would strip off his gear and crawl in headfirst with a flashlight and Lieutenant Cross's .45-caliber pistol... They would sit down or kneel, not facing the hole, listening to the ground beneath them, imagining cobwebs and ghosts, whatever was down there—the tunnel walls squeezing in—how the flashlight seemed impossibly heavy in the hand and how it was tunnel vision in the very strictest sense, compression in all ways, even time, and how you had to wiggle in—ass and elbows—a swallowed-up feeling—and how you find yourself worrying about odd things: Will your flashlight go dead? Do rats carry rabies? If you screamed, how far would the sound carry? Would your buddies hear it? ... (Charters 1999, 610)

The second-person point of view, though unpopular, turns to the imperative mood and the second-person pronouns "you" ("your" and "yours") to speak to readers directly. In this situation, the narrator takes at least one character directly as "you" and regards the readership as a character within the story. Tom Robbins' novel *Half Asleep in Frog Pajamas* (published in 1994 by Bantam Books) is one with a second-person narration.

Questions for Reflection

1. What effects will come out if Hawthorne had chosen to tell his story from the point of view of Goodman Brown?

2. Find the short story of "Bartleby, the Scrivener" by Herman Melville, read it carefully, and make comments on its first-person narrator.

3. Discuss the omniscient point of view that occurs in Le Guin's "The Ones Who Walk Away from Omelas."

4. Considering the story "A Good Man Is Hard to Find," what is the dominant point of view from which the story is told? Is the narrator a character in the story? If so, is he or she a participant in the story's events or just a witness? Does the story's point of view create irony? What are the advantages of the story's point of view? How does the point of view achieve the

intention of the text?

5. Find a story chiefly with a second-person narration and analyze its effects achieved by this point of view.

■ Setting

> Many authors find it hard to write about environments that they did not know in childhood. The voices reheard from childhood have a truer pitch. And the foliage— the trees of childhood—are remembered more exactly. When I work from within a different locale from the South, I have to wonder what time the flowers are in bloom—and what flowers? I hardly let characters speak unless they are Southern.
>
> —Carson McCullers, "The Flowering Dream"
>
> (Kirszner & Mandell 2006, 171)

Generally speaking the setting is the place and time of the story. When a story is set or where it takes place often affects the readers' understanding of the events and characters. However, the setting is more than place and time. It also involves many physical and cultural elements. Setting is actually the physical, spiritual or cultural background against which the action of a story takes place. The elements that constitute a setting are:

(1) the actual geographical location, its typography, scenery, and such physical arrangements as the location of the windows and doors in a room; (2) the occupations and daily manners of living of the characters; (3) the time and period in which the action takes place, for example, epoch in history season of the year; (4) the general environment of the characters, for example, religious, mental, moral, social and emotional conditions through which the people in the narrative move (Holman & Harmon 1986, 465).

The following story of Kate Chopin presents a good example of setting (as presented in Paragraphs 4-7).

The Story of an Hour (1894)

—Kate Chopin (1851-1904)

[1] Knowing that Mrs. Mallard was afflicted with a heart trouble, great care was taken to break to her as gently as possible the news of her husband's death.

[2] It was her sister Josephine who told her, in broken sentences, veiled hints that revealed in half concealing. Her husband's friend Richards was there, too, near her. It was he who had been in the newspaper office when intelligence of the railroad disaster was received, with Brently Mallard's name leading the list of "killed." He had only taken the time to assure himself of its truth by a second telegram, and had hastened to forestall any less careful, less

tender friend in bearing the sad message.

[3] She did not hear the story as many women have heard the same, with a paralyzed inability to accept its significance. She wept at once, with sudden, wild abandonment, in her sister's arms. When the storm of grief had spent itself she went away to her room alone. She would have no one follow her.

[4] There stood, facing the open window, a comfortable, roomy armchair. Into this she sank, pressed down by a physical exhaustion that haunted her body and seemed to reach into her soul.

[5] She could see in the open square before her house the tops of trees that were all aquiver with the new spring life. The delicious breath of rain was in the air. In the street below a peddler was crying his wares. The notes of a distant song which some one was singing reached her faintly, and countless sparrows were twittering in the eaves.

[6] There were patches of blue sky showing here and there through the clouds that had met and piled one above the other in the west facing her window.

[7] She sat with her head thrown back upon the cushion of the chair, quite motionless, except when a sob came up into her throat and shook her, as a child who has cried itself to sleep continues to sob in its dreams.

[8] She was young, with a fair, calm face, whose lines bespoke repression and even a certain strength. But now there was a dull stare in her eyes, whose gaze was fixed away off yonder on one of those patches of blue sky. It was not a glance of reflection, but rather indicated a suspension of intelligent thought.

[9] There was something coming to her and she was waiting for it, fearfully. What was it? She did not know; it was too subtle and elusive to name. But she felt it, creeping out of the sky, reaching toward her through the sounds, the scents, the color that filled the air.

[10] Now her bosom rose and fell tumultuously. She was beginning to recognize this thing that was approaching to possess her, and she was striving to beat it back with her will—as powerless as her two white slender hands would have been.

[11] When she abandoned herself a little whispered word escaped her slightly parted lips. She said it over and over under her breath: "Free, free, free!" The vacant stare and the look of terror that had followed it went from her eyes. They stayed keen and bright. Her pulses beat fast, and the coursing blood warmed and relaxed every inch of her body.

[12] She did not stop to ask if it were or were not a monstrous joy that held her. A clear and exalted perception enabled her to dismiss the suggestion as trivial.

[13] She knew that she would weep again when she saw the kind, tender hands folded in death; the face that had never looked save with love upon her, fixed and gray and dead. But she saw beyond that bitter moment a long procession of years to come that would belong to her absolutely. And she opened and spread her arms out to them in welcome.

[14] There would be no one to live for during those coming years; she would live for herself. There would be no powerful will bending her in that blind persistence with which men and women believe they have a right to impose a private will upon a fellow-creature. A kind intention or a cruel intention made the act seem no less a crime as she looked upon it in that brief moment of illumination.

[15] And yet she had loved him—sometimes. Often she had not. What did it matter! What could love, the unsolved mystery, count for in the face of this possession of self-assertion which she suddenly recognized as the strongest impulse of her being!

[16] "Free! Body and soul free!" she kept whispering.

[17] Josephine was kneeling before the closed door with her lips to the keyhole, imploring for admission. "Louise, open the door! I beg; open the door—you will make yourself ill. What are you doing, Louise? For heaven's sake open the door."

[18] "Go away. I am not making myself ill." No; she was drinking in a very elixir of life through that open window.

[19] Her fancy was running riot along those days ahead of her. Spring days, and summer days, and all sorts of days that would be her own. She breathed a quick prayer that life might be long. It was only yesterday she had thought with a shudder that life might be long.

[20] She arose at length and opened the door to her sister's importunities. There was a feverish triumph in her eyes, and she carried herself unwittingly like a goddess of Victory. She clasped her sister's waist, and together they descended the stairs. Richards stood waiting for them at the bottom.

[21] Some one was opening the front door with a latchkey. It was Brently Mallard who entered, a little travel-stained, composedly carrying his grip sack and umbrella. He had been far from the scene of the accident, and did not even know there had been one. He stood amazed at Josephine's piercing cry; at Richards' quick motion to screen him from the view of his wife.

[22] But Richards was too late.

[23] When the doctors came they said she had died of heart disease—of the joy that kills.

In Kate Chopin's "The Story of an Hour," the room of Mrs. Malland speaks metaphorically to her homebound life. She was once restricted to the small enclosure. At the news of her husband's supposed death in a railroad accident, she bursts into tears and later withdraws into her room. When she looks out of the window, she catches sight of the trees, the rainy street, the paddler crying his ware, and the sparrows. All these give her a great sense of light-heartedness and freshness. The setting symbolizes her emotional state. The sharp contrast between the restricted space of her room and the outside world suggests a tension "between Mrs. Mallard's subjugation and her desire for freedom" (DiYanni 2000, 62). She seems to be suffocated by the chained marital life and she thus harbors a great hope for freedom as symbolized by the natural world outside the window.

Another example is found in Nathaniel Hawthorne's *Scarlet Letter* (1850). The novel is set in Puritan Boston, Massachusetts in the middle of the 17th century. It tells the story of Hester Prynne, who gives birth to an illegitimate daughter after her adultery with a man whose name she never reveals. Hester confesses but she struggles to live a new life of dignity though she has to put on a piece of cloth with a red letter "A" on her bosom. The setting immediately reminds readers of the harsh Puritanical morality and legalism of Boston at that time when adultery was regarded as serious subject of moral degeneration. The setting corresponds with the concerns of the subjects like sin, shame, humiliation, fear, oppression, hypocrisy, humanity, courage, hope, freedom, and spiritual rebirth.

Questions for Reflection

1. What is meant by the setting of a story?
2. How does Nathaniel Hawthorne set the scene in "Young Goodman Brown?"
3. Read the story of "A Rose for Emily" and comment on the function of its setting.

A Rose for Emily (1931)

—William Faulkner (1897−1962)

I

When Miss Emily Grierson died, our whole town went to her funeral: the men through a sort of respectful affection for a fallen monument, the women mostly out of curiosity to see the inside of her house, which no one save an old man-servant—a combined gardener and cook—had seen in at least ten years.

It was a big, squarish frame house that had once been white, decorated with cupolas and spires and scrolled balconies in the heavily lightsome style of the seventies, set on what had once been our most select street. But garages and cotton gins had encroached and obliterated even the august names of that neighborhood; only Miss Emily's house was left, lifting its stubborn and coquettish decay above the cotton wagons and the gasoline pumps—an eyesore among eyesores. And now Miss Emily had gone to join the representatives of those august names where they lay in the cedar-bemused cemetery among the ranked and anonymous graves of Union and Confederate soldiers who fell at the battle of Jefferson.

Alive, Miss Emily had been a tradition, a duty, and a care; a sort of hereditary obligation upon the town, dating from that day in 1894 when Colonel Sartoris, the mayor—he who fathered the edict that no Negro woman should appear on the streets without an apron—remitted her taxes, the dispensation dating from the death of her father on into perpetuity. Not that Miss Emily would have accepted charity. Colonel Sartoris invented an involved tale to the effect that Miss Emily's father had loaned money to the town, which the town, as a matter of business, preferred this way of repaying. Only a man of Colonel Sartoris' generation and thought could have invented it, and only a woman could have believed it.

When the next generation, with its more modern ideas, became mayors and aldermen, this arrangement created some little dissatisfaction. On the first of the year they mailed her a tax notice. February came, and there was no reply. They wrote her a formal letter, asking her to call at the sheriff's office at her convenience. A week later the mayor wrote her himself, offering to call or to send his car for her, and received in reply a note on paper of an archaic shape, in a thin, flowing calligraphy in faded ink, to the effect that she no longer went out at all. The tax notice was also enclosed, without comment.

They called a special meeting of the Board of Aldermen. A deputation waited upon her, knocked at the door through which no visitor had passed since she ceased giving china-painting lessons eight or ten years earlier. They were admitted by the old Negro into a dim hall from which a stairway mounted into still more shadow. It smelled of dust and disuse—a close, dank smell. The Negro led them into the parlor. It was furnished in heavy, leather-covered furniture. When the Negro opened the blinds of one window, they could see that the leather was cracked; and when they sat down, a faint dust rose sluggishly about their thighs, spinning with slow motes in the single sunray. On a tarnished gilt easel before the fireplace stood a crayon portrait of Miss Emily's father.

They rose when she entered—a small, fat woman in black, with a thin gold chain descending to her waist and vanishing into her belt, leaning on an ebony cane with a tarnished gold head. Her skeleton was small and spare; perhaps that was why what would have been merely plumpness in another was obesity in her. She looked bloated, like a body long submerged in motionless water, and of that pallid hue. Her eyes, lost in the fatty ridges of her face, looked like two small pieces of coal pressed into a lump of dough as they moved from one face to another while the visitors stated their errand.

She did not ask them to sit. She just stood in the door and listened quietly until the spokesman came to a stumbling halt. Then they could hear the invisible watch ticking at the end of the gold chain.

Her voice was dry and cold. "I have no taxes in Jefferson. Colonel Sartoris explained it to me. Perhaps one of you can gain access to the city records and satisfy yourselves."

"But we have. We are the city authorities, Miss Emily. Didn't you get a notice from the sheriff, signed by him?"

"I received a paper, yes," Miss Emily said. "Perhaps he considers himself the sheriff... I have no taxes in Jefferson."

"But there is nothing on the books to show that, you see. We must go by the—"

"See Colonel Sartoris. I have no taxes in Jefferson."

"But, Miss Emily—"

"See Colonel Sartoris." (Colonel Sartoris had been dead almost ten years.) "I have no taxes in Jefferson. To be!" The Negro appeared. "Show these gentlemen out."

II

So she vanquished them, horse and foot, just as she had vanquished their fathers thirty years before about the smell. That was two years after her father's death and a short time after her sweetheart—the one we believed would marry her—had deserted her. After her father's death she went out very little; after her sweetheart went away, people hardly saw her at all. A few of the ladies had the temerity to call, but were not received, and the only sign of life about the place was the Negro man—a young man then—going in and out with a market basket.

"Just as if a man—any man—could keep a kitchen properly,"the ladies said; so they were not surprised when the smell developed. It was another link between the gross, teeming world and the high and mighty Griersons.

A neighbor, a woman, complained to the mayor, Judge Stevens, eighty years old.

"But what will you have me do about it, madam?" he said.

"Why, send her word to stop it," the woman said. "Isn't there a law?"

"I'm sure that won't be necessary," Judge Stevens said. "It's probably just a snake or a rat that nigger of hers killed in the yard. I'll speak to him about it."

The next day he received two more complaints, one from a man who came in diffident deprecation. "We really must do something about it, Judge. I'd be the last one in the world to bother Miss Emily, but we've got to do something." That night the Board of Aldermen met— three graybeards and one younger man, a member of the rising generation.

"It's simple enough," he said. "Send her word to have her place cleaned up. Give her a certain time to do it in, and if she don't..."

"Dammit, sir," Judge Stevens said, "will you accuse a lady to her face of smelling bad?"

So the next night, after midnight, four men crossed Miss Emily's lawn and slunk about the house like burglars, sniffing along the base of the brickwork and at the cellar openings while one of them performed a regular sowing motion with his hand out of a sack slung from his shoulder. They broke open the cellar door and sprinkled lime there, and in all the outbuildings. As they recrossed the lawn, a window that had been dark was lighted and Miss Emily sat in it, the light behind her, and her upright torso motionless as that of an idol. They crept quietly across the lawn and into the shadow of the locusts that lined the street. After a week or two the smell went away.

That was when people had begun to feel really sorry for her. People in our town, remembering how old lady Wyatt, her great-aunt, had gone completely crazy at last, believed that the Griersons held themselves a little too high for what they really were. None of the young men were quite good enough for Miss Emily and such. We had long thought of them as a tableau, Miss Emily a slender figure in white in the background, her father a spraddled silhouette in the foreground, his back to her and clutching a horsewhip, the two of them framed by the back-flung front door. So when she got to be thirty and was still single, we were not pleased exactly, but vindicated; even with insanity in the family she wouldn't have turned down all of her chances if they had really materialized.

When her father died, it got about that the house was all that was left to her; and in a way, people were glad. At last they could pity Miss Emily. Being left alone, and a pauper, she had become humanized. Now she too would know the old thrill and the old despair of a penny more or less.

The day after his death all the ladies prepared to call at the house and offer condolence and aid, as is our custom Miss Emily met them at the door, dressed as usual and with no trace of grief on her face. She told them that her father was not dead. She did that for three days, with the ministers calling on her, and the doctors, trying to persuade her to let them dispose of the body. Just as they were about to resort to law and force, she broke down, and they buried her father quickly.

We did not say she was crazy then. We believed she had to do that. We remembered all the young men her father had driven away, and we knew that with nothing left, she would have to cling to that which had robbed her, as people will.

III

She was sick for a long time. When we saw her again, her hair was cut short, making her look like a girl, with a vague resemblance to those angels in colored church windows—sort of tragic and serene.

The town had just let the contracts for paving the sidewalks, and in the summer after her father's death they began the work. The construction company came with riggers and mules and machinery, and a foreman named Homer Barron, a Yankee—a big, dark, ready man, with a big voice and eyes lighter than his face. The little boys would follow in groups to hear him cuss the riggers, and the riggers singing in time to the rise and fall of picks. Pretty soon he knew everybody in town. Whenever you heard a lot of laughing anywhere about the square, Homer Barron would be in the center of the group. Presently we began to see him and Miss Emily on Sunday afternoons driving in the yellow-wheeled buggy and the matched team of bays from the livery stable.

At first we were glad that Miss Emily would have an interest, because the ladies all said, "Of course a Grierson would not think seriously of a Northerner, a day laborer." But there were still others, older people, who said that even grief could not cause a real lady to forget noblesse oblige—without calling it noblesse oblige. They just said, "Poor Emily. Her kinsfolk should come to her." She had some kin in Alabama; but years ago her father had fallen out with them over the estate of old lady Wyatt, the crazy woman, and there was no communication between the two families. They had not even been represented at the funeral.

And as soon as the old people said, "Poor Emily," the whispering began. "Do you suppose it's really so?" they said to one another. "Of course it is. What else could..." This behind their hands; rustling of craned silk and satin behind jalousies closed upon the sun of Sunday afternoon as the thin, swift clop-clop-clop of the matched team passed: "Poor Emily."

She carried her head high enough—even when we believed that she was fallen. It was as if she demanded more than ever the recognition of her dignity as the last Grierson; as if it had wanted that touch of earthiness to reaffirm her imperviousness. Like when she bought the rat poison, the arsenic. That was over a year after they had begun to say "Poor Emily," and while the two female cousins were visiting her.

"I want some poison," she said to the druggist. She was over thirty then, still a slight woman, though thinner than usual, with cold, haughty black eyes in a face the flesh of which was strained across the temples and about the eye-sockets as you imagine a lighthouse-keeper's face ought to look. "I want some poison," she said.

"Yes, Miss Emily. What kind? For rats and such? I'd recom—"

"I want the best you have. I don't care what kind."

The druggist named several. "They'll kill anything up to an elephant. But what you want is—"

"Arsenic," Miss Emily said. "Is that a good one?"

"Is… arsenic? Yes, ma'am. But what you want—"

"I want arsenic."

The druggist looked down at her. She looked back at him, erect, her face like a strained flag. "Why, of course," the druggist said. "If that's what you want. But the law requires you to tell what you are going to use it for."

Miss Emily just stared at him, her head tilted back in order to look him eye for eye, until he looked away and went and got the arsenic and wrapped it up. The Negro delivery boy brought her the package; the druggist didn't come back. When she opened the package at home there was written on the box, under the skull and bones: "For rats."

IV

So the next day we all said, "She will kill herself"; and we said it would be the best thing. When she had first begun to be seen with Homer Barron, we had said, "She will marry him." Then we said, "She will persuade him yet," because Homer himself had remarked—he liked men, and it was known that he drank with the younger men in the Elks' Club—that he was not a marrying man. Later we said, "Poor Emily" behind the jalousies as they passed on Sunday afternoon in the glittering buggy, Miss Emily with her head high and Homer Barron with his hat cocked and a cigar in his teeth, reins and whip in a yellow glove.

Then some of the ladies began to say that it was a disgrace to the town and a bad example to the young people. The men did not want to interfere, but at last the ladies forced the Baptist minister—Miss Emily's people were Episcopal—to call upon her. He would never divulge what happened during that interview, but he refused to go back again. The next Sunday they again drove about the streets, and the following day the minister's wife wrote to Miss Emily's relations in Alabama.

So she had blood-kin under her roof again and we sat back to watch developments. At first nothing happened. Then we were sure that they were to be married. We learned that Miss Emily had been to the jeweler's and ordered a man's toilet set in silver, with the letters H. B. on each piece. Two days later we learned that she had bought a complete outfit of men's clothing, including a nightshirt, and we said, "They are married." We were really glad. We were glad because the two female cousins were even more Grierson than Miss Emily had ever been.

So we were not surprised when Homer Barron—the streets had been finished some time since—was gone. We were a little disappointed that there was not a public blowing-off, but we believed that he had gone on to prepare for Miss Emily's coming, or to give her a chance to get rid of the cousins. (By that time it was a cabal, and we were all Miss Emily's allies to help circumvent the cousins.) Sure enough, after another week they departed. And, as we had expected all along, within three days Homer Barron was back in town. A neighbor saw the Negro man admit him at the kitchen door at dusk one evening.

And that was the last we saw of Homer Barron. And of Miss Emily for some time. The Negro man went in and out with the market basket, but the front door remained closed. Now and then we would see her at a window for a moment, as the men did that night when they sprinkled the lime, but for almost six months she did not appear on the streets. Then we knew that this was to be expected too; as if that quality of her father which had thwarted her woman's life so many times had been too virulent and too furious to die.

When we next saw Miss Emily, she had grown fat and her hair was turning gray. During the next few years it grew grayer and grayer until it attained an even pepper-and-salt iron-gray, when it ceased turning. Up to the day of her death at seventy-four it was still that vigorous iron-gray, like the hair of an active man.

From that time on her front door remained closed, save for a period of six or seven years, when she was about forty, during which she gave lessons in china-painting. She fitted up a studio in one of the downstairs rooms, where the daughters and granddaughters of Colonel Sartoris' contemporaries were sent to her with the same regularity and in the same spirit that they were sent to church on Sundays with a twenty-five-cent piece for the collection plate. Meanwhile her taxes had been remitted.

Then the newer generation became the backbone and the spirit of the town, and the painting pupils grew up and fell away and did not send their children to her with boxes of color and tedious brushes and pictures cut from the ladies' magazines. The front door closed upon the last one and remained closed for good. When the town got free postal delivery, Miss Emily alone refused to let them fasten the metal numbers above her door and attach a mailbox to it. She would not listen to them.

Daily, monthly, yearly we watched the Negro grow grayer and more stooped, going in and out with the market basket. Each December we sent her a tax notice, which would be returned by the post office a week later, unclaimed. Now and then we would see her in one of the downstairs windows—she had evidently shut up the top floor of the house—like the carven torso of an idol in a niche, looking or not looking at us, we could never tell which. Thus she passed from generation to generation—dear, inescapable, impervious, tranquil, and perverse.

And so she died. Fell ill in the house filled with dust and shadows, with only a doddering Negro man to wait on her. We did not even know she was sick; we had long since given up trying to get any information from the Negro. He talked to no one, probably not even to her, for his voice had grown harsh and rusty, as if from disuse.

She died in one of the downstairs rooms, in a heavy walnut bed with a curtain, her gray head propped on a pillow yellow and moldy with age and lack of sunlight.

V

The Negro met the first of the ladies at the front door and let them in, with their hushed, sibilant voices and their quick, curious glances, and then he disappeared. He walked right through the house and out the back and was not seen again.

The two female cousins came at once. They held the funeral on the second day, with the town coming to look at Miss Emily beneath a mass of bought flowers, with the crayon face of her father musing profoundly above the bier and the ladies sibilant and macabre; and the very old men—some in their brushed Confederate uniforms—on the porch and the lawn, talking of Miss Emily as if she had been a contemporary of theirs, believing that they had danced with her and courted her perhaps, confusing time with its mathematical progression, as the old do, to whom all the past is not a diminishing road but, instead, a huge meadow which no winter ever quite touches, divided from them now by the narrow bottle-neck of the most recent decade of years.

Already we knew that there was one room in that region above stairs which no one had seen in forty years, and which would have to be forced. They waited until Miss Emily was decently in the ground before they opened it.

The violence of breaking down the door seemed to fill this room with pervading dust. A thin, acrid pall as of the tomb seemed to lie everywhere upon this room decked and furnished as for a bridal: upon the valance curtains of faded rose color, upon the rose-shaded lights, upon the dressing table, upon the delicate array of crystal and the man's toilet things backed with tarnished silver, silver so tarnished that the monogram was obscured. Among them lay a collar and tie, as if they had just been removed, which, lifted, left upon the surface a pale crescent in the dust. Upon a chair hung the suit, carefully folded; beneath it the two mute shoes and the discarded socks.

The man himself lay in the bed.

For a long while we just stood there, looking down at the profound and fleshless grin. The body had apparently once lain in the attitude of an embrace, but now the long sleep that outlasts love, that conquers even the grimace of love, had cuckolded him. What was left of him, rotted beneath what was left of the nightshirt, had become inextricable from the bed in which he lay; and upon him and upon the pillow beside him lay that even coating of the patient and biding dust.

Then we noticed that in the second pillow was the indentation of a head. One of us lifted something from it, and leaning forward, that faint and invisible dust dry and acrid in the nostrils, we saw a long strand of iron-gray hair.

■ Language and Style

> When a writer starts in very young, his problems apart from his story are those of technique, of words, of rhythms, of story methods, of transition, of characterization, of ways of creating effects. But after years of trial and error most of these things are solved and one gets what is called a style. It is then that a story conceived falls into place neatly and is written down having the indelible personal hallmark of the writer.
>
> —*John Steinbeck*, *Letter*
> (Kirszner & Mandell 2006, 276)

Style is the featured way of an author in his or her habitual use of language to create a literary work. It reflects the unique ways that the writers see people, society and nature. Style is one of the elements of literature and it often refers to

> the way in which the writer uses language, selecting and arranging words to say what he or she wants to say. Style encompasses elements such as word choice; syntax; sentence length and structure; and the presence, frequency, and prominence of imagery and figures of speech (Kirszner & Mandell 2006, 276).

With a certain style, a voice is created to represent the idea of the narrator, the character, or even the author. Creative use of language in fiction enriches the contents of the story and highlights its overall effects. The out-of-the-way diction or sentence pattern has special stylistic features and connotes extra meanings. The language speaks itself in an implied way. In Toni Morrison's first novel *The Bluest Eye* (1970), the *Dick-and-Jane Primer* for children arranged orderly in Standard English printing gives a picture of the happy middle-class white family and the warm and sweet love among family members.

> Here is the house. It is green and white. It has a red door. It is very pretty. Here is the family. Mother, father, Dick, and Jane live in the green-and-white house. They are very happy. See Jane. She has a red dress. She wants to play. Who will play with Jane? See the cat. It goes meow-meow. Come and play. Come play with Jane (Morrison 1994, 5).

However, the messy printing of the primer at the very beginning of different chapters in *The Bluest Eye* speaks itself, implying the miseries and the spiritual distortions of the poverty-stricken African Americans. For example, in this chapter of the Section entitled "Autumn," the first three lines are printed in a mess, with capitalized, non-spaced, and non-punctuated "sentences" of the *Dick-and-Jane Primer*.

HEREISTHEFAMILYMOTHERFATHER

DICK AND JANE LIVE IN THE GREE

NANDWHITEHOUSETHEYAREVERYH

(Morrison 1994, 38)

This messily printed part concerns the pretty green house. It gives a list of the family members, describes their house, and is broken up with the word "happy." The happy scene of the Dick-and-Jane family is in sharp contrast with the messy state of the Breedlove family. The distorted sentence pattern corresponds well with the distorted relations in the Breedlove family, witnessed by the domestic violence of the Breedlove couple who often quarrel and fight in front of their kids and the painful and fearful response of the daughter Pecola described later in this chapter. In other chapters of the novel, such a printing is frequently seen at the very beginning of the text, each distorted pattern alluding to the poor situation of the characters as depicted in the corresponding part.

In Zora Neale Hurston's *Their Eyes Were Watching God* (1937), African American vernacular English goes side by side with Standard English, particularly in the dialogues between the characters. It is a style of Hurston's works.

> "Naw, Jody, it jus' looks lak it keeps us in some way we ain't natural wid one 'nother. You'se always of talkin' and fix' things, and Ah feels lak Ah'm jus' markin' time. Hope it soon gits over."
>
> "Over, Janie? I god, Ah ain't even started good. Ah told you in de very first beginning dat Ah aimed tuh be uh big voice. You oughta be glad, 'cause dat makes uh big woman outa you."
> (Hurston 1990, 46)
>
> ...
>
> Janie loved the conversation and sometimes she thought up good stories on the mule, but Joe had forbidden her to indulge. He didn't want her talking after such trashy people. "You'se Mrs. Mayor Starks, Janie. I god, Ah can't see what uh woman uh yo' stability would want tuh be treasurin' all dat gum-grease from folks dat don't even own de house dey sleep in. 'Tain't no early use. They's jus' some puny humans playin' round de toes uh Time." (Hurston 1990, 53−54)
>
> ...

The vernacular language sheds much light on the characters and underscores the African American folklore (especially the oral tradition). Meanwhile it accentuates the voices of the African American people who hope to establish themselves either in the local community or in the white-dominant American society. The mixed use of vernacular English with Standard English implies (the expectation of) white-and-black integration on the part of the (implied) author.

In the novel *Ulysses*, James Joyce experiments with the stream-of-consciousness style, imitating thought and

> allowing ideas run into one another as random associations are made so that readers may follow and participate in the thought processes of the narrator (Kirszner & Mandell 2006, 277).

Take for example the following selection from *Ulysses*.

Frseeeeeeeefronnnng train somewhere whistling the strength those engines have in them like big giants and the water rolling all over and out of them all sides like the end of Loves old sweet sonnnng the poor men that have to be out all the night from their wives and families in those roasting engines stifling it was today (Kirszner & Mandell 2006, 277).

It is a stream-of-consciousness passage. The fierce sound of the running train mixes with the noisy running water on both sides, and the noises are connected simultaneously with the sweet singing of the homesick men crowded in the sweltering and uncomfortable car. The narrator's thoughts jump from here to there. The narrative sequence winds itself up and forward, reflecting the thoughts and (somewhat positive) reactions of the characters ("poor men") in the annoying situation.

In the discussion of language style in fiction, it is equally important to include such elements as formal and informal diction, and figures of speech (especially figurative comparisons like simile and metaphor).

Formal diction is characterized by elaborate, complex sentences; a learned vocabulary; and a serious, objective, detached tone. The speaker avoids contractions, shortened word forms (like phone), regional expressions, and slang... [It] may indicate erudition, a high educational level, a superior social or professional position, or emotional detachment (Kirszner & Mandell 2006, 279).

The following passage from "The Birthmark," a short story by Nathaniel Hawthorne, is an example of formal writing, with long, complex sentences, and learned words. Moreover, no colloquialism is applied. The style fits well with the concern of the story, the obsession with human perfection.

In the latter part of the last century there lived a man of science, an eminent proficient in every branch of natural philosophy, who not long before our story opens had made experience of a spiritual affinity more attractive than any chemical one. He had left his laboratory to the care of an assistant, cleared his fine countenance from the furnace smoke, washed the stain of acids from his fingers, and persuaded a beautiful woman to become his wife. In those days when the comparatively recent discovery of electricity and other kindred mysteries of Nature seemed to open paths into the region of miracle, it was not unusual for the love of science to rival the love of a woman in its depth and absorbing energy. The higher intellect, the imagination, the spirit, and even the heart might all find their congenial ailment in pursuits which, as some of their ardent votaries believed, would ascend from one step of powerful intelligence to another, until the philosopher should lay his hand on the secret of creative force and perhaps make new worlds for himself (Kirszner & Mandell 2006, 279).

However, in fiction, a first-person narration can be formal too, though quite often third-person narration is popular when expressing a formal tone. Take for example the following paragraph from "The Loons", a story by Margaret Laurence (1926–1987), a Canadian novelist and short story writer.

Just below Manawaka, where the Wachakwa River ran brown and noisy over the pebbles, the scrub oak and grey-green willow and chokecherry bushes grew in a dense thicket. In a clearing at the centre of the thicket stood the Tonnerre family's shack. The basis at this dwelling was a small square cabin made of poplar poles and chinked with mud, which had been built by Jules Tonnerre some fifty years before, when he came back from Batoche with a bullet in his thigh, the year that Riel was hung and the voices of the Metis entered their long silence. Jules had only intended to stay the winter in the Wachakwa Valley, but the family was still there in the thirties, when I was a child. As the Tonnerres had increased, their settlement had been added to, until the clearing at the foot of the town hill was a chaos of lean-tos, wooden packing cases, warped lumber, discarded car tyres, ramshackle chicken coops, tangled strands of barbed wire and rusty tin cans. (Para. 1)

Despite the clause "when I was a child," the whole paragraph is formally written and the narrator sounds objective and detached.

What's more, even when a subjective tone is predominant in narration, the use of language is formal too. For example, the following paragraphs from *No Signposts in the Sea* by V. Sackville-West, a British poet and novelist, best embody the formal way of writing though narrated from the first-person perspective.

Dismissive as Pharisee, I regarded as moonlings all those whose life was lived on a less practical plane. Protests about damage to "natural beauty" froze me with contempt, for I believed in progress and could spare no regrets for a lake dammed into hydraulic use for the benefit of an industrial city in the Midlands. And so it was for all things. A hard materialism was my creed, accepted as a law of progress; any ascription of disinterested motives aroused not only my suspicion but my scorn (Zhang 1995, 289–290).

Sometimes we follow a coastline, it may be precipitous bluffs of grey limestone rising sheer out of the sea, or a low-lying arid stretch with miles of white sandy beach, and no sign of habitation, very bleached and barren. These coasts remind me of people; either they are forbidding and unapproachable, or else they present no mystery and show all they have to give at a glance, you feel the country would continue to be flat and featureless however far you penetrated inland. What I like best are the stern cliffs, with ranges of mountains soaring behind them, full of possibilities, peaks to be scaled only by the most daring. What plants of the high altitudes grow unravished among their crags and valleys? So do I let my imagination play over the recesses of Laura's Character, so austere in the foreground but nurturing what treasures of tenderness, like delicate flowers, for the discovery of the venturesome (Zhang 1995, 291–292).

Sometimes, formal language may appear stiff and it is uncommon in daily speech. Moreover, with extreme formal diction or expressions, a narrator or a character may sound pedantic, pretentious or condescending.

Informal language in fiction is consistent with daily speech and it is featured by colloquialisms, short forms or abbreviations, slangs, regional expressions, and sentence fragments. In Flannery O'Connor's "A Good Man Is Hard to Find," the expressions "aloose" (Para. 1), "you all" (Paras. 2, 51, 57, 73 and 77), and "britches" (Para. 19) are informal and the characters' speech pattern suggests their identities of southern middle-class people. Moreover, informal style may draw the readers closer to the text and shorten their distance. Again in "The Loons," the father's informal or slangy expressions sound warm and sincere.

> "I don't know what to do about that kid," my father said at dinner one evening. "Piquette Tonnerre, I mean. The <u>damn</u> bone's flared up again. I've had her in hospital for quite a while now, and it's under control all right, but I hate <u>like the dickens</u> to send her home again."
> (Para. 4)

However, formal and informal diction and expressions are used simultaneously in fiction, short or long. Since they have different stylistic functions, a writer may choose freely the way of language use considering his or her purpose of literary writing.

In creative writing, the author tends to take advantage of figures of speech to produce artistic effect, inspiring rich imagination of the reader and revealing further information about characters, plots, and themes. Since there are a variety of figurative usages, the discussion here will cover only some of them, such as simile, metaphor, and personification, because of limited space.

In "A Good Man Is Hard to Find," the simile in the sentence "the face was as broad and innocent as a cabbage" implies a dehumanized description of the mother by the narrator and the expression "like a rabbit's ears" at the end of the whole sentence corresponds to the dehumanized image.

> Bailey didn't look up from his reading so she wheeled around then and faced the children's mother, a young woman in slacks, <u>whose face was as broad and innocent as a cabbage</u> and was tied around with a green head-kerchief that had two points on the top <u>like rabbit's ears</u>.
> (Para. 2)

Other examples of simile used in the story to dehumanize the character can be found in Alice Walker's "Everyday Use for Your Grandmamma" too.

> I am the way my daughter would want me to be: a hundred pounds lighter, my skin <u>like an uncooked barley pancake</u>. (Para. 5)
>
> From the other side of the car comes a short, stocky man. Hair is all over his head a foot long and hanging from his chin <u>like a kinky mule tail</u>. (Para. 19)
>
> I hear Maggie go "Uhnnnh" again. It is her sister's hair. It stands straight up <u>like the wool on a sheep</u>. It is black as night and around the edges are two long pigtails that rope about <u>like small lizards</u> disappearing behind her ears. (Para. 20)

This way of language use also produces a humorous effect.

The metaphorical usage of words also helps to convey the attitude of the narrator or the (implied) author toward characters and events. For example, in "The Loons," the metaphor in the sentences conveys the attitude of "I" toward the Indian girl Piquette.

> It seemed to me that Piquette must be in some way <u>a daughter of the forest</u>, a kind of junior prophetess of the wilds, who might impart to me, if I took the right approach, some of the

secrets which she undoubtedly knew… (Para. 22)

In another paragraph of "The Loons," the narrator is describing their cottage and her love of it as well as the natural scene is well expressed in the metaphor "the filigree of the spruce trees."

> Our cottage was not named, as many were, "Dew Drop Inn" or "Bide-a-Wee," or "Bonnie Doon". The sign on the roadway bore in austere letters only our name, MacLeod. It was not a large cottage, but it was on the lakefront. You could look out the windows and see, through the filigree of the spruce trees, the water glistening greenly as the sun caught it. (Para. 17)

Personification is another popular figure of speech

> that endows inanimate objects or abstract ideas with life or with human characteristics… [It] expands the readers' vision of the story's setting and gives a dreamlike quality to the passage (Kirszner & Mandell 2006, 281).

Examples of personification are seen in the following selection from "The Loons."

> The two grey squirrels were still there, gossiping at us from the tall spruce beside the cottage, and by the end of the summer they would again be tame enough to take pieces of crust from my hands. (Para. 17)
>
> At the end of my first year, I came back home for the summer. I spent the first few days in talking non-stop with my mother, as we exchanged all the news that somehow had not found its way into letters… (Para. 63)

The personified expressions make the narration vivid and lively.

On the whole, in the discussion of language use in a story, because of the unique or even the deliberate choice of diction and sentence pattern by the authors, it is very important to put all these examples in their specific context so as to give a proper and reasonable interpretation.

Questions for Reflection

Read the following selections ("Araby" and "The Loons") and answer the questions.

Araby (1914)

—James Joyce(1884−1941)

North Richmond Street, being blind, was a quiet street except at the hour when the Christian Brothers' School set the boys free. An uninhabited house of two storeys stood at the blind end, detached from its neighbours in a square ground. The other houses of the street, conscious of decent lives within them, gazed at one another with brown imperturbable faces.

The former tenant of our house, a priest, had died in the back drawing-room. Air, musty from having been long enclosed, hung in all the rooms, and the waste room behind the kitchen was littered with old useless papers. Among these I found a few paper-covered books, the pages of which were curled and damp: The Abbot, by Walter Scott, The Devout Communicant and The

Memoirs of Vidocq. I liked the last best because its leaves were yellow. The wild garden behind the house contained a central apple-tree and a few straggling bushes under one of which I found the late tenant's rusty bicycle-pump. He had been a very charitable priest; in his will he had left all his money to institutions and the furniture of his house to his sister.

When the short days of winter came dusk fell before we had well eaten our dinners. When we met in the street the houses had grown sombre. The space of sky above us was the colour of ever-changing violet and towards it the lamps of the street lifted their feeble lanterns. The cold air stung us and we played till our bodies glowed. Our shouts echoed in the silent street. The career of our play brought us through the dark muddy lanes behind the houses where we ran the gauntlet of the rough tribes from the cottages, to the back doors of the dark dripping gardens where odours arose from the ashpits, to the dark odorous stables where a coachman smoothed and combed the horse or shook music from the buckled harness. When we returned to the street light from the kitchen windows had filled the areas. If my uncle was seen turning the corner we hid in the shadow until we had seen him safely housed. Or if Mangan's sister came out on the doorstep to call her brother in to his tea we watched her from our shadow peer up and down the street. We waited to see whether she would remain or go in and, if she remained, we left our shadow and walked up to Mangan's steps resignedly. She was waiting for us, her figure defined by the light from the half-opened door. Her brother always teased her before he obeyed and I stood by the railings looking at her. Her dress swung as she moved her body and the soft rope of her hair tossed from side to side.

Every morning I lay on the floor in the front parlour watching her door. The blind was pulled down to within an inch of the sash so that I could not be seen. When she came out on the doorstep my heart leaped. I ran to the hall, seized my books and followed her. I kept her brown figure always in my eye and, when we came near the point at which our ways diverged, I quickened my pace and passed her. This happened morning after morning. I had never spoken to her, except for a few casual words, and yet her name was like a summons to all my foolish blood.

Her image accompanied me even in places the most hostile to romance. On Saturday evenings when my aunt went marketing I had to go to carry some of the parcels. We walked through the flaring streets, jostled by drunken men and bargaining women, amid the curses of labourers, the shrill litanies of shop-boys who stood on guard by the barrels of pigs' cheeks, the nasal chanting of street-singers, who sang a come-all-you about O'Donovan Rossa, or a ballad about the troubles in our native land. These noises converged in a single sensation of life for me: I imagined that I bore my chalice safely through a throng of foes. Her name sprang to my lips at moments in strange prayers and praises which I myself did not understand. My eyes were often full of tears (I could not tell why) and at times a flood from my heart seemed to pour itself out into my bosom. I thought little of the future. I did not know whether I would ever speak to her or not or, if I spoke to her, how I could tell her of my confused adoration. But my body was like a harp and her words and gestures were like fingers running upon the wires.

One evening I went into the back drawing-room in which the priest had died. It was a dark rainy evening and there was no sound in the house. Through one of the broken panes I heard the rain impinge upon the earth, the fine incessant needles of water playing in the sodden beds. Some distant lamp or lighted window gleamed below me. I was thankful that I could see so little. All my senses seemed to desire to veil themselves and, feeling that I was about to slip from them, I pressed the palms of my hands together until they trembled, murmuring: "O love! O love!" many times.

At last she spoke to me. When she addressed the first words to me I was so confused that I did not know what to answer. She asked me was I going to Araby. I forgot whether I answered yes or no. It would be a splendid bazaar, she said she would love to go.

"And why can't you?" I asked.

While she spoke she turned a silver bracelet round and round her wrist. She could not go, she said, because there would be a retreat that week in her convent. Her brother and two other boys were fighting for their caps and I was alone at the railings. She held one of the spikes, bowing her head towards me. The light from the lamp opposite our door caught the white curve of her neck, lit up her hair that rested there and, falling, lit up the hand upon the railing. It fell over one side of her dress and caught the white border of a petticoat, just visible as she stood at ease.

"It's well for you," she said.

"If I go," I said, "I will bring you something."

What innumerable follies laid waste my waking and sleeping thoughts after that evening! I wished to annihilate the tedious intervening days. I chafed against the work of school. At night in my bedroom and by day in the classroom her image came between me and the page I strove to read. The syllables of the word Araby were called to me through the silence in which my soul luxuriated and cast an Eastern enchantment over me. I asked for leave to go to the bazaar on Saturday night. My aunt was surprised and hoped it was not some Freemason affair. I answered few questions in class. I watched my master's face pass from amiability to sternness; he hoped I was not beginning to idle. I could not call my wandering thoughts together. I had hardly any patience with the serious work of life which, now that it stood between me and my desire, seemed to me child's play, ugly monotonous child's play.

On Saturday morning I reminded my uncle that I wished to go to the bazaar in the evening. He was fussing at the hallstand, looking for the hat brush, and answered me curtly:

"Yes, boy, I know."

As he was in the hall I could not go into the front parlour and lie at the window. I left the house in bad humour and walked slowly towards the school. The air was pitilessly raw and already my heart misgave me.

When I came home to dinner my uncle had not yet been home. Still it was early. I sat staring at the clock for some time and. when its ticking began to irritate me, I left the room. I mounted the staircase and gained the upper part of the house. The high cold empty gloomy rooms liberated me and I went from room to room singing. From the front window I saw my companions playing below in the street. Their cries reached me weakened and indistinct and, leaning my forehead against the cool glass, I looked over at the dark house where she lived. I may have stood there for an hour, seeing nothing but the brown-clad figure cast by my imagination, touched discreetly by the lamplight at the curved neck, at the hand upon the railings and at the border below the dress.

When I came downstairs again I found Mrs. Mercer sitting at the fire. She was an old garrulous woman, a pawnbroker's widow, who collected used stamps for some pious purpose. I had to endure the gossip of the tea-table. The meal was prolonged beyond an hour and still my uncle did not come. Mrs. Mercer stood up to go: she was sorry she couldn't wait any longer, but it was after eight o'clock and she did not like to be out late as the night air was bad for her. When she had gone I began to walk up and down the room, clenching my fists. My aunt said:

"I'm afraid you may put off your bazaar for this night of Our Lord."

At nine o'clock I heard my uncle's latchkey in the halldoor. I heard him talking to himself and heard the hallstand rocking when it had received the weight of his overcoat. I could interpret these signs. When he was midway through his dinner I asked him to give me the money to go to the bazaar. He had forgotten.

"The people are in bed and after their first sleep now," he said.

I did not smile. My aunt said to him energetically:

"Can't you give him the money and let him go? You've kept him late enough as it is."

My uncle said he was very sorry he had forgotten. He said he believed in the old saying: "All work and no play makes Jack a dull boy." He asked me where I was going and, when I had told him a second time he asked me did I know The Arab's Farewell to his Steed. When I left the kitchen he was about to recite the opening lines of the piece to my aunt.

I held a florin tightly in my hand as I strode down Buckingham Street towards the station. The sight of the streets thronged with buyers and glaring with gas recalled to me the purpose of my journey. I took my seat in a third-class carriage of a deserted train. After an intolerable delay the train moved out of the station slowly. It crept onward among ruinous house and over the twinkling river. At Westland Row Station a crowd of people pressed to the carriage doors; but the porters moved them back, saying that it was a special train for the bazaar. I remained alone in the bare carriage. In a few minutes the train drew up beside an improvised wooden platform. I passed out on to the road and saw by the lighted dial of a clock that it was ten minutes to ten. In front of me was a large building which displayed the magical name.

I could not find any sixpenny entrance and, fearing that the bazaar would be closed, I passed in quickly through a turnstile, handing a shilling to a weary-looking man. I found myself in a big hall girdled at half its height by a gallery. Nearly all the stalls were closed and the greater part of the hall was in darkness. I recognised a silence like that which pervades a church after a service. I walked into the centre of the bazaar timidly. A few people were gathered about the stalls which were still open. Before a curtain, over which the words Cafe Chantant were written in coloured lamps, two men were counting money on a salver. I listened to the fall of the coins.

Remembering with difficulty why I had come I went over to one of the stalls and examined porcelain vases and flowered tea-sets. At the door of the stall a young lady was talking and laughing with two young gentlemen. I remarked their English accents and listened vaguely to their conversation.

"O, I never said such a thing!"

"O, but you did!"

"O, but I didn't!"

"Didn't she say that?"

"Yes. I heard her."

"O, there's a... fib!"

Observing me the young lady came over and asked me did I wish to buy anything. The tone of her voice was not encouraging; she seemed to have spoken to me out of a sense of duty. I looked humbly at the great jars that stood like eastern guards at either side of the dark entrance to the stall and murmured:

"No, thank you."

The young lady changed the position of one of the vases and went back to the two young men. They began to talk of the same subject. Once or twice the young lady glanced at me over her shoulder.

I lingered before her stall, though I knew my stay was useless, to make my interest in her wares seem the more real. Then I turned away slowly and walked down the middle of the bazaar. I allowed the two pennies to fall against the sixpence in my pocket. I heard a voice call from one end of the gallery that the light was out. The upper part of the hall was now completely dark.

Gazing up into the darkness I saw myself as a creature driven and derided by vanity; and my eyes burned with anguish and anger.

Questions

1. What do you think of the use of language in "Araby" of *Dubliners* by James Joyce? Please illustrate in detail.

2. What words and expressions convey the boy's extreme idealism and romantic view of the world?

3. How does the language of "Araby" help to express its theme?

4. Look at the following paragraph from William Faulkner's "A Rose for Emily" and discuss its style of language use.

   Alive, Miss Emily had been a tradition, a duty, and a care; a sort of hereditary obligation upon the town, dating from that day in 1894 when Colonel Sartoris, the mayor—he who fathered the edict that no Negro woman should appear on the streets without an apron—remitted her taxes, the dispensation dating from the death of her father on into perpetuity. Not that Miss Emily would have accepted charity. Colonel Sartoris invented an involved tale to the effect that Miss Emily's father had loaned money to the town, which the town, as a matter of business, preferred this way of repaying. Only a man of Colonel Sartoris' generation and thought could have invented it, and only a woman could have believed it.

5. Read the following selection ("The Loons") carefully, find examples of hyperbole, synecdoche, metonymy, and transferred epithet, parallelism, sarcasm, self-mockery, and comment on their effects in story-telling.

The Loons

—Margaret Laurence (1926-1987)

[1] Just below Manawaka, where the Wachakwa River ran brown and noisy over the pebbles, the scrub oak and grey-green willow and chokecherry bushes grew in a dense thicket. In a clearing at the centre of the thicket stood the Tonnerre family's shack. The basis at this dwelling was a small square cabin made of poplar poles and chinked with mud, which had been built by Jules Tonnerre some fifty years before, when he came back from Batoche with a bullet in his thigh, the year that Riel was hung and the voices of the Metis entered their long silence. Jules had only intended to stay the winter in the Wachakwa Valley, but the family was still there in the thirties, when I was a child. As the Tonnerres had increased, their settlement had been added to, until the clearing at the foot of the town hill was a chaos of lean-tos, wooden packing cases, warped lumber, discarded car tyres, ramshackle chicken coops, tangled strands of barbed wire and rusty tin cans.

[2] The Tonnerres were French half-breeds, and among themselves they spoke a patois that was neither Cree nor French. Their English was broken and full of obscenities. They did not belong among the Cree of the Galloping Mountain reservation, further north, and they did not belong among the Scots-Irish and Ukrainians of Manawaka, either. They were, as my Grandmother MacLeod would have put it, neither flesh, fowl, nor good salt herring. When their men were not working at odd jobs or as section hands on the C. P. R. they lived on relief. In the summers, one of the Tonnerre youngsters, with a face that seemed totally unfamiliar with laughter, would knock at the doors of the town's brick houses and offer for sale a lard-pail full of bruised wild strawberries, and if he got as much as a quarter he would grab the coin and run before the customer had time to change her mind. Sometimes old Jules, or his son Lazarus, would get mixed up in a Saturday-night brawl, and would hit out at whoever was nearest or howl drunkenly among the offended shoppers on Main Street, and then the Mountie would put them for the night in the barred cell underneath the Court House, and the next morning they would be quiet again.

[3] Piquette Tonnerre, the daughter of Lazarus, was in my class at school. She was older than I, but she had failed several grades, perhaps because her attendance had always been sporadic and her interest in schoolwork negligible. Part of the reason she had missed a lot of school was that she had had tuberculosis of the bone, and had once spent many months in hospital. I knew this because my father was the doctor who had looked after her. Her sickness was almost the only thing I knew about her, however. Otherwise, she existed for me only as a vaguely embarrassing

presence, with her hoarse voice and her clumsy limping walk and her grimy cotton dresses that were always miles too long. I was neither friendly nor unfriendly towards her. She dwelt and moved somewhere within my scope of vision, but I did not actually notice her very much until that peculiar summer when I was eleven.

[4] "I don't know what to do about that kid," my father said at dinner one evening. "Piquette Tonnerre, I mean. The damn bone's flared up again. I've had her in hospital for quite a while now, and it's under control all right, but I hate like the dickens to send her home again."

[5] "Couldn't you explain to her mother that she has to rest a lot?" my mother said.

[6] "The mother's not there," my father replied. "She took off a few years back. Can't say I blame her. Piquette cooks for them, and she says Lazarus would never do anything for himself as long as she's there. Anyway, I don't think she'd take much care of herself, once she got back. She's only thirteen, after all. Beth, I was thinking—what about taking her up to Diamond Lake with us this summer? A couple of months rest would give that bone a much better chance."

[7] My mother looked stunned.

[8] "But Ewen—what about Roddie and Vanessa?"

[9] "She's not contagious," my father said. "And it would be company for Vanessa."

[10] "Oh dear," my mother said in distress, "I'll bet anything she has nits in her hair."

[11] "For Pete's sake," my father said crossly, "do you think Matron would let her stay in the hospital for all this time like that? Don't be silly, Beth."

[12] Grandmother MacLeod, her delicately featured face as rigid as a cameo, now brought her mauve-veined hands together as though she were about to begin prayer.

[13] "Ewen, if that half-breed youngster comes along to Diamond Lake, I'm not going," she announced. "I'll go to Morag's for the summer."

[14] I had trouble in stifling my urge to laugh, for my mother brightened visibly and quickly tried to hide it. If it came to a choice between Grandmother MacLeod and Piquette, Piquette would win hands down, nits or not.

[15] "It might be quite nice for you, at that," she mused. "You haven't seen Morag for over a year, and you might enjoy being in the city for a while. We'll Ewen dear, you do what you think best. If you think it would do Piquette some good, then we'll be glad to have her, as long as she behaves herself."

[16] So it happened that several weeks later, when we all piled into my father's old Nash, surrounded by suitcases and boxes of provisions and toys for my ten-month-old brother, Piquette was with us and Grandmother MacLeod, miraculously, was not. My father would only be staying at the cottage for a couple of weeks, for he had to get back to his practice, but the rest of us would stay at Diamond Lake until the end of August.

[17] Our cottage was not named, as many were, "Dew Drop Inn" or "Bide-a-Wee," or

"Bonnie Doon". The sign on the roadway bore in austere letters only our name, MacLeod. It was not a large cottage, but it was on the lakefront. You could look out the windows and see, through the filigree of the spruce trees, the water glistening greenly as the sun caught it. All around the cottage were ferns, and sharp-branched raspberry bushes, and moss that had grown over fallen tree trunks, if you looked carefully among the weeds and grass, you could find wild strawberry plants which were in white flower now and in another month would bear fruit, the fragrant globes hanging like miniature scarlet lanterns on the thin hairy stems. The two grey squirrels were still there, gossiping at us from the tall spruce beside the cottage, and by the end of the summer they would again be tame enough to take pieces of crust from my hands. The broad moose antlers that hung above the back door were a little more bleached and fissured after the winter, but otherwise everything was the same. I raced joyfully around my kingdom, greeting all the places I had not seen for a year. My brother, Roderick, who had not been born when we were here last summer, sat on the car rug in the sunshine and examined a brown spruce cone, meticulously turning it round and round in his small and curious hands. My mother and father toted the luggage from car to cottage, exclaiming over how well the place had wintered, no broken windows, thank goodness, no apparent damage from storm-felled branches or snow.

[18] Only after I had finished looking around did I notice Piquette. She was sitting on the swing her lame leg held stiffly out, and her other foot scuffing the ground as she swung slowly back and forth. Her long hair hung black and straight around her shoulders, and her broad coarse-featured face bore no expression—it was blank, as though she no longer dwelt within her own skull, as though she had gone elsewhere. I approached her very hesitantly.

[19] "Want to come and play?"

[20] Piquette looked at me with a sudden flash of scorn.

[21] "I ain't a kid," she said.

[22] Wounded, I stamped angrily away, swearing I would not speak to her for the rest of the summer. In the days that followed, however, Piquette began to interest me, and I began to want to interest her. My reasons did not appear bizarre to me. Unlikely as it may seem, I had only just realised that the Tonnerre family, whom I had always heard called half-breeds, were actually Indians, or as near as made no difference. My acquaintance with Indians was not extensive. I did not remember ever having seen a real Indian, and my new awareness that Piquette sprang from the people of Big Bear and Poundmaker, of Tecumseh, of the Iroquois who had eaten Father Brébeuf's heart—all this gave her an instant attraction in my eyes. I was devoted reader of Pauline Johnson at this age, and sometimes would orate aloud and in an exalted voice, West wind, blow from your prairie nest, blow from the mountains, blow from the west—and so on. It seemed to me that Piquette must be in some way a daughter of the forest, a kind of junior prophetess of the wilds, who might impart to me, if I took the right approach, some of the secrets which she undoubtedly knew—where the whippoorwill made her nest, how the coyote reared her young, or whatever it was that it said in Hiawatha.

[23] I set about gaining Piquette's trust. She was not allowed to go swimming, with her bad leg, but I managed to lure her down to the beach—or rather, she came because there was nothing else to do. The water was always icy, for the lake was fed by springs, but I swam like a dog, thrashing my arms and legs around at such speed and with such an output of energy that I never grew cold. Finally, when I had enough, I came out and sat beside Piquette on the sand. When she saw me approaching, her hands squashed flat the sand castle she had been building, and she looked at me sullenly, without speaking.

[24] "Do you like this place?" I asked, after a while, intending to lead on from there into the question of forest lore.

[25] Piquette shrugged. "It's okay. Good as anywhere."

[26] "I love it," I said. "We come here every summer."

[27] "So what?" Her voice was distant, and I glanced at her uncertainly, wondering what I could have said wrong.

[28] "Do you want to come for a walk?" I asked her. "We wouldn't need to go far. If you walk just around the point there, you come to a bay where great big reeds grow in the water, and all kinds of fish hang around there. Want to? Come on."

[29] She shook her head.

[30] "Your dad said I ain't supposed to do no more walking than I got to." I tried another line.

[31] "I bet you know a lot about the woods and all that, eh?" I began respectfully.

[32] Piquette looked at me from her large dark unsmiling eyes.

[33] "I don't know what in hell you're talkin' about," she replied. "You nuts or somethin'? If you mean where my old man, and me, and all them live, you better shut up, by Jesus, you hear?"

[34] I was startled and my feelings were hurt, but I had a kind of dogged perseverance. I ignored her rebuff.

[35] "You know something, Piquette? There's loons here, on this lake. You can see their nests just up the shore there, behind those logs. At night, you can hear them even from the cottage, but it's better to listen from the beach. My dad says we should listen and try to remember how they sound, because in a few years when more cottages are built at Diamond Lake and more people come in, the loons will go away."

[36] Piquette was picking up stones and snail shells and then dropping them again.

[37] "Who gives a good goddamn?" she said.

[38] It became increasingly obvious that, as an Indian, Piquette was a dead loss. That evening I went out by myself, scrambling through the bushes that overhung the steep path, my feet slipping on the fallen spruce needles that covered the ground. When I reached the shore, I walked along the firm damp sand to the small pier that my father had built, and sat down there. I heard someone else crashing through the undergrowth and the bracken, and for a moment I

thought Piquette had changed her mind, but it turned out to be my father. He sat beside me on the pier and we waited, without speaking.

[39] At night the lake was like black glass with a streak of amber which was the path of the moon. All around, the spruce trees grew tall and close-set, branches blackly sharp against the sky, which was lightened by a cold flickering of stars. Then the loons began their calling. They rose like phantom birds from the nests on the shore, and flew out onto the dark still surface of the water.

[40] No one can ever describe that ululating sound, the crying of the loons, and no one who has heard it can ever forget it. Plaintive, and yet with a quality of chilling mockery, those voices belonged to a world separated by aeons from our neat world of summer cottages and the lighted lamps of home.

[41] "They must have sounded just like that," my father remarked, "before any person ever set foot here."

[42] Then he laughed. "You could say the same, of course, about sparrows or chipmunks, but somehow it only strikes you that way with the loons."

[43] "I know," I said.

[44] Neither of us suspected that this would be the last time we would ever sit here together on the shore, listening. We stayed for perhaps half an hour, and then we went back to the cottage. My mother was reading beside the fireplace. Piquette was looking at the burning birch log, and not doing anything.

[45] "You should have come along," I said, although in fact I was glad she had not.

[46] "Not me," Piquette said. "You wouldn' catch me walkin' way down there jus' for a bunch of squawkin' birds."

[47] Piquette and I remained ill at ease with one another. I felt I had somehow failed my father, but I did not know what was the matter, nor why she would not or could not respond when I suggested exploring the woods or playing house. I thought it was probably her slow and difficult walking that held her back. She stayed most of the time in the cottage with my mother, helping her with the dishes or with Roddie, but hardly ever talking. Then the Duncans arrived at their cottage, and I spent my days with Mavis, who was my best friend. I could not reach Piquette at all, and I soon lost interest in trying. But all that summer she remained as both a reproach and a mystery to me.

[48] That winter my father died of pneumonia, after less than a week's illness. For some time I saw nothing around me, being completely immersed in my own pain and my mother's. When I looked outward once more, I scarcely noticed that Piquette Tonnerre was no longer at school. I do not remember seeing her at all until four years later, one Saturday night when Mavis and I were having Cokes in the Regal Cafe. The jukebox was booming like tuneful thunder, and beside it, leaning lightly on its chrome and its rainbow glass, was a girl.

[49] Piquette must have been seventeen then, although she looked about twenty. I stared at her, astounded that anyone could have changed so much. Her face, so stolid and expressionless

before, was animated now with a gaiety that was almost violent. She laughed and talked very loudly with the boys around her. Her lipstick was bright carmine, and her hair was cut short and frizzily permed. She had not been pretty as a child, and she was not pretty now, for her features were still heavy and blunt. But her dark and slightly slanted eyes were beautiful, and her skin-tight skirt and orange sweater displayed to enviable advantage a soft and slender body.

[50] She saw me, and walked over. She teetered a little, but it was not due to her once-tubercular leg, for her limp was almost gone.

[51] "Hi, Vanessa," her voice still had the same hoarseness. "Long time no see, eh?"

[52] "Hi," I said. "Where've you been keeping yourself, Piquette?"

[53] "Oh, I been around," she said. "I been away almost two years now. Been all over the place—Winnipeg, Regina, Saskatoon. Jesus, what I could tell you! I come back this summer, but I ain't stayin'. You kids go in to the dance?"

[54] "No," I said abruptly, for this was a sore point with me. I was fifteen, and thought I was old enough to go to the Saturday-night dances at the Flamingo. My mother, however, thought otherwise.

[55] "Y'oughta come," Piquette said. "I never miss one. It's just about the on'y thing in this jerkwater town that's any fun. Boy, you couldn' catch me stayin' here. I don' give a shit about this place. It stinks."

[56] She sat down beside me, and I caught the harsh over-sweetness of her perfume.

[57] "Listen, you wanna know something, Vanessa?" she confided, her voice only slightly blurred. "Your dad was the only person in Manawaka that ever done anything good to me."

[58] I nodded speechlessly. I was certain she was speaking the truth. I knew a little more than I had that summer at Diamond Lake, but I could not reach her now any more than I had then. I was ashamed, ashamed of my own timidity, the frightened tendency to look the other way. Yet I felt no real warmth towards her—I only felt that I ought to, because of that distant summer and because my father had hoped she would be company for me, or perhaps that I would be for her, but it had not happened that way. At this moment, meeting her again, I had to admit that she repelled and embarrassed me, and I could not help despising the self-pity in her voice. I wished she would go away. I did not want to see her. I did not know what to say to her. It seemed that we had nothing to say to one another.

[59] "I'll tell you something else," Piquette went on. "All the old bitches an' biddies in this town will sure be surprised. I'm getting' married this fall—my boy friend, he's an English fella, works in the stockyards in the city there, a very tall guy, got blond wavy hair. Gee, is he ever handsome. Got this real classy name. Alvin Gerald Cummings—some handle, eh? They call him Al."

[60] For the merest instant, then I saw her. I really did see her, for the first and only time in all the years we had both lived in the same town. Her defiant face, momentarily, became unguarded and unmasked, and in her eyes there was a terrifying hope.

[61] "Gee, Piquette—" I burst out awkwardly, "that's swell. That's really wonderful. Congratulations—good luck—I hope you'll be happy—"

[62] As I mouthed the conventional phrases, I could only guess how great her need must have been, that she had been forced to seek the very things she so bitterly rejected.

[63] When I was eighteen, I left Manawaka and went away to college. At the end of my first year, I came back home for the summer. I spent the first few days in talking non-stop with my mother, as we exchanged all the news that somehow had not found its way into letters—what had happened in my life and what had happened here in Manawaka while I was away. My mother searched her memory for events that concerned people I knew.

[64] "Did I ever write you about Piquette Tonnerre, Vanessa?" she asked one morning.

[65] "No, I don't think so," I replied. "Last I heard of her, she was going to marry some guy in the city. Is she still there?"

[66] My mother looked perturbed, and it was a moment before she spoke, as though she did not know how to express what she had to tell and wished she did not need to try.

[67] "She's dead," she said at last. Then, as I stared at her, "Oh, Vanessa, when it happened, I couldn't help thinking of her as she was that summer—so sullen and gauche and badly dressed. I couldn't help wondering if we could have done something more at that time—but what could we do? She used to be around in the cottage there with me all day, and honestly it was all I could do to get a word out of her. She didn't even talk to your father very much, although I think she liked him in her way."

[68] "What happened?" I asked.

[69] "Either her husband left her, or she left him," my mother said. "I don't know which. Anyway, she came back here with two youngsters, both only babies—they must have been born very close together. She kept house, I guess, for Lazarus and her brothers, down in the valley there, in the old Tonnerre place. I used to see her on the street sometimes, but she never spoke to me. She'd put on an awful lot of weight, and she looked a mess, to tell you the truth, a real slattern, dressed any old how. She was up in court a couple of times—drunk and disorderly, of course. One Saturday night last winter, during the coldest weather, Piquette was alone in the shack with the children. The Tonnerres made home-brew all the time, so I've heard, and Lazarus said later she'd been drinking most of the day when he and the boys went out that evening. They had an old woodstove there—you know the kind, with exposed pipes. The shack caught fire. Piquette didn't get out, and neither did the children."

[70] I did not say anything. As so often with Piquette, there did not seem to be anything to say. There was a kind of silence around the image in my mind of the fire and the snow, and I wished I could put from my memory the look that I had seen once in Piquette's eyes.

[71] I went up to Diamond Lake for a few days that summer, with Mavis and her family. The MacLeod cottage had been sold after my father's death, and I did not even go to look at it, not wanting to witness my long-ago kingdom possessed now by strangers. But one evening I went

down to the shore by myself.

[72] The small pier which my father had built was gone, and in its place there was a large and solid pier built by the government, for Galloping Mountain was now a national park, and Diamond Lake had been re-named Lake Wapakata, for it was felt that an Indian name would have a greater appeal to tourists. The one store had become several dozen, and the settlement had all the attributes of a flourishing resort—hotels, a dance-hall, cafes with neon signs, the penetrating odours of potato chips and hot dogs.

[73] I sat on the government pier and looked out across the water. At night the lake at least was the same as it had always been, darkly shining and bearing within its black glass the streak of amber that was the path of the moon. There was no wind that evening, and everything was quiet all around me. It seemed too quiet, and then I realized that the loons were no longer here. I listened for some time, to make sure, but never once did I hear that long-drawn call, half mocking and half plaintive, spearing through the stillness across the lake.

[74] I did not know what had happened to the birds. Perhaps they had gone away to some far place of belonging. Perhaps they had been unable to find such a place, and had simply died out, having ceased to care any longer whether they lived or not.

[75] I remembered how Piquette had scorned to come along, when my father and I sat there and listened to the lake birds. It seemed to me now that in some unconscious and totally unrecognized way, Piquette might have been the only one, after all, who had heard the crying of the loons.

■ Imagery

Imagery has a great significance to a story and it influences the understanding of the story on the part of the readership. Generally imagery refers to "words and phrases that describe what is seen, heard, smelled, tasted, or touched" (Kirszner & Mandell 2006, 280). In other words, imagery in fiction involves the senses of the readers in their understanding of the story and it refers to the language helping to produce pictures in the minds of people. In "A Good Man Is Hard to Find" by Flannery O'Connor, the visual imagery such as "hearse-like automobile" (Para. 69) and the audio imagery like "Toombsboro" (Para. 45) are used to evoke a deadly atmosphere.

The story tells the unfortunate encounter of a family with criminals and the death of the whole family. Throughout the story, the imagery associated with death is easily understood. Some of the images are described indirectly while others, presented through symbolism. In the text, there are many descriptions implying death especially in the family. For example,

> her collars and cuffs were white organdy trimmed with lace and at her neckline she had pinned a purple spray of cloth violets containing a sachet. In case of an accident, anyone seeing

her <u>dead</u> on the highway would know at once that she was a lady. (Para. 12)

They passed a large cotton field with five or six <u>graves</u> fenced in the middle of it, like a small island. "Look at the <u>graveyard</u>!" the grandmother said, pointing it out. "That was the old family <u>burying ground</u>. That belonged to the plantation." (Para. 22)

"Where is the plantation?" John Wesley asked. (Para. 23)

"<u>Gone with Wind</u>," said the grandmother. "Ha, Ha." (Para. 24)

They drove off again into the hot afternoon... Outside of <u>Toombsboro</u> [tomb?] she woke up and recalled an old plantation that she had visited in this neighborhood once when she was a young lady (Para. 45).

Moreover, when the family had an accident, the car "turned over" but "nobody <u>killed</u>." A vehicle coming towards them appears to be strange and dismal. "The car... was a big black battered <u>hearse</u>-like automobile." (Para. 69) In the car there are three men with guns in hand. This seems to be a bad omen.

The mother and her children are ordered by the gangsters to sit together in front of a (horrible) forest. "Behind them the line of woods <u>gaped like a dark open mouth</u>" (Para. 79). The chief criminal, The Misfit, seems not to care about being recognized by the grandmother. But his words suggest he will harm the family.

"Yes'm," the man said, smiling slightly as if he were pleased in spite of himself to be known, "but it would have been better for all of you, lady, if you hadn't of reckernized me." (Para. 82)

While the Grandmother talks to The Misfit, "there was <u>a pistol shot</u> from the woods, followed closely by another. Then <u>silence</u>" (Para. 107). Further, from their conversation, it is obvious that The Misfit thinks it natural to commit crimes.

"I found out the crime don't matter. You can do one thing or you can do another, <u>kill</u> a man or take a tire off his car, because sooner or later you're going to forget what it was you done and just be punished for it." (Para. 122)

They continue their talk but before long, "there was <u>a piercing scream</u> from the woods, followed closely by <u>a pistol report</u>" (Para. 129). The scream and gunshot imply the death of the family members.

When the Grandmother offers The Misfit all the money, he answers, "Lady, there never was a body that give the <u>undertaker</u> a tip" (Para. 131). Finally The Misfit shot the Grandmother too.

As is shown, the visual as well as sound imagery throughout the story foreshadows the fatal outcome of the family.

Questions for Reflection

1. Where and why is imagery used?
2. Read the following passage from T. Coraghessan Boyle's "Greasy Lake" and make comments

on its imagery.

Through the center of town, up the strip, past the housing developments and shopping malls, street lights giving way to the thin streaming illumination of the headlights, trees crowding the asphalt in a black unbroken wall: that was the way out to Greasy Lake. The Indians had called it Wakan, a reference to the clarity of its waters. Now it was fetid and murky, the mud banks glittering with broken glass and strewn with beer cans and the charred remains of bonfires. There was a single ravaged island a hundred yards from shore, so stripped of vegetation it looked as if the air force had strafed it. We went up to the lake because everyone went there, because we wanted to snuff the rich scent of possibility on the breeze, watch a girl [swimmer] plunge into the festering murk, drink beer, smoke pot, howl at the stars, savor the incongruous full-throated roar of rock and roll against the primeval susurrus of frogs and crickets. This was nature (Kirszner & Mandell 2006, 280).

Symbol and Irony

> Symbols and metaphors share several qualities, but they are far from being synonymous. Both are figurative expressions that transcend literal language. Both rely heavily on implication and suggestion. Both present the abstract in concrete terms, and both can be interpreted with varying degrees of openness or specificity. They differ, however, in important ways. A symbol expands language by substitution, and metaphor by comparison and interaction. A symbol does not ask a reader to merge two concepts but rather to let one thing suggest another. A symbol derives its meaning through development and consensus, a metaphor through invention and originality. A symbol is strengthened by repetition, but a metaphor is destroyed by it.
> —Roland Bartel, Metaphors and Symbols

> The truth is, I do indeed include images in my work, but I don't think of them as symbols. To me, symbols are stand-in's for abstract ideas. They belong to the High School of Hidden Meanings: vases symbolize female orifices, broken vases symbolizes a loss of virginity and innocence. Heavy stuff. I prefer using images. My writing tends toward the Elementary School of Word Pictures: the accidental shattering of a vase in an empty room changes the emotions of a scene from sanity to uneasiness, perhaps even to dread. The point is, if there are symbols in my work they exist largely by accident or through someone else's interpretative design.
> —Amy Tan, The Threepenny Review
> (Kirszner & Mandell 2006, 330)

As for the elements of fictional works, the previously discussed facets like plot, character, language and style, point of view and so on are very common. However, other elements like symbol, irony, and allegory are also of great importance. They enable the writers to convey the rich and varied meanings in brief and in abstraction, and to remind the readership of the intentional personalized manipulation of language which helps to convey the actual meaning of the text.

> A symbol is a person, object, action, place, or event that, in addition to its literal meaning, suggests a more complex meaning or range of meaning (Kirszner & Mandell 2006, 330).

The meaning they connote goes beyond their literal sense. In Alice Walker's "Everyday Use for Your Grandmamma," the quilt means more than an everyday use or an ordinary piece of bedding. Rather, it alludes to the family heirloom and represents traditional heritage. The (possible) marital relationship between Dee (Wangero) and Asalamalakim implies the expectation of the (implied) author that the radical and the moderate young activists would reunite in the Civil Rights Movement.

There are universal and conventional symbols. A universal symbol involves that part of human experience shared by almost all people. For example, the Old Man, the Mother, and the River, all symbols of nurturing, are universal for people across the world, who all mostly agree about their implications. Sometimes, a universal symbol is also called an archetypal symbol. A conventional symbol means the part of human experience shared by people with common cultural and social conceptions or expectations. For instance, a rose stands for love, an olive branch for peace, and the skull-and-crossbones, for poison. Conventional symbols are culturally specific.

In literature, symbols are used in much the same way to enable

> writers to convey particular emotions or messages with a high degree of predictability (Kirszner & Mandell 2006, 331).

If the readers share the same cultural and social background, they may be able to figure out the intentions of the writers' symbolic expressions. For example, in literary works, "spring" suggests rebirth, hope and promise, while "summer" stands for youth and beauty. Due to cultural differences, the same symbol may have different connotations. For example, an owl implies wisdom in the US but unluckiness in China. In Hawthorne's "Young Goodman Brown,"

> Faith's pink ribbons may symbolize her youth and innocence to one reader and her femininity and coquettishness to another... Some readers may even see them as an example of Hawthorne's exploration of the ambiguous nature of signs, similar to the ambiguous nature of Goodman Brown's night in the forest (Charters 1999, 949).

When something comes out in a fictional work, possibly it becomes a symbol if it

> keeps appearing again and again in the story, at key moments; if the narrator devotes a good deal of time to describing it; if it is placed in a conspicuous physical location; if characters keeps noticing it and commenting on its presence; if its lost (or found) at a critical moment; if its function in some way parallels the development of plot or character (for instance if it stops as a relationship ends or as a character dies); if the story's opening or closing paragraph

focuses on [this something]; if the story is called "this something" (Kirszner & Mandell 2006, 332).

Symbols enrich the possible meanings of a story. A literary symbol can be anything in a story's setting, plot, or characterization.

Irony is also an important element of fiction. It

> always involves a contrast or discrepancy between one thing and another... The contrast may be between what is said and what is meant or between what happens and what is expected to happen (DiYanni 2000, 93).

Irony is one of the figures of speech too. It permeates a story and emerges quite often in language and events.

In Alice Walker's "Everyday Use for Your Grandmamma," When the house caught fire, Mama would have asked Dee, "Why don't you do a dance around the ashes?" (Para. 10) But she did not. Mama actually does not mean to encourage Dee to dance. She just conveys her upsetness and disappointment in Dee who appears not to value the family heritage symbolized by the old house that has now burnt down to the ground. Further, Dee's reaction here seems to be in sharp contrast with her later eagerness to have the quilt (a symbol of their cultural heritage).

Another example is seen in Ursula K. Le Guin's "The Ones Who Walk Away from Omelas."

> They would like to do something for the child. But there is nothing they can do. If the child were brought up into the sunlight out of the vile place, if it were cleaned and fed and comforted, that would be a good thing, indeed; but if it were done, in that day and hour all the prosperity and beauty and delight of Omelas would wither and be destroyed. Those are the terms. To exchange all the goodness and grace of every life in Omelas for that single, small improvement; to throw away the happiness of thousands for the chance of the happiness of one: that would be to let guilt within the walls indeed.

The underlined sentence, "that would be to let guilt within the walls indeed," is an instance of irony. In a so-called city of bliss, happiness depends totally on the sacrifice of a scapegoat. Sympathy and mutual care become "guilt." It is no happy city at all.

Questions for Reflection

1. In William Faulkner's "A Rose for Emily," what does the watch symbolize?
2. In Kate Chopin's "The Story of an Hour," what does Mrs. Malard's room symbolize?
3. The discrepancies between what it seems to be and what it is involve the irony of circumstance (or situation). Find an example of the irony of circumstance in Chopin's "The Story of an Hour" and make some comments.

■ Allegory

An allegory communicates a doctrine, message, or moral principle by making it into a narrative in which the characters personify ideas, concepts, qualities, or other abstractions. Thus an allegory is a story with two parallel and consistent levels of meaning—one literal and one figurative.

(Kirszner & Mandell 2006, 333)

The figurative meaning connotes some moral, political, literary, or religious senses.

As discussed previously, a symbol has a literal meaning but meanwhile it may also have many symbolic associations. Thus a symbol is open to varied interpretations. However, an allegorical figure, for example, a character, an object, a place, or an event, "has just one meaning within an allegorical framework, the set of ideas that conveys the allegory's message" (Kirszner & Mandell 2006, 333). If a character stands for good, he or she cannot stand for evil at the same time. In Nathaniel Hawthorne's "Young Goodman Brown," the male protagonist Goodman stands for a good person on the whole though he goes somewhat astray into the evil forest, while his wife Faith represents the qualities they are expected to have, for example, the quality to resist temptation. The older man's stuff, the stick featuring the design of a black snake, may have different implications. It is symbolic.

This staff, carried by a Satanic figure who represents evil and temptation, suggests the snake in the Garden of Eden, an association that neatly fits into the allegorical framework of the story. Alternately, however, the staff could suggest the "slippery," ever-changing nature of sin, the difficulty people have in perceiving the sin, or sexuality (which may explain Young Goodman Brown's susceptibility to temptation). This range of possible meanings suggests that the staff functions as a symbol (not an allegorical figure) that enriches Hawthorne's allegory (Kirszner & Mandell 2006, 333).

Fable, or usually a beast fable, is a kind of popular allegory. It is a story, with animals as the characters, that implies some moral lessons. *Aesop's Fables* have many good examples of beast fables.

Questions for Reflection

1. Find the examples of allegory from a story you have read and make some comments.
2. Study the fable "The Gentlemen of the Jungle" by Jomo Kenyatta and illustrate how the allegorical figures work within the framework of the allegory.

The Gentlemen of the Jungle

An African View of European Expansion
—by Jomo Kenyatta (1890–1978)

In the late 19th century the chief European powers divided Africa among themselves. They could do this because European arms were superior and because African chiefs did not understand the meaning of the treaties they were asked to sign. As a result Africans lost the lands they have traditionally lived on and cultivated. Their attitude toward European "expansion" is made clear in the following fable, which reflects the attitude of the Kikuyu people of Kenya toward European laws and commissions.

Once upon a time an elephant made a friendship with a man. One day a heavy thunderstorm broke out, the elephant went to his friend, who had a little hut at the edge of the forest, and said to him: "My dear good man, will you please let me put my trunk inside your hut to keep it out of this torrential rain?"

The man, seeing what situation his friend was in, replied: "My dear good elephant, my hut is very small, but there is room for your trunk and myself. Please put your trunk in gently."

The elephant thanked his friend, saying: "You have done me a good deed and one day I shall return your kindness."

But what followed? As soon as the elephant put his trunk inside the hut, slowly he pushed his head inside, and finally flung the man out in the rain, and then lay down comfortably inside his friend's hut, saying: "My dear good friend, your skin is harder than mine, and as there is not enough room for both of us, you can afford to remain in the rain while I am protecting my ' delicate skin from the hailstorm.'"

The man, seeing what his friend had done to him, started to grumble; the animals in the nearby forest heard the noise and came to see what was the matter. All stood around listening to the heated argument between the man and his friend the elephant. In this turmoil the lion came along roaring, and said in a loud voice: "Don't you all know that I am the King of the Jungle! How dare anyone disturb the peace of my kingdom?"

On hearing this, the elephant, who was one of the high ministers in the jungle kingdom, replied in a soothing voice, and said: "My lord, there is no disturbance of the peace in your kingdom. I have only been having a little discussion with my friend here as to the possession of this little hut which your lordship sees me occupying." The lion, who wanted to have "peace and tranquility" in his kingdom, replied in a noble voice, saying: "I command my ministers to appoint a Commission of Enquiry to go thoroughly into this matter and report accordingly… I am sure that you will be pleased with the findings of the Commission." The man was very pleased by these sweet words from the King of the Jungle, and innocently waited for his opportunity, in the belief that naturally the hut would be returned to him.

The elephant, obeying the command of his master, got busy with other ministers to appoint the Commission of Enquiry. The following elders of the jungle were appointed to sit in the

Commission: (1) Mr. Rhinoceros; (2) Mr. Buffalo; (3) Mr. Alligator; (4) The Rt. Hon. Mr. Fox to act as chairman; and (5) Mr. Leopard to act as Secretary to the Commission. On seeing the personnel, the man protested and asked if it was not necessary to include in this Commission a member from his side. But he was told that it was impossible, since no one from his side was well enough educated to understand the intricacy of jungle law. Further, that there was nothing to fear, for the members of the Commission were all men of repute for their impartiality in justice, and as they were gentlemen chosen by God to look after the interests of races less adequately endowed with teeth and claws, he might rest assured that they would investigate the matter with the greatest care and report impartially.

The Commission sat to take the evidence. The Rt. Hon. Mr. Elephant was first called. He came along with a superior air, brushing his tusks with a sapling which Mrs. Elephant had provided, and in an authoritative voice said: "Gentlemen of the Jungle, there is no need for me to waste your valuable time in relating a story which I am sure you all know. I have always regarded it as my duty to protect the interests of my friends, and this appears to have caused the misunderstanding between myself and my friend here. He invited me to save his hut from being blown away by a hurricane. As the hurricane had gained access owing to the unoccupied space in the hut, I considered it necessary, in my friend's own interests, to turn the undeveloped space to a more economic use by sitting in it myself: a duty which any of you would undoubtedly have performed with equal readiness in similar circumstances."

After hearing the Rt. Hon. Mr. Elephant's conclusive evidence, the Commission called Mr. Hyena and other elders of the jungle, who all supported what Mr. Elephant had said. They then called the man, who began to give his own account of the dispute. But the Commission cut him short, saying: "My good man, please confine yourself to relevant issues. We have already heard the circumstances from various unbiased sources; all we wish you to tell us is whether the undeveloped space in your hut was occupied by anyone else before Mr. Elephant assumed his position?"

The man began to say: "No, but..."

But at this point the Commission declared that they had heard sufficient evidence from both sides and retired to consider their decision. After enjoying a delicious meal at the expense of the Rt. Hon. Mr. Elephant, they reached their verdict, called the man, and declared as follows: "In our opinion this dispute has arisen through a regrettable misunderstanding due to the backwardness of your ideas. We consider that Mr. Elephant has fulfilled his sacred duty of protecting your interests. As it is clearly for your good that the space should be put to its most economic use, and as you yourself have not reached the stage of expansion which would enable you to fill it, we consider it necessary to arrange a compromise to suit both parties. Mr. Elephant shall continue his occupation of your hut, but we give you permission to look for a site where you can build another hut more suited to your needs, and we will see that you are well protected."

The man, having no alternative, and fearing that his refusal might expose him to the teeth and claws of members of the Commission, did as they suggested. But no sooner had he built another hut than Mr. Rhinoceros charged in with his horn lowered and ordered the man to quit. A Royal Commission was again appointed to look into the matter, and the same finding was given. This procedure was repeated until Mr. Buffalo, Mr. Leopard, Mr. Hyena and the rest were all were accommodated with new huts. Then the man decided that he must adopt an effective method of protection, since Commissions of Enquiry did not seem to be of any use to him. He sat down and said: "Ng-enda thi ndeagaga motegi," which literally means, "there is nothing that treads on the earth that cannot be trapped," or in other words, you can fool people for a time, but not forever.

Early one morning, when the huts already occupied by the jungle lords were all beginning to decay and fall to pieces, he went out and built a bigger and better hut a little distance away. No sooner had Mr. Rhinoceros seen it than he came rushing in, only to find that Mr. Elephant was already inside, sound asleep. Mr. Leopard next came to the window, Mr. Lion, Mr. Fox and Mr. Buffalo entered the doors, while Mr. Hyena howled for a place in the shade and Mr. Alligator basked on the roof. Presently they all began disputing about their rights of penetration, and from disputing they came to fighting, and while they were all embroiled together the man set the hut on fire and burnt it to the ground, jungle lords and all. Then he went home, saying: "Peace is costly, but it's worth the expense," and lived happily ever after.

■ Theme

> The truth about any subject only comes when all the sides of the story are put together, and all their different meanings make one new meaning.
>
> —Alice Walker, Discovering Fiction
>
> The concepts of beauty and ugliness are mysterious to me. Many people write about them. In mulling over them, I try to get underneath them and see what they mean, understand the impact they have on what people do. I also write about love and death. The problem I face as a writer is to make my stories mean something.
>
> —Toni Morrison, Discovering Fiction
>
> (Kirszner & Mandell 2006, 381)

In fiction reading, readers usually intend to summarize the main idea of the story. To sum up means to generalize the meaning of the story. Theme is the result of such a generalization. While the plot of a story is a general summary of what happened in the action, the theme of the story is more general. Further, the theme

> has to convey the values and ideas expressed by the story... and [it] applies to the world outside [the story too]... [Quite often it] is a general observation about humanity (Kirszner & Mandell 2006, 382).

For example, considering "Young Goodman Brown" by Nathaniel Hawthorne, the plot can be summed up as

> a young Puritan husband loses his faith in God and humankind after attending a witches'
> coven [but] the theme is an even more general statement of meaning of the story (losing faith
> can destroy a person's life) (Charters 1999, 950).

However, it is quite often difficult to generalize the exact meaning or make a well-established statement of the theme because of the varied perspectives of different readers. What's more, many stories have more than one theme. Still, since literature can have many different interpretations, generalization is possible and practicable. But to establish a statement that summarizes the meaning of a story, it is necessary to support it with sufficient and convincing evidence from the text.

It is worth noting that the theme is the co-product of literary creation by the author and interpretation by the readership. An author may present a theme in the story, but quite often the theme is not directly stated in the text, meaning that a generalization is necessary.

Considering the decision on the theme(s) of a story, other elements of a story play crucial parts.

> A story's theme, that is, grows out of the relationship of the other elements. To formulate
> a story's theme, we try to explain what these elements collectively suggest (DiYanni 2000, 86).

These other elements usually involve the title, the statement (especially the comments) of the narrator or character, the action, the arrangement of events, conflict, point of view, symbols and other details. Some featured points or components in terms of these elements will help reveal or strengthen the theme(s).

Questions for Reflection

1. Please illustrate how the elements of a story help to suggest its theme(s).
2. How does a story's conflict offer clues to the theme of "Araby" by James Joyce?
3. Read the story "Doe Season" by David Michael Kaplan and decide on the possible themes of it. Find enough evidence from the text to support your analysis and argument.

Doe Season (1985)

—David Michael Kaplan(1946—)

[1] They were always the same woods, she thought sleepily as they drove through the early morning darkness—deep and immense, covered with yesterday's snowfall, which had frozen overnight. They were the same woods that lay behind her house, and they stretch all the way to here, she thought, for miles and miles, longer than I could walk in a day, or a week even, but they are still the same woods. The thought made her feel good: it was like thinking of God; it was like thinking of the space between here and the moon; it was like thinking of all the foreign

countries from her geography book where even now, Andy knew, people were going to bed, while they—she and her father and Charlie Spoon and Mac, Charlie's eleven-year-old son—were driving deeper into the Pennsylvania countryside, to go hunting.

[2] They had risen long before dawn. Her mother, yawning and not trying to hide her sleepiness, cooked them eggs and French toast. Her father smoked a cigarette and flicked ashes into his saucer while Andy listened, wondering *Why doesn't he come?* and *Won't he ever come?* until at last a car pulled into the graveled drive and honked. "That will be Charlie Spoon," her father said; he always said "Charlie Spoon," even though his real name was Spreun, because Charlie was, in a sense, shaped like a spoon, with a large head and a narrow waist and chest.

[3] Andy's mother kissed her and her father and said, "Well, have a good time" and "Be careful." Soon they were outside in the bitter dark, loading gear by the back-porch light, their breath steaming. The woods behind the house were then only a black streak against the wash of night.

[4] Andy dozed in the car and woke to find that it was half light. Mac—also sleeping—had slid against her. She pushed him away and looked out the window. Her breath clouded the glass, and she was cold; the car's heater didn't work right. They were riding over gentle hills, the woods on both sides now—the same woods, she knew, because she had been watching the whole way, even while she slept. They had been in her dreams, and she had never lost sight of them.

[5] Charlie Spoon was driving. "I don't understand why she's coming," he said to her father. "How old is she anyway—eight?"

[6] "Nine," her father replied. "She's small for her age."

[7] "So—nine. What's the difference? She'll just add to the noise and get tired besides."

[8] "No, she won't," her father said. "She can walk me to death. And she'll bring good luck, you'll see. Animals—I don't know how she does it, but they come right up to her. We go walking in the woods, and we'll spot more raccoons and possums and such than I ever see when I'm alone."

[9] Charlie grunted.

[10] "Besides, she's not a bad little shot, even if she doesn't hunt yet. She shoots the 22 real good."

[11] "Popgun," Charlie said, and snorted. "And target shooting ain't deer hunting."

[12] "Well, she's not gonna be shooting anyway, Charlie," her father said. "Don't worry. She'll be no bother."

[13] "I still don't know why she's coming," Charlie said.

[14] "Because she wants to, and I want her to. Just like you and Mac. No difference."

[15] Charlie turned onto a side road and after a mile or so slowed down. "That's it!" he cried. He stopped, backed up, and entered a narrow dirt road almost hidden by trees. Five hundred yards down, the road ran parallel to a fenced-in field. Charlie parked in a cleared area

deeply rutted by frozen tractor tracks. The gate was locked. In the spring, Andy thought, there will be sows here, and a dog that chases them, but now the field was unmarked and bare.

[16] "This is it," Charlie Spoon declared. "Me and Mac was up here just two weeks ago, scouting it out, and there's deer. Mac saw the tracks."

[17] "That's right," Mac said.

[18] "Well, we'll just see about that," her father said, putting on his gloves. He turned to Andy. "How you doing, honeybun?"

[19] "Just fine," she said.

[20] Andy shivered and stamped as they unloaded: first the rifles, which they unsheathed and checked, sliding the bolts, sighting through scopes, adjusting the slings; then the gear, their food and tents and sleeping bags and stove stored in four backpacks—three big ones for Charlie Spoon and her father and Mac, and a day pack for her.

[21] "That's about your size," Mac said, to tease her.

[22] She reddened and said, "Mac, I can carry a pack big as yours any day." He laughed and pressed his knee against the back of hers, so that her leg buckled. "Cut it out," she said. She wanted to make an iceball and throw it at him, but she knew that her father and Charlie were anxious to get going, and she didn't want to displease them.

[23] Mac slid under the gate, and they handed the packs over to him. Then they slid under and began walking across the field toward the same woods that ran all the way back to her home, where even now her mother was probably rising again to wash their breakfast dishes and make herself a fresh pot of coffee. She is there, and we are here: the thought satisfied Andy. There was no place else she would rather be.

[24] Mac came up beside her. "Over there's Canada," he said, nodding toward the woods.

[25] "Huh!" she said. "Not likely."

[26] "I don't mean right over there. I mean farther up north. You think I'm dumb?"

[27] Dumb as your father, she thought.

[28] "Look at that," Mac said, pointing to a piece of cow dung lying on a spot scraped bare of snow. "A frozen meadow muffin." He picked it up and sailed it at her. "Catch!"

[29] "Mac!" she yelled. His laugh was as gawky as he was. She walked faster. He seemed different today somehow, bundled in his yellow-and-black-checkered coat, a rifle in hand, his silly floppy hat not quite covering his ears. They all seemed different as she watched them trudge through the snow—Mac and her father and Charlie Spoon—bigger, maybe, as if the cold landscape enlarged rather than diminished them, so that they, the only figures in that landscape, took on size and meaning just by being there. If they weren't there, everything would be quieter, and the woods would be the same as before. *But they are here*, Andy thought, looking behind her at the boot prints in the snow, *and I am too*, *and so it's all different*.

[30] "We'll go down to the cut where we found those deer tracks," Charlie said as they entered the woods. "Maybe we'll get lucky and get a late one coming through."

[31] The woods descended into a gully. The snow was softer and deeper here, so that often Andy sank to her knees. Charlie and Mac worked the top of the gully while she and her father walked along the base some thirty yards behind them. "If they miss the first shot, we'll get the second," her father said, and she nodded as if she had known this all the time. She listened to the crunch of their boots, their breathing, and the drumming of a distant woodpecker. And the crackling. In winter the woods crackled as if everything were straining, ready to snap like dried chicken bones.

[32] We are hunting, Andy thought. The cold air burned her nostrils. They stopped to make lunch by a rock outcropping that protected them from the wind. Her father heated the bean soup her mother had made for them, and they ate it with bread already stiff from the cold. He and Charlie took a few pulls from a flask of Jim Beam while she scoured the plates with snow and repacked them. Then they all had coffee with sugar and powdered milk, and her father poured her a cup too. "We won't tell your momma," he said, and Mac laughed. Andy held the cup the way her father did, not by the handle but around the rim. The coffee tasted smoky. She felt a little queasy, but she drank it all.

[33] Charlie Spoon picked his teeth with a fingernail. "Now, you might've noticed one thing," he said.

[34] "What's that?" her father asked.

[35] "You might've noticed you don't hear no rifles. That's because there ain't other hunters here. We've got the whole damn woods to ourselves. Now, I ask you—do I know how to find 'em?"

[36] "We haven't seen deer yet, neither."

[37] "Oh, we will," Charlie said, "but not for a while now." He leaned back against the rock. "Deer're sleeping, resting up for the evening feed."

[38] "I seen a deer behind our house once, and it was afternoon," Andy said.

[39] "Yeah, honey, but that was *before* deer season," Charlie said, grinning. "They know something now. They're smart that way."

[40] "That's right," Mac said.

[41] Andy looked at her father—had she said something stupid?

[42] "Well, Charlie," he said, "if they know so much, how come so many get themselves shot?"

[43] "Them's the ones that don't *believe* what they know," Charlie replied. The men laughed. Andy hesitated, and then laughed with them.

[44] They moved on, as much to keep warm as to find a deer. The wind became even stronger. Blowing through the treetops, it sounded like the ocean, and once Andy thought she could smell salt air. But that was impossible; the ocean was *hundreds* of miles away, farther than Canada even. She and her parents had gone last summer to stay for a week at a motel on the New Jersey shore. That was the first time she'd seen the ocean, and it frightened her. It was huge and

empty, yet always moving. Everything lay hidden. If you walked in it, you couldn't see how deep it was or what might be below; if you swam, something could pull you under and you'd never be seen again. Its musky, rank smell made her think of things dying. Her mother had floated beyond the breakers, calling to her to come in, but Andy wouldn't go farther than a few feet into the surf. Her mother swam and splashed with animal-like delight while her father, smiling shyly, held his white arms above the waist-deep water as if afraid to get them wet. Once a comber rolled over and sent them both tossing, and when her mother tried to stand up, the surf receding behind, Andy saw that her mother's swimsuit top had come off, so that her breasts swayed free, her nipples like two dark eyes. Embarrassed, Andy looked around: except for two women under a yellow umbrella farther up, the beach was empty. Her mother stood up unsteadily, regained her footing. Taking what seemed the longest time, she calmly refixed her top. Andy lay on the beach towel and closed her eyes. The sound of the surf made her head ache.

[45] And now it was winter; the sky was already dimming, not just with the absence of light but with a mist that clung to the hunters' faces like cobwebs. They made camp early. Andy was chilled. When she stood still, she kept wiggling her toes to make sure they were there. Her father rubbed her arms and held her to him briefly, and that felt better. She unpacked the food while the others put up the tents.

[46] "How about rounding us up some firewood, Mac?" Charlie asked.

[47] "I'll do it," Andy said. Charlie looked at her thoughtfully and then handed her the canvas carrier.

[48] There wasn't much wood on the ground, so it took her a while to get a good load. She was about a hundred yards from camp, near a cluster of high, lichen-covered boulders, when she saw through a crack in the rock a buck and two does walking gingerly, almost daintily, through the alder trees. She tried to hush her breathing as they passed not more than twenty yards away. There was nothing she could do. If she yelled, they'd be gone; by the time she got back to camp, they'd be gone. The buck stopped, nostrils quivering, tail up and alert. He looked directly at her. Still she didn't move, not one muscle. He was a beautiful buck, the color of late-turned maple leaves. Unafraid, he lowered his tail, and he and his does silently merged into the trees. Andy walked back to camp and dropped the firewood.

[49] "I saw three deer," she said. "A buck and two does."

[50] "Where?" Charlie Spoon cried, looking behind her as if they might have followed her into camp.

[51] "In the woods yonder. They're gone now."

[52] "Well, hell!" Charlie banged his coffee cup against his knee.

[53] "Didn't I say she could find animals?" her father said, grinning.

[54] "Too late to go after them," Charlie muttered. "It'll be dark in a quarter hour. Damn!"

[55] "Damn!" Mac echoed.

[56] "They just walk right up to her," her father said.

[57] "Well, leastwise this proves there's deer here." Charlie began snapping long branches into shorter ones. "You know, I think I'll stick with you," he told Andy, "since you're so good at finding deer and all. How'd that be?"

[58] "Okay, I guess," Andy murmured. She hoped he was kidding; no way did she want to hunt with Charlie Spoon. Still, she was pleased he had said it.

[59] Her father and Charlie took one tent, she and Mac the other. When they were in their sleeping bags, Mac said in the darkness, "I bet you really didn't see no deer, did you?"

[60] She sighed. "I did, Mac. Why would I lie?"

[61] "How big was the buck?"

[62] "Four point. I counted."

[63] Mac snorted.

[64] "You just believe what you want, Mac," she said testily.

[65] "Too bad it ain't buck season," he said. "Well, I got to go pee."

[66] "So pee."

[67] She heard him turn in his bag. "You ever see it?" he asked.

[68] "It? What's 'it'?"

[69] "It. A pecker."

[70] "Sure," she lied.

[71] "Whose? Your father's?"

[72] She was uncomfortable. "No," she said.

[73] "Well, whose then?"

[74] "Oh I don't know! Leave me be, why don't you?"

[75] "Didn't see a deer, didn't see a pecker," Mac said teasingly.

[76] She didn't answer right away. Then she said, "My cousin Lewis. I saw his."

[77] "Well, how old's he?"

[78] "One and a half."

[79] "Ha! A baby! A baby's is like a little worm. It ain't a real one at all."

[80] If he says he'll show me his, she thought, I'll kick him. I'll just get out of my bag and kick him.

[81] "I went hunting with my daddy and Versh and Danny Simmons last year in buck season," Mac said, "and we got ourselves one. And we hog-dressed the thing. You know what that is, don't you?"

[82] "No," she said. She was confused. What was he talking about now?

[83] "That's when you cut him open and take out all his guts, so the meat don't spoil. You make him lighter to pack out, too."

[84] She tried to imagine what the deer's guts might look like, pulled from the gaping hole. "What do you do with them?" she said. "The guts?"

[85] "Oh, just leave 'em for the bears."

[86] She ran her finger like a knife blade along her belly.

[87] "When we left them on the ground," Mac said, "they smoked. Like they were cooking."

[88] "Huh," she said.

[89] "They cut off the deer's pecker, too, you know."

[90] Andy imagined Lewis's pecker and shuddered. "Mac, you're disgusting."

[91] He laughed. "Well, I gotta to pee." She heard him rustle out of his bag. "Broo!" he cried, flapping his arms. "It's cold!"

[92] *He makes so much noise,* she thought, *just noise and more noise.*

[93] Her father woke them before first light. He warned them to talk softly and said that they were going to the place where Andy had seen the deer, to try to cut them off on their way back from their night feeding. Andy couldn't shake off her sleep. Stuffing her sleeping bag into its sack seemed to take an hour, and tying her boots was the strangest thing she'd ever done. Charlie Spoon made hot chocolate and oatmeal with raisins. Andy closed her eyes and, between beats of her heart, listened to the breathing of the forest. *When I open my eyes, it will be lighter,* she decided. But when she did, it was still just as dark, except for the swaths of their flashlights and the hissing blue flame of the stove. *There has to be just one moment when it all changes from dark to light,* Andy thought. She had missed it yesterday, in the car, today she would watch more closely.

[94] But when she remembered again, it was already first light and they had moved to the rocks by the deer trail and had set up shooting positions—Mac and Charlie Spoon on the up-trail side, she and her father behind them, some six feet up on a ledge. The day became brighter, the sun piercing the tall pines, raking the hunters, yet providing little warmth. Andy now smelled alder and pine and the slightly rotten odor of rock lichen. She rubbed her hand over the stone and considered that it must be very old, had probably been here before the giant pines, *before anyone was in these woods at all.* A chipmunk sniffed on a nearby branch. She aimed an imaginary rifle and pressed the trigger. The chipmunk froze, then scurried away. Her legs were cramping on the narrow ledge. Her father seemed to doze, one hand in his parka, the other cupped lightly around the rifle. She could smell his scent of old wool and leather. His cheeks were speckled with gray-black whiskers, and he worked his jaws slightly, as if chewing a small piece of gum.

[95] *Please let us get a deer,* she prayed.

[96] A branch snapped on the other side of the rock face. Her father's hand stiffened on the rifle, startling her—*He hasn't been sleeping at all,* she marveled—and then his jaw relaxed, as did the lines around his eyes, and she heard Charlie Spoon call, "Yo, don't shoot, it's us." He and Mac appeared from around the rock. They stopped beneath the ledge. Charlie solemnly crossed his arms.

[97] "I don't believe we're gonna get any deer here," he said drily.

[98] Andy's father lowered his rifle to Charlie and jumped down from the ledge. Then he reached up for Andy. She dropped into his arms and he set her gently on the ground.

[99] Mac sidled up to her. "I knew you didn't see no deer," he said.

[100] "Just because they don't come when you want'em to don't mean she didn't see them," her father said.

[101] Still, she felt bad. Her telling about the deer had caused them to spend the morning there, cold and expectant, with nothing to show for it.

[102] They tramped through the woods for another two hours, not caring much about noise. Mac found some deer tracks, and they argued about how old they were. They split up for a while and then rejoined at an old logging road that deer might use, and followed it. The road crossed a stream, which had mostly frozen over but in a few spots still caught leaves and twigs in an icy swirl. They forded it by jumping from rock to rock. The road narrowed after that, and the woods thickened.

[103] They stopped for lunch, heating up Charlie's wife's corn chowder. Andy's father cut squares of applesauce cake with is hunting knife and handed them to her and Mac, who ate his almost daintily. Andy could faintly taste knife oil on the cake. She was tired. She stretched her leg; the muscle that had cramped on the rock still ached.

[104] "Might as well relax," her father said, as if reading her thoughts. "We won't find deer till suppertime."

[105] Charlie Spoon leaned back against his pack and folded his hands across his stomach. "Well, even if we don't get a deer," he said expansively, "it's still great to be out here, breathe some fresh air, clomp around a bit. Get away from the house and the old lady." He winked at Mac, who looked away.

[106] "That's what the woods are all about, anyway," Charlie said. "It's where the women don't want to go." He bowed his head toward Andy. "With your exception, of course, little lady." He helped himself to another piece of applesauce cake.

[107] "She ain't a woman," Mac said.

[108] "Well, she damn well's gonna be," Charlie said. He grinned at her. "Or will you? You're half a boy anyway. You go by a boy's name. What's your real name? Andrea, ain't it?"

[109] "That's right," she said. She hoped that if she didn't look at him, Charlie would stop.

[110] "Well, which do you like? Andy or Andrea?"

[111] "Don't matter," she mumbled. "Either."

[112] "She's always been Andy to me," her father said.

[113] Charlie Spoon was still grinning. "So what are you gonna be, Andrea? A boy or a girl?"

[114] "I'm a girl," she said.

[115] "But you want to go hunting and fishing and everything, huh?"

[116] "She can do whatever she likes," her father said.

[117] "Hell, you might as well have just had a boy and be done with it!" Charlie exclaimed.

[118] "That's funny," her father said, and chuckled. "That's just what her momma tells me."

[119] They were looking at her, and she wanted to get away from them all, even from her father, who chose to joke with them.

[120] "I'm going to walk a bit," she said.

[121] She heard them laughing as she walked down the logging trail. She flapped her arms; she whistled. *I don't care how much noise I make*, she thought. Two grouse flew from the underbrush, startling her. A little farther down, the trail ended in a clearing that enlarged into a frozen meadow; beyond it the woods began again. A few moldering posts were all that was left of a fence that had once enclosed the field. The low afternoon sunlight reflected brightly off the snow, so that Andy's eyes hurt. She squinted hard. A gust of wind blew across the field, stinging her face. And then, as if it had been waiting for her, the doe emerged from the trees opposite and stepped cautiously into the field. Andy watched: it stopped and stood quietly for what seemed a long time and then ambled across. It stopped again about seventy yards away and began to browse in a patch of sugar grass uncovered by the wind. Carefully, slowly, never taking her eyes from the doe, Andy walked backward, trying to step into the boot prints she'd already made. When she was far enough back into the woods, she turned and walked faster, her heart racing. *Please let it stay*, she prayed.

[122] "There's doe in the field yonder," she told them.

[123] They got their rifles and hurried down the trail.

[124] "No use," her father said. "We're making too much noise any way you look at it."

[125] "At least we got us the wind in our favor," Charlie Spoon said, breathing heavily.

[126] But the doe was still there, grazing.

[127] "Good Lord," Charlie whispered. He looked at her father. "Well, whose shot?"

[128] "Andy spotted it," her father said in a low voice. "Let her shoot it."

[129] "What!" Charlie's eyes widened.

[130] Andy couldn't believe what her father had just said. She'd only shot tin cans and targets; she'd never even fired her father's .30.30, and she'd never killed anything.

[131] "I can't," she whispered.

[132] "That's right, she can't," Charlie Spoon insisted. "She's not old enough and she don't have a license even if she was!"

[133] "Well, who's to tell?" her father said in a low voice. "Nobody's going to know but us." He looked at her. "Do you want to shoot it, punkin?"

[134] *Why doesn't it hear us?* She wondered. *Why doesn't it run away?* "I don't know," she

said.

[135] "Well, I'm sure as hell gonna shoot it," Charlie said. Her father grasped Charlie's rifle barrel and held it. His voice was steady.

[136] "Andy's a good shot. It's her deer. She found it, not you. You'd still be sitting on your ass back in camp." He turned to her again. "Now—do you want to shoot it, Andy? Yes or no."

[137] He was looking at her; they were all looking at her. Suddenly she was angry at the deer, who refused to hear them, who wouldn't run away even when it could. "I'll shoot it," she said. Charlie turned away in disgust.

[138] She lay on the ground and pressed the rifle stock against her shoulder bone. The snow was cold through her parka; she smelled oil and wax and damp earth. She pulled off one glove with her teeth. "It sights just like the 22," her father said gently. "Cartridge's already chambered." As she had done so many times before, she sighted down the scope; now the doe was in the reticle. She moved the barrel until the cross hairs lined up. Her father was breathing beside her.

[139] "Aim where the chest and legs meet, or a little above, punkin," he was saying calmly. "That's the killing shot."

[140] But now, seeing it in the scope, Andy was hesitant. Her finger weakened on the trigger. Still, she nodded at what her father said and sighted again, the cross hairs lining up in exactly the same spot—the doe had hardly moved, its brownish-gray body outlined starkly against the blue-backed snow. *It doesn't know*, Andy thought. *It just doesn't know*. And as she looked, deer and snow and faraway trees flattened within the circular frame to become like a picture on a calendar, not real, and she felt calm, as if she had been dreaming everything—the day, the deer, the hunt itself. And she, finger on trigger, was only a part of that dream.

[141] "Shoot!" Charlie hissed.

[142] Through the scope she saw the deer look up, ears high and straining.

[143] Charlie groaned, and just as he did, and just at the moment when Andy knew— *knew*—the doe would bound away, as if she could feel its haunches tensing and gathering power, she pulled the trigger. Later she would think, *I felt the recoil, I smelled the smoke, but I don't remember pulling the trigger*. Through the scope the deer seemed to shrink into itself, and then slowly knelt, hind legs first, head raised as if to cry out. It trembled, still straining to keep its head high, as if that alone would save it; failing, it collapsed, shuddered, and lay still.

[144] "Whoee!" Mac cried.

[145] "One shot! One shot!" her father yelled, clapping her on the back. Charlie Spoon was shaking his head and smiling dumbly.

[146] "I told you she was a great little shot!" her father said. "I told you!" Mac danced and clapped his hands. She was dazed, not quite understanding what had happened. And then they were crossing the field toward the fallen doe, she walking dreamlike, the men laughing and

joking, released now from the tension of silence and anticipation. Suddenly Mac pointed and cried out, "Look at that!"

[147] The doe was rising, legs unsteady. They stared at it, unable to comprehend, and in that moment the doe regained its feet and looked at them, as if it too were trying to understand. Her father whistled softly. Charlie Spoon unslung his rifle and raised it to his shoulder, but the doe was already bounding away. His hurried shot missed, and the deer disappeared into the woods.

[148] "Damn, damn, damn," he moaned.

[149] "I don't believe it," her father said. "That deer was dead."

[150] "Dead, hell!" Charlie yelled. "It was gutshot, that's all. Stunned and gutshot. Clean shot, my ass!"

[151] *What have I done?* Andy thought.

[152] Her father slung his rifle over his shoulder. "Well, let's go. It can't get too far."

[153] "Hell, I've seen deer run ten miles gunshot," Charlie said. He waved his arms, "We may never find her!"

[154] As they crossed the field, Mac came up to her and said in a low voice, "Gutshoot a deer, you'll go to hell."

[155] "Shut up, Mac," she said, her voice cracking. It was a terrible thing she had done, she knew. She couldn't bear to think of the doe in pain and frightened. *Please let it die*, she prayed.

[156] But though they searched all the last hour of daylight, so that they had to recross the field and go up the logging trail in a twilight made even deeper by thick, smoky clouds, they didn't find the doe. They lost its trail almost immediately in the dense stands of alderberry and larch.

[157] "I am cold, and I am tired," Charlie Spoon declared. "And if you ask me, that deer's in another county already."

[158] "No one's asking you, Charlie," her father said.

[159] They had a supper of hard salami and ham, bread, and the rest of the applesauce cake. It seemed a bother to heat the coffee, so they had cold chocolate instead. Everyone turn in early.

[160] "We'll find it in the morning, honeybun," her father said, as she went to her tent.

[161] "I don't like to think of it suffering." She was almost in tears.

[162] "It's dead already, punkin. Don't even think about it." He kissed her, his breath sour and his beard rough against her cheek.

[163] Andy was sure she wouldn't get to sleep; the image of the doe falling, falling, then rising again, repeated itself whenever she closed her eyes. Then she heard an owl hoot and realized that it had awakened her, so she must have been asleep after all. She hoped the owl would hush, but instead it hooted louder. She wished her father or Charlie Spoon would wake

up and do something about it, but no one moved in the other tent, and suddenly she was afraid that they had all decamped, wanting nothing more to do with her. She whispered, "Mac, Mac," to the sleeping bag where he should be, but no one answered. She tried to find the flashlight she always kept by her side, but couldn't, and she cried in panic, "Mac, are you there?" He mumbled something, and immediately she felt foolish and hoped he wouldn't reply.

[164] When she awoke again, everything had changed. The owl was gone, the woods were still, and she sensed light, blue and pale, light where before there had been none. *The moon must have come out*, she thought. And it was warm, too, warmer than it should have been. She got out of her sleeping bag and took off her parka—it was that warm. Mac was asleep, wheezing like an old man. She unzipped the tent and stepped outside.

[165] The woods were more beautiful than she had ever seen them. The moon made everything ice-rimmed glimmer with a crystallized, immanent light, while underneath that ice the branches of trees were as stark as skeletons. She heard a crunching in the snow, the one sound in all that silence, and there, walking down the logging trail into their camp, was the doe. Its body, like everything around her, was silvered with frost and moonlight. It walked past the tent where her father and Charlie Spoon were sleeping and stopped no more than six feet from her. Andy saw that she had shot it, yes, had shot it cleanly, just where she thought she had, the wound a jagged, bloody hole in the doe's chest.

[166] *A heart shot*, she thought.

[167] The doe stepped closer, so that Andy, if she wished, could have reached out and touched it. It looked at her as if expecting her to do this, and so she did, running her hand, slowly at first, along the rough, matted fur, then down to the edge of the wound, where she stopped. The doe stood still. Hesitantly, Andy felt the edge of the wound. The torn flesh was sticky and warm. The wound parted under her touch. And then, almost without her knowing it, her fingers were within, probing, yet still the doe didn't move. Andy pressed deeper, through flesh and muscle and sinew, until her whole hand and more was inside the wound and she had found the doe's heart, warm and beating. She cupped it gently in her hand. *Alive*, she marveled. *Alive*.

[168] The heart quickened under her touch, becoming warmer and warmer until it was hot enough to burn. In pain, Andy tried to remove her hand, but the wound closed about it and held her fast. Her hand was burning. She cried out in agony, sure they would all hear and come help, but they didn't. And then her hand pulled free, followed by a steaming rush of blood, more blood than she ever could have imagined—it covered her hand and arm, and she saw to her horror that her hand was steaming. She moaned and fell to her knees and plunged her hand into the snow. The doe looked at her gently and then turned and walked back up the trail.

[169] In the morning, when she woke, Andy could still smell the blood, but she felt no pain. She looked at her hand. Even though it appeared unscathed, it felt weak and withered. She couldn't move it freely and was afraid the others would notice. *I will hide it in my jacket pocket*, she

decided; *so nobody can see*. She ate the oatmeal that her father cooked and stayed apart from them all. No one spoke to her, and that suited her. A light snow began to fall. It was the last day of their hunting trip. She wanted to be home.

[170] Her father dumped the dregs of his coffee. "Well, let's go look for her," he said.

[171] Again they crossed the field. Andy lagged behind. She averted her eyes from the spot where the doe had fallen, already filling up with snow. Mac and Charlie entered the woods first, followed by her father. Andy remained in the field and considered the smear of gray sky, the nearby flock of crows pecking at unyielding stubble. *I will stay here*, she thought, *and not move for a long while*. But now someone—Mac—was yelling. Her father appeared at the wood's edge and waved for her to come. She ran and pushed through a brake of alderberry and larch. The thick underbrush scratched her face. For a moment she felt lost and looked wildly about. Then, where the brush thinned, she saw them standing quietly in the falling snow. They were staring down at the dead doe. A film covered its upturned eye, and its body was lightly dusted with snow.

[172] "I told you she wouldn't get too far," Andy's father said triumphantly. "We must've just missed her yesterday. Too blind to see."

[173] "We're just damn lucky no animal got to her last night," Charlie muttered.

[174] Her father lifted the doe's foreleg. The wound was blood-clotted, brown, and caked like frozen mud. "Clean shot," he said to Charlie. He grinned. "My little girl."

[175] Then he pulled out his knife, the blade gray as the morning. Mac whispered to Andy, "Now watch this," while Charlie Spoon lifted the doe from behind by its forelegs so that its head rested between his knees, its underside exposed. Her father's knife sliced thickly from chest to belly to crotch, and Andy was running from them, back to the field and across, scattering the crows who cawed and circled angrily. And now they were all calling to her—Charlie Spoon and Mac and her father—crying Andy, Andy (but that wasn't her name, she would no longer be called that); yet louder than any of them was the wind blowing through the treetops, like the ocean where her mother floated in green water, also calling "Come in, come in", while all around her roared the mocking of the terrible, now inevitable, sea.

Part 2

Poetry

❧ Chapter 5 ❧
An Overview

To begin with, it may be of some help to enjoy the following poem concerning the idea of poetry.

Poetry (1921)

    Marianne Moore (1887−1972)

I, too, dislike it: there are things that are important beyond all
    this fiddle.
Reading it, however, with a perfect contempt for it, one discovers that there is
in it after all, a place for the genuine.
    Hands that can grasp, eyes
    that can dilate, hair that can rise
      if it must, these things are important not because a

high-sounding interpretation can be put upon them but because they are
    useful. When they become so derivative as to become unintelligible,
    the same thing may be said for all of us, that we
      do not admire what
      we cannot understand: the bat,
        holding on upside down or in quest of something to

eat, elephants pushing, a wild horse taking a roll, a tireless wolf under
    a tree, the immovable critic twinkling his skin like a horse that feels
    a flea, the base-
ball fan, the statistician—
    nor is it valid
      to discriminate against "business documents and

school-books"; all these phenomena are important. One must make
    a distinction
    however: when dragged into prominence by half poets, the result
    is not poetry,
nor till the autocrats among us can be
    "literalists of
    the imagination" —above

insolence and triviality and can present

for inspection, "imaginary gardens with real toads in them,"
    shall we have
  it. In the meantime, if you demand on the one hand,
  the raw material of poetry in
    all its rawness, and
    that which is on the other hand
      genuine, then you are interested in poetry.

Moore's poem may throw some light on the nature of poetry. Then again, what does it mean by poetry?

> *Sir, what is Poetry?*
> *Why, Sir, it is much easier to say what it is not. We all know what light is: but it is not easy to tell what it is.*
>
> —Samuel Johnson

Throughout history, poetry, as a literary genre, has had a predominant place in different cultures since ancient time. It has thus aroused the great interest among poets and critics who have offered definitions of poetry from their perspectives. It is evident that a definite one is almost impossible, but a working definition is likely and helpful. Poetry, as a genre of literature, takes advantage of aesthetic and rhythmic qualities of language to express meanings and evoke feelings. According to *Oxford English Dictionary* (OED), poetry in existing has many implications. It is

> the art or work of the poet: [a] With special reference to its form: Composition in verse or metrical language, or in some equivalent patterned arrangement of language; usually also with choice of elevated words and figurative uses, and option of a syntactical order, differing more or less from those of ordinary speech or prose writing. [b] The product of this art as a form of literature; the writings of a poet or poets; poems collectively or generally; metrical work or composition; verse. (Opp. to prose.) [c] With special reference to its function: The expression or embodiment of beautiful or elevated thought, imagination, or feeling, in language adapted to stir the imagination and emotions, both immediately and also through the harmonic suggestions latent in or implied by the words and connexions of words actually used, such language containing a rhythmical element and having usually a metrical form (as in sense 3 a); though the term is sometimes extended to include expression in non-metrical language having similar harmonic and emotional qualities (prose-poetry).

This definition highlights the metrical form and the arrangement pattern of poetic works that usually express rich meanings and convey profound feelings. Poetry is also featured by sound.

> Poetry is a cultural form where the placing of the words is driven by their sound as well as by their sense or meaning (Strachan & Terry 2000, 10).

These interpretations at least help with a general understanding of poetry and its basic features.

Questions for Reflection

Read the following poem and answer the questions.

Ars Poetica (1926)

—Archibald MacLeish (1892—1982)

A poem should be palpable and mute
As a globed fruit,

Dumb
As old medallions to the thumb,

Silent as the sleeve-worn stone
Of casement ledges where the moss has grown—

A poem should be wordless
As the flight of birds.

A poem should be motionless in time
As the moon climbs,

Leaving, as the moon releases
Twig by twig the night-entangled trees,

Leaving, as the moon behind the winter leaves,
Memory by memory the mind—

A poem should be motionless in time
As the moon climbs.

A poem should be equal to
Not true.

For all the history of grief
An empty doorway and a maple leaf.

For love
The leaning grasses and two lights above the sea—

A poem should not mean

But be

Questions

1. How do you understand the poem "Ars Poetica"?
2. To what extent do you agree with Archibald MacLeish considering the nature of poetry?

Chapter 6
Types of Poetry

Poetry can be classified as narrative or lyric. Narrative poems highlight action while lyrics, song.

Most poems are either narrative poems which recounts a story, or lyric poems, which communicate a speaker's mood, feelings or state of mind (Kirszner & Mandell 2006, 773).

Narrative Poetry

Any poem, if it tells a story, can be considered narrative, though it may be a short one. Take the following poem as an example.

Richard Cory (1897)
—Edwin Arlington Robinson (1869−1935)

Whenever Richard Cory went down town,
We people on the pavement looked at him:
He was a gentleman from sole to crown,
Clean favored, and imperially slim.

And he was always quietly arrayed,
And he was always human when he talked;
But still he fluttered pulses when he said,
"Good-morning," and he glittered when he walked.

And he was rich—yes, richer than a king—
And admirably schooled in every grace:
In fine, we thought that he was everything
To make us wish that we were in his place.

So on we worked, and waited for the light,
And went without the meat, and cursed the bread;
And Richard Cory, one calm summer night,
Went home and put a bullet through his head.

"Richard Cory", though brief, is a narrative poem because it mainly recounts the story of a man called Richard Cory. However, the most familiar forms of narrative poetry are the epic, the ballad and the romance.

Epic poems recount the accomplishment of heroic figures, typically including expansive settings, superhuman feats, and gods and supernatural beings. The language of epic poems tends to be formal, even elevated, and often quite elaborate (Kirszner & Mandell 2006, 773).

Epic poems are usually long and they deal with important subjects. They record in chronological order the origins of a civilization and manifest its central beliefs and values. In Western cultures, the famous epics are Homer's *Iliad* and *Odyssey* (Greek), Virgil's *Aeneid* (Roman), Dante's *Divine Comedy* (Italian), *Beowulf* (Anglo Saxon), *The Epic of Gilgamesh* (Babylonian), *Das Nibelungenlied* (German), and Milton's *Paradise Lost*. Moreover, in recent time, people follow the same tradition and create new epics. A good example is seen in *Omeros* (1990), an epic poem by Caribbean writer Derek Walcott, a poet who received Nobel Prize for Literature in 1992.

Another kind of narrative poetry is the ballad which was rooted in oral tradition, and it is perhaps the most popular type of narrative poetry. Originally a ballad was meant to be sung or recited and later it was put down in written forms. A ballad is usually characterized by repeated words and phrases, including a refrain, the line or lines repeated in verse. There are folk ballads and literary ballads. Examples of literary ballads are "La Belle Dame sans Merci" by John Keats, "Ballad of Birmingham" by Dudley Randall, "The Ballad of Rudolph Reed" by Gwendolyn Brooks, and "The Ballad of Reading Gaol" by Oscar Wilde.

Literary ballads imitate the folk ballad by adhering basic conventions—repeated lines and stanza in a refrain, swift action with occasional surprise endings, extraordinary events evoked in direct, simple language, and scant characterization—but are more polished stylistically and more self-conscious in their use of poetic techniques (DiYanni 2000, 411).

Romance is also a type of narrative poetry and it features adventure. The plot is complex, often with surprising and magical actions. The main characters are human who are face to face with monsters. Romance was once popular in the Middle Ages. However, some of its features have remained in modern adventure fictions and love stories.

◼ Lyric Poetry

Considering narrative poems, especially literary ballads, the story is told with songs, and action occurs with emotion, but story and action are the protruding elements. In lyric poetry, song and emotion take the major place. Lyrics are

subjective poems, often brief, that express the feelings and thoughts of a single speaker (who may or may not represent the poet). The lyric is more a poetic manner than a form; it is more variable and less subjective to strict convention than narrative poetry. Lyric poetry is typically characterized by brevity, melody, and emotional intensity (DiYanni 2000, 411).

Lyric poems take different forms too.

> Forms of lyric poetry range from the epigram, a brief witty poem that is often satirical, such as Alexander Pope's "On the Collar of a Dog," to the elegy, a lament for the dead, such as Seamus Heaney's "Mid-Term Break." Lyric forms also include the ode, a long stately poem in stanza of varied length, meter, and form; and the aubade, a love lyric expressing complaint that dawn means the speaker must part from his lover. An example of the ode is John Keats's "Ode to a Nightingale;" the aubade is represented by John Donne's "The Sun Rising" (DiYanni 2000, 411).

Of the lyric poems, the sonnet has a classical European flavor, characterized by strict rules and forms of poetic composition.

> The sonnet, for example, condenses into fourteen lines an expression of emotion or articulation of idea according to one of two basic patterns: the Italian (or Petrarchan) and the English (or Shakespearean). An Italian sonnet is composed of an eight-line octave and a six-line sestet. A Shakespearean sonnet is composed of three four-line quatrainsand and a concluding two-line couplet... an Italian sonnet may state a problem in the octave and present a solution in its sestet. A Shakespearean sonnet will usually introduce a subject in the first quatrain, expand and develop it in the second and third quatrains, and conclude something about it in its final couplet (DiYanni 2000, 411−412).

Sonnets reached their peak popularity during the Renaissance. Later, writers who were interested in the sonnet form began to make some changes to them.

Questions for Reflection

1. Read the opening lines from Virgil's *Aeneid* and Milton's *Paradise Lost*. Write down your response as to the epic's subjects and language.

(1) from Virgil's *Aeneid*

> I sing of warfare and a man at war.
>
> From the sea-coast of Troy in early days
>
> He came to Italy by destiny,
>
> To our Lavinian western shore,
>
> A fugitive, this captain, buffeted
>
> Cruelly on land as on the sea
>
> By blows from powers of the air—behind them
>
> Baleful Juno in her sleepless rage.
>
> And cruel losses were his lot in war,

Till he could found a city and bring home
His gods to Latium, land of the Latin race,
The Alban lords, and the high walls of Rome.
Tell me the causes now, O Muse, how galled
In her divine pride, and how sore at heart
From her old wound, the queen of gods compelled him—
A man apart, devoted to his mission—
To undergo so many perilous days
And enter on so many trials.

(2) from Milton's *Paradise Lost*

Of Man's first disobedience, and the fruit
Of that forbidden tree whose mortal taste
Brought death into the world, and all our woe,
With loss of Eden, till one greater Man
Restore us, and regain the blissful seat,
Sing, Heavenly Muse, that, on the secret top
Of Oreb, or of Sinai, didst inspire
That shepherd who first taught the chosen seed
In the beginning how the Heavens and Earth
Rose out of Chaos: or, if Sion hill
Delight thee more, and Siloa's brook that flowed
Fast by the oracle of God, I thence
Invoke thy aid to my adventurous song,
That with no middle flight intends to soar
Above th' Aonian mount, while it pursues
Things unattempted yet in prose or rhyme.
And chiefly thou, O Spirit, that dost prefer
Before all temples th' upright heart and pure,
Instruct me, for thou know'st; thou from the first
Wast present, and, with mighty wings outspread,
Dovelike sat'st brooding on the vast abyss,
And mad'st it pregnant: what in me is dark
Illumine; what is low, raise and support;
That, to the height of this great argument,
I may assertth' Eternal Providence,
And justify the ways of God to men.

2. How do you understand a ballad? Read the following ballad and pay attention to its features.

The Ballad of Rudolph Reed (1960)

—Gwendolyn Brooks (1917－2000)

Rudolph Reed was oaken.
His wife was oaken too.
And his two girls and his good little man
Oakened as they grew.

"I am not hungry for berries.
I am not hungry for bread.
But hungry hungry for a house
Where at night a man in bed

"May never hear the plaster
Stir as if in pain.
May never hear the roaches
Falling like fat rain.

"Where never wife and children need
Go blinking through the gloom.
Where every room of many rooms
Will be full of room.

"Oh my home may have its east or west
Or north or south behind it.
All I know is I shall know it,
And fight for it when I find it."

It was in a street of bitter white
That he made his application.
For Rudolph Reed was oakener
Than others in the nation.

The agent's steep and steady stare
Corroded to a grin.
Why, you black old, tough old hell of a man,

Move your family in !

Nary a grin grinned Rudolph Reed,
Nary a curse cursed he,
But moved in his House. With his dark little wife,
And his dark little children three.

A neighbor would *look*, with a yawning eye
That squeezed into a slit.
But the Rudolph Reeds and the children three
Were too joyous to notice it.

For were they not firm in a home of their own
With windows everywhere
And a beautiful banistered stair
And a front yard for flowers and a back yard for grass?

The first night, a rock, big as two fists.
The second, a rock big as three.
But nary a curse cursed Rudolph Reed.
(Though oaken as man could be.)

The third night, a silvery ring of glass.
Patience ached to endure.
But he looked, and lo! small Mabel's blood
Was staining her gaze so pure.

Then up did rise our Rudolph Reed
And pressed the hand of his wife,
And went to the door with a thirty-four
And a beastly butcher knife.

He ran like a mad thing into the night.
And the words in his mouth were stinking.
By the time he had hurt his first white man
He was no longer thinking.

By the time he had hurt his fourth white man

Rudolph Reed was dead.

His neighbors gathered and kicked his corpse.

"Nigger——" his neighbors said.

Small Mabel whimpered all night long,

For calling herself the cause.

Her oak-eyed mother did no thing

But change the bloody gauze.

3. Read "Ode to the West Wind" by Percy Bysshe Shelley and make some comments on the theme and language.

Ode to the West Wind (1820)

—Percy Bysshe Shelley (1792–1822)

I

O wild West Wind, thou breath of Autumn's being,

Thou, from whose unseen presence the leaves dead

Are driven, like ghosts from an enchanter fleeing,

Yellow, and black, and pale, and hectic red,

Pestilence-stricken multitudes: O Thou,

Who chariotest to their dark wintry bed

The winged seeds, where they lie cold and low,

Each like a corpse within its grave, until

Thine azure sister of the Spring shall blow

Her clarion o'er the dreaming earth, and fill

(Driving sweet buds like flocks to feed in air)

With living hues and odours plain and hill:

Wild Spirit, which art moving everywhere;

Destroyer and Preserver; hear, O hear!

II

Thou on whose stream, mid the steep sky's commotion,

Loose clouds like Earth's decaying leaves are shed,

Shook from the tangled boughs of Heaven and Ocean,

Angels of rain and lightning: there are spread
On the blue surface of thine aery surge,
Like the bright hair uplifted from the head

Of some fierce Maenad, even from the dim verge
Of the horizon to the zenith's height,
The locks of the approaching storm. Thou dirge

Of the dying year, to which this closing night
Will be the dome of a vast sepulcher,
Vaulted with all thy congregated might

Of vapours, from whose solid atmosphere
Black rain and fire and hail will burst: O hear!

III

Thou who didst waken from his summer dreams
The blue Mediterranean, where he lay,
Lulled by the coil of his crystalline streams,

Beside a pumice isle in Baiae's bay,
And saw in sleep old palaces and towers
Quivering within the wave's intenser day,

All overgrown with azure moss and flowers
So sweet, the sense faints picturing them! Thou
For whose path the Atlantic's level powers

Cleave themselves into chasms, while far below
The sea-blooms and the oozy woods which wear
The sapless foliage of the ocean, know

Thy voice, and suddenly grow grey with fear,
And tremble and despoil themselves: O hear!

IV

If I were a dead leaf thou mightest bear;
If I were a swift cloud to fly with thee;
A wave to pant beneath thy power, and share

The impulse of thy strength, only less free
Than thou, O Uncontrollable! If even
I were as in my boyhood, and could be

The comrade of thy wanderings over Heaven,
As then, when to outstrip thy skiey speed
Scarce seemed a vision; I would ne'er have striven

As thus with thee in prayer in my sore need,
Oh! lift me as a wave, a leaf, a cloud!
I fall upon the thorns of life! I bleed!

A heavy weight of hours has chained and bowed
One too like thee: tameless, and swift, and proud.

V

Make me thy lyre, even as the forest is:
What if my leaves are falling like its own!
The tumult of thy mighty harmonies

Will take from both a deep, autumnal tone,
Sweet though in sadness. Be thou, Spirit fierce,
My spirit! Be thou me, impetuous one!

Drive my dead thoughts over the universe
Like withered leaves to quicken a new birth!
And, by the incantation of this verse,

Scatter, as from an unextinguished hearth
Ashes and sparks, my words among mankind!
Be through my lips to unawakened Earth

The trumpet of a prophecy! O Wind,

If Winter comes, can Spring be far behind?

4. Read the following sonnet and pay attention to the themes and language.

Shall I Compare Thee to a Summer's Day? (Sonnet 18) (1609)

—William Shakespeare (1564−1616)

Shall I compare thee to a summer's day?
Thou art more lovely and more temperate.
Rough winds do shake the darling buds of May,
And summer's lease hath all too short a date.
Sometime too hot the eye of heaven shines,
And often is his gold complexion dimmed;
And every fair from fair sometime declines,
By chance, or nature's changing course, untrimmed.
But thy eternal summer shall not fade,
Nor lose possession of that fair thou ow'st;
Nor shall death brag thou wander'st in his shade,
When in eternal lines to time thou grow'st.
    So long as men can breathe or eyes can see,
    So long lives this, and this gives life to thee.

∂ Chapter 7 ∾
Reading Poetry : the Basic Approaches

The basic approaches to the study of poetry involve experiencing, interpreting and evaluating.

When reading poetry, like when reading fiction and drama, readers immediately respond and associate meanings with details of action and language, and they make connections and draw inferences in the piece of literature. It is both an emotional and intellectual activity. Some conclusions are reached with considerations about the elements of poetry. However, since poetry is a compact art, the linguistic evidence is of great importance to understanding and appreciating it. Therefore, concerning poetry, readers pay more attention to the connotations of words and the expressive qualities of sound and rhythm in lines and stanzas along with the syntax and structure.

In terms of reading poetry, the basic approaches, experiencing, interpreting, and evaluating, are usually applied. Considering these three methods in terms of poetry, the following questions are helpful.

1. What feelings does the poem evoke? What sensations, associations, and memories does it give rise to? [Experiencing]
2. What ideas does the poem express, either directly or indirectly? What sense does it make? What do we understand it to say and suggest? [Interpreting]
3. What view of the world does the poet present? Does it agree with your view? What do you think of the poet's view? What value does the poem hold for you as a work of art and as an influence on your way of understanding yourself and others? [Evaluating]

(DiYanni 2000, 395)

In other words, experiencing highlights the feelings evoked by the poem. It means subjective responses or personal reactions which touch on sensations, associations and memories. It is impressionistic, as well as rational. Actually, it concerns how the poems may be related to our lives.

In view of interpreting, it emphasizes what ideas are expressed or what sense is made. Interpretation involves intellectual understanding and it is analytical and rational.

Considering evaluating, it focuses on what view of the world is presented. In this sense, viewpoint or standpoint and value are the key terms. It also concerns the significance of the poem. It is sort of aesthetical assessment.

Examples are given below as far as the three approaches are concerned.

Those Winter Sundays (1962)

—Robert Hayden (1913—1980)

Sundays too my father got up early
and put his clothes on in the blueblack cold,
then with cracked hands that ached
from labor in the weekday weather made
banked fires blaze. No one ever thanked him.   5

I'd wake and hear the cold splintering, breaking.
When the rooms were warm, he'd call,
and slowly I would rise and dress,
fearing the chronic angers of that house,

Speaking indifferently to him,   10
who had driven out the cold
and polished my good shoes as well.
What did I know, what did I know
of love's austere and lonely offices?

The Experience of Poetry

To "experience the poem" means to have an initial response to it. It is subjective, personal and impressionistic. It arouses the memories and feelings of the reader.

Reading the poem, readers may immediately share the feelings of the speaker. They will associate the scene of the poem with their own experiences. They may have a memory of their own childhood when their hard-working fathers, possibly weather beaten, used to do the housework for the family day by day. Even on cold days, the fathers never gave up their task for they took it to be their duties to take good care of the family. But quite often, as the speaker shows, the family members seemed to take it for granted what the father had done for them. As a result, they ignored the paternal love for them. They may also feel sorry for their ignorance of the paternal love because they may not have chances to return the favor.

The Interpretation of Poetry

To interpret a poem means to understand its meaning and its implications. Readers explain the poem to themselves and derive what it means or suggests as far as the speaker and the subject are concerned. It is an intellectual and rational understanding, instead of a mere emotional response. In interpretation readers pay more attention to the details of description and action, to the language and form and consider how these details work together to produce meaning and significance. They often draw a conclusion with references to the elements of poetry. This is the process of close reading.

In "Those Winter Sundays," the word "wake" ("I'd wake and hear the cold splintering, breaking." Line 6) suggests the meaning of the poem. It is about the awakening of the speaker (a boy then, and an adult now), and his realization of paternal love and his reminiscence on his past experiences. The word "warm" ("When the rooms were warm," Line 7) has both physical and symbolic suggestions, the warmth of the house from the stove lit by the father in the cold morning, and the warmth of the family because of the father's care and dedication.

The poem, with vivid language, presents a contrast between "my father" and "I", between the past and the present, and between misunderstanding and appreciation. The expressions like "Sundays too," "with cracked hands that ached from labor," "in the blackblue cold," "driven out the cold," "polished my good shoes," and "lonely offices" protrude the image of "my father" who is diligent, persevering, caring and dedicated. The lines "fearing the chronic angers of that house" (Line 9) and "Speaking indifferently to him" (Line 10) suggest the inevitable problems or even misunderstandings within the family. Possibly the father was often angry with the speaker, the son, so that he responded coldly to the father despite the efforts the father had been making for family. Though the poem does not show why so, the speaker finally realizes the paternal care and love. The last two lines of Stanza 3, "What did I know, what did I know/of love's austere and lonely offices?" best embody the feelings of the speaker and the meaning of the poem. The emphasis via repetition (of "what did I know") and use of the big word "austere" sheds light on the speaker's attitude. He may regret his delayed realization of his father's love, a meaning that is omnipresent, but simple.

Interpretation as this may go on and on for readers are likely to make a satisfying explanation which is readable, sensible, logical and reasonable to both the reader himself and other readers. The convincibility of an interpretation lies heavily with sufficient evidence from the text. Readers usually attach great importance to what matters to them the most so that interpretations will differ. Hence the value in poetry.

The Evaluation of Poetry

To evaluate a poem involves the literariness, the writing effects, the significance, and the views of world that are present in it. Readers make assessments about the cultural value presented or implied in the poem.

> When we evaluate a poem, first, we assess its literary quality and make a judgment about how good it is and how successful it realizes its poetic intentions. We examine its language and structure, for example, and consider how well they work together to embody meaning and convey feeling. Second, we consider how much significance the poem has for us personally, and what significance it may have for other readers... We also consider the significance the poem may have had for the poet, both its general value as part of a body of writing and its particular expression of feelings, attitudes, ideas, and values—its perspective on experience

(DiYanni 2000, 402).

Readers pay attention to a poem because they find connections of the poetic world with their world, and they share the experiences presented in it. As mentioned before, in reading poetry, readers may associate a poem with their lives and respond to it from their cultural, moral, political, religious, and aesthetical perspectives. Different readers understand a poem in their own ways. Consideration for such differences is itself a form of evaluation. Moreover, the readers are also concerned with the background, style, and purpose in a poem. Different poems may have different effects on readers and the same readers at different ages may have different interpretations and evaluations

> In evaluating poems, we explore the how and why of such differences. In so doing, we turn to a consideration of the various cultural assumptions, moral attitudes, and political convictions that animate particular poems. We consider the perspective from which they were written. Our consideration involves an investigation into the circumstances of its composition, the external facts and internal experiences of the poet's life, the attitudes and beliefs he or she may have expressed in letters or other comments, the audience and occasion for which a particular poem was written, its publication history and reception by readers past and present (DiYanni 2000, 402).

In this sense, readers may draw different conclusions after reading a poem.

> We may agree or disagree with the speaker's response to the woods in Frost's "Stopping by Woods on a Snowy Evening." We may confirm or deny the models of experience illustrated in Hayden's "Those Winter Sundays." Invariably, however, we measure the sentiments of a poem against our own. We may or may not appreciate responsibility as much as Frost's speaker seems to (DiYanni 2000, 403).

What's more, the cultural values and worldview of the readers influence their interpretation and evaluation of poetry.

> In evaluating a poem, we appraise it according to our own special combination of cultural, moral, and aesthetic values which derive from our place in family and society. These values are affected by race, gender and language. Our moral values reflect our ethical norms—what we consider good and evil, right and wrong. They are influenced by our religious beliefs and perhaps by our political convictions as well. Our aesthetic values concern what we see as beautiful or ugly, well or poorly made (DiYanni 2000, 403).

It should be noted that the aesthetic value of a poem is hard to discuss because the standards of aesthetics may differ from person to person and from culture to culture. In other words, since it involves personal and subjective interpretations of beauty, goodness, ugliness, and even truth, it is really difficult to make a final decision. Still, it is safe to say that a better evaluation, armed with a better knowledge of the elements of poetry, is possible and thus some evaluations may sound more reasonable than others.

Measuring a poem's achievement requires some knowledge of how poets exploit diction, imagery, syntax, and sound; how they establish form and control tone; how they work within or against a literary tradition... What we should strive for in evaluating poems is to understand the merits of different kinds of poems, to judge them fairly against what they are meant to be rather than what we think they should be (DiYanni 2000, 404).

Despite the difficulties in determining the aesthetic value of poetry for the sake of subjective reading, it is worthwhile to have a try and the experience gained from such attempts will surely benefit both the readers and the literary practices. Moreover, it should be remembered that

our goal should be, ultimately, to develop a sense of literary tact, the kind of informed and balanced judgment that comes with experience in reading and living, coupled with continued thoughtful reflection on both (DiYanni 2000, 404).

In other words, the evaluation or assessment of poetry, and other forms of literature too, does not mean to make a unanimous final decision on the aesthetics, but to practice to develop a sense and to train in the skill of literary appreciation to make balanced judgment out of the varied ways of evaluation, and to give thoughtful considerations of the literary work.

Now please look at the poem "The Red Wheelbarrow" by William Carlos Williams (1883−1963) and pay attention to its literary quality, significance, values, and language and structure.

The Red Wheelbarrow

—William Carlos Williams

so much depends

upon

a red wheel

barrow

glazed with rain   5

water

beside the white

chickens

"The Red Wheelbarrow" presents a visual image like a still life painting of the countryside, highlighting the wheelbarrow and the chickens with a contrast of colors of red and white. The lines "glazed with rain / water" (Lines 5−6) imply that the hardship, severe but temporary, has finally gone and life has returned to normality. The poem highlights the beauty in simplicity, in nature, and in harmony and it expresses the value that agriculture or farming is the fundamental pillar of human society and civilization. In this way it is like a minimalist artwork, featured by the uses of diminished and consequently simplified design elements.

The poem best embodies the idea that form carries meaning and sound suggests sense.

The poem is actually one sentence broken up at various intervals, characterized by enjambment, or "the carrying over of a sentence from one line to the next" (OED 2009). All the 16 words are typed in lower case, featuring the free style, and meanwhile highlighting the sense of depicting ordinary things in ordinary writing. The poem, sawtoothed, is composed of four stanzas, each with four words. Further, in each stanza, the last word of the first line ("depends," "wheel," "rain," and "white") functions as a stress to the main points of the poem.

In terms of its sound, the poem takes advantage of the (long) vowels and consonants to create musical and poetic effects, as seen in "so" and "barrow"; in "upon" and "a"; in "glazed" and "rain"; in "beside" and "white"; and in "much" and "chickens", in "red" and "barrow", and in "wheel" and "glazed". The first line of the poem stops with "depends" and ends in the last line with "chickens", two similar sounds matching well with each other. The interlaced vowels and consonants make the poem well rhymed and rhythmic. The distinctions in these sounds reveal that "the central stanzas are mellifluous, the frame stanzas choppy…, however, the honeyed and the choppy are linked in the third and fourth stanzas" (Ahearn 1988). Besides, the sound effects help the readers to catch the overall quality of the poem.

On the whole, the poem presents an image of a poet who has

> the artistic conception of a painter, the sense of fluent rhythm of a musician, and the calm and objective quality of a physician in the observation of the reality (Liu 2003, 51).

This poem may also have some implications. Banal or ordinary things, once placed in a new and sometimes incongruous scene, will have new values and significances, and they bring people into the imaginative world and will inevitably induce people to think. What's more, the poem concerns the relationship between man and nature. "So much depends / upon" suggests a sense of emotional possibilities, but

> ultimately, so much depends upon our recognizing the complex ways in which we depend on the scene (as the farmer depends on these specific objects for his sustenance) (Ahearn 1988).

The foundations of civilization lie on the simple existence which is embodied by simple agricultural instruments like the wheelbarrow, and by the simple activities of farming and poultry raising. Man's recognition of "the scene," the natural surroundings, reveals the interactions between man and nature.

The interpretation and evaluation of poetry may go on along with the readers' increased knowledge and their growth of experience. There are no definite, final interpretations and evaluations.

Questions for Reflection

Read the following poem in terms of the experiencing, interpreting, and evaluating approaches, and answer the questions.

My Grandmother's Love Letters

—Hart Crane (1899—1932)

There are no stars tonight
But those of memory.
Yet how much room for memory there is
In the loose girdle of soft rain.

There is even room enough
For the letters of my mother's mother,
Elizabeth,
That have been pressed so long
Into a corner of the roof
That they are brown and soft,
And liable to melt as snow.

Over the greatness of such space
Steps must be gentle.
It is all hung by an invisible white hair.
It trembles as birch limbs webbing the air.

And I ask myself:

"Are your fingers long enough to play
Old keys that are but echoes:
Is the silence strong enough
To carry back the music to its source
And back to you again
As though to her?"

Yet I would lead my grandmother by the hand
Through much of what she would not understand;
And so I stumble. And the rain continues on the roof
With such a sound of gently pitying laughter.

Questions

Experiencing

1. What feelings appear as you read this poem?

2. What words, phrases, and details induce your strongest responses?

3. What associations about your own grandma and mother do you bring to the poem?

4. Can the situation described here apply to your parents? Why or why not?

Interpreting

1. What words, phrases, lines, and details may have confused you? Why?

2. What observations can you make about the poem's details?

3. What words and phrases appear again? How? Why?

4. What connections can you establish among the details of action and language?

5. How do you understand "My Grandmother's Love Letters"?

Evaluating

1. What values are associated with "My Grandmother's Love Letters?"

2. What is the speaker's attitudes toward his grandmother (and his mother)? To what extent do you think the speaker's attitudes are those of the author? Why so?

3. How do your own ideas and standards influence your experience, interpretation, and evaluation of the poem?

4. Write an essay to comment on the poem's aesthetic accomplishment.

5. When you have enough knowledge about the life and work of Hart Crane and about the critical studies of his works, you are suggested to re-examine this poem and write an essay about your new findings considering the interpretation and evaluation of the poem.

Chapter 8
Elements of Poetry

To better understand poems in view of experience, interpretation and evaluation, it is important to have sufficient knowledge of the essential elements of poetry which usually involve

a speaker whose voice we hear in it; its diction or selection of words; its syntax or the order of those words; its imagery or details of sight, sound, taste, smell, and touch; its figures of speech or nonliteral ways of expressing one thing in terms of another, such as symbol and metaphor; its sound effects, especially rhyme, assonance, and alliteration; its rhythm and meter or the pattern of accents we hear in the poem's words, phrases, lines, and sentences; and its structure or formal pattern of organization (DiYanni 2000, 413).

The elements of a poem, inside or outside, work together, directly or indirectly, to express feeling and embody meaning in ways tangible or intangible.

■ Voice: Speaker and Tone

What makes a poem significant? What makes it memorable? Passion and thought, emotionally charged language, fresh imagery, surprising use of metaphor… Yes. But also, I think, the very sure sense that the moment we enter the world of the poem we are participating another episode of the myth-journey of humankind; that a voice has taken up the tale once more. The individual experience as resulted or presented in the poem renews our deep, implicit faith in that greater experience. A poem remains with us to the extent that it allows us to feel that we are all listening to a voice at once contemporary and ancient. This makes all the difference.

—*John Haines, "The Hole in the Bucket"*

(Kirszner & Mandell 2006, 822)

The speaker is the voice or "persona" of a poem, or "a mask that a poet assumes" (Kirszner & Mandell 2006, 823). It is not necessarily the poet because the poet may be writing from a perspective entirely different from his own. A male poet may write from the perspective of a woman and a white poet may give the voice of black people, or vice versa. Further, an adult poet may write from the perspective of a child, or even a poet may write from the perspective of an animal, a plant, or an object. Of course there are some poems whose speaker's voice goes close to the poet's and in some of these cases the speaker and the poet share greatly in common so that the distance between the poet and the speaker becomes very little. However, they are quite different in the vast majority of cases.

Whatever the case, the speaker is not the poet but rather a creation that the poet uses to convey his or her ideas. (For this reason, poems by a single poet may have very different voices.) (Kirszner & Mandell 2006, 824)

To identify the speaker, readers are expected to consider comprehensively the poem's elements concerned. The title and subject of a poem, the general meaning it expresses, the repeated words or images it involves, and the metrical pattern it adopts may all help reveal the identity of the speaker as well as its attitude and inclination.

A poem always has a speaker's voice.

It is this voice that conveys the poem's *tone*, its implied attitude toward its subject. Tone is an abstraction we make from the details of a poem's language: the use of meter and rhyme (or lack of them); the inclusion of certain kinds of details and exclusion of other kinds; particular choices of words and sentence pattern, of imagery and figurative language. When we listen to a poem's language and hear the voice of its speaker, we catch its tone and feeling and ultimately its meaning (DiYanni 2000, 413).

Now please look at Roethke's "My Papa's Waltz" and pay attention to its speaker and tone.

My Papa's Waltz (1948)

—Theodore Roethke (1908–1963)

The whiskey on your breath
Could make a small boy dizzy;
But I hung on like death:
Such waltzing was not easy.

We romped until the pans
Slid from the kitchen shelf;
My mother's countenance
Could not unfrown itself.

The hand that held my wrist
Was battered on one knuckle;
At every step you missed
My right ear scraped a buckle.

You beat time on my head
With a palm caked hard by dirt,
Then waltzed me off to bed
Still clinging to your shirt.

In this poem, the speaker recounts a good memory of his father and he enjoys the spirited scene in which he and his father "danced." The tone here is light, playful and joyful. Another example of a kid who remembers his father is found in Hayden's "Those Winter Sundays." However, the tone of Hayden's poem is different, suggesting a sense of regret, disappointment and anger (for his childish coldness to his father).

Poetry can enjoy a wide range of possible tones. For instance,

> a poem's speaker may be joyful, sad, playful, serious, comic, intimate, formal, relaxed, condescending, or ironic (Kirszner & Mandell 2006, 837).

Considering the range of tones in a poem, one of the more important and lasting is the ironic tone of voice. Irony is

> a way of speaking that implies a discrepancy or opposition between what is said and what is meant (DiYanni 2000, 414).

One of such examples is Stephen Crane's "Do Not Weep, Maiden, for War Is Kind."

"Do Not Weep, Maiden, for War Is Kind" (1899)

—from "War Is Kind" by Stephen Crane (1871−1900)

Do not weep, maiden, for war is kind.
Because your lover threw wild hands toward the sky
And the affrighted steed ran on alone,
Do not weep.
War is kind.   5

      Hoarse, booming drums of the regiment,
      Little souls who thirst for fight,
      These men were born to drill and die.
      The unexplained glory flies above them,
      Great is the battle-god, great, and his kingdom— 10
      A field where a thousand corpses lie.

Do not weep, babe, for war is kind.
Because your father tumbled in the yellow trenches,
Raged at his breast, gulped and died,
Do not weep.   15
War is kind.

      Swift blazing flag of the regiment,
      Eagle with crest of red and gold,
      These men were born to drill and die.
      Point for them the virtue of slaughter,   20
      Make plain to them the excellence of killing

And a field where a thousand corpses lie.

Mother whose heart hung humble as a button
On the bright splendid shroud of your son,
Do not weep.   25
War is kind.

In the poem, the ironic tone is found in the depiction of details of death ("the affrighted steed"; "men... born to drill and die"; "a thousand corpses"; "your father... gulped and died"; "slaughter"; "killing"; and "shroud") which are sharply contrasted with the "comforting or encouraging" repetition of "Do not weep/War is kind." The image of "glorious war" is counterbalanced with the image of death.

The speaker's voice reveals its character, personality, value, attitude and feeling. Sometimes, the speaker speaks alone, or at other times, the speaker speaks to someone else. In a poem when a speaker addresses a silent listener, it is called a dramatic monologue (DiYanni 2000, 415). Robert Browning's "My Last Duchess" is a good example in which the speaker is developed as a character.

My Last Duchess (1842)

—Robert Browning (1812–1889)

FERRARA

That's my last Duchess painted on the wall,
Looking as if she were alive. I call
That piece a wonder, now; Fra Pandolf's hands
Worked busily a day, and there she stands.
Will't please you sit and look at her? I said
"Fra Pandolf" by design, for never read
Strangers like you that pictured countenance,
The depth and passion of its earnest glance,
But to myself they turned (since none puts by
The curtain I have drawn for you, but I)
And seemed as they would ask me, if they durst,
How such a glance came there; so, not the first
Are you to turn and ask thus. Sir, 'twas not
Her husband's presence only, called that spot
Of joy into the Duchess' cheek; perhaps
Fra Pandolf chanced to say, "Her mantle laps
Over my lady's wrist too much," or "Paint
Must never hope to reproduce the faint
Half-flush that dies along her throat." Such stuff
Was courtesy, she thought, and cause enough
For calling up that spot of joy. She had

A heart—how shall I say? —too soon made glad,

Too easily impressed; she liked whate'er

She looked on, and her looks went everywhere.

Sir, 'twas all one! My favor at her breast,

The dropping of the daylight in the West,

The bough of cherries some officious fool

Broke in the orchard for her, the white mule

She rode with round the terrace—all and each

Would draw from her alike the approving speech,

Or blush, at least. She thanked men—good! but thanked

Somehow—I know not how—as if she ranked

My gift of a nine-hundred-years-old name

With anybody's gift. Who'd stoop to blame

This sort of trifling? Even had you skill

In speech—which I have not—to make your will

Quite clear to such an one, and say "Just this

Or that in you disgusts me; here you miss,

Or there exceed the mark"—and if she let

Herself be lessoned so, nor plainly set

Her wits to yours, forsooth, and made excuse—

E'en then would be some stooping; and I choose

Never to stoop. Oh sir, she smiled, no doubt,

Whene'er I passed her; but who passed without

Much the same smile? This grew; I gave commands;

Then all smiles stopped together. There she stands

As if alive. Will't please you rise? We'll meet

The company below, then. I repeat,

The Count your master's known munificence

Is ample warrant that no just pretense

Of mine for dowry will be disallowed;

Though his fair daughter's self, as I avowed

At starting, is my object. Nay, we'll go

Together down, sir. Notice Neptune, though,

Taming a sea-horse, thought a rarity,

Which Claus of Innsbruck cast in bronze for me!

Sometimes a speaker has a set identity such as a small boy in Roethke's "My Papa's Waltz" or the Duke in Browning's "My Last Duchess" while at other times it is anonymous like the speaker in "The Red Wheelbarrow" by Williams. Since the speaker of a poem describes events, feelings, and ideas to readers, the more readers get to know the speaker, the better they can interpret and evaluate the poem.

Questions for Reflection

Read the following poems and answer the questions.

Poem 1

I'm Nobody! Who Are You?

—Emily Dickinson (1830−1886)

I'm nobody! Who are you?
Are you nobody, too?
Then there's a pair of us—don't tell!
They'd banish—you know!

How dreary to be somebody!
How public like a frog
To tell one's name the livelong June
To an admiring bog!

Questions

1. How many voices are there in the poem? What do they represent?
2. How close is the speaker's voice to the poet's?

Poem 2

Nice Car, Camille (2001)

—James Tate (1943−   )

Camille drove by in her sports car with
the top down. I waved to her, but she didn't
see me, or else she just chose not to wave back.
She's an incredibly beautiful woman, but always
Seems sad, sad or angry, it's hard to tell. I
went to school with her. We'd talk sometimes.
Her father had owned an oil company. It had been
in the family for three generations. But one of
his employees had killed him when she was six.
Then her mother married some bum and he squandered
most of her money gambling. Camille didn't really
make friends in school. She didn't want any. She
Always managed to drive a really sexy car. She'd
always have her sunglasses on, speeding through

town as if late for an appointment. And I'd always
wave if I saw her. Hello, Camille. Goodbye,
Camille. That was my contribution to making her
life unforgettable.

Questions

1. From the poem what do you know about Camille and the speaker?
2. When the speaker says in the last two lines "That was my contribution to making her/life unforgettable," what is the tone, serious or sarcastic?

■ Word Choice (Diction)

> *What is known in a poem is its language, that is, the words it uses. Yet those words seem different in a poem. Even the most familiar will seem strange. In a poem, each word, being equally important, exists in absolute focus, having a weight it rarely achieves in fiction... Words in a novel are subordinate to broad slices of action or characterization that pushes the plot forward. In a poem, they are the action.*
> —Mark Strand, *Introduction to Best American Poems of* 1991
> (Kirszner & Mandell 2006, 865)

Diction means the choice of words or phrases. Since poems are usually brief and highly compact, good poems often embody the idea of "the best words in the best order" as said by Samuel Taylor Coleridge. To understand a poem means to understand, first of all, the meaning and implications of words. Usually, for both poets and readers

> the "best words" are those that do the most work; they convey feeling and indirectly imply ideas rather than state them outright (DiYanni 2000, 422).

Word choices in poems are made intentionally by the poets who have thought them proper in terms of sound, degree of correctness or abstract, extent of specificity or generation, or the connotations they involve. Sometimes, a poet may deliberately make it ambiguous for the sake of poetic effect to achieve an artistic meaning.

Take for example the following analysis of the second stanza of Roethke's "My Papa's Waltz" in terms of its diction, which owes much to DiYanni's interpretation (DiYanni 2000, 422-423).

> We romped until the pans
> Slid from the kitchen shelf;
> My mother's countenance
> Could not unfrown itself.

Words like "romped," "countenance," and "unfrown" are used properly and they are certainly chosen intentionally by the poet for special effects. Here, can "romped" be replaced by *danced* since the poem is describing a dance, specifically a waltz? Definitely not! The word "romped" indicates play or frolic of a boisterous nature. In this situation, although "romped" is not a word for dance, it actually suggests a kind of rough, crude dancing, in contrast with elegant and systematic waltzing. Moreover, "romped" connotes a kind of vigorous (half drunken) father-(little) son roughhousing. "Romped" reveals the speaker's attitude toward that unusual childhood experience.

The words "countenance" and "unfrown" produce important effects. "Countenance" is less familiar and more surprising than face, and "unfrown" is a word possibly coined by the poet. One is a big word and the other, uncommon. They appear somewhat strange in the lines because other lines of the stanza are in plain language. "Countenance" suggests the mother's formality as she watches the informal play of her husband and son. "Not unfrown," but actually "frown", would possibly reveal the mother's disapproval and annoyance.

DiYanni gives further explanations of the poem considering the definitions of "countenance" in the *Random House College Dictionary*:

noun	1. appearance, esp. the expression of the face...
	2. the face; visage
	3. calm facial expression; composure
	4. (obsolete) bearing; behavior
trans. verb	5. To permit or tolerate
	6. to approve, support, or encourage... (DiYanni 2000, 423)

As DiYanni pointed out, considering definitions 3 and 4, a problem or complication comes. Does the mother's "frown" suggest "discomposure" instead of "calm facial expression"? Or the word "countenance" used here by Roethke has double senses at the same time: "facial expression" and "tolerate and permit, approve and encourage"? In this way, it matches with the boy's double sense of the experience for the child as both pleasurable and frightening (DiYanni 2000, 423).

Questions for Reflection

Read the following poems and answer the questions.

Poem 1

When I Heard the Learn'd Astronomer (1865)

—Walt Whitman (1819–1892)

When I heard the learn'd astronomer,

When the proofs, the figures, were ranged in columns before me,

When I was shown the charts and diagrams, to add, divide, and measure them,

When I sitting heard the astronomer where he lectured with much applause in the lecture-room,

How soon unaccountable I became tired and sick,

Till rising and gliding out I wander'd off by myself,

In the mystical moist night-air, and from time to time,

Look'd up in perfect silence at the stars.

Questions

1. How are words chosen for their sounds?
2. How are words chosen for their connotations?
3. How are words chosen for their relationships to other words?

Poem 2

Sears Life (2001)

—Wanda Coleman (1946−2013)

it makes me nervous to go into a store
because i never know if i'm going to
come out. have you noticed how much
they look like prisons these days? no display
windows anymore. all that cold soulless   5
lighting—as atmospheric as county jail—
and all that ground-breaking status-quo
shattering rock 'n' roll reduced to neuron
pablum and piped in over the escalators.
breaks my rebel heart. and i especially   10
hate the aroma of fresh-nuked popcorn
rushing my nose, throwing my stomach
off balance. eyes follow me everywhere
like i'm a neon sign that shouts shoplifter.
and so many snide counter rats want to   15
service me, it almost makes me feel rich
and royal. that's why i rarely bother to
browse. i go straight to the department
of object of conjecture, make my decision
quick, throw down the cash and split   20

one time i had barely left this store
when i heard somebody yelling stop! stop!
i turned around and this dough-fleshed
armed security guard was waving me down.
i waited while he caught his breath and   25
demanded to search my purse i stared him
into his socks. we're outside the store,
i reminded him. if you search me, you'd

better find some goddamned something.

he took a minute to examine my eyes, turned   30

around and went back to his job, snorting

dust and coondogging teenage loiterers

Questions

1. Is this poem informal? Explain why in terms of its diction.

2. If the poem is informal, is this informality a strength or a weakness? Why?

3. How does the poem's structure, lack of capitalization and punctuation, influence the overall effect?

4. What can you infer about the speaker from the poem's language, such as "neuron"/"pablum" (Lines 8-9), "counter rats" (Line 15), and "dough-fleshed" (Line 23)?

5. What do you think about the speaker's observations?

■ Word Order

Besides diction, the order of words in a poem is also important for the departure from conventional word order may produce poetic effects. This is a way of emphasis in favor of the relationship between words, rhyme or meter, sound correspondence, and revelation of a speaker's mood. Take for example again the poem "Dust of Snow."

Dust of Snow

—Robert Frost (1874-1963)

The way a crow
Shook down on me
The dust of snow
From a hemlock tree

Has given my heart
A change of mood
And saved some part
Of a day I had rued.

The poem is actually a single sentence broken down into lines for the sake of rhyme (for example, crow/snow, me/tree, heart/part, and mood/rued). In this way, it highlights the sound correspondence. If arranged in a different way, the sound effect will disappear. Further, the irregular syntactic pattern gives a playful quality of the poem, casting light on the speaker's change of state of mind. This is exemplified by the vertical location of the two vowels of /eɪ/ and also the two words of "change" and "save". The two words contain the same vowels and particularly they have the most important connotations of the poem. They are displayed with one on top the other (two important words arranged longitudinally together). The syntax of the poems helps highlight the idea that nature is beneficial to the improvement of disposition or state of mind.

Questions for Reflection

Read the following poems and answer the questions.

Poem 1

One Day I Wrote Her Name upon the Strand (Sonnet 75) (1595)

—Edmund Spenser (1552–1599)

One day I wrote her name upon the strand,
But came the waves and washed it away:
Again I wrote it with a second hand,
But came the tide and made my pains his prey.
"Vain man," said she, "that doest in vain assay,   5
A mortal thing so to immortalize,
For I myself shall like to this decay,
And eke my name be wiped out likewise."
"Not so," quod I, "let baser things devise,
To die in dust, but you shall live by fame: 10
My verse your virtues rare shall eternize,
And in the heavens write your glorious name.
Where whenas death shall all the world subdue,
Our love shall live, and later life renew."

Questions

1. Point out the words in this poem that depart from conventional English syntax.
2. Discuss the functions of the intentional placement of these words.

Poem 2

Anyone Lived in a Pretty How Town (1940)

—E. E. Cummings (1894–1962)

anyone lived in a pretty how town
(with up so floating many bells down)
spring summer autumn winter
he sang his didn't he danced his did.

Women and men (both little and small)   5

cared for anyone not at all
they sowed their isn't they reaped their same
sun moon stars rain

children guessed (but only a few
and down they forgot as up they grew   10
autumn winter spring summer)
that noone loved him more by more

when by now and tree by leaf
she laughed his joy she cried his grief
bird by snow and stir by still   15
anyone's any was all to her

someones married their everyones
laughed their cryings and did their dance
(sleep wake hope and then) they
said their nevers they slept their dream   20

stars rain sun moon
(and only the snow can begin to explain
how children are apt to forget to remember
with up so floating many bells down)

one day anyone died i guess   25
(and noone stooped to kiss his face)
busy folk buried them side by side
little by little and was by was

all by all and deep by deep
and more by more they dream their sleep   30
noone and anyone earth by april
wish by spirit and if by yes.

Women and men (both dong and ding)
summer autumn winter spring
reaped their sowing and went their came   35
sun moon stars rain

Questions

1. In Line 10, the inverted sequence means to respond to the demands of what?
2. The poem has unconventional syntax, or unexpected departures from the musical metrical pattern (in Line 3 and Line 8) and from the rhyme scheme (in Lines 3 and 4), and the use of parts of speech in unfamiliar contexts. What effects have these techniques produced?

■ Imagery

The difference between a literature that includes the image, and a literature that excludes the image (such as the newspaper or the scientific Newtonian essay) is that the first helps us to bridge the gap between ourselves and nature, and the second encourages us to remain isolated, living despairingly in the gap. Many philosophers and critics urge us to remain in the gap, and let the world of nature and the world of men fall further and further apart. We can do that; or a human being can reach out with his right hand to the natural world, and with his left hand to the world of human intelligence, and touch both at the same moment. Apparently no one but human beings can do this.

—Robert Bly, "What the Image Can Do"

(Kirszner & Mandell 2006, 897)

Poems owe greatly to the concrete or specific details that stimulate the readers' senses and manipulate their responses. Such specific details in poetry are called imagery. A purpose of literature is to expand the perception of readers. Images appeal to the senses and they help readers develop a sense of the scenes. For this sake,

a poet uses imagery, language that evoke a physical sensation produced by one or more of the five senses—sight, hearing, taste, touch, and smell (Kirszner & Mandell 2006, 899).

For example, Hayden's "Those Winter Sundays" arouses the readers' sense of touch (the feeling of cold and heat as suggested by words like "blueblack cold" and "fires blaze"). Frost's "Stopping by Woods on a Snowy Evening" stimulates the senses of sight and touch (with depictions like "between the woods and frozen lake", "the sweep of easy wind," and "downy" snowflakes).

The following poem contains two aural images ("a ringing" and "Whang"), a tactile image ("brushed on limbs") and a gustatory image ("the taste/of rust").

Some Good Things to Be
Said for the Iron Age (1970)

—Gary Snyder (1930－)

A ringing tire iron
　　dropped on the pavement

Whang of a saw
brusht on limbs
the taste
of rust

Images induce emotional and imaginative associations and influence the readers' responses which may be similar or different considering their individual experiences. The associations help create the atmosphere or mood of the poem, such as quiet, boisterous, mystical, jubilant, or melancholy.

Imagery can make up the deficiency of wording. Often, "just a few words enable poets to evoke a range of emotions and reaction" (Kirszner & Mandell 2006, 900). Williams's "The Red Wheelbarrow" and Ezra Pound's "In a Station of the Metro" are good examples in which rich connotations and images are there despite the economical use of words. "The Red Wheelbarrow" uses simple imagery to create a scene on which "so much depends."

The wheelbarrow establishes a momentary connection between the poet and his world. Like a still-life painting, the red wheelbarrow beside the white chickens gives order to a world that is full of seemingly unrelated objects. By asserting the importance of the objects in the poem, the poet suggests that our ability to perceive the objects of this world gives our lives meaning and that our ability to convey our perceptions to others is central to our lives as well as to art (Kirszner & Mandell 2006, 900).

Williams, via the small poem, highlights the relationship between man and his world and emphasizes the importance of human perception of the objects of the world to produce meaning in life.

Questions for Reflection

Read the following poems and answer the questions.

Poem 1

Vignette (1996)

—Maxine Kumin (1925–2014)

Every morning the Head Start van
rattles down the ruts of Poorhouse Road
to collect Emmet, who is first on
and last off and suffers from attention
deficit disorder but loves the schoolyard   5
slides and swings, lunchtime, and Sue, his driver.

Every afternoon where Poorhouse Road
spirals down to dirt, old foundered Radar

uproots himself from the muck of his pasture

And focuses his one good eye uphill.   10

The van pulls over. Emmet, clutching the apple

Sue unfailingly provides,

scrambles over the sagging fence rail.

No attention deficit on either side.

Questions

1. In what way is this poem a vignette, a brief literary description or a literary sketch?

2. What images are found in the poem and what roles do they play in creating meaning or a theme?

Poem 2

In a Station of the Metro (1913)

—Ezra Pound (1885–1972)

The apparition of these faces in the crowd:

Petals on a wet, black bough.

Questions

1. What does the word "apparition" suggest?

2. What images are there in the poem?

■ Figures of Speech

Poetry is made of comparisons, simple or complex, open or concealed. The richness of poetry is obtained by mixing or interweaving or juxtaposing these comparisons... In poetry all metaphors are mixed metaphors.

—J. Isaacs, *The Background*

I suppose we shall never be able to distinguish absolutely and with a hard edge the image from the metaphor, anymore than anyone has so distinguished prose from poetry... We shall very often be able to tell, just as we can very often tell the difference between snow and rain; but there are some weathers which are either-neither, and so here there is an area where our differences will mingle. If the poet says, simply, "The red bird," we shall probably take that as an image. But as soon as we read the rest of the line—"The red bird flies across the golden floor"—there arises obscure thoughts of relationships that lead in the direction of parable: the line alone is not, strictly, a metaphor, but its resonances take it prospectively beyond a pure perception... Metaphor stands somewhat as a mediating term squarely between a thing and a thought, which may be why it is so likely to compose itself about a word of sense and a word of thought, as in this example of a common Shakespearean formula: "Even to the teeth and forehead of my fault."

—Howard Nemerov, "On Metaphor"

(Kirszner & Mandell 2006, 916)

In literature, figures of speech abound. The language in literature can be literal and figurative. The difference is seen between what exactly the words convey and what the actual meanings of the words are.

Rhetoricians have catalogued more than 250 different *figures of speech*, expressions or ways of using words in a nonliteral sense. They include *hyperbole* or exaggeration ("I'll die if I miss that game"); *litotes* or understatement ("Being flayed alive is somewhat painful"); *synecdoche* or using a part to signify the whole ("Lend me a hand"); *metonymy* or substituting an attribute of a thing for the thing itself ("Step on the gas"); *personification*, endowing inanimate objects or abstract concepts with animate characteristics or qualities ("The lettuce was lonely without tomatoes and cucumbers for company") (DiYanni 2000, 436).

Literature is a world of figures of speech and it is hard and unnecessary to give a full list of all the figurative devices here. For preliminary studies, examples of simile, metaphor, hyperbole, and personification are shown in terms of poetry.

Simile and metaphor involve chiefly comparison, "the making of connections between normally unrelated things, seeing one thing in terms of another" (DiYanni 2000, 436). That's why Robert Burns once remarked that, essentially, poetry was a way of "saying one thing and meaning another, saying one thing in terms of another" (DiYanni 2000, 436). Simile, using words or expressions such as "like," "as," "seemingly," or "as if," establishes the comparison more evidently than metaphor as for which the comparison is always implied. Moreover, "the simile is more restricted in its comparative suggestion than is the metaphor" (DiYanni 2000, 436). For example, if one says "Smith is as cunning as a fox," the comparison highlights almost entirely the cunning features between the two. On the other hand, if the sentence is put in the form of a metaphor, say, "Smith is a fox," the comparison may suggest more than the cunning features between the two. In this situation, Smith may have other traits of a fox despite the evident cunning feature of the animal. Metaphor may carry a more extensive sense.

Questions for Reflection

Read the following poems and answer the questions.

Poem 1

I Wandered Lonely as a Cloud (1807)

—William Wordsworth (1770–1850)

I wandered lonely as a cloud
  That floats on high o'er vales and hills,

When all at once I saw a crowd,
  A host, of golden daffodils;
Beside the lake, beneath the trees,   5
Fluttering and dancing in the breeze.

Continuous as the stars that shine
  And twinkle on the milky way,
They stretched in never-ending line
  Along the margin of a bay: 10
Ten thousand saw I at a glance,
Tossing their heads in sprightly dance.

The waves beside them danced; but they
  Out-did the sparkling waves in glee;
A Poet could not but be gay,   15
  In such a jocund company;
I gazed—and gazed—but little thought
What wealth the show to me had brought:

For oft, when on my couch I lie
  In vacant or in pensive mood,   20
They flash upon that inward eye
  Which is the bliss of solitude;
And then my heart with pleasure fills,
And dances with the daffodils.

Questions

1. Identify the simile and metaphor in the poem and make sure of their comparisons.

2. Give a detailed analysis on the use of simile and metaphor in this poem.

3. Are there any other figurative devices? What are they?

Poem 2

My Father as a Guitar (2000)

—Martin Espada (1957–)

The cardiologist prescribed
a new medication
and lectured my father

that he had to stop working.
And my father said: *I can't.*
The landlord won't let me.
The heart pills are dice
in my father's hand,
gambler who needs cash
by the first of the month.

On the night his mother died
in faraway Puerto Rico,
my father lurched upright in bed,
heart hammering
like the fist of a man at the door
with an eviction notice.
Minutes later,
the telephone sputtered
with news of the dead.

Sometimes I dream
my father is a guitar,
with a hole in his chest
where the music throbs
between my fingers.

Questions

1. Identify the figures of speech (e.g. simile, metaphor, or personification) in the poem.
2. The speaker's father is compared to a guitar. In the poem this is done with a metaphor instead of a simile. Why so? How does this help the speaker express his feelings?

Poem 3

A Red, Red Rose (1796)

—Robert Burns (1759−1796)

Oh, my love is like a red, red rose
  That's newly sprung in June;
Oh, my love is like the melody
  That's sweetly played in tune.

So fair art thou, my bonny lass,

So deep in love am I;
And I will love thee still, my dear,
  Till a' the seas gang dry.

Till a' the seas gang dry, my dear,
  And the rocks melt wi' the sun;   10
And I will love thee still, my dear,
  While the sands o' life shall run.

And fare thee weel, my only love!
  And fare thee weel awhile!
And I will come again, my love   15
  Though it were ten thousand mile.

Questions

1. In the poem, why does the speaker compare his love to a rose?
2. Besides simile, hyperbole is also used in the poem in the exaggeration of the extent of the speaker's love. Does the exaggeration strengthen or weaken the effectiveness of the poem? Why?

Poem 4

That Time of Year Thou Mayst in Me Behold (Sonnet 73) (1609)

—William Shakespeare (1564–1616)

That time of year thou mayst in me behold
When yellow leaves, or none, or few, do hang
Upon those boughs which shake against the cold,
Bare ruined choirs, where late the sweet birds sang.
In me thou see'st the twilight of such day   5
As after sunset fadeth in the west,
Which by and by black night doth take away,
Death's second self that seals up all in rest.
In me thou see'st the glowing of such fire,
That on the ashes of his youth doth lie,   10
As the deathbed whereon it must expire,
Consumed with that which it was nourished by
  This thou perceiv'st, which makes thy love more strong,
  To love that well which thou must leave ere long.

Questions

1. Identify the poem's metaphorical language.
2. Discuss the connections between metaphor and imagery in this poem.
3. How does the figurative language help with your understanding?

■ Symbolism

Symbolism and symbols are easily seen in literary works.

> Symbolism, in its broad sense, is the use of one object to represent or suggest another; or in literature, the use of symbols in writing, particularly the serious and extensive use of such symbols (Holman & Harmon 1986, 494).

> A symbol is any object or action that means more than itself, any objection or action that represents something beyond itself (DiYanni 2000, 442).

Put in another way, a symbol refers to an idea or image that suggests something else and it is an image that goes beyond the literal sense in a complex way (Kirszner & Mandell 2006, 1013). For example, an olive branch symbolizes peace, a rose, beauty, love, or transience, and water, life (fertility or food) but also death (floods). These are universal symbols popular in different parts of the world. Universal or archetypal symbols come from the images or ideas that exist in a hidden way in the subconscious of all people. However, many symbols are the products of a given environment. In other words, the meaning of any symbol is restricted by its context which is often cultural and aesthetic.

The Sick Rose (1794)

—William Blake (1757−1827)

O Rose, thou art sick!
The invisible worm
That flies in the night,
In the howling storm:
Has found out thy bed   5
Of crimson joy:
And his dark secret love
Does thy life destroy.

Usually a rose stands for love, and it is simply a sign of love. Considering Blake's "The Sick Rose," the rose may encompass a variety of meanings, such as beauty (of a woman), perfection, passion, (dark or mysterious) love, or pleasant sensations. These possible meanings can be both contradictory and complementary.

Quite often, it is hard to determine whether a person or an object is symbol or not. Sometimes, even if it is determined as symbols, it is still difficult to make sure what they stand for. However, it is this uncertainty that gives life and vitality to literature. Interpretations may go on from person to person, and from culture to culture.

Questions for Reflection

Read the following poem and answer the questions.

For Once, Then, Something (1923)

—Robert Frost (1874—1963)

Others taunt me with having knelt at well-curbs
Always wrong to the light, so never seeing
Deeper down in the well than where the water
Gives me back in a shining surface picture
Me myself in the summer heaven, godlike,   5
Looking out of a wreath of fern and cloud puffs.
Once, when trying with chin against a well-curb,
I discerned, as I thought, beyond the picture,
Through the picture, a something white, uncertain,
Something more of the depths—and then I lost it.   10
Water came to rebuke the too clear water.
One drop fell from a fern, and lo, a ripple
Shook whatever it was lay there at bottom,
Blurred it, blotted it out. What was that whiteness?
Truth? A pebble of quartz? For once, then, something.   15

Questions

1. What's the central symbol in this poem?
2. How the symbol in the poem is different from the traditional image of a well?
3. Does the speaker find significance of what he saw?

At the same time, it must be noted that it is not enough to just determine the symbolic significance of a particular item in a poem. The determination or interpretation depends heavily on the evidence from the text. Furthermore, the symbol is expected to correspond to the theme of the poem.

Questions for Reflection

Read the following poem and answer the questions.

Volcanoes Be in Sicily

—Emily Dickinson (1830−1886)

Volcanoes be in Sicily
And South America
I judge from my Geography—
Volcanoes nearer here
A Lava step at any time   5
Am I inclined to climb—
A Crater I may contemplate
Vesuvius at Home.

Questions

1. What do the volcanoes represent?
2. How does the image of the volcano help with the understanding of the theme?

■ Allegory

An allegory is a type of symbolism. In *Merriam-Webster Dictionary*, the definitions go as:

1. the expression by means of symbolic fictional figures and actions of truths or generalizations about human existence · a writer known for his use of allegory; also: an instance (as in a story or painting) of such expression · The poem is an allegory of love and jealousy.

2. a symbolic representation: emblem[2]

Related to symbolism, an allegory is a form of narrative in which people, places, and events have (half) hidden or symbolic meaning. It uses people, places or events to represent abstract ideas.

Allegorical figures, each with a strict equivalent, form an allegorical framework, a set of ideas that conveys the allegory's message or lesson... Allegorical figures can always be assigned specific meanings... Thus, symbols open up possibilities for interpretation, whereas allegories tend to restrict possibility (Kirszner & Mandell 2006, 1018).

In allegorical poems the details of action directly correspond to certain meanings, while in symbolic poems the meanings of symbols are more open-ended.

Quite often an allegory involves a journey or adventure, as in the case of Dante's *Divine Comedy*, which traces a journey through Hell, Purgatory, and Heaven. Within an allegory, everything can have meaning: the road on which the characters walk, the people they encounter, or a phrase that one of them repeats throughout the journey (Kirszner & Mandell 2006, 1018).

In reading an allegorical poem, the reader is expected to direct their attention to how well these elements correspond to the allegorical framework. The meaning of allegorical poems can be either explicit or implicit.

Questions for Reflection

Read the following poems and answer the questions.

Poem 1

Uphill (1861)

—Christina Rossetti (1830—1894)

Does the road wind uphill all the way?
   Yes, to the very end.
Will the day's journey take the whole long day?
   From morn to night, my friend.

But is there for the night a resting-place?   5
   A roof for when the slow dark hours begin.
May not the darkness hide it from my face?
   You cannot miss that inn.

Shall I meet other wayfarers at night?
   Those who have gone before.   10
Then must I knock, or call when just in sight?
   They will not keep you standing at that door.

Shall I find comfort, travel-sore and weak?
   Of labour you shall find the sum.
Will there be beds for me and all who seek?   15
   Yea, beds for all who come.

Questions

1. What does the "uphill road" stand for?
2. What do "day" and "night" stand for?

3. What kind of journey is depicted and what does it suggest?

4. What do you know about the structure and tone of the poem?

Poem 2

The Road Not Taken (1915)

—Robert Frost (1874–1963)

Two roads diverged in a yellow wood,
And sorry I could not travel both
And be one traveler, long I stood
And looked down one as far as I could
To where it bent in the undergrowth;   5

Then took the other, as just as fair,
And having perhaps the better claim,
Because it was grassy and wanted wear;
Though as for that the passing there
Had worn them really about the same,   10

And both that morning equally lay
In leaves no step had trodden black.
Oh, I kept the first for another day!
Yet knowing how way leads on to way,
I doubted if I should ever come back.   15

I shall be telling this with a sigh
Somewhere ages and ages hence:
Two roads diverged in a wood, and I—
I took the one less traveled by,
And that has made all the difference.   20

Questions

1. Do you think that the poem is about more than just walking in the woods and choosing a path to follow? Why?

2. Identify the possible symbolic meanings of the poem.

3. What kind of human problem is implied in the poem?

■ Sound

> *A primary pleasure in poetry is… the pleasure of saying something over for its own sweet sake and because it sounds just right.*
>
> (Kirszner & Mandell 2006, 948)

Sound is the soul of poetry, and sound holds together the meanings of lines of a poem.

Rhyme

Considering the elements of poetry, rhyming sounds often become the center of attention.

> Rhyme can be defined as the matching of final vowel and consonant sounds in two or more words (DiYanni 2000, 457).

A rhyme can be classified in different ways depending on the degree, position, and number of rhyming syllables. When final vowel and consonant sounds are the same, like "born" and "horn," "tight" and "might," or "sleep" and "deep," it is called a perfect rhyme. When the final consonant sounds in two words are the same but the vowels are different, such as "learn" and "barn," "pads" and "lids," or even "road" and "dead," it is called an imperfect rhyme (also named near rhyme, approximate rhyme, slant rhyme, or consonance) (Kirszner & Mandell 2006, 961).

Considering the position of the rhyming syllables in a poem,

> when the corresponding sounds occur at the ends of lines we have end rhyme; when they occur within the lines we have internal rhyme (DiYanni 2000, 457).

Furthermore, a beginning rhyme appears at the beginning of the line. The following selections are examples of the three kinds of rhymes: end, internal, and beginning rhyme, respectively.

> Tyger! Tyger! Burning <u>bright</u>
> In the forests of the <u>night</u>
> —William Blake, "The Tyger"

> The sun came up upon the left,
> Out of the sea came he!
> And he shone <u>bright</u> and on the <u>right</u>
> Went down in to the sea.
> —Samuel Taylor Coleridge, "The Rime on the Ancient Mariner"

> Red river, red river,
> <u>Slow</u> flow heat is silence
> <u>No</u> will is still as a river

Still. Will hear move

    —T. S. Eliot, "Virginia"

(Kirszner & Mandell 2006, 962)

As for the numbers of corresponding syllables in a poem, there are masculine, feminine, and triple rhymes.

      Masculine thyme (also called rising rhyme) occurs when single syllables correspond ("can" / "ran"; "descend" / "contend"). Feminine rhyme (also called double rhyme or falling rhyme) occurs when two syllables, a stressed one followed by an unstressed one, correspond ("ocean" / "motion"; "leaping" / "sleeping"). Triple rhyme occurs when three syllables correspond ("paragon" / "Aragon") (Kirszner & Mandell 2006, 962).

A rhyme can produce the feeling of harmony, incongruity, humor, or satire.

Questions for Reflection

Read Robert Frost's "Stopping by Woods on a Snowy Evening" and answer the questions.

Stopping by Woods on a Snowy Evening (1923)

—Robert Frost (1874−1963)

Whose woods these are I think I know.
His house is in the village though;
He will not see me stopping here
To watch his woods fill up with snow.

My little horse must think it queer   5
To stop without a farmhouse near
Between the woods and frozen lake
The darkest evening of the year.

He gives his harness bells a shake
To ask if there is some mistake.   10
The only other sound's the sweep
Of easy wind and downy flake.

The woods are lovely, dark and deep,
But I have promises to keep,
And miles to go before I sleep,   15
And miles to go before I sleep.

Questions

1. Read the poem and analyze its rhyme.

2. How does the rhyme pattern support the poem's meaning?

Alliteration and Assonance

Alliteration and assonance are also important ways of "playing with sound."

Alliteration [refers to] the repetition of consonant sounds, especially at the beginning of words, and assonance, the repetition of vowel sounds, as described by John Hollander in *Rhyme's Reason*: Assonance is the spirit of a rhyme, /A common vowel, hovering like a sigh/ After its consonantal body dies ... /Alliteration lightly links /Stressed syllables with common consonants (DiYanni 2000, 458).

Questions for Reflection

Read the third stanza of Robert Frost's "Stopping by Woods on a Snowy Evening" and answer the questions.

He gives his harness bells a shake

To ask if there is some mistake.

The only other sound's the sweep

Of easy wind and downy flake.

Questions

1. Identify the examples of alliteration and assonance.

2. How does the repetition of vowels help to highlight the images?

3. What are the effects of the repeated consonant "s"?

Rhyme Scheme

A rhyme scheme refers to

the pattern, or sequence, in which the rhyme sounds occur in a stanza or poem. Rhyme schemes, for the purpose of analysis, are usually presented by the assignment of the same letter of the alphabet to each similar sound in a stanza (Holman & Harmon 1986, 433).

For example, the rhyme scheme pattern of the Spenserian stanza is *ababbcbcc*.

He durst not enter into th'open greene,

For dread of them unwares to be descryde,

For breaking of their daunce, if he were seene;

But in the covert of the wood did byde,

Beholding all, yet of them unespyde.

There he did see, that pleased much his sight,

That even he himselfe his eyes envyde,

A hundred naked maked lilly white,

All raunged in a ring, and dauncing in delight. (*The Faerie Queene*)

The above stanza is a typical example showing the rhyme scheme pattern of the Spenserian stanza, taken from *The Faerie Queene* by Edmund Spenser, the 16th-century English poet who invented the Spenserian rhyme scheme pattern.

The Spenserian stanza is iambic, with the first eight lines in pentameters (five/stress lines) and the last line having the defining characteristic of a concluding longer line of six feet (an "alexandrine") (Starchan & Terry 2009, 47).

In Thomas Moore's "The Time I've Lost in Wooing," the rhyme pattern of each stanza, (taken separately), goes as *aabbaccddc*. In this poem, each stanza repeats the same rhyme scheme twice, and some rhymes in the first stanza are repeated in the second and third stanzas. This suggests the connections in form as well as meaning throughout. The rhyme scheme strengthens the poem's meaning by linking lines into structural units.

The Time I've Lost in Wooing

—Thomas Moore (1779−1852)

The time I've lost in wooing,
In watching and pursuing
The light that lies
In woman's eyes,
Has been my heart's undoing.
Though Wisdom oft has sought me,
I scorn'd the lore she brought me,
My only books
Were woman's looks,
And folly's all they've taught me.

Her smile, when Beauty granted,
I hung with gaze enchanted,
Like him, the sprite,
Whom maids by night
Oft meet in glen that's haunted,
Like him, too, Beauty won me;
But, while her eyes were on me,
If once their ray
Was turn'd away,
Oh! winds could not outrun me.

And are those follies going?

And is my proud heart growing

Too cold or wise

For brilliant *eyes*

Again to set it glowing?

No—vain, alas! th'endeavour,

From bonds so sweet to sever;

Poor Wisdom's chance

Against a glance

Is now as weak as ever!

Questions for Reflection

Read the following poem carefully and answer the questions.

In the Valley of the Elwy

Gerard Manley Hopkins (1844—1889)

I remember a house where all were good

    To me, God knows, deserving no such thing:

    Comforting smell breathed at very entering,

Fetched fresh, as I suppose, off some sweet wood.

That cordial air made those kind people a hood   5

    All over, as a bevy of eggs the mothering wing

    Will, or mild nights the new morsels of Spring:

Why, it seemed of course; seemed of right it should.

Lovely the woods, waters, meadows, combes, vales,

All the air things wear that build this world of Wales;   10

    Only the inmate does not correspond:

God, lover of souls, swaying considerate scales,

Complete thy creature dear O where it fails,

    Being mighty a master, being a father and fond.

Questions

1. What is the rhyme scheme of this poem? Make detailed explanations.

2. Identify the examples of alliteration and assonance. What effect do they have on the content?

3. What is the central theme of the poem? How does the rhyme scheme reflect the central theme?

Rhythm and Meter

        The most obvious function of the line is rhythmic: it can record the slight (but meaningful) hesitations between word and word that are characteristic of the mind's dance among perceptions but which are not noted by grammatical punctuation... The line-break is a form of punctuation additional to the punctuation that forms part of the logic of completed thoughts.

—Denise Levertov, "On the Function of Line"

(Kirszner & Mandell 2006, 948)

To start, look at the common examples of rhythm using stressed and unstressed syllables. These phrases are also common in spoken English as well as literary texts.

Good EVening, DEAR. (Iamb)

HOW'S it GOing? (Trochee)

CHECK, PLEASE. (Spondee)

BEAUtiful WEAther we're HAving now. (Dactyl)

To inFINity and beYOND. (Anapest)

Rhythm refers to the regular recurrence of the accent or the stressed sound in a poem. Quite often poetic rhythm is created by meter. "[Rhythm] is the pulse or beat we feel in a phrase of music or a line of poetry (DiYanni 2000, 465)." Poetry explores natural phenomena and human experiences and it aims to reflect the rhythms of the natural and human worlds. Rhythm captures the attention of readers by producing musical effects, and thus playing an important role in the expression of feelings and conveying of meanings.

Rhythm in poetry is usually achieved via repetition of rhyming sounds, words, phrases or lines, or via the arrangement of words.

Gwendolyn Brooks's poem "We Real Cool" (1960), for example, has a strong rhythmic effect.

We Real Cool (1960)

—Gwendolyn Brooks (1917–2000)

THE POOL PLAYERS.

SEVEN AT THE GOLDEN SHOVEL.

We real cool. We

Left school. We

Lurk late. We

Strike straight. We

Sing sin. We

Thin gin. We

Jazz June. We

Die soon.

The rhythm of this poem is achieved by the monosyllabic words, enjambment (running-on lines) and rhyme, all of which produce a strong sense of force. It is both poetic and musical.

Another example is seen in a selected part of a poem by E. E. Cummings, considering the rhythmic effect produced by unusual arrangement of words.

> the moon is hiding
> in her hair.
> The
> lily
> of heaven
> full of all dreams,
> draws down.

Because of the enjambment, readers must alternate the speed of reading. The adjustment of a slow or fast pace in recitation creates a rhythm, highlighting the key concept of "the lily" in Cummings's poem.

A meter is "the recurrence of regular units of stressed and unstressed syllables" (Kirszner & Mandell 2006, 951). It is "a count of the stresses we feel in the poem's rhythm" (DiYanni 2000, 467). Conventionally, the unit of poetic meter in English is the foot, which is "a fixed pattern of stressed and unstressed syllables" (Kirszner & Mandell 2006, 951). The analysis of the metrical structure of a poem line is called scansion, which touches on the patterns of stressed and unstressed syllables. In printing, a stressed syllable is put in capitalization and an unstressed one, in lowercase (e.g. "WINdows," "CURtains;" MY COUN-TRY 'tis of THEE). Or a stressed syllable is marked up above with a "ˈ," and an unstressed one, a "◡"

(e.g. Shăll Í cŏmpáre thée tŏ ă súmmĕr's dáy).

A poetic foot may be either iambic or trochaic, anapestic or dactylic.

> Iamb [is] defined as an unaccented syllable followed by an accented one as in the word "preVENT, conTAIN;" reversing the order of accented and unaccented syllables we get a trochee, [with] an accented syllable followed by an unaccented one, as in "FOOTball, LIquor."... An anapest consists of two unaccented syllables followed by an accented one as in "compreHEND, or interVENE." A dactylic reverses the anapest, beginning with an accented syllable followed by two unaccented ones (DANgerous, ANapest) (Diyanni 2000, 467).

With two syllables per foot, iambic and trochaic feet are called duple (or double) meters. Three-syllable meters are called triple meters like anapestic and dactylic meters.

It is necessary to add a bit more about poetic meter. The first is about rising and falling meters.

> Iambic and anapestic meters are called rising meters because they progress from unstressed syllables to stressed syllables. Trochaic and dactylic meters are called falling meters because they progress from stressed syllables to unstressed syllables. (Kirszner & Mandell 2006, 951)

The second is that a poem's meter is often flexible despite the strict convention. For example,

Shakespeare's sonnet "That Time of Year Thou Mayst in Me Behold" does not, in each line, follow exactly the metrical pattern.

The third point is that a metric line of a poem is measured by the number of feet it has.

We give names to lines of poetry based on the number of feet they contain. [For instance,]

Number of feet per line

one foot	monometer
two feet	dimeter
three feet	trimeter
four feet	tetrameter
five feet	pentameter
six feet	hexameter
seven feet	heptameter
eight feet	octameter

(DiYanni 2000, 468)

Many passages in Shakespeare's plays are written in unrhymed lines of iambic pentameter called blank verse. However, poets tend to choose different meters based on their preference. Quite often, a poet may change the length of a line in order to avoid monotony or emphasize something.

Questions for Reflection

Read the following poems carefully and answer the questions.

Poem 1
Stopping by Woods on a Snowy Evening
—Robert Frost (1874−1963) (the last stanza)

The woods are lovely, dark and deep,
But I have promises to keep,
And miles to go before I sleep,
And miles to go before I sleep.

Poem 2
I Like to See It Lap the Miles—
—Emily Dickinson (1830−1886)

I like to see it lap the Miles—
And lick the Valleys up—

And stop to feed itself at Tanks—
And then—prodigious step

Around a Pile of Mountains—   5
And supercilious peer
In Shanties—by the sides of Roads—
And then a Quarry pare

To fit its Ribs
And crawl between   10
Complaining all the while
In horrid—hooting stanza—
Then chase itself down Hill—

And neigh like Boanerges—
Then—prompter than a Star   15
Stop—docile and omnipotent
At it's own stable door—

Questions

1. Read the two poems carefully and analyze their metrical patterns.
2. How do the metrical patterns help with the expression of feeling and conveying of idea?

■ Form

> No verse can be free; it must be governed by some measure, but not by the old measure.
>
> —Williams Carlos Williams, "On Measure"
>
> (Kirszner & Mandell 2006, 976)

The form of a literary text refers to its structure or shape. Different parts of the text come together to form a whole. Poetic form means the design of a poem described considering rhyme, meter, and stanzaic pattern (Kirszner & Mandell 2006, 977).

The form of poetry involves its patterns of organization which touch on sound, image, syntax, structure (closed form and open form) and stanza(s).

Syntax refers to

the grammatical structure of words in sentences and the deployment of sentences in longer units throughout the poem (DiYanni 2000, 449).

Certain syntax, say, featured by repeated or abruptly broken off lines, may somehow help to express meanings and convey feelings. For example, "Those Winter Sundays" is featured by normal word order and varied length of sentence (short sentences for emphasis), question and repetition (to emphasize remembrance of the speaker's father, and his regret at his belated understanding). In "Stopping by Woods on a Snowy Evening," emphasis is made via inversion or the reversal of the standard order of words in a line. Further, the syntax is characterized by the variations in tempo among the four stanzas via punctuation and grammatical form, which help to heighten its expressiveness and to control its tone (DiYanni 2000, 449−450).

Structure: Closed Form and Open Form

Until the 20th century, poems were mostly written in closed (or fixed) form, "characterized by regular patterns of meter, rhyme, line and stanzaic divisions" (Kirszner & Mandell 2006, 978). Further,

A closed form (or fixed form) poem looks symmetrical; it has an identifiable, repeated pattern, with lines of similar length arranged in groups of two, three, four, or more. Such poems also tend to rely on regular metrical patterns and rhyme schemes (Kirszner & Mandell 2006, 978).

Regular form helps with recitation and memory and it is also a way to differentiate poetry from prose. However, excessive regularity may lead to poems constrained and filled with "dull rhyme" as commented by Keats in his poem "If by Dull Rhymes Our English Must Be Chain'd (1819)."

If by Dull Rhymes Our English Must Be Chain'd

—John Keats (1795−1821)

If by dull rhymes our English must be chain'd,
  And, like Andromeda, the Sonnet sweet
Fetter'd, in spite of pained loveliness;
Let us find out, if we must be constrain'd,
  Sandals more interwoven and complete
To fit the naked foot of poesy;
Let us inspect the lyre, and weigh the stress
Of every chord, and see what may be gain'd
  By ear industrious, and attention meet:
Misers of sound and syllable, no less
  Than Midas of his coinage, let us be
Jealous of dead leaves in the bay wreath crown;
So, if we may not let the Muse be free,
  She will be bound with garlands of her own.

Some poets choose to follow the regularity so as to highlight its significance. For example, Billy Collins (1941–), "in the playful sonnet, experimented with imagery, figures of speech, allusion, and other techniques, stretching closed form to its limits" (Kirszner & Mandell 2006, 978).

Sonnet (1999)

—Billy Collins

All we need is fourteen lines, well, thirteen now,
and after this one just a dozen
to launch a little ship on love's storm-tossed seas,
then only ten more left like rows of beans.
How easily it goes unless you get Elizabethan   5
and insist the iambic bongos must be played
and rhymes positioned at the ends of lines,
one for every station of the cross.
But hang on here while we make the turn
into the final six where all will be resolved,   10
where longing and heartache will find an end,
where Laura will tell Petrarch to put down his pen,
take off those crazy medieval tights,
blow out the lights, and come at last to bed.

Throughout the history of literature, poets have been practicing new ways to express their ideas. Many poets learned from other cultures as well as carrying on traditional approaches. Take British and American poets for example.

[They] adopted (and still use) early French forms, such as the villanelle and the sestina, and early Italian forms, such as the Petrarchan sonnet and ternza rima. The 19th-century American poet Henry Wadsworth studied Icelandic epics; the 20th-century poet Ezra Pound studied the works of French troubadours; and Pound and other 20th-century American poets, such as Richard Wright and Carolyn Kizer, were inspired by Japanese Haiku. Other American poets, such as Vachel Lindsay, Langston Hughes, and Maya Angelou, looked closer to home —to the rhythms of blues, jazz, and spirituals—for inspiration (Kirszner & Mandell 2006, 978).

Despite the consistant popularity of closed form poetry throughout history, more poets have begun to experiment with new ways of expression. One type is called open form poetry (sometimes called free verse or vers libre),

varying line length within a poem, dispensing with stanzaic division, breaking lines in unexpected places, and even abandoning any semblance of formal structure (Kirszner & Mandell 2006, 978).

Poets such as William Blake and Mathew Arnold practiced writing poems with irregular meter and length, while Walt Whitman used long lines in his poems, similar to prose. Poetry of Imagism often tends to have unconventional rhythms and meters. These practices demonstrate the typical features of open form poems.

Poets, then and now, may prefer closed or open forms based on their aesthetical, cultural or idiosyncratic preferences. Innovation always takes place. For example, some poets may mix the two forms together within a single poem. They may use irregular meter or a traditional sonnet rhyme scheme, or change its lines and stanzas. They may have a preference for blank verse which is

unrhymed poetry with each line written in a set of five stressed and five unstressed syllables called iambic pentameter (Kirszner & Mandell 2006, 979).

The following selection of Shakespeare's *Hamlet* is an example of blank verse.

To sleep! Perchance to dream:—ay, there's the rub;
For in that sleep of death what dreams may come,
When we have shuffled off this mortal coil,
Must give us pause: there's the respect
That makes calamity of so long life[.]

(Kirszner & Mandell 2006, 979)

Questions for Reflection

Read the following poem carefully and answer the questions.

Ex-Basketball Player (1958)

—John Updike (1932−2009)

Pearl Avenue runs past the high-school lot,
Bends with the trolley tracks, and stops, cut off
Before it has a chance to go two blocks,
At Colonel McComsky Plaza. Berth's Garage
Is on the corner facing west, and there,   5
Most days, you'll find Flick Webb, who helps Berth out.

Flick stands tall among the idiot pumps—
Five on a side, the old bubble-head style,
Their rubber elbows hanging loose and low.
One's nostrils are two S's, and his eyes   10
An E and O. And one is squat, without
A head at all—more of a football type.

Once Flick played for the high-school team, the Wizards.
He was good: in fact, the best. In '46

He bucketed three hundred ninety points, 15

A county record still. The ball loved Flick.

I saw him rack up thirty-eight or forty

In one home game. His hands were like wild birds.

He never learned a trade, he just sells gas,

Checks oil, and changes flats. Once in a while, 20

As a gag, he dribbles an inner tube,

But most of us remember anyway.

His hands are fine and nervous on the lug wrench.

It makes no difference to the lug wrench, though.

Off work, he hangs around Mae's Luncheonette. 25

Grease-gray and kind of coiled, he plays pinball,

Smokes those thin cigars, nurses lemon phosphates.

Flick seldom says a word to Mae, just nods

Beyond her face toward bright applauding tiers

Of Necco Wafers, Nibs, and Juju Beads. 30

Questions

1. What are the characteristics of "Ex-Basketball Player" as a blank verse?
2. How do the formal features help highlight the theme of the poem?

In the contemporary period, open form sometimes turns into prose poems. Milosz's "Christopher Robin" is an example.

Christopher Robin (1998)

—Czeslaw Milosz (1911–2004)

In April of 1996 the international press carried the news of the death,
at age seventy-five, of Christopher Robin Milne, immortalized
in a book by his father, A. A. Milne, Winnie-the-Pooh, as Christopher Robin.

I must think suddenly of matters too difficult for a bear of little
brain. I have never asked myself what lies beyond the place
where we live, I and Rabbit, Piglet and Eeyore, with our friend
Christopher Robin. That is, we continued to live here, and
nothing changed, and I just ate my little something. Only 5
Christopher Robin left for a moment.

Owl says that immediately beyond our garden Time begins,

and that it is an awfully deep well. If you fall in it, you go
down and down, very quickly, and no one knows what happens
to you next. I was a bit worried about Christopher Robin falling   10
in, but he came back and then I asked him about the well.
"Old bear," he answered. "I was in it and I was falling and I
was changing as I fell. My legs became long, I was a big person,
I wore trousers down to the ground, I had a gray beard, then
I grew old, hunched, and I walked with a cane, and then I   15
died. It was probably just a dream, it was quite unreal. The
only real thing was you, old bear, and our shared fun. Now I
won't go anywhere, even if I'm called for an afternoon snack."

Questions for Reflection

Read the poem "The Colonel" and then answer the questions.

The Colonel (1978)

—Carolyn Forche (1950–   )

What you have heard is true. I was in his house. His wife carried
a tray of coffee and sugar. His daughter filed her nails, his son went
out for the night. There were daily papers, pet dogs, a pistol on the
cushion beside him. The moon swung bare on its black cord over
the house. On the television was a cop show. It was in English.   5
Broken bottles were embedded in the walls around the house to
scoop the kneecaps from a man's legs or cut his hands to lace. On
the windows there were gratings like those in liquor stores. We had
dinner, rack of lamb, good wine, a gold bell was on the table for
calling the maid. The maid brought green mangoes, salt, a type of   10
bread. I was asked how I enjoyed the country. There was a brief
commercial in Spanish. His wife took everything away. There was
some talk then of how difficult it had become to govern. The parrot
said hello on the terrace. The colonel told it to shut up, and pushed
himself from the table. My friend said to me with his eyes: say   15
nothing. The colonel returned with a sack used to bring groceries
home. He spilled many human ears on the table. They were like
dried peach halves. There is no other way to say this. He took one
of them in his hands, shook it in our faces, dropped it into a water
glass. It came alive there. I am tired of fooling around he said. As   20
for the rights of anyone, tell your people they can go fuck themselves. He swept the ears to the floor with his arm and held the last
of his wine in the air. Something for your poetry, no? he said. Some

of the ears on the floor caught this scrap of his voice. Some of the

ears on the floor were pressed to the ground.   25

Questions

1. Is this poetry or prose? Why?
2. What is the form?
3. How does the form of the "The Colonel" help to communicate its theme?

The form of poetry also has much to do with its stanza.

[Generally,] a stanza is a group of two or more lines with the same metrical pattern—and often with a regular rhyme as well—separated by blank space from other such groups of lines. The stanza in poetry is like the paragraph in prose: it groups related thoughts into units (Kirszner & Mandell 2006, 979).

A stanza may have different lines, from two to eight, and rhyme plays an important role.

A two-line stanza with rhyming lines of similar length and meter is called a couplet. The heroic couplet, first used by Geoffrey Chaucer and especially popular throughout the eighteenth century, consists of two rhymed lines of iambic pentameter, with a weak pause after the first line and a strong pause after the second. For example,

True ease in writing comes from art, not chance,

As those move easiest who have learned to dance.

(from Alexander Pope's *An Essay on Criticism*)

A three-line stanza with lines of similar length and a set rhyme scheme is called a tercet. Percy Bysshe Shelley's "Ode to the West Wind" is built largely on tercets.

O wild West Wind, thou breath of Autumn's being,

Thou, from whose unseen presence the leaves dead

Are driven, like ghosts from an enchanter fleeing,

Yellow, and black, and pale, and hectic red,

Pestilence-stricken multitudes: O thou,

Who chariotest to their dark wintry bed

A four-line stanza with lines of similar length and a set rhyme scheme is called a quatrain. For example, Wadsworth's "She Dwelt among the Untrodden Ways":

A violet by a mossy stone

Half hidden from the eye!

—Fair as a star, when only one

Is shining in the sky.

(Kirszner & Mandell 2006, 980)

Contemporary poets also prefer quatrains. Examples can be found in Roethke's "My Papa's Waltz," Adrienne Rich's "Aunt Jennifer's Tiger," and Robert Frost's "Stopping by Woods on a

Snowy Evening."

Sonnet

A most popular form of poetry is sonnet, a fourteen-line poem usually written in iambic pentameter. A sonnet is strictly constrained in form so that it is considered poetry with a closed or fixed form.

The Shakespearean or English sonnet falls into three quatrains or four-line sections with rhyme pattern *abab cdcd efef* followed by a couplet or pair of rhymed lines with the pattern *gg*.... the Petrarchan or Italian sonnet... falls into two parts: an octave of eight lines and a sestet of six. The octave thyme pattern is *abba abba* (two sets of four lines); the sestet's lines are more variable: *cde cde*; or *ced ced*; or *cd cd cd* (DiYanni 2000, 474).

Questions for Reflection

Read the following poems and analyze their structural features.

Poem 1

That Time of Year Thou Mayst in Me Behold (Sonnet 73) (1609)

—William Shakespeare (1564–1616)

That time of year thou mayst in me behold
When yellow leaves, or none, or few, do hang
Upon those boughs which shake against the cold,
Bare ruined choirs, where late the sweet birds sang.
In me thou see'st the twilight of such day   5
As after sunset fadeth in the west;
Which by and by black night doth take away,
Death's second self, that seals up all in rest.
In me thou see'st the glowing of such fire,
That on the ashes of his youth doth lie,   10
As the deathbed whereon it must expire,
Consumed with that which it was nourished by.
  This thou perceiv'st, which makes thy love more strong,
  To love that well which thou must leave ere long.

Poem 2

On First Looking into Chapman's Homer

—John Keats(1795–1821)

Much have I traveled in the realms of gold,

And many goodly states and kingdoms seen;

    Round many western islands have I been

Which bards in fealty to Apollo hold.

Oft of one wide expanse had I been told   5

    That deep-brow'd Homer ruled as his demesne;

    Yet did I never breathe its pure serene

Till I heard Chapman speak out loud and bold:

Then felt I like some watcher of the skies

    When a new planet swims into his ken;   10

Or like stout Cortez when with eagle eyes

    He star'd at the Pacific—and all his men

Look'd at each other with a wild surmise—

    Silent, upon a peak in Darien.

■ Theme

In reading poetry, discovering the theme(s) is of great importance. As discussed before, a theme is defined as

> an abstraction or generalization drawn from the details of a literary work... [It] refers to an idea or intellectually apprehensible meaning inherent and implicit in a work (DiYnanni 2000, 86−87).

Or put another way,

> in general terms, theme refers to the ideas the poet explores, the concerns the poem examines. More specifically, a poem's theme is its main point or idea (Kirszner & Mandell 2006, 775).

Poems may deal with a variety of subjects such as love, war, heroism, nature, gender identity, courage, perseverance, or the folly of human desires. Meanwhile, themes are the concerns and ideas of these subjects. For example,

> poems "about nature" may praise the beauty of nature, assert the superiority of its simplest creatures over humans, consider its evanescence, or mourn its destruction. Similarly, poems "about death" may examine the difficulty of facing one's own mortality, eulogize a friend, assert the need for the acceptance of life's cycles, cry out against death's inevitability, or explore the carpe diem theme ("Life is brief, so let us seize the day") (Kirszner & Mandell 2006, 775).

It should be noted that over simplicity or distortion must be avoided considering the analysis of the theme(s). A single perspective is quite often incomplete. The alleged "theme" or "themes" may vary from person to person due to the differences in experiences, aesthetically or culturally.

Determining a theme is a complex task involving profound consideration to the elements of the literary work, say, certain poems here, as well as to the extra-text information of or concerning the work (poem).

For example, Langston Hughes's "Dream Deferred" emphasizes African American people's indignation against racial oppression. William Wordsworth's "Daffodils" manifests a strong appreciation for integration of man and nature. Hayden's "Those Winter Sundays" highlights "a father's loving concern for his family," or "the speaker's remorse about his indifference to his father;" Roethke's "My Papa's Waltz" reveals "the complexity of the speaker's response to his memories of father and their bedtime ritual" rather than "a child's terror at his father's horseplay" (DiYnanni 2000, 482−483). Frost's "Stopping by Woods on a Snowy Evening" may underline (possibly simultaneously)

> the necessity to face the responsibilities inherent in adult life [...]; a tension in our lives between our desire for rest and peace and our need to fulfill responsibilities and meet obligations [...]; the seductiveness of death as an attractive way of escaping the pressures of circumstance and the weight of responsibility [...]; [and / or] the ability of man to appreciate [...] the beauty of nature (DiYnanni 2000, 483).

Further, perhaps more can be said as to the central ideas expressed in Frost's "Stopping by Woods on a Snowy Evening." Life is intermingled with beautiful things and difficulties and hardship. Though life is not easy, people should go ahead and struggle to the last minute. Life is tiring though sometimes it is pleasurable. Perhaps to be a human means to fight, to toil, and to struggle in the earthly world. Or life means long-time labor plus temporary enjoyment. Interpretations may go on along with the change of readers or the change of their experiences. Different interpretations of the theme suggest varied perspectives.

To give further illustrations, Robinson's "Miniver Cheevy" is taken as another example to the discovery of the possible themes.

Miniver Cheevy (1910)
—Edwin Arlington Robinson (1869−1935)

Miniver Cheevy, child of scorn,
   Grew lean while he assailed the seasons;
He wept that he was ever born,
   And he had reasons.

Miniver loved the days of old   5
   When swords were bright and steeds were prancing;
The vision of a warrior bold
   Would set him dancing.

Miniver sighed for what was not,
    And dreamed, and rested from his labors;   10
He dreamed of Thebes and Camelot,
    And Priam's neighbors.

Miniver mourned the ripe renown
    That made so many a name so fragrant;
He mourned Romance, now on the town,   15
    And Art, a vagrant.

Miniver loved the Medici,
    Albeit he had never seen one;
He would have sinned incessantly
    Could he have been one.   20

Miniver cursed the commonplace
    And eyed a khaki suit with loathing;
He missed the medieval grace
    Of iron clothing.

Miniver scorned the gold he sought,   25
    But sore annoyed was he without it;
Miniver thought, and thought, and thought,
    And thought about it.

Miniver Cheevy, born too late,
    Scratched his head and kept on thinking;   30
Miniver coughed, and called it fate,
    And kept on drinking.

The theme of the poem is modern men's vexation and despair as caused by their sense of misplacement in time and by their strong emotional affiliation to the past. These people seem to have been born in wrong times so that they become incongruous in the present. Moreover, they have developed a strong love of the past time so that they seem to be suited more to an earlier time or style. The poem also alludes to the contradiction of modern men who worship money but meanwhile cherish the noble spirit disregarding for wealth. Miniver Cheevy is the one that best represents such kind of people.

Miniver Cheevy regretted that he was born in a world of defiance and resentment ["He wept that he was ever born" (Line 3)], and it was in a wrong place and wrong time for him ["child of scorn" (Line 1), "born too late" (Line 29)]. As a result, he seemed to have passed his days in a miserable way ["grew lean while he assailed the seasons" (Line 2)]. Why? He had his own reasons because he bore with him good hopes and dreams. He expected he should have been born in the ancient heroic age. So, he would become wild with joy at the thought of the ancient time when the brave soldiers with iron clothes fought on robust horses ["the vision of a warrior bold/ Would set him dancing" (Lines 7−8)]. He dreamed to be one of them. Unfortunately, he was not ["Miniver sighed for what was not" (Line 9), "born too late" (Line 29)]. What a pity! Miniver had a painful longing for the highly advanced ancient time when so many fighters became well-known (Lines 4−7). He admired their heroic deeds, exploits, glory and fame ["the ripe renown," "That made so many a name so fragrant" (Lines 13−14)]. Consequently, he even disliked the ordinary people simply because they wore common clothes made of khaki. They did not wear iron clothes like the ancient warriors ["cursed the commonplace", "eyed a khaki suit with loathing", "missed the medieval grace/Of iron clothing" (Lines 21−24)]! He felt very much sorry that Romance had been reduced to be chargeable to the parish ["on the town" (Line 15)]. He had a strong love for arts, but unfortunately it had become something unsettled. In other words, the holy, sacred nature was gone ["And Art, a vagrant" (Line 16)]. His passion for art drove him to love the Medici for the noble and powerful family in Florence always made donations to the art field. But he despised the Medici members perhaps because of the treacherous and tricky characters of these rich businessmen. Here, together with Miniver's attitude toward money in later lines, the man's paradoxical state of mind was distinctly displayed ["loved the Medici... / He would have sinned incessantly/Could he have been one." (Lines 17−20) and "Miniver scorned the gold he sought, /But sore annoyed was he without it;" (Lines 25−26)]. Like many people, he loved money but in the meantime showed strong resentment toward money. Facing all the puzzlement, difficulties, what did he do? Miniver did nothing but just keep on thinking. He blamed his bad fortune. He put all his failure and inability down to the alleged poor fate. To top it off, he drowned his worries in drink. He became numb. The image of Miniver Cheevy corresponds well to the possible themes of the poem.

Questions for Reflection

Read the following poems carefully and answer the questions.

Poem 1

Crumbling Is not an Instant's Act

—Emily Dickinson (1830−1886)

Crumbling is not an instant's Act
A fundamental pause
Dilapidation's processes
Are organized Decays—

'Tis first a Cobweb on the Soul

A Cuticle of Dust
A Borer in the Axis
An Elemental Rust—

Ruin is formal—Devil's work
Consecutive and slow—
Fail in an instant, no man did
Slipping—is Crashe's law—

Questions

1. How do you understand the opening line of the poem?
2. What do you think the theme of the poem is? Why?

Poem 2

A Woman Mourned by Daughters (1984)

—Adrienne Rich (1929–2012)

Now, not a tear begun,
we sit here in your kitchen,
spent, you see, already.
You are swollen till you strain
this house and the whole sky.   5
You, whom we so often
succeeded in ignoring!
You are puffed up in death
like a corpse pulled from the sea;
we groan beneath your weight.   10
And yet you were a leaf,
a straw blown on the bed,
you had long since become
crisp as a dead insect.
What is it, if not you,   15
that settles on us now
like satins you pulled down
over our bridal heads?
What rises in our throats
like food you prodded in?   20
Nothing could be enough.
You breathe upon us now

through solid assertions
of yourself: teaspoons, goblets,
seas of carpet, a forest   25
of old plants to be watered,
an old man in an adjoining
room to be touched and fed.
And all this universe
dares us to lay a finger   30
anywhere, save exactly
as you would wish it done.

Questions

1. What are the possible themes of the poem?
2. Which elements of poetry help with your interpretation of the themes?
3. In reading the poem, what attract(s) your attention the most? Why?

Part 3

Drama

♂ Chapter 9 ♥
An Overview

Drama is a staged art, but it is meant to be read whereas a play is written to be performed. According to Professor J. M. Manly, there are three necessary elements in drama: "(1) a story (2) told in action (3) by actors who impersonate the characters of the story" (Holman & Harmon 1986, 154).

Drama develops primarily via dialogue. The plot and action of drama unfold on stage when the characters interact with each other. A dramatic work does not have a narrator like in fiction. Instead the absence of a narrator is made up using the dramatic techniques such as monologue, soliloquy, and asides as well as stage directions, makeup, costumes, scenery, and lighting. Here it is worth noting that monolgue is different from soliloquy.

> By convention, a monologue is a speech that represents what someone would speak aloud in a situation with listeners, although they do not speak; the monologue therefore differs somewhat from the soliloquy, which is a speech that represents what someone is thinking inwardly, without listener... Hamlet's famous soliloquy, "To be or not to be," is an obvious example (Holman & Harmon 1986, 311; 475).

Simply speaking, monologue means that the speaker speaks to the audience while soliloquy, the speaker speaks to himself (or he thinks aloud).

Asides refer to "brief comments by an actor who addresses the audience but is not heard by the other characters" (Kirszner & Mandell 2006, 1289). This technique is used to reveal the thoughts of the speaker. "By a custom of the theater, the speaker of an aside is assumed to be telling the truth" (Holman & Harmon 1986, 41).

Questions for Reflection

1. How much do you know about drama?
2. What is your favorite play? Why?

❦ Chapter 10 ❦
Types of Drama

Traditionally there are two types of drama: tragedy and comedy. Tragedy, just as the name suggests, refers to an event with a poor or sad ending while comedy, a happy ending. Tragedy induces tears while comedy calls forth laughter. Tragedy and comedy stand for different ways of looking at the world.

> The comic view celebrates life and affirms it; it is typically joyous and festive. The tragic view highlights life's sorrows; it is typically brooding and solemn. Tragic plays end unhappily, often with the death of the hero; comedies usually end happily, often with a celebration such as a marriage. Both comedy and tragedy contain changes of fortune, with the fortunes of comic characters turning from bad to good and those of tragic characters from good to bad (DiYanni 2000, 740).

■ Tragedy

In literature, tragedy, as defined in *Merriam-Webster's Collegiate Dictionary*, traditionally refers to

> a serious drama [that] typically describing a conflict between the protagonist and a superior force (as destiny) and haing a sorrowful or disastrous conclusion that excites pity or terror (*Merriam-Webster's Collegiate Dictionary*).

According to Aristotle, a tragedy is a drama "treating a serious subject and involving persons of significance" (Kirszner & Mandell 2006, 1298). Moreover, the protagonist of a tragedy, as Aristotle put it,

> is neither all good nor all evil, but a mixture of the two. [He or she] is... more exalted and [possesses] some weakness or flaw—perhaps narrowness of vision or overwhelming pride, [which] is typically the element that creates the condition for tragedy (Kirszner & Mandell 2006, 1298).

In Shakespeare's plays, the tragic protagonists are vividly portrayed. Macbeth was once a brave general of King Duncan's army. But his greediness for the crown and his cruelty to maintain his position led to his downfall. Finally Macbeth was disrupted by wronged ghosts and tortured by guilt for his crimes. He was killed by the avenger Macduff in action. Timon's unscrupulous generosity and his narrow vision of friendship brought him betrayal by his alleged "friends" whom he had once helped. Timon was also hypocritical for he gave money to those (hangers-on) who merely showed a slight love or gratitude to him. His eagerness to earn a reputation as a generous and affectionate nobleman was the root of his tragedy.

Irony is an integral part of tragedy. There are dramatic irony (or tragic irony) and cosmic irony (or irony of fate).

> Dramatic irony emerges from a situation in which the audience knows more about the dramatic situation than a character does (Kirszner & Mandell 2006, 1298) .

In other words, the meaning of the words or acts of a character may be

> unperceived by the character but understood by the audience. The irony resides in the contrast between the meaning intended by the speaker and the different significance by others (Holman & Harmon 1986, 158) .

When Oedipus declares that anybody who violates the gods shall be exiled as punishment, the audience knows that he is actually saying something about himself, though of course Oedipus does not know that.

Cosmic irony has something to do with fate and naivety of the characters. It

> occurs when God, fate, or some larger, uncontrollable force seems to be intentionally deceiving characters into believing that they can escape their fate. Too late, they realize that trying to avoid their destiny is futile (Kirszner & Mandell 2006, 1299) .

Oedipus's birth parents (King Laius and Queen Jocasta of Thebes), as well as Oedipus later, believed that they could prevent the occurrence of Apollo's prophecy so that they made endeavors to change the situation. Ironically all their efforts were in vain. Oedipus finally ended up killing his father and marrying his mother. His errors damaged his city and family.

There is another point in a tragedy that is also of great importance. It is the ultimate recognition of the reasons for his or her unfortunate outcome by the tragic protagonist.

> This recognition (and accompanying acceptance) elevate tragic protagonists to grandeur and give their suffering meaning. Without this recognition, there would be no tragedy, just pathos—suffering that exists simply to satisfy the sentimental or morbid sensibilities of the audience (Kirszner & Mandell 2006, 1299) .

As a result, King Lear died "a humbled but enlightened man" (Kirszner & Mandell 2006, 1298) for he realized (in his insanity) the nature of power and his vanity in the past. Othello, having recognized his fault, died honorably and bravely with his love, whom he had killed because of his misunderstanding of her. Tragedy may strike a responsive chord in the hearts of readers or an audience who may possibly have similar reactions to that of the tragic heroes. They watch (in their mind's eye) the dramatic action which will somehow help them remove strong or violent emotions. That is why tragedies are not discouraging. As commented by Aristotle,

> the pity and fear aroused in the audience are purged or released and the audience experiences a cleansing of those emotions and a sense of relief that the action is over (DiYanni

2000, 741).

Perhaps tragedy helps to improve human character and morality. Either that or people feel exalted along with tragic heroes.

Ideas about tragic protagonists have been changing. Traditionally, the protagonist, as Aristotle put it, should be someone exceptional, say, a king, or a noble figure. Thus, historical personage, mythical figures, kings, princes, dukes, or great generals are the central characters in the play. However these figures are quite often replaced later by protagonists of lesser rank such as Romeo and Juliet, and ordinary people like Willy Loman in Arthur Miller's *Death of a Salesman*. The change in characterization shed much light on the shift in the themes of tragedy too. The deep-rooted social restrictions in contrast with the courage of ordinary people to rise from the mediocre lives, and their sufferings have also become the themes. For instances, the protagonists of the Naturalist plays are destroyed "not by the gods or by fate but by poverty, animal drives or social class" (Kirszner & Mandell 2006, 1300).

■ Comedy

In contrast with tragedy, comedy refers to "a light form of drama that aims to amuse and that ends happily" (Holman & Harmon 1986, 98). To amuse, it is inevitable and necessary to appeal to wit and humor.

> In general, the comic effect arises from a recognition of some incongruity of speech, action, or character... Viewed in another sense, comedy may be considered to deal with people in their human state, restrained and often made ridiculous by their limitations, faults, bodily functions, and animal nature (Holman & Harmon 1986, 98).

In comedy, the reversals of fortunes and misjudgment finally bring about success, victory, and happiness. Comic protagonists are often ordinary figures. Sometimes comic characters are stereotypical and seem to be flat or one-dimensional. More often than not, the narrative is stereotypical too.

> Cinderella stories like these are the staples of comedy: an impoverished student inherits a fortune; a beggar turns out to be a prince; a wife (or husband or child) presumed dead turns up alive and well; the war (between nations, classes, families, the sexes) ends, the two sides are reconciled and everybody lives happily ever after (DiYanni 2000, 742).

However, it is evident that not all the characters in a comedy have a happy ending. At least one character suffers or many undergo hardships. In this sense, comedy can be classified into satiric comedy and romantic comedy.

Satiric comedy "exposes human folly, criticizes human conduct, and aims to correct it" (DiYanni 2000, 742). Examples are seen in Oliver Goldsmith's *She Stoops to Conquer*, George

Bernard Shaw's *Pygmalion*, Moliere's *Tartuffe* and the Russian comedic plays such as *The Milliner's Shop* by Ivan Krylov and *The Headstrong Turk* by Kozma Prutkov.

Romantic comedy "portrays characters gently, even generously; its spirit is more tolerant and its tone more genial" (DiYanni 2000, 742). Despite the hardships the protagonists have gone through or the tortures they have endured, the tone is generally delightful and entertaining. Shakespeare's *A Midsummer Night's Dream* is a typical example of romantic comedy.

Questions for Reflection

1. In terms of Aristotle's remarks, how is *Oedipus* regarded as a typical tragedy?
2. Read Shakespeare's *A Midsummer Night's Dream* and then write an essay to comment on its comedy effects.

♂ Chapter 11 ♄
Reading Drama: the Basic Approaches

Like reading fiction and poetry, reading drama also involves the three approaches of experiencing, interpreting, and evaluating. Though classified as three steps, they usually take place around the same time. While reading, readers show their emotional response, associating personal or shared experiences to the text (script). Further, readers try to interpret it, to make sense of the script and to figure out the implied meanings. There are the varied possible meanings to be examined, so readers are expected to have a good knowledge of the basic elements and characteristics of drama in order to interpret a script reasonably and understand it better. Finally, readers often make judgments about what they are reading in accordance to their subjective response and intellectual interpretation of the script. They make comments on the quality of the dramatic script and assess the cultural, social and moral values embodied in the monologue, soliloquy, or dialogue of characters, the voiceover, stage directions, and the plot. Readers pay attention to the literary and theatrical artistry of the drama/play. The three approaches all involve the individual elements of a drama and their functions within a dramatic work. Each approach affects the other and they are interconnected to form the whole process of reading drama. Since a play is meant to be performed, reading drama concerns the "apprehension of the ongoing performance either on stage or in [the] mind's eye [of readers]" (DiYanni 2000, 730).

To sum up, the approach of experiencing is mostly concerned with how a drama affects the readers, the interpretation involves what the drama means or signifies to the readers, and the evaluation depends on what values are displayed in the drama (for example in its speech and action). These values may refer to both those of the character(s) and those of the (implied) author.

To show the different but quite often simultaneous steps in reading drama, the first Act of *Death of a Salesman* (1949) by Arthur Miller (1915 −2005) is analyzed. The examples in the analyses hereafter from the playscript may include those from other parts of the text which, because of limited space, have not been included in the excerpt. For this reason, examples quoted from the playscript are noted in reference to Kirszner & Mandell's book rather than this selection.

Death of a Salesman (1949)
—Arthur Miller

Act Ⅰ

A melody is heard, played upon a flute. It is small and fine, telling of grass and trees and the horizon. The curtain rises.

Before us is the Salesman's house. We are aware of towering, angular shapes behind it, surrounding it on all sides. Only the blue light of the sky falls upon the house and forestage; the surrounding area shows an angry glow of orange. As more light appears, we see a solid vault of apartment houses around the small, fragile-seeming home. An air of the dream clings to the place, a dream rising out of reality. The kitchen at center seems actual enough, for there is a kitchen table with three chairs, and a refrigerator. But no other fixtures are seen. At the back of the kitchen there is a draped entrance, which leads to the living room. To the right of the kitchen, on a level raised two feet, is a bedroom furnished only with a brass bedstead and a straight chair. On a shelf over the bed a silver athletic trophy stands. A window opens onto the apartment house at the side.

Behind the kitchen, on a level raised six and a half feet, is the boys' bedroom, at present barely visible. Two beds are dimly seen, and at the back of the room a dormer window. (This bedroom is above the unseen living room.) At the left a stairway curves up to it from the kitchen.

The entire setting is wholly or, in some places, partially transparent. The roofline of the house is one-dimensional; under and over it we see the apartment buildings. Before the house lies an apron, curving beyond the forestage into the orchestra. This forward area serves as the back yard as well as the locale of all Willy's imaginings and of his city scenes. Whenever the action is in the present the actors observe the imaginary wall-lines, entering the house only through the door at the left. But in the scenes of the past these boundaries are broken, and characters enter or leave a room by stepping "through" a wall onto the forestage.

From the right, Willy Loman, the Salesman, enters, carrying two large sample cases. The flute plays on. He hears but is not aware of it. He is past sixty years of age, dressed quietly. Even as he crosses the stage to the doorway of the house, his exhaustion is apparent. He unlocks the door, comes into the kitchen, and thankfully lets his burden down, feeling the soreness of his palms. A word-sigh escapes his lips—it might be "Oh, boy, oh, boy." He closes the door, then carries his cases out into the living room, through the draped kitchen doorway.

Linda, his wife, has stirred in her bed at the right. She gets out and puts on a robe, listening. Most often jovial, she has developed an iron repression of her exceptions to Willy's behavior—she more than loves him, she admires him, as though his mercurial nature, his temper, his massive dreams and little cruelties, served her only as sharp reminders of the turbulent longings within him, longings which she shares but lacks the temperament to utter and follow to their end.

LINDA (hearing Willy outside the bedroom, calls with some trepidation): Willy!

WILLY: It's all right. I came back.

LINDA: Why? What happened? (Slight pause.) Did something happen, Willy?

WILLY: No, nothing happened.

LINDA: You didn't smash the car, did you?

WILLY (with casual irritation): I said nothing happened. Didn't you hear me?

LINDA: Don't you feel well?

WILLY: I am tired to the death. (The flute has faded away. He sits on the bed beside her, a little numb.) I couldn't make it. I just couldn't make it, Linda.

LINDA (*very carefully, delicately*): Where were you all day? You look terrible.

WILLY: I got as far as a little above Yonkers. I stopped for a cup of coffee.
Maybe it was the coffee.

LINDA: What?

WILLY (*after a pause*): I suddenly couldn't drive any more. The car kept going off onto the shoulder, y'know?

LINDA (*helpfully*): Oh. Maybe it was the steering again. I don't think Angelo knows the Studebaker.

WILLY: No, it's me, it's me. Suddenly I realize I'm goin' sixty miles an hour and I don't remember the last five minutes. I'm—I can't seem to—keep my mind to it.

LINDA: Maybe it's your glasses. You never went for your new glasses.

WILLY: No, I see everything. I came back ten miles an hour. It took me nearly four hours from Yonkers.

LINDA (*resigned*): Well, you'll just have to take a rest. Willy, you can't continue this way.

WILLY: I just got back from Florida.

LINDA: But you didn't rest your mind. Your mind is overactive, and the mind is what counts, dear.

WILLY: I'll start out in the morning. Maybe I'll feel better in the morning. (*She is taking off his shoes.*) These goddam arch supports are killing me.

LINDA: Take an aspirin. Should I get you an aspirin? It'll soothe you.

WILLY (*with wonder*): I was driving along, you understand? And I was fine. I was even observing the scenery. You can imagine, me looking at scenery, on the road every week of my life. But it's so beautiful up there. Linda, the trees are so thick, and the sun is warm. I opened the windshield and just let the warm air bathe over me. And then all of a sudden I'm goin' off the road! I'm tellin'ya, I absolutely forgot I was driving. If I'd've gone the other way over the white line I might've killed somebody. So I went on again—and five minutes later I'm dreamin' again, and I nearly... (*He presses two fingers against his eyes.*) I have such thoughts, I have such strange thoughts.

LINDA: Willy, dear. Talk to them again. There's no reason why you can't work in New York.

WILLY: They don't need me in New York. I'm the New England man. I'm vital in New England.

LINDA: But you're sixty years old. They can't expect you to keep travelling every week.

WILLY: I'll have to send a wire to Portland. I'm supposed to see Brown and Morrison tomorrow morning at ten o'clock to show the line. Goddammit, I could sell them! (*He starts putting on his jacket.*)

LINDA (*taking the jacket from him*): Why don't you go down to the place tomorrow and tell Howard you've simply got to work in New York? You're too accommodating, dear.

WILLY: If old man Wagner was alive I'd a been in charge of New York now! That man was a prince, he was a masterful man. But that boy of his, that Howard, he don't appreciate. When I went north the first time, the Wagner Company didn't know where New England was!

LINDA: Why don't you tell those things to Howard, dear?

WILLY (*encouraged*): I will, I definitely will. Is there any cheese?

LINDA: I'll make you a sandwich.

WILLY: No, go to sleep. I'll take some milk. I'll be up right away. The boys in?

LINDA: They're sleeping. Happy took Biff on a date tonight.

WILLY (*interested*): That so?

LINDA: It was so nice to see them shaving together, one behind the other, in the bathroom. And going out together. You notice? The whole house smells of shaving lotion.

WILLY: Figure it out. Work a lifetime to pay off a house. You finally own it, and there's nobody to live in it.

LINDA: Well, dear, life is a casting off. It's always that way.

WILLY: No, no, some people-some people accomplish something. Did Biff say anything after I went this morning?

LINDA: You shouldn't have criticised him, Willy, especially after he just got off the train. You mustn't lose your temper with him.

WILLY: When the hell did I lose my temper? I simply asked him if he was making any money. Is that a criticism?

LINDA: But, dear, how could he make any money?

WILLY (*worried and angered*): There's such an undercurrent in him. He became a moody man. Did he apologize when I left this morning?

LINDA: He was crestfallen, Willy. You know how he admires you. I think if he finds himself, then you'll both be happier and not fight any more.

WILLY: How can he find himself on a farm? Is that a life? A farmhand? In the beginning, when he was young, I thought, well, a young man, it's good for him to tramp around, take a lot of different jobs. But it's more than ten years now and he has yet to make thirty-five dollars a week!

LINDA: He's finding himself, Willy.

WILLY: Not finding yourself at the age of thirty-four is a disgrace!

LINDA: Shh!

WILLY: The trouble is he's lazy, goddammit!

LINDA: Willy, please!

WILLY: Biff is a lazy bum!

LINDA: They're sleeping. Get something to eat. Go on down.

WILLY: Why did he come home? I would like to know what brought him home.

LINDA: I don't know. I think he's still lost, Willy. I think he's very lost.

WILLY: Biff Loman is lost. In the greatest country in the world a young man with such— personal attractiveness, gets lost. And such a hard worker. There's one thing about Biff— he's not lazy.

LINDA: Never.

WILLY (*with pity and resolve*): I'll see him in the morning; I'll have a nice talk with him. I'll get him a job selling. He could be big in no time. My God! Remember how they used to follow him around in high school? When he smiled at one of them their faces lit up. When he walked down the street... (*He loses himself in reminiscences.*)

LINDA (*trying to bring him out of it*): Willy, dear, I got a new kind of American-type cheese today. It's whipped.

WILLY: Why do you get American when I like Swiss?

LINDA: I just thought you'd like a change...

WILLY: I don't want a change! I want Swiss cheese. Why am I always being contradicted?

LINDA (*with a covering laugh*): I thought it would be a surprise.

WILLY: Why don't you open a window in here, for God's sake?

LINDA (*with infinite patience*): They're all open, dear.

WILLY: The way they boxed us in here. Bricks and windows, windows and bricks.

LINDA: We should've bought the land next door.

WILLY: The street is lined with cars. There's not a breath of fresh air in the neighborhood. The grass don't grow any more. You can't raise a carrot in the back yard. They should've had a law against apartment houses. Remember those two beautiful elm trees out there? When I and Biff hung the swing between them?

LINDA: Yeah, like being a million miles from the city.

WILLY: They should've arrested the builder for cutting those down. They massacred the neighbourhood. (*Lost.*) More and more I think of those days, Linda. This time of year it was lilac and wisteria. And then the peonies would come out, and the daffodils. What fragrance in this room!

LINDA: Well, after all, people had to move somewhere.

WILLY: No, there's more people now.

LINDA: I don't think there's more people. I think.

WILLY: There's more people! That's what's ruining this country! Population is getting out of control. The competition is maddening! Smell the stink from that apartment house! And another one on the other side... How can they whip cheese?

On Willy's last line, Biff and Happy raise themselves up in their beds, listening.

LINDA: Go down, try it. And be quiet.

WILLY (*turning to Linda, guiltily*): You're not worried about me, are you, sweetheart?

BIFF: What's the matter?

HAPPY: Listen!

LINDA: You've got too much on the ball to worry about.

WILLY: You're my foundation and my support, Linda.

LINDA: Just try to relax, dear. You make mountains out of molehills.

WILLY: I won't fight with him any more. If he wants to go back to Texas, let him go.

LINDA: He'll find his way.

WILLY: Sure. Certain men just don't get started till later in life. Like Thomas Edison; I think. Or B. F. Goodrich. One of them was deaf. (*He starts for the bedroom doorway.*) I'll put my money on Biff.

LINDA: And Willy—if it's warm Sunday we'll drive in the country. And we'll open the windshield, and take lunch.

WILLY: No, the windshields don't open on the new cars.

LINDA: But you opened it today.

WILLY: Me? I didn't. (*He stops.*) Now isn't that peculiar! Isn't that a remarkable... (*He breaks off in amazement and fright as the flute is heard distantly.*)

LINDA: What, darling?

WILLY: That is the most remarkable thing.

LINDA: What, dear?

WILLY: I was thinking of the Chevvy. (*Slight pause.*) Nineteen twenty-eight... when I had that red Chevvy... (*Breaks off.*) That funny? I coulda sworn I was driving that Chevvy today.

LINDA: Well, that's nothing. Something must've reminded you.

WILLY: Remarkable. Ts. Remember those days? The way Biff used to simonize that car? The dealer refused to believe there was eighty thousand miles on it. (*He shakes his head.*) Heh! (*To Linda.*) Close your eyes. I'll be right up. (*He walks out of the bedroom.*)

HAPPY (*to Biff*): Jesus, maybe he smashed up the car again!

LINDA (*calling after Willy*): Be careful on the stairs, dear! The cheese is on the middle shelf. (*She turns, goes over to the bed, takes his jacket, and goes out of the bedroom.*)

Light has risen on the boys' room. Unseen, Willy is heard talking to himself, "eighty thousand miles," and a little laugh. Biff gets out of bed, comes downstage a bit, and stands attentively. Biff is two years older than his brother Happy, well built, but in these days bears a worn air and seems less self-assured. He has succeeded less, and his dreams are stronger and less acceptable than Happy's. Happy is tall, powerfully made. Sexuality is like a visible color on him, or a scent that many women have discovered. He, like his brother, is lost, but in a different way, for he has never allowed himself to turn his face toward defeat and is thus more confused and hard-skinned, although seemingly more content.

HAPPY (*getting out of bed*): He's going to get his license taken away if he keeps that up. I'm getting nervous about him, y'know, Biff?

BIFF: His eyes are going.

HAPPY: No, I've driven with him. He sees all right. He just doesn't keep his mind on it. I drove into the city with him last week. He stops at a green light and then it turns red and he goes. (*He laughs.*)

BIFF: Maybe he's color-blind.

HAPPY: Pop? Why he's got the finest eye for color in the business. You know that.

BIFF (*sitting down on his bed*): I'm going to sleep.

HAPPY: You're not still sour on Dad, are you, Biff?

BIFF: He's all right, I guess.

WILLY (*underneath them, in the living room*): Yes, sir, eighty thousand miles—eighty-two thousand!

BIFF: You smoking?

HAPPY (*holding out a pack of cigarettes*): Want one?

BIFF: (*taking a cigarette*): I can never sleep when I smell it.

WILLY: What a simonizing job, heh?

HAPPY (*with deep sentiment*): Funny, Biff, y'know? Us sleeping in here again? The old beds. (*He pats his bed affectionately.*) All the talk that went across those two beds, huh? Our whole lives.

BIFF: Yeah. Lotta dreams and plans.

HAPPY (*with a deep and masculine laugh*): About five hundred women would like to know what was said in this room.

They share a soft laugh.

BIFF: Remember that big Betsy something—what the hell was her name—over on Bushwick Avenue?

HAPPY (*combing his hair*): With the collie dog!

BIFF: That's the one. I got you in there, remember?

HAPPY: Yeah, that was my first time—I think. Boy, there was a pig. (*They laugh, almost crudely.*) You taught me everything I know about women. Don't forget that.

BIFF: I bet you forgot how bashful you used to be. Especially with girls.

HAPPY: Oh, I still am, Biff.

BIFF: Oh, go on.

HAPPY: I just control it, that's all. I think I got less bashful and you got more so. What happened, Biff? Where's the old humor, the old confidence? (*He shakes Biff's knee. Biff gets up and moves restlessly about the room.*) What's the matter?

BIFF: Why does Dad mock me all the time?

HAPPY: He's not mocking you, he...

BIFF: Everything I say there's a twist of mockery on his face. I can't get near him.

HAPPY: He just wants you to make good, that's all. I wanted to talk to you about Dad for a long time, Biff. Something's—happening to him. He—talks to himself.

BIFF: I noticed that this morning. But he always mumbled.

HAPPY: But not so noticeable. It got so embarrassing I sent him to Florida. And you know something? Most of the time he's talking to you.

BIFF: What's he say about me?

HAPPY: I can't make it out.

BIFF: What's he say about me?

HAPPY: I think the fact that you're not settled, that you're still kind of up in the air...

BIFF: There's one or two other things depressing him, Happy.

HAPPY: What do you mean?

BIFF: Never mind. Just don't lay it all to me.

HAPPY: But I think if you just got started—I mean—is there any future for you out there?

BIFF: I tell ya, Hap, I don't know what the future is. I don't know—what I'm supposed to want.

HAPPY: What do you mean?

BIFF: Well, I spent six or seven years after high school trying to work myself up. Shipping clerk, salesman, business of one kind or another. And it's a measly manner of existence. To get on that subway on the hot mornings in summer. To devote your whole life to keeping stock, or making phone calls, or selling or buying. To suffer fifty weeks of the year for the sake of a two-week vacation, when all you really desire is to be outdoors, with your shirt off. And always to have to get ahead of the next fella. And still—that's how you build a future.

HAPPY: Well, you really enjoy it on a farm? Are you content out there?

BIFF (*with rising agitation*): Hap, I've had twenty or thirty different kinds of jobs since I left home before the war, and it always turns out the same. I just realized it lately. In Nebraska when I herded cattle, and the Dakotas, and Arizona, and now in Texas. It's why I came home now, I guess, because I realized it. This farm I work on, it's spring there now, see? And they've got about fifteen new colts. There's nothing more inspiring or—beautiful than the sight of a mare and a new colt. And it's cool there now, see? Texas is cool now, and it's spring. And whenever spring comes to where I am, I suddenly get the feeling, my God, I'm not gettin' anywhere! What the hell am I doing, playing around with horses, twenty-eight dollars a week! I'm thirty-four years old, I oughta be makin' my future. That's when I come running home. And now, I get here, and I don't know what to do with myself. (*After a pause.*) I've always made a point of not wasting my life, and every time I come back here I know that all I've done is to waste my life.

HAPPY: You're a poet, you know that, Biff? You're a—you're an idealist!

BIFF: No, I'm mixed up very bad. Maybe I oughta get married. Maybe I oughta get stuck into something. Maybe that's my trouble. I'm like a boy. I'm not married. I'm not in business, I just—I'm like a boy. Are you content, Hap? You're a success, aren't you? Are you content?

HAPPY: Hell, no!

BIFF: Why? You're making money, aren't you?

HAPPY (*moving about with energy, expressiveness*): All I can do now is wait for the merchandise manager to die. And suppose I get to be merchandise manager? He's a good friend of mine, and he just built a terrific estate on Long Island. And he lived there about two months and sold it, and now he's building another one. He can't enjoy it once it's finished. And I know that's just what I would do. I don't know what the hell I'm workin' for. Sometimes I sit in my apartment—all alone. And I think of the rent I'm paying. And it's crazy. But then, it's what I always wanted. My own apartment, a car, and plenty of women. And still, goddammit, I'm lonely.

BIFF (*with enthusiasm*): Listen, why don't you come out West with me?

HAPPY: You and I, heh?

BIFF: Sure, maybe we could buy a ranch. Raise cattle, use our muscles. Men built like we are should be working out in the open.

HAPPY (*avidly*): The Loman Brothers, heh?

BIFF (*with vast affection*): Sure, we'd be known all over the counties!

HAPPY (*enthralled*): That's what I dream about, Biff. Sometimes I want to just rip my clothes off in the middle of the store and outbox that goddam merchandise manager. I mean I can outbox, outrun, and outlift anybody in that store, and I have to take orders from those common, petty sons-of-bitches till I can't stand it any more.

BIFF: I'm tellin' you, kid, if you were with me I'd be happy out there.

HAPPY (*enthused*): See, Biff, everybody around me is so false that I'm constantly lowering my ideals...

BIFF: Baby, together we'd stand up for one another, we'd have someone to trust.

HAPPY: If I were around you...

BIFF: Hap, the trouble is we weren't brought up to grub for money. I don't know how to do it.

HAPPY: Neither can I!

BIFF: Then let's go!

HAPPY: The only thing is—what can you make out there?

BIFF: But look at your friend. Builds an estate and then hasn't the peace of mind to live in it.

HAPPY: Yeah, but when he walks into the store the waves part in front of him. That's fifty-two thousand dollars a year coming through the revolving door, and I got more in my pinky finger than he's got in his head.

BIFF: Yeah, but you just said...

HAPPY: I gotta show some of those pompous, self-important executives over there that Hap Loman can make the grade. I want to walk into the store the way he walks in. Then I'll go with you, Biff. We'll be together yet, I swear. But take those two we had tonight. Now weren't they gorgeous creatures?

BIFF: Yeah, yeah, most gorgeous I've had in years.

HAPPY: I get that any time I want, Biff. Whenever I feel disgusted. The only trouble is, it gets like bowling or something. I just keep knockin' them over and it doesn't mean anything. You still run around a lot?

BIFF: Naa. I'd like to find a girl—steady, somebody with substance.

HAPPY: That's what I long for.

BIFF: Go on! You'd never come home.

HAPPY: I would! Somebody with character, with resistance! Like Mom, y'know? You're gonna call me a bastard when I tell you this. That girl Charlotte I was with tonight is engaged to be married in five weeks. (*He tries on his new hat.*)

BIFF: No kiddin'!

HAPPY: Sure, the guy's in line for the vice-presidency of the store. I don't know what gets into me, maybe I just have an overdeveloped sense of competetion or something, but I went and ruined her, and furthermore I can't get rid of her. And he's the third executive I've done that to. Isn't that a crummy characteristic? And to top it all, I go to their weddings! (*Indignantly, but laughing.*) Like I'm not supposed to take bribes. Manufacturers offer me a hundred-dollar bill now and then to throw an order their way. You know how honest I am, but it's like this girl, see. I hate myself for it. Because I don't want the girl, and still, I take it and—I love it!

BIFF: Let's go to sleep.

HAPPY: I guess we didn't settle anything, heh?

BIFF: I just got one idea that I think I'm going to try.

HAPPY: What's that?

BIFF: Remember Bill Oliver?

HAPPY: Sure, Oliver is very big now. You want to work for him again?

BIFF: No, but when I quit he said something to me. He put his arm on my shoulder, and he said, "Biff, if you ever need anything, come to me."

HAPPY: I remember that. That sounds good.

BIFF: I think I'll go to see him. If I could get ten thousand or even seven or eight thousand dollars I could buy a beautiful ranch.

HAPPY: I bet he'd back you. Cause he thought highly of you, Biff. I mean, they all do. You're well liked, Biff. That's why I say to come back here, and we both have the apartment. And I'm tellin' you, Biff, any babe you want...

BIFF: No, with a ranch I could do the work I like and still be something. I just wonder though. I wonder if Oliver still thinks I stole that carton of basketballs.

HAPPY: Oh, he probably forgot that long ago. It's almost ten years. You're too sensitive. Anyway, he didn't really fire you.

BIFF: Well, I think he was going to. I think that's why I quit. I was never sure whether he knew or not. I know he thought the world of me, though. I was the only one he'd let lock up the place.

WILLY (*below*): You gonna wash the engine, Biff?

HAPPY: Shh!

Biff looks at Happy, who is gazing down, listening. Willy is mumbling in the parlor.

HAPPY: You hear that?

They listen. Willy laughs warmly.

BIFF (*growing angry*): Doesn't he know Mom can hear that?

WILLY: Don't get your sweater dirty, Biff!

A look of pain crosses Biff's face.

HAPPY: Isn't that terrible? Don't leave again, will you? You'll find a job here. You gotta stick around. I don't know what to do about him, it's getting embarrassing.

WILLY: What a simonizing job!

BIFF: Mom's hearing that!

WILLY: No kiddin', Biff, you got a date? Wonderful!

HAPPY: Go on to sleep. But talk to him in the morning, will you?

BIFF (*reluctantly getting into bed*): With her in the house. Brother!

HAPPY (*getting into bed*): I wish you'd have a good talk with him.

The light of their room begins to fade.

BIFF (*to himself in bed*): That selfish, stupid...

HAPPY: Sh... Sleep, Biff.

Their light is out. Well before they have finished speaking, Willy's form is dimly seen below in the darkened kitchen. He opens the refrigerator, searches in there, and takes out a bottle of milk. The apartment houses are fading out, and the entire house and surroundings become covered with leaves. Music insinuates itself as the leaves appear.

WILLY: Just wanna be careful with those girls, Biff, that's all. Don't make any promises. No promises of any kind. Because a girl, y'know, they always believe what you tell 'em, and you're very young, Biff, you're too young to be talking seriously to girls.

Light rises on the kitchen. Willy, talking, shuts the refrigerator door and comes downstage to the kitchen table. He pours milk into a glass. He is totally immersed in himself, smiling faintly.

WILLY: Too young entirely, Biff. You want to watch your schooling first. Then when you're all set, there'll be plenty of girls for a boy like you. (*He smiles broadly at a kitchen chair.*) That so? The girls pay for you? (*He laughs.*) Boy, you must really be makin' a hit.

Willy is gradually addressing—physically—a point offstage, speaking through the wall of the kitchen, and his voice has been rising in volume to that of a normal conversation.

WILLY: I've been wondering why you polish the car so careful. Ha! Don't leave the hubcaps, boys. Get the chamois to the hubcaps. Happy, use newspaper on the windows, it's the easiest thing. Show him how to do it Biff! You see, Happy? Pad it up, use it like a pad. That's it, that's it, good work. You're doin' all right, Hap. (*He pauses, then nods in approbation for a few seconds, then looks upward.*) Biff, first thing we gotta do when we get time is clip that big branch over the house. Afraid it's gonna fall in a storm and hit the roof. Tell you what. We get a rope and sling her around, and then we climb up there with a couple of saws and take her down. Soon as you finish the car, boys, I wanna see ya. I got a surprise for you, boys.

BIFF (*offstage*): Whatta ya got, Dad?

WILLY: No, you finish first. Never leave a job till you're finished—remember that. (*Looking toward the "big trees."*) Biff, up in Albany I saw a beautiful hammock. I think I'll buy it next trip, and we'll hang it right between those two elms. Wouldn't that be something? Just swingin' there under those branches. Boy, that would be...

Young Biff and Young Happy appear from the direction Willy was addressing. Happy carries rags and a pail of water. Biff, wearing a sweater with a block "S," carries a football.

...

The Experience of Drama

To experience a play means to see how it affects the readers/audience emotionally and what subjective responses they have.

At first glance, the title of the play *Death of a Salesman* suggests that something bad is going to happen. In fact the salesman (finally) dies for whatever reason. It immediately causes the audience to feel bad. Something must have gone wrong with the salesman and his family. Eventually it turns out that the trouble has a lot to do with (lack of) money.

In the opening scene, Willy Loman drives his car back home from work. He is a salesman and has to drive a long distance, selling products at a firm. He seems to be exhausted as success appears distant for him. For all this, he still knows his worth at the age of sixty. He has a family to take care of, especially his sons, the unsettled Biff and the cynical Happy, whom he hopes to make a rise in life one day.

Willy looks down on Biff's job on the farm as poor and degrading. "How can he find himself on a farm? Is that a life? A farmhand?" (Kirszner & Mandell 2006, 1566) In Willy's eyes, Biff could have been successful because Biff was believed to be brilliant and promising. Willy harbored a great hope on Biff.

At the scene of Biff and Happy's bedroom, they have a conversation. From their talk the audience learns that a generation gap lies between the sons and their father. The brothers disagree on what Biff should do to build a future. The gap is particularly evident between Biff and his father. Happy seems to be more confident, though his confidence seems problematic. He is sort of cynical and frivolous. He takes women from his executives and he takes bribes too. Happy appears to be a good-for-nothing man.

The scene comes back to Willy who is recalling the good old days when he was more fresh and energetic and when Biff was still an excellent football player. Willy has great ambitions for his son Biff. Based on dialogues between Willy and Linda, Linda shows herself to be a kindhearted woman and considerate wife and mother.

A generation gap also exists between Happy and Willy. Happy once promised Willy that he would earn enough money so that Willy could retire comfortably, but Willy does not believe Happy.

> HAPPY: Pop, I told you I'm gonna retire you for life.
> WILLY: You'll retire me for life on seventy goddam dollars a week? And your women and
> your car and your apartment, and you'll retire me for life! Christ's sake, I couldn't get
> past Yonkers today! Where are you guys, where are you? The woods are burning! I
> can't drive a car!
>
> (Miller, *Death of a Salesman*; Kirszner & Mandell 2006, 1580)

The generation gap comes from disagreement regarding the family's future plan, and Biff's discovery of his father's secret. Biff gets angry at his father so that he does not take his father's excuse. Linda then becomes angry with Biff, who does not show respect to his hard-working father, and Biff answers by calling his father a fake.

> HAPPY: Mom!
> LINDA: That's all you are, my baby! (*To Biff.*) And you! What happened to the love you
> had for him? You were such pals! How you used to talk to him on the phone every
> night! How lonely he was till he could come home to you!
>
> ...
>
> BIFF: Because I know he's a fake and he doesn't like anybody around who knows!
>
> (Miller, *Death of a Salesman*; Kirszner & Mandell 2006, 1589)

Planning the future causes the family members to argue with each other but finally, mutual understanding gains the upper hand and Willy's martyred spirit has moved the sons. The play has struck a responsive chord in the hearts of its readers or audience. The situation is so familiar to the readers because it contains good practical implications.

The Interpretation of Drama

Interpretation goes with the discovery of meaning or sense of a play with regard to the theme, plot, characterization, or language. From the first Act of *Death of a Salesman*, readers can understand Willy and his ambitions for himself and especially for his son Biff. Willy's thoughts and behavior suggest that he, an ordinary man, can be a hero too, even though his image is different from the traditional hero who is supposed to be noble and high-ranking. This is testified in Miller's comments that

> tragic feeling is evoked in the audience by a character who is ready to lay down his life, if need be, to secure one thing—his sense of person dignity (Last 1991, 26).

The play *Death of a Salesman* reveals the conflict between ambition and reality, and it also challenges the idea of success merely based on money or wealth. Willy's high expectation and the confusion of the sons in their future plan touch on issues of ambition and reality. In the play and in daily life, they seem often to go against each other. Willy places high hopes on his son Biff and he imagines Biff as a "Hercules."

> (*Biff enters the darkened kitchen, takes a cigarette, and leaves the house. He comes downstage into a golden pool of light. He smokes, staring at the night.*)
> WILLY: Like a young god. Hercules—something like that. And the sun, the sun all around him. Remember how he waved to me? Right up from the field, with the representatives of three colleges standing by? And the buyers I brought, and the cheers when he came out—Loman, Loman, Loman! God Almighty, he'll be great yet. A star like that, magnificent, can never really fade away!
>
> (Miller, *Death of a Salesman*; Kirszner & Mandell 2006, 1595)

However, Biff disregards his father's expectation. Biff has his own plan for the future but at the moment, in his thirties, he has not settled down yet. The situations in which Willy and Biff are involved signifies a contradiction between ambition and reality.

Whether it is planning future or Willy's hope for his sons' successes, they all imply that in modern American society, money is one sign of success. This finds good expressions in the abundant references to "money" or words about it in the dialogue between Willy and Linda, such as "sell," "five hundred gross," "seven hundred gross," "commission," "Two hundred and twelve dollars," "How much," "a hundred and eighty gross," "seventy dollars and some pennies," "sixteen dollars," "owe," and "a dollar eighty." (Kirszner & Mandell 2006, 1577) Moreover, money and wealth have become a symbol of manhood for Willy.

The setting of countryside and (farm) life in the play implies the enjoyment of nature and the good old days. Memories of the countryside suggest the characters' temporary reminiscence of the simple, free-of-fierce-competition life. For becoming successful, the countryside is not an ideal place. So, despite the ruthless competition, urban life is an inevitable choice of the characters who are in search of opportunities for success.

The Evaluation of Drama

To evaluate a play, readers consider the play's values, beliefs, and theatrical artistry.

Death of a Salesman examines American middle-class beliefs and values. These in the middle-class firmly believe in the American Dream, which is a combination of beliefs in the unity of the family, the healthiness of competition in a society, the need for success and money, and the view that America is the great land in which free opportunity for all exists (Last 1991, 6).

This belief was very popular in the 20th century and is still accepted today. Competition is part of life, and money and success have become the source of stability. Willy Loman's idea of stability and success is closely related to family. In other words, family comes first when considering the pursuit of happiness and success. That is why Willy takes great care of his sons and is ready to sacrifice for his family, especially for his children. According to Willy Loman, if the family has a stable financial situation, they will feel emotionally stable. Willy cannot make "enough" money to run the family. He regrets that he was not as courageous as his brother Ben, who went to Africa and made a fortune.

However, the (implied) author seems to challenge these ideas. In the play, Willy, a hard-working and ambitious salesman, loses his job. Biff is angry at his father's intention and endeavor to push him toward "success." These events suggest that the prevalent idea of success by Americans in pursuit of the American Dram may not be true. They should not go all out to join in the fierce competition in the consumption society of big cities. Money and wealth are not the single standard for alleged success.

The play also touches on the ethics of family. Loyalty and unity are important principles for a family. However, infidelity and betrayal have been found in a persona (the protagonist Willy). Willy loves his family so much so that he would sacrifice his life for them. He loves his wife.

> WILLY (*with great feeling*): You're the best there is, Linda, you're a pal, you know that? On the road — on the road I want to grab you sometimes and just kiss the life outa you. (Miller, *Death of a Salesman*; Kirszner & Mandell 2006, 1578)

Paradoxically, he is not loyal to his wife Linda. In the recalling scene later, a woman appears. She has a kind of special relationship with Willy. They have had an illicit love affair. Willy's excuses to Biff are that he is so lonely. Biff is unable to pardon his father and calls Willy a fake. His anger at his father's infidelity implies the values of the (implied) author who seems to maintain that mutual loyalty and fidelity are the basic principles in a strong marital relationship.

Characters' values are also shown in the dialogue. For example, Ben expresses his idea and value about the "business" competition. He seems to cherish tricky and unfair approaches in business.

> BEN (*Patting Biff's knee*): Never fight fair with a stranger, boy. You'll never get out of the jungle that way. (*Taking Linda's hand and bowing.*) It was an honor and a pleasure to meet you, Linda.
> LINDA (*withdrawing her hand coldly, frightened*): Have a nice trip.
> (Miller, *Death of a Salesman*; Kirszner & Mandell 2006, 1585)

Linda's fear and indifferent attitude toward Ben imply her disregard for Ben's values and behavior.

Besides the moral and ethical comment which involves certain values and beliefs in *Death of a Salesman*, analysis of the play's theatrical features is also necessary in view of the approach of evaluation. It touches on the elements of stage directions, lighting, music, presentation of characters' speech, time, and space.

In the stage directions of Act I, for example, a particular form of the music and light helps suggest the message of the play.

Music appears frequently in the text from stage directions at the beginning through the end of the script. Take the beginning stage directions for example.

> *A melody is heard, played upon a flute. It is small and fine, telling of grass and trees and the horizon.* (Kirszner & Mandell 2006, 1563)

The flute here means more than a tune to play in the background. It is "a representation of life in the open, a life full of hope and peace" (Last 1991, 50). Another use of the flute is when Linda and Willy have a conversation and Willy suddenly remembers something in the past.

LINDA: And Willy— if it's warm Sunday we'll drive in the country. And we'll open the windshield, and take lunch.

WILLY: No, the windshields don't open on the new cars.

LINDA: But you opened it today.

WILLY: Me? I didn't. (*He stops.*) Now isn't that peculiar! Isn't that a remarkable… (*He breaks off in amazement and fright as the flute is heard distantly.*)

LINDA: What, darling?

WILLY: That is the most remarkable thing.

LINDA: What, dear?

WILLY: I was thinking of the Chevvy. (*Slight pause.*) Nineteen twenty–eight… when I had that red Chevvy… (*Breaks off.*) That funny? I coulda sworn I was driving that Chevvy today.

LINDA: Well, that's nothing. Something must've reminded you.

WILLY: Remarkable. Ts. Remember those days? The way Biff used to simonize that car? The dealer refused to believe there was eighty thousand miles on it. (*He shakes his head.*) Heh! (*To Linda.*) Close your eyes. I'll be right up. (*He walks out of the bedroom.*)

(Miller, Death of a Salesman; Kirszner & Mandell 2006, 1567−1568)

Along with the flute, Willy begins to recall the past, those happy old days.

> The flute is particularly suited to this, as it is an instrument which can be easily-associated with nostalgia (Last 1991, 50).

The tune of the flute corresponds well to Willy's reminiscing, which is highlighted by the flashback.

Flashbacks are used in the play to demonstrate "the recurrence of memories in Willy's mind, to explain the present through events in the past" (Last, 1991, 7). For example, Willy's affair with the woman is revealed through flashbacks. In Act I, Willy is talking to Linda and Linda is praising Willy for his handsome appearance. Then, along with the music, Willy, while still talking to Linda, speaks (in his memory) to the woman and gradually Willy and the woman begin to flirt. (Kirszner & Mandell 2006, 1578—1579). Time flashes from present to past.

> The flashback is part of the explanation of Willy's behavior [and it] is [also] used to reveal Willy's conscience (Last 1991, 48).

Besides the music of flute, the device of flashback strengthens Willy's memory of the good old days when he had a good time in the countryside, in the time of booming business, and of course in the company of the other woman.

Light is another key element in theatrical artistry. In the opening part of Act I, the stage directions repeat a certain form of "light."

> We are aware of towering, angular shapes behind it, surrounding it on all sides. Only the blue light of the sky falls upon the house and forestage; the surrounding area shows an angry glow of orange. As more light appears, we see a solid vault of apartment houses around the small, fragile-seeming home. An air of the dream clings to the place, a dream rising out of reality. (Miller, *Death of a Salesman*; Kirszner & Mandell 2006, 1563)

Here "light" carries a strong sense of hope or dream, foreshadowing the aspirations and endeavors of the Lomans for a bright future. In the text, the image of light appears again and again to reinforce this sense of hope in Willy's words when he compares Biff to "Hercules," and "the sun all around him," or "A star... [that] can never really fade away" (Kirszner & Mandell 2006, 1595). The sun and star are immediately associated with bright light, shining above, signifying Willy's ardent hope for his son. At the end of Act I, the image of light appears again, highlighting Willy's strong hope for a prosperous future.

> WILLY (*staring through the window into the moonlight*): Gee, look at the moon moving between the buildings! (Miller, *Death of a Salesman*; Kirszner & Mandell 2006, 1595)

Moonlight, together with the sunlight and the light of the star, well conveys Willy's strong hope.

In *Death of a Salesman*, manipulation of time and space is another theatrical feature. Despite the traditional methods of the characters' interactions and clear plot development and the standard dramatic elements such as exposition, rising action, conflict, climax, and so forth, the insertion of Willy's stream of conscious is non-traditional. It helps the audience to perceive his mental instability and get involved in it. This mental instability suggests that Willy quite often can not distinguish past from present. At first glance, it seems that the past and present are happening at the same time on stage. However, for the benefit of the readers or audience, memories of past events are made clear from present action via stage directions.

> *Light rises on the kitchen. Willy, talking, shuts the refrigerator door and comes downstage*

to the kitchen table. He pours milk into a glass. He is totally immersed in himself, smiling faintly.

WILLY: Too young entirely, Biff. You want to watch your schooling first. Then when you're all set, there'll be plenty of girls for a boy like you. (*He smiles broadly at a kitchen chair.*) That so? The girls pay for you? (*He laughs*) Boy, you must really be makin' a hit.

Willy is gradually addressing — physically — a point offstage, speaking through the wall of the kitchen, and his voice has been rising in volume to that of a normal conversation.

WILLY: I been wondering why you polish the car so careful. Ha! Don't leave the hubcaps, boys. Get the chamois to the hubcaps. Happy, use newspaper on the windows, it's the easiest thing. Show him how to do it Biff! You see, Happy? ...

(Miller, *Death of a Salesman*; Kirszner & Mandell 2006, 1573)

In this scene (Act I), both past and present happen on the same stage but the space and boundaries of the rooms are cleverly divided. In the first stage directions quoted above, Willy's talk and movement happen in the present. In the second stage directions, Willy returns to the past via his imagination. He remembers the old days when he talked to his sons and gave them advice. Since this conversation happened in the past, Willy now has to direct his speech through the wall to a point offstage. This theatrical device helps the audience to understand that Willy is turning aside from now to the past.

Last but not the least, the portrayal of ordinary people like the Lomans in the play inevitably evokes the readers or audience to consider their own situations in life. It also indicates that "Miller is able to show that everyday people can rise above the ordinary when challenged" (Last, 1991, 7).

Questions for Reflection

Read the following excerpt and answer the questions in terms of experiencing, interpreting and evaluating.

A Doll's House (1879)

—Henrik Ibsen (1828–1906)

CHARACTERS

TORVALD HELMER, *A LAWYER*

NORA, *HIS WIFE*

DR. RANK

MRS. LINDE

NILS KROGSTAD, *A BANK CLERK*

THE HELMERS' THREE SMALL CHILDREN

ANNE-MARIE, *THEIR NURSE*

HELENE, *A MAID*

A DELIVERY BOY

The action takes place in HELMER'S residence.

Act I

A comfortable room, tastefully but not expensively furnished. A door to the right in the back wall leads to the entryway, another to the left leads to HELMER'S study. Between these doors, a piano. Midway in the left-hand wall a door, and further back a window. Near the window a round table with an armchair and a small sofa. In the right-hand wall, toward the rear a door, and nearer the foreground a porcelain stove with two armchairs and a rocking chair beside it. Between the stove and the side door, a small table. Engravings on the walls. And etagère with china figures and other small art objects; a small bookcase with richly bound books; the floor carpeted; a fire burning in the stove. It is a winter day.

A bell rings in the entryway; shortly after we hear the door being unlocked. NORA comes into the room, humming happily to herself; she is wearing street clothes and carries an armload of packages, which she puts down on the table to the right. She has left the hall door open; and through it a DELIVERY BOY is seen, holding a Christmas tree and a basket which he gives to the MAID who let them in.

NORA: Hide the tree well, Helene. The children mustn't get a glimpse of it till this evening, after it's trimmed. (*To the DELIVERY BOY, taking out her purse.*) How much?

DELIVERY BOY: Fifty, ma'am.

NORA: There's a crown. No, keep the change. (*The BOY thanks her and leaves. NORA shuts the door. She laughs softly to herself while taking off her street things. Drawing a bag of macaroons from her pocket, she eats a couple; then steals over and listens at her husband's study door.*) Yes, he's home. (*Hums again as she moves to the table, right.*)

HELMER (*from the study*): Is that my little lark twittering out there?

NORA (*busy opening some packages*): Yes, it is.

HELMER: Is that my squirrel rummaging around?

NORA: Yes!

HELMER: When did my squirrel get in?

NORA: Just now. (*Putting the macaroon bag in her pocket and wiping her mouth.*) Do come in, Torvald, and see what I've bought.

HELMER: Can't be disturbed. (*After a moment he opens the door and peers in, pen in hand.*) Bought, you say? All that there? Has the little spendthrift been out throwing money around again?

NORA: Oh, but Torvald, this year we really should let ourselves go a bit. It's the first Christmas we haven't had to economize.

HELMER: But you know we can't go squandering.

NORA: Oh yes, Torvald, we can squander a little now. Can't we? Just a tiny, wee bit. Now that you've got a big salary and are going to make piles and piles of money.

HELMER: Yes—starting New Year's. But then it's a full three months till the raise comes through.

NORA: Pooh! We can borrow that long.

HELMER: Nora! (*Goes over and playfully takes her by the ear.*) Are you scatterbrains off again? What if today I borrowed a thousand crowns, and you squandered them over Christmas week, and then on New Year's Eve a roof tile fell on my head, and I lay there—

NORA (*putting her hand on his mouth*): Oh! Don't say such things!

HELMER: Yes, but what if it happened—then what?

NORA: If anything so awful happened, then it just wouldn't matter if I had debts or not.

HELMER: Well, but the people I'd borrowed from?

NORA: Them? Who cares about them! They're strangers.

HELMER: Nora, Nora, how like a woman! No, but seriously, Nora, you know what I think about that. No debts! Never borrow! Something of freedom's lost—and something of beauty, too—from a home that's founded on borrowing and debt. We've made a brave stand up to now, the two of us; and we'll go right on like that the little while we have to.

NORA (*going toward the stove*): Yes, whatever you say, Torvald.

HELMER (*following her*): Now, now, the little lark's wings mustn't droop. Come on, don't be a sulky squirrel. (*Taking out his wallet.*) Nora, guess what I have here.

NORA (*turning quickly*): Money!

HELMER: There, see. (*Hands her some notes.*) Good grief, I know how costs go up in a house at Christmas time.

NORA: Ten—twenty—thirty—forty. Oh, thank you, Torvald; I can manage no end on this.

HELMER: You really will have to.

NORA: Oh yes, I promise I will! But come here so I can show you everything I bought. And so cheap! Look, new clothes for Ivar here—and a sword. Here a horse and a trumpet for Bob. And a doll and doll's bed here for Emmy; they're nothing much, but she'll tear them to bits in no time anyway. And here I have dress material and handkerchiefs for the maids. Old Anne-Marie really deserves something more.

HELMER: And what's in that package there?

NORA (*with a cry*): Torvald, no! You can't see that till tonight!

HELMER: I see. But tell me now, you little prodigal, what have you thought of for yourself?

NORA: For myself? Oh, I don't want anything at all.

HELMER: Of course you do. Tell me just what—within reason—you'd most like to have.

NORA: I honestly don't know. Oh, listen, Torvald—

HELMER: Well?

NORA (*fumbling at his coat buttons, without looking at him*): If you want to give me something, then maybe you could—you could—

HELMER: Come on, out with it.

NORA (*hurriedly*): You could give me money, Torvald. No more than you think you can spare, and then one of these days I'll buy something with it.

HELMER: But Nora—

NORA: Oh, please, Torvald darling, do that! I beg you, please. Then I could hang the bills in pretty gilt paper on the Christmas tree. Wouldn't that be fun?

HELMER: What are those little birds called that always fly through their fortunes?

NORA: Oh yes, spendthrifts; I know all that. But let's do as I say, Torvald; then I'll have time to decide what I really need most. That's very sensible, isn't it?

HELMER (*smiling*): Yes, very—that is, if you actually hung onto the money I give you, and you actually used it to buy yourself something. But it goes for the house and for all sorts of foolish things, and then I only have to lay out some more.

NORA: Oh, but Torvald—

HELMER: Don't deny it, my dear little Nora. (*Putting his arm around her waist.*) Spendthrifts are sweet, but they use up a frightful amount of money. It's incredible what it costs a man to feed such birds.

NORA: Oh, how can you say that! Really, I save everything I can.

HELMER (*laughing*): Yes, that's the truth. Everything you can. But that's nothing at all.

NORA (*humming, with a smile of quiet satisfaction*): Hm, if you only knew what expenses we larks and squirrels have, Torvald.

HELMER: You're an old little one. Exactly the way your father was. You're never at a loss for scaring up money; but the moment you have it, it runs right out through your fingers; you never know what you've done with it. Well, one takes you as you are. It's deep in your blood. Yes, these things are hereditary, Nora.

NORA: Ah, I could wish I'd inherited many of Papa's qualities.

HELMER: And I couldn't wish you anything but just what you are, my sweet little lark. But wait; it seems to me you have a very—what should I call it? —a very suspicious look today—

NORA: I do?

HELMER: You certainly do. Look me straight in the eye.

NORA (*looking at him*): Well?

HELMER (*shaking an admonitory finger*): Surely my sweet tooth hasn't been running riot in town today, has she?

NORA: No. Why do you imagine that?

HELMER: My sweet tooth really didn't make a little detour through the confectioner's?

NORA: No, I assure you, Torvald—

HELMER: Hasn't nibbled some pastry?

NORA: No, not at all.

HELMER: Not even munched a macaroon or two?

NORA: NO, Torvald, I assure you, really—

HELMER: There, there now. Of course I'm only joking.

NORA (*going to the table, right*): You know I could never think of going against you.

HELMER: No, I understand that; and you have given me your word. (*Going over to her.*) Well, you keep your little Christmas secrets to yourself, Nora darling. I expect they'll come to light this evening, when the tree is lit.

NORA: Did you remember to ask Dr. Rank?

HELMER: No. But there's no need for that; it's assumed he'll be dining with us. All the same, I'll ask him when he stops by here this morning. I've ordered some fine wine. Nora, you can't imagine how I'm looking forward to this evening.

NORA: So am I. And what fun for the children, Torvald!

HELMER: Ah, it's so gratifying to know that one's gotten a safe, secure job, and with a comfortable salary. It's a great satisfaction, isn't it?

NORA: Oh, it's wonderful!

HELMER: Remember last Christmas? Three whole weeks before, you shut yourself in every evening till long after midnight, making flowers for the Christmas tree, and all the other decorations to surprise us. Ugh, that was the dullest time I've ever lived through.

NORA: It wasn't at all dull for me.

HELMER (*smiling*): But the outcome was pretty sorry, Nora.

NORA: Oh, don't tease me with that again. How could I help it that the cat came in and tore everything to shreds.

HELMER: No, poor thing, you certainly couldn't. You wanted so much to please us all, and that's what counts. But it's just as well that the hard times are past.

NORA: Yes, it's really wonderful.

HELMER: Now I don't have to sit here alone, boring myself, and you don't have to tire your precious eyes and your fair little delicate hands—

NORA (*clapping her hands*): No, is it really true, Torvald, I don't have to? Oh, how wonderfully lovely to hear! (*Taking his arm.*) Now I'll tell you just how I've thought we should plan things. Right after Christmas—(*The doorbell rings.*) Oh, the bell. (*Straightening the room up a bit.*) Somebody would have to come. What a bore!

HELMER: I'm not at home to visitors, don't forget.

MAID (*from the hall doorway*): Ma'am, a lady to see you—

NORA: All right, let her come in.

MAID (*to HELMER*): And the doctor's just come too.

HELMER: Did he go right to my study?

MAID: Yes, he did.

Questions

The Experience of Drama

1. What does the title suggest?
2. What does the cast of characters suggest?
3. What do the stage directions reveal about the world of the play?
4. With the unfolding of initial incidents, what inferences can you make about the characters?
5. What do you think about the large tip that Nora gives to the delivery boy?
6. What do you know about Torvald, Nora's husband, based on their conversations?
7. What do you know about the relationship between Nora and her husband?
8. What is Torvald's general attitude toward Nora?

The Interpretation of Drama

1. What do the characters' speech and actions signify?
2. What does *A Doll's House* suggest about the marital relationship?
3. What does *A Doll's House* suggest more generally?
4. Why do the characters behave as they do?

The Evaluation of Drama

1. What are your comments on the values of the characters shown by their speech and actions?
2. What are the attitudes and personalities of Torvald and Nora?
3. What are the attitudes of the play or of the implied author?
4. How do your social and cultural perspectives influence your evaluation of the play?
5. How does gender influence your perspective on Torvald and Nora?
6. How do your experiences as a member of a family influence your evaluation of the relationship between Torvald and Nora?
7. Find the entire script of *Death of a Salesman* and read it carefully. Compare the literary and theatrical artistry of it with *A Doll's House*.

☙ Chapter 12 ❧
Elements of Drama

The elements of drama generally comprise plot, character, dialogue, staging, and theme. A discussion of these elements and others will help shed light on its features.

 ## Plot

> Great character creation is a fine thing in a drama, but the sum of all its characters is the story that they enact. Aristotle puts the plot at the head of the dramatic elements; of all these he thinks plot the most difficult and the most expressive. And he is right.
>
> —Stark Young, The Theatre
> (Kirszner & Mandell 2006, 1336)

Plot is the essential framework of a play. Plot refers to the structure of a play's action especially the arrangement of events. A plot has a structure and the structure may vary depending on the playwright and time.

> Traditional plot structure consists of an exposition, presentation of background information necessary for the development of the plot; rising action, a set of conflicts and crises; climax, the play's most decisive crisis; falling action, a follow-up that moves toward the play resolution or denouement (DiYanni 2000, 743).

Many plays do not follow the exact pattern of starting with exposition, going through the rising action, climax and falling action, and ending with a resolution or denouement. The plot of some complex plays may start with the conflict, like that of *Oedipus the King*, or the falling action after the climax ends quickly after the death of the protagonist, like in *Hamlet*.

The plot attracts the attention of the readers or audience.

> By the arrangement of incidents, a dramatist may create suspense, evoke laughter, cause anxiety, or elicit surprise (DiYanni 2000, 744).

The readers or audience are activated by the suspense and surprise as they make speculations about the events and try to figure out the possible resolution. Suspense is brought about by conflict. Conflict is the "raw material out of which plot is constructed" (Holman & Harmon 1986, 108). Conflicts are generally seen as between man vs. man, man vs. nature, man vs. self, and man vs.

society. In some plays, the conflict is explicit, like Sophocles' *Antigone*, while in some others, it is implicit, like the opening scene of *A Doll's House*.

Plot development is achieved through action, or "what characters say and do" (Kirszner & Mandell 2006, 1338) and quite often "dialogue, stage directions, and staging techniques work together to move the play's action along." (Kirszner & Mandell 2006, 1338) Stage directions refer to

> notes added to the script of a play to convey information about its performance not already explicit in the dialogue (Hartnoll & Found 2000, 478).

In English theatre, stage directions

> are all relative to the position of an actor facing the audience... and they all date from the time when the stage was raked, or sloped upwards towards the back. Thus movement towards the audience is said to be "down stage," movement away from the audience "up stage..." The simplest examples of stage directions are such singles words as "enters," "turns,"... [and] "exit" (Hartnoll & Found 2000, 478).

At the opening scene of *Death of a Salesman*, the long stage directions provide detailed information about the characters and also foreshadow what will happen.

Staging techniques usually involve the design of the performance, the projection of words, background music, the selection of props, lighting or sound, the adjustment of scenery, and the modification of performance space.

On the whole, dialogue (often in flashbacks and foreshadowing), stage directions, and staging techniques help advance the action of a play and make clear the time, place, personalities of characters, or happenings and possible results.

Questions for Reflection

1. Find the entire script of the play *Wit* (1991) by Margret Edson (1961–), read it carefully, and then answer the following questions.
   (1) In what order does the playwright put the incidents of the play?
   (2) What is the effect of this arrangement of incidents?
   (3) Where is the play's climax? How is the climax set up?
   (4) Does the play's dialogue involve summaries of past events (flashbacks) or references to events in the future (foreshadowing)? How do they advance the plot of the play?
2. How is the opening scene of *A Doll's House* related to its developing action, its concluding scene, and its themes?
3. In *A Doll's House*, how do the upcoming costume party and Nora's dance influence the development of the play's plot?

■ Character

> *A character living on stage is a union of the creative talents of the actor and the dramatist. Any argument over which of the two is more important is futile because they are completely interdependent. The actor requires the character created by the dramatist to provide the initial and vital stimulus. The dramatist requires the embodiment of the character by the actor to bring his creation to fulfillment. The result of this collaboration is the finished performance to which both the actor and the dramatist have made a unique contribution. The result can be neither Shakespeare's Macbeth nor the actor's Macbeth. It must be the actor as Shakespeare's Macbeth.*
>
> —Charles McGraw, *Acing Is Believing*, 2nd ed.
>
> (Kirszner & Mandell 2006, 1457)

The character are the center of a play. In fact, "characters are literary imitations of human beings" (DiYanni 2000, 745). They play the roles of the human being in real life. Their appearance, speech, behavior, or action all reveal a lot about themselves and most importantly about the (real) people they stand for. The characters in play embody human qualities on which the audience develop associations and make inferences with consideration to the life experiences. To know a character is to know something of the humanity. To a great extent, to understand a character lies heavily with a good knowledge of the words and deeds of the character in relation to other characters.

In some plays, like *The Glass Menagerie* (1944) by Tennessee Williams, the leading character, Tom Wingfield, also plays the role of narrator (Kirszner & Mandell 2006, 1457). He speaks directly to the audience as a character, but he introduces the background information of the play to the audience as a narrator. For most plays, there are no narrators. Characters are presented to the audience immediately via their physical appearance, behavior, speech, action and/or other characters' words. In the opening scene of Act I, *Pygmalion* (1912), the presentation of the Flower Girl Eliza Doolittle seems to be discouraging because her speech and manners are not proper and her appearance is uncomely. She speaks with a strong local accent and behaves aggressively and unforgivingly. It is hard to imagine that she will later become (or be turned into) a fair lady.

> THE FLOWER GIRL: Nah then, Freddy: look wh' y' gowin, deah.
>
> FREDDY: Sorry. (*He rushes off.*)
>
> THE FLOWER GIRL: (*picking up her scattered flowers and replacing them in the basket*):
>   There's menners f ' yer! Te-oo banches o voylets trod into the mad. (*She sits down on the plinth of the column, sorting her flowers, on the lady's right. She is not at all*

an attractive person. She is perhaps eighteen, perhaps twenty, hardly older. She wears a little sailor hat of black straw that has long been exposed to the dust and soot of London and has seldom if ever been brushed. Her hair needs washing rather badly: its mousy color can hardly be natural. She wears a shoddy black coat that reaches nearly to her knees and is shaped to her waist. She has a brown skirt with a coarse apron. Her boots are much the worse for wear. She is no doubt as clean as she can afford to be; but compared to the ladies she is very dirty. Her features are no worse than theirs; but their condition leaves something to be desired; and she needs the services of a dentist.)

THE MOTHER: How do you know that my son's name is Freddy, pray?

THE FLOWER GIRL: Ow, eez ye-ooa san, is e? Wal, fewd dan y' de-ooty bawmz a mather should, eed now bettern to spawl a pore gel's flahrzn than ran awy athaht pyin. Will ye-oo py me f' them?

The speech of characters shows much about themselves. A characters' speech can include monologue, soliloquy, and dialogue. Hamlet's famous soliloquy ("to be or not to be") highlights his hesitant personality. Romeo uses monologue (in the garden of Capulet while waiting for Juliet to appear on the balcony) to express his ardent feelings for Juliet and to shares his thoughts with the audience.

ROMEO: He jests at scars that never felt a wound.

(Enter JULIET above)

But, soft! what light through yonder window breaks?
It is the east, and Juliet is the sun.
Arise, fair sun, and kill the envious moon,
Who is already sick and pale with grief,
That thou her maid art far more fair than she:
Be not her maid, since she is envious;
Her vestal livery is but sick and green
And none but fools do wear it; cast it off.
It is my lady, O, it is my love!
O, that she knew she were!
She speaks yet she says nothing: what of that?
Her eye discourses; I will answer it.
I am too bold, 'tis not to me she speaks:
Two of the fairest stars in all the heaven,
Having some business, do entreat her eyes
To twinkle in their spheres till they return.
What if her eyes were there, they in her head?
The brightness of her cheek would shame those stars,
As daylight doth a lamp; her eyes in heaven
Would through the airy region stream so bright

That birds would sing and think it were not night.

See, how she leans her cheek upon her hand!

O, that I were a glove upon that hand,

That I might touch that cheek!

(Shakespeare, Act Ⅱ Scene One, *Romeo and Juliet*; Bate & Rasmussen 2008, 1696)

Certainly the speech of a character concerns interpretations on other characters, and it also involves the review of past events, the prediction of future happening, or the comments on the on-going events. One character may be presented from another character's perspective. For example, in the Requiem of *Death of a Salesman*, Willy's character is well displayed via the comments about him from Charlie, Linda, Biff and Happy.

CHARLEY: It was a very nice funeral.

LINDA: But where are all the people he knew? Maybe they blame him.

CHARLEY: Naa. It's a rough world, Linda. They wouldn't blame him.

LINDA: I can't understand it. At this time especially. First time in thirty-five years we were just about free and clear. He only needed a little salary. He was even finished with the dentist.

CHARLEY: No man only needs a little salary.

LINDA: I can't understand it.

BIFF: There were a lot of nice days. When he'd come home from a trip; or on Sundays, making the stoop; finishing the cellar; putting on the new porch; when he built the extra bathroom; and put up the garage. You know something, Charley, there's more of him in that front stoop than in all the sales he ever made.

CHARLEY: Yeah. He was a happy man with a batch of cement.

LINDA: He was so wonderful with his hands.

BIFF: He had the wrong dreams. All, all, wrong.

HAPPY (*almost ready to fight Biff*): Don't say that!

BIFF: He never knew who he was.

CHARLEY (*Stopping Happy's movement and reply. To Biff*): Nobody dast blame this man. You don't understand: Willy was a salesman. And for a salesman, there is no rock bottom to the life. He doesn't put a bolt to a nut, he doesn't tell you the law or give you medicine. He's man way out there in the blue, riding on a smile and a Shoeshine. And when they start not smiling back—that's an earthquake. And then you get yourself a couple of spots on your hat, and you're finished. Nobody dast blame this man. A salesman is got to dream, boy. It comes with the territory.

BIFF: Charley, the man didn't know who he was.

HAPPY (*infuriated*): Don't say that!

(Miller, *Death of a Salesman*; Kirszner & Mandell 2006, 1633−1634)

A character's language can be formal or informal depending on the situation of the drama. For example, in the opening scene of Act Ⅰ, *Pygmalion*, Eliza's regional accent and the gentlemen's Standard English are heard at the same time to shed light on the different social classes. In other words, characterization is made vivid via the application of learned, foreign, figurative words and expressions or the use of plain, slang or vernacular terms. Moreover, the language of characters suggests a certain kind of tone to convey their mood or attitude. For example, at the end of *A Doll's House*, Nora's words suggest that she appears calm but decisive while those of her husband Torvald Helmer reveal that he is emotional and disappointed. Nora sounds resolute while Torvald Helmer, desperate.

> HELMER: But to part! To part from you! No, Nora, no—I can't imagine it.
> NORA: (*going out, right*) All the more reason why I have to be.
> HELMER: Over! All over! Nora, won't you ever think about me?
> NORA: I'm sure I'll think of you often, and about the children and the house here.
>
> (Ibsen, *A Doll's House*; Kirszner & Mandell 2006, 1462)

They all have undergone some radical changes so that their tones are quite different from the beginning of the play.

Questions for Reflection

1. Find some examples from *A Doll's House* by Henrik Ibsen to show how dialogue reveals a great deal about the characters' personalities.
2. Sometimes what some characters say to or about another character can reveal more of the character to the audience than that character's own words. Find some examples from *Death of a Salesman* to illustrate this.
3. Minor characters are often flat but they still play important roles. Find a minor character from *Death of a Salesman* and discuss how the play would be different without this character.
4. Read again the following stage directions from the opening scene of *Pygmalion* and write a small essay on what is revealed about the character through the stage directions.

   She is not at all an attractive person. She is perhaps eighteen, perhaps twenty, hardly older. She wears a little sailor hat of black straw that has long been exposed to the dust and soot of London and has seldom if ever been brushed. Her hair needs washing rather badly: its mousy color can hardly be natural. She wears a shoddy black coat that reaches nearly to her knees and is shaped to her waist. She has a brown skirt with a coarse apron. Her boots are much the worse for wear. She is no doubt as clean as she can afford to be; but compared to the ladies she is very dirty. Her features are no worse than theirs; but their condition leaves something to be desired; and she needs the services of a dentist.

5. Look at the following example from Act Ⅳ Scene Three of Shakespeare's *Othello* and consider the dialogue between Desdemona (wife of Othello) and Emilia (maid to Desdemona and wife of Iago). Please illustrate how the dialogue helps reveal the characters' personalities.

   > DESDEMONA (*singing*): I called my love false love, but what said he then?
   >   Sing willow, willow, willow:
   >   If I court more women, you'll couch with more men! —

So get thee gone, goodnight. Mine eyes do itch:

Doth that bode weeping?

EMILIA: 'Tis neither here nor there.

DESDEMONA: I have heard it said so. O' these men, these men!

Dost thou in conscience think—tell me, Emilia—

That there be women do abuse their husbands

In such gross kind?

EMILIA: There be some such, no question.

DESDEMONA: Wouldst thou do such a deed for all the world?

EMILIA: Why, would not you?

DESDEMONA: No, by this heavenly light!

EMILIA: Nor I neither by this heavenly light:

I might do't as well i' the dark.

DESDEMONA: Wouldst thou do such a deed for all the world?

EMILIA: The world's a huge thing: it is a great price

For a small vice.

DESDEMONA: In troth, I think thou wouldst not.

EMILIA: In troth, I think I should; and undo't when I had done. Marry, I would not do
such a thing for a joint-ring, not for measures of lawn, nor for gowns, petticoats, nor
caps, nor any petty exhibition; but for all the whole world—why, who would not make
her husband a cuckold to make him a monarch? I should venture purgatory for't.

DESDEMONA: Beshrew me if I would do such a wrong

For the whole world.

EMILIA: Why, the wrong is but a wrong i' th' world; and having the world for your
labor, 'tis a wrong in your own world, and you might quickly make it right.

DESDEMONA: I do not think there is any such woman.

■ Staging

*In reading a play rather than witnessing it on stage, we... have to imagine what
it might look like in performance, projecting in our mind's eye an image of the
setting and the props, as well as the movements, gestures, facial expressions, and
vocal intonations of the characters ... And we—like the director, designer, and
actors—must develop our understanding of the play and our idea of the play in
performance primarily from a careful reading of the dialogue, as well as from
whatever stage directions and other information the dramatist might provide about*

the characters and the setting.

—*Carl H. Klaus, Miriam Gilbert, and Braford S. Field, Jr., Stages of Drama*
(Kirszner & Mandell 2006, 1638)

Staging refers to a vision of dramatic performance with the help of objects, sound, and music. It touches on "the spectacle a play presents in performance, its visual detail" (DiYanni 2000, 748). As an element of drama, staging includes

> the stage setting, or sets—scenery and props—as well as the costumes, lighting, sound effects, and music that bring the play to life on stage. In short, staging is everything that goes into making a written script a play (Kirszner & Mandell 2006, 1638).

Usually a play depends on stage directions to set the atmosphere for the audience. Some stage directions are long and detailed, such as those at the very beginning of Scene One of *Death of a Salesman* or *A Raisin in the Sun* (by Lorraine Hansberry in 1958). Some are fairly short and brief, such as those in Act I of Samuel Beckett's 1952 absurdist play *Waiting for Godot*, like "*A country road. A tree. Evening*" (Kirszner & Mandell 2006, 1639).

Staging gives important information about characters (about their intentions and motivations), the events, and the theme(s) of the play. Costumes give information about the time and social customs. In Act II Scene One of *A Raisin in the Sun*, Beneatha, a young African American girl who has become infatuated with African culture and deliberately wears the traditional Nigerian costume that Asagai brought for her.

> BENEATHA (*Emerging grandly from the doorway so that we can see her thoroughly robed in the costume Asagai brought*): You are looking at what a well-dressed Nigerian woman wears… Isn't that beautiful?
>
> (Hansberry 1994, 54)

The Nigerian costume corresponds well to the theme of heritage, identification among some African Americans, and Africa. It accounts for Beneatha's ultimate departure for Africa later in the play.

Costume also helps reveal the emotions of the characters. For example, when Hamlet enters for the first time, he seems to be upset and sad through his clothes which reveal his state of mind. This fact was immediately apparent to Shakespeare's audience because Hamlet is dressed in sable, which to the Elizabethans signified a melancholy nature.

Props can throw light on a play's characters and themes. The handkerchief in *Othello* was once something showing Desdemona's affection for Othello, but later became (the so-called) proof for fictitious love between Desdemona and Michael Cassio. The flowers that Eliza sells at the opening scene of Shaw's *Pygmalion* are actually the symbol of lower class, foreshowing that a Cinderella story will happen. Willy's house in *Death of a Salesman* has some implications too. It is "sparsely furnished, revealing financial status of the family" (Kirszner & Mandell 2006, 1641).

Staging includes music and sound effects too. In the stage directions of Scene Two of *A Raisin in the Sun*, the blues music highlights the African American culture in the house of the Youngers.

> *It is the following morning; a Saturday morning, and house cleaning is in progress at the Youngers … As they work, the radio is on and a Southside disk-jockey program is inappropriately filling the house with a rather exotic saxophone blues…*

> (Hansberry 1994, 54)

At the very beginning of Act I of *Death of a Salesman*, the stage directions start with the background information about music. "A melody is heard, played upon a flute. It is small and fine, telling of grass and trees and the horizon" (Kirszner & Mandell 2006, 1563). As mentioned before, the flute suggests a sense of nostalgia, which suggests Willy's inner thoughts though it is temporary ("small"). However, it is good. In other words, both the music and past are good. In *A Doll's House*, Ibsen makes good use of sound.

> He asks for music to accompany Nora's frenzied dancing as she attempts to delay Torvald's discovery of Kroonstad's letter. In his same scene Ibsen also uses sound to heighten suspense as he has Torvald open the mailbox off-stage: we hear but don't see the mailbox click open (DiYanni 2000, 748).

Staging, combined with other dramatic elements, is conducive to a comprehensive understanding of the play.

Questions for Reflection

1. In *A Raisin in the Sun*, the Youngers (the African American family) have bought a house in a white community and they are preparing the moving. Read the following stage directions of Scene Three and find out what the directions reveal about the characters.

   Scene Three

   Time: Saturday, moving day, one week later.

   Before the curtain rises, RUTH's voice, a strident, dramatic church alto, cuts through the silence.

   It is, in the darkness, a triumphant surge, a penetrating statement of expectation: "Oh, Lord, I don't feel no ways tired! Children, oh, glory hallelujah!"

   As the curtain rises we see that RUTH is alone in the living room, finishing up the family's packing. It is moving day. She is nailing crates and tying cartons. BENEATHA enters, carrying a guitar case, and watches her exuberant sister-in-law.

2. Find a script of *Hamlet* and read Act IV. In Act IV of *Hamlet*, Ophelia has gone mad and she gives flowers to the characters like Claudius (the King) and the Queen. What do her flowers signify?

3. How does the use of scenery and lighting help create imaginative settings in *Death of a Salesman*?

4. Find a script of *A Doll's House* and read the end. Answer the question below.

   HELMER (*sinks down on a chair by the door, face buried in his hands*): *Nora! Nora!*

   (*Looking about and rising.*) Empty. She's gone. (*A sudden hope leaps in him.*)

The greatest miracle—?

From below, the sound of a door slamming shut.

How does the final sound effect in the stage directions cut short Helmer's attempt as self-deluding optimism?

Theme

> *... I think that when we speak of dramatic significance we're really talking about, either openly or unknowingly, about the dilemma of living together, of living a social existence, and the conflict is endless between Man and his fellows and between his own instincts and the social necessity.*
>
> —Arthur Miller, *The Playwrights Speak*
>
> *I can't even count how many times I've heard the line, "where did the idea for this play come from?" ... Ideas emerge from plays—not the other way around... I think explanation destroys [a play] and makes it less than it is.*
>
> —Sam Shepard, *Fool for Love and Other Plays*
>
> (Kirszner & Mandell 2006, 1767)

In reading a dramatic script, readers look for a theme. Any attempt may seem unclear because opinions are diverse and the same reader may change his / her mind later. It is risky to generalize the theme of a play but a summary of the central ideas is necessary and conducive to understanding the play.

A complex play usually has more than one theme. Just as in fiction, all the elements of a dramatic work allude to its themes. In drama, it is often practicable to infer the main idea(s) that a play embodies from the plot (particularly the development of conflict) and the language of the characters (their monologue, soliloquy, and especially dialogue).

Shakespeare's *Othello*, for example, is a play that examines the true nature of the human soul.

The dominant themes of *Othello* involve the harm of racism and the detrimental effects of human vulnerability. It is the racial discrimination of the Venetians against foreigners, especially the Moors, and the flawed human nature embodied in different characters that bring about the tragic ending of the play. The play's conflicts in the plot and action (characters' words and behaviors) correspond to the themes of racial problem and human vulnerability, the root for the downfall of the protagonists. Characterization of minor figures in the play also helps highlight the themes. In *Othello*, the words and behaviors of two minor figures, Rodorigo and Emilia, play an integral part in the revelation of the play's central ideas.

There are several conflicts in the play, the conflict between Othello, the leading protagonist, and the Venetian society overwhelmed by racism, the inconspicuous conflict between Othello and his wife Desdemona, and the conflict between the heroic Othello and the domestic Othello (or Othello's inner conflict after marriage). All of these conflicts allude to the impending tragic consequences.

Othello, the hero who was victorious over the enemies in battle, is highly praised by the Duke of Venice and he is thus commissioned by the Duke as Chief General of Cyprus. Meanwhile, Desdemona, daughter of a Venetian senator Brabantio, is trying to elope with Othello because they have fallen in love with each other so sincerely and ardently. They decide to marry and live together. However, their marital union immediately incurs resistance from Desdemona's father, Brabantio, who will not tolerate their differences in race, age, and experience. It also triggers resentment from Rodorigo, a jealous suitor of Desdemona, and Iago, Othello's Ensign and a narrow-minded villain who is resentful that Othello has appointed Cassio, rather than him, as lieutenant.

The first conflict comes between Othello, a warrior of Moor nobility, and the racist white Christians in Venetian society. The objection of Brabantio and the like implies the rampant racism in Venice against the Moors.

Rodorigo shows discrimination against Othello by calling him "the thick-lips," and "an extravagant wheeling stranger" (Shakespeare, *Othello*; Bate & Rasmussen 2008, 2089; 2090).

Brabantio gets very angry with his daughter and Othello, regarding their union as "evil" and deceptive. He abuses Othello, saying "the sooty bosom/Of such a thing as thou (Shakespeare, *Othello*; Bate & Rasmussen 2008, 2093)." He condemns Othello, the Moor, as pagan and believes that the Duke and others will naturally support the racism.

> BRABANTIO:
>> ... the duke himself,
>> Or any of my brothers of the state,
>> Cannot but feel this wrong as 'twere their own;
>> For if such actions may have passage free,
>> Bond-slaves and pagans shall our statesmen be.

>>>>> (Act I Scene Two, *Othello*)

From Brabantio's words, it can be inferred that if it were not for the urgent warfare in Cyprus, Othello would be punished. This shows that racial discrimination is severe in Venice. The Duke's intervention causes Brabantio to change his mind immediately and approve the marriage between his daughter and Othello. However, he seems to accept the Duke's directions reluctantly and he still harbors a secret grudge against the marriage. This is shown in Gratiano's words. Gratiano, one of the kinsmen of Brabantio, speaks near the end of the play after Desdemona's tragic death.

> GRATIANO: Poor Desdemona! I am glad thy father's dead:
>> Thy match was mortal to him, and pure grief
>> Shore his old thread in twain: did he live now,

This sight would make him do a desperate turn,

Yea, curse his better angel from his side,

And fall to reprobation.

(Act V, Scene Two, Othello)

Gratiano announces the real cause of Brabantio's death. Brabantio was extremely annoyed by the marriage between Desdemona and Othello. Brabantio's rigid racial discrimination against the Moors reveals the prevalent prejudice on the outsiders in the Venetian society. The conflict between Othello and the white Venetian Christians is a good example of white racism against the foreigners. It is actually the conflict between social inclusion and exclusion.

Another conflict, though subtle and hidden, is perceptible in the marital relationship between Othello and his wife Desdemona.

In his heart, Othello takes marital life as a sort of bondage. He actually loves the freedom he used to enjoy before marriage. He confides this to Iago at the scene in which Othello appears for the first time and is confronted by the cursing Brabantio.

> OTHELLO: ... for know, Iago,
>
> But that I love the gentle Desdemona,
>
> I would not my unhoused free condition
>
> Put into circumscription and confine
>
> For the sea's worth.

(Act I, Scene Two, Othello)

Though possibly Othello speaks these words casually, they reveal his inner thoughts, dormant somewhere in his mind. His consideration of marital life as a sort of limitation hinders his further efforts to improve his marriage with Desdemona. Unfortunately, Othello, as well as lots of couples, does not realize the importance of working a relationship. When the idea of bondage in marriage reappears, it has negative effects on the marital relationship, foreshadowing the possible incongruity between Othello and Desdemona.

Desdemona loves Othello because of his heroic experiences, which is manifested in Othello's words.

> OTHELLO: ... these things to hear
>
> Would Desdemona seriously incline:
>
> But still the house-affairs would draw her thence:
>
> Which ever as she could with haste dispatch,
>
> She'd come again, and with a greedy ear
>
> Devour up my discourse:
>
> ...
>
> She loved me for the dangers I had pass'd,
>
> And I loved her that she did pity them.

(Act I, Scene Three, Othello)

Worship can produce love. Desdemona's admiration and love for Othello and Othello's appreciation of Desdemona's beauty and virtue were the fundamental elements for their marital union. But while their love for each other comes from mutual appreciation, the two seem to be different in their social orientation. Othello tries his best, armed with his military excellence, to get integrated into Venetian society, while Desdemona defies Venetian social customs. This subtle difference can be seen as an underlying conflict between the two characters and may account for their misfortune in family life.

Moreover, the ways of loving seem to be slightly problematic considering Othello and Desdemona in their marital life. It is possibly more proper if one of the lovers or couples could try, first of all, to understand the other and could try to love him or her in their preferred ways. Othello and Desdemona go to Cyprus and stay together happily. But they seem to remain the same as usual and they do not change their roles from enthusiastic lovers into husband and wife. They still love each other but they have not tried to consider the other's feelings. No evidence from the play suggests that they consider questions about what he/she actually cares about or likes. They get along with each other in the usual ways that are taken for granted. The dialogue between Desdemona and Othello concerning the punishment of Cassio implies that they have not been prepared well for such a conversation. Cassio is framed by Iago and Rodorigo for drinking while on duty. This is a new incidence that Desdemona and Othello meet in their new life, and new things alike will certainly occur again and again as time passes by. However, neither of them intended to understand what the other was actually thinking about. Desdemona hastens to beg Othello for leniency and she urges Othello to accept her request immediately, ignoring the fact that Othello may have his own difficulties and considerations concerning this case of Cassio. In their dialogue, he answers Desdemona curtly.

> DESDEMONA: Why, your lieutenant, Cassio. Good my lord,
>
>   …
>
>   I prithee, call him back.
> OTHELLO: Went he hence now?
> DESDEMONA: Ay, sooth; so humbled
>   That he hath left part of his grief with me,
>   To suffer with him. Good love, call him back.
> OTHELLO: Not now, sweet Desdemona; some other time.
> DESDEMONA: But shall't be shortly?
> OTHELLO: The sooner, sweet, for you.
> DESDEMONA: Shall't be to-night at supper?
> OTHELLO: No, not to-night.
> DESDEMONA: To-morrow dinner, then?
> OTHELLO: I shall not dine at home;
>   I meet the captains at the citadel.
> DESDEMONA: Why, then, to-morrow night; or Tuesday morn;

On Tuesday noon, or night; on Wednesday morn:
I prithee, name the time, but let it not
Exceed three days: in faith, he's penitent;

...

To incur a private cheque. When shall he come?
Tell me, Othello: I wonder in my soul,
What you would ask me, that I should deny,
Or stand so mammering on.

...

OTHELLO: Prithee, no more: let him come when he will;
I will deny thee nothing.
DESDEMONA: Why, this is not a boon;

...

OTHELLO: I will deny thee nothing:
Whereon, I do beseech thee, grant me this,
To leave me but a little to myself.

(Act III, Scene Three, *Othello*)

Thus misunderstanding will inevitably occur as witnessed by what happens in the play. The case of Othello and Desdemona is also an expression of human vulnerability, persisting one's old ways or being unwilling or unable to pursue mutual understanding.

The third conflict is found in Othello's heart. After Iago's divisive seductions, Othello feels confused. This inner conflict of Othello corresponds to the play's theme of human vulnerability.

At the beginning of the play Othello is a very confident man. When he first appears (in the scene in which he is going to confront the angry Brabantio and his relatives or attendants), Othello remains cool, self-contained and confident.

OTHELLO: Let him do his spite:
My services which I have done the signiory
Shall out-tongue his complaints. 'Tis yet to know—
Which, when I know that boasting is an honour,
I shall promulgate—I fetch my life and being
From men of royal siege, and my demerits
May speak unbonneted to as proud a fortune
As this that I have reach'd: ...

...

OTHELLO: Not I: I must be found:
My parts, my title and my perfect soul
Shall manifest me rightly.

...

(Act I, Scene Two, *Othello*)

Othello also has complete faith in Desdemona when they first marry and he says " My life upon her faith!" Later, he remains confident even when Iago insinuates that Desdemona may be disloyal.

> OTHELLO: ...
>> When I shall turn the business of my soul
>> To such exsufflicate and blown surmises,
>> Matching thy inference. 'Tis not to make me jealous
>> To say my wife is fair, feeds well, loves company,
>> Is free of speech, sings, plays and dances well;
>> Where virtue is, these are more virtuous:
>> Nor from mine own weak merits will I draw
>> The smallest fear or doubt of her revolt;
>> For she had eyes, and chose me.
>>
>> ...

(Act Ⅲ, Scene Three, *Othello*)

However, under Iago's constant instigation, Othello begins to become suspicious of Desdemona. He becomes gullible and his confidence fades away. He begins to doubt himself and question his choice. Inner conflict is working now.

> IAGO: ...
>> My lord, I see you're moved.
> OTHELLO:
>> No, not much moved:
>> I do not think but Desdemona's honest.
>
> ...
>
> OTHELLO:
>> And yet, how nature erring from itself—
>
> ...
>
> OTHELLO: Why did I marry? This honest creature doubtless
>> Sees and knows more, much more, than he unfolds.
>
> ...
>
> OTHELLO: ... Haply, for I am black
>> And have not those soft parts of conversation
>> That chamberers have, or for I am declined
>> Into the vale of years—yet that's not much—
>> She's gone. I am abused; and my relief
>> Must be to loathe her. O curse of marriage,
>> That we can call these delicate creatures ours,
>> And not their appetites! ...

(Act Ⅲ, Scene Three, *Othello*)

Later Othello is overwhelmed by inner conflict and he gradually loses his rationality. His racial identity, corroded by Venetian racism, seems to be the direct cause of his self-debased inclination.

Though he still demands evidence from Iago on Desdemona's infidelity, his confidence has become feeble. In Iago's words, "He is much changed." Consequently, Othello cannot contain his insanity and he murders his beloved wife before committing suicide after realizing the truth. Human weakness, when stimulated in certain circumstances, can become disastrous.

Characterization is a very important element that contributes to the theme of the play. The main character's words and actions shed light on the central idea of the theme. Minor characters may also play an important role in highlighting the theme.

Flawed human nature finds its best expressions in Iago who is greedy (for power and reputation), self-conceited, selfish, jealous, double-faced, and cruel. Iago's words and his actions are vivid examples of his moral weaknesses.

> IAGO: Despise me,
>> if I do not. Three great ones of the city,
>> In personal suit to make me his lieutenant,
>> Off-capp'd to him: and, by the faith of man,
>> I know my price, I am worth no worse a place:
>> But he; as loving his own pride and purposes,
>> Evades them, with a bombast circumstance
>> Horribly stuff'd with epithets of war;
>> Nonsuits my mediators; for, "Certes," says he,
>> "I have already chose my officer."
>> And what was he?
>> Forsooth, a great arithmetician,
>> One Michael Cassio, a Florentine,
>> A fellow almost damn'd in a fair wife;
>> That never set a squadron in the field,
>> Nor the division of a battle knows
>> More than a spinster; unless the bookish theoric,
>> Wherein the toged consuls can propose
>> As masterly as he: mere prattle, without practise,
>> Is all his soldiership. But he, sir, had the election:
>> And I, of whom his eyes had seen the proof
>> At Rhodes, at Cyprus and on other grounds
>> Christian and heathen, must be be-lee'd and calm'd
>> By debitor and creditor: this counter-caster,
>> He, in good time, must his lieutenant be,
>> And I—God bless the mark! —his Moorship's ancient.

(Act I, Scene One, Othello)

Iago flatters himself as an able man (bragging that "I know my price"). Iago becomes extremely jealous of Cassio and harbors hostility toward Othello (who did not recognize his "price") and Cassio (who seems to have taken his position). In his dialogue with Roderigo, a

Venetian gentleman who has failed to woo Desdemona, Iago speaks his mind and reveals his evil purpose for following Othello.

> RODERIGO: I would not follow him then.
> IAGO: O, sir, content you;
>> I follow him to serve my turn upon him:
>> We cannot all be masters, nor all masters
>> Cannot be truly follow'd. You shall mark
>> Many a duteous and knee-crooking knave,
>> That, doting on his own obsequious bondage,
>> Wears out his time, much like his master's ass,
>> For nought but provender, and when he's old, cashier'd:
>> Whip me such honest knaves. Others there are
>> Who, trimm'd in forms and visages of duty,
>> Keep yet their hearts attending on themselves,
>> And, throwing but shows of service on their lords,
>> Do well thrive by them,
>> And when they have lined their coats
>> Do themselves homage: these fellows have some soul;
>> And such a one do I profess myself. For, sir,
>> It is as sure as you are Roderigo,
>> Were I the Moor, I would not be Iago:
>> In following him, I follow but myself;
>> Heaven is my judge, not I for love and duty,
>> But seeming so, for my peculiar end:
>> For when my outward action doth demonstrate
>> The native act and figure of my heart
>> In compliment extern, 'tis not long after
>> But I will wear my heart upon my sleeve
>> For daws to peck at: I am not what I am.

(Act I, Scene One, Othello)

Iago loses no time to make trouble and he, together with his complice Roderigo, manages to irritate Senator Brabantio, who will not tolerate his daughter's engagement to Othello.

> RODERIGO: What a full fortune does the thicklips owe
>> If he can carry't thus!
> IAGO: Call up her father,
>> Rouse him: make after him, poison his delight,
>> Proclaim him in the streets; incense her kinsmen,
>> And, though he in a fertile climate dwell,
>> Plague him with flies: though that his joy be joy,
>> Yet throw such changes of vexation on't,

As it may lose some colour.

RODERIGO: Here is her father's house; I'll call aloud.

IAGO: Do, with like timorous accent and dire yell
    As when, by night and negligence, the fire
    Is spied in populous cities.

(Act I, Scene One, Othello)

Moreover, to meet his vicious demands, Iago goes with double-dealing, saying to Brabantio that:

Though I do hate him as I do hell-pains,
Yet, for necessity of present life,
I must show out a flag and sign of love,
Which is indeed but sign.

(Act I, Scene One, Othello)

Soon after, he stands by the side of Othello, pretending to be angry at Brabantio.

IAGO: Though in the trade of war I have slain men,
    Yet do I hold it very stuff o' the conscience
    To do no contrived murder: I lack iniquity
    Sometimes to do me service: nine or ten times
    I had thought to have yerk'd him here under the ribs.

OTHELLO: 'Tis better as it is.

IAGO: Nay, but he prated,
    And spoke such scurvy and provoking terms
    Against your honour
    That, with the little godliness I have,
    I did full hard forbear him. But, I pray you, sir,
    Are you fast married? Be assured of this,
    That the magnifico is much beloved,
    And hath in his effect a voice potential
    As double as the duke's: he will divorce you;
    Or put upon you what restraint and grievance
    The law, with all his might to enforce it on,
    Will give him cable.

(Act I, Scene Two, Othello)

Another example of Iago's duplicity is found in his interpretation of reputation and good name. Iago says to Cassio, pretending to comfort him.

IAGO: ... Reputation is an idle and most false imposition: oft got without merit, and lost
    without deserving:...

(Act II, Scene Three, Othello)

Later Iago changes his idea about fame and reputation when he speaks to Othello. At this time he is making his evil plan to frame up Desdemona and Cassio.

> IAGO: Good name in man and woman, dear my lord,
>> Is the immediate jewel of their souls:
>> Who steals my purse steals trash; 'tis something, nothing;
>> 'Twas mine, 'tis his, and has been slave to thousands:
>> But he that filches from me my good name
>> Robs me of that which not enriches him
>> And makes me poor indeed.

> (Act III, Scene Three, *Othello*)

Now Iago claims that reputation is so important, to him and to others. A third example of his duplicity is seen when he blames Othello and condemns Othello's maltreatment of Desdemona.

> IAGO: Beshrew him for it!
>> How comes this trick upon him?
>> (Act IV, Scene Two, *Ohtello*)
>> These examples cast much light on Iago's capricious and sinister personality.
>> Besides power and high status, Iago lusts for wealth. He takes advantage of Roderigo
>> and steals a lot of money from Roderigo.
> IAGO: Thus do I ever make my fool my purse:
>> For I mine own gain'd knowledge should profane,
>> If I would time expend with such a snipe.
>> But for my sport and profit...

> (Act I, Scene Three, *Othello*)

Iago plots to trap Cassio into a pit, hoping to take Cassio's place as lieutenant.

> IAGO: (*Aside*) He takes her by the palm: ay, well said, whisper: with as little a web as this will I ensnare as great a fly as Cassio. Ay, smile upon her, do; I will gyve thee in thine own courtship...

> (Act II, Scene One, *Othello*)

Iago exploits Othello's weaknesses and manages to irritate Othello with the made-up story about the illicit love affair between Desdemona and Cassio. Othello begins to fly into a rage, but Iago, with evil intentions, goes on to persuade Othello not to be angry.

> IAGO: Stand you awhile apart;
>> Confine yourself but in a patient list.
>> Whilst you were here o'erwhelmed with your grief—
>> A passion most unsuiting such a man—
>>
>> ...

> (Act IV, Scene One, *Othello*)

Iago is actually pouring oil on the flames and Othello is conflicted.

OTHELLO: Dost thou hear, Iago?
    I will be found most cunning in my patience;
    But—dost thou hear? —most bloody.

                     (Act Ⅳ, Scene One, *Othello*)

Finally when Iago finds that his secret was disclosed by Emilia, he gets desperate and brings death upon her. His cruelty is fully manifested. Iago's moral weaknesses drive him into criminal offences. They are the major and direct causes to the tragic ending of Desdemona and Othello as well as Emilia and Roderigo.

Othello reveals human nature and sheds light on the damage caused by human moral weaknesses. However, to err is human. In other words, humanity is complex and humans have the characteristics of both angels and devils. It is the human conscience that will finally overcome the weakness so that the glory of human nature will triumph. In *Othello*, the characterization of a minor figure Emilia, expresses this idea about human nature.

Emilia, deceived by her husband Iago, stole Desdemona's handkerchief. Then she lied about it to Desdemona. Emilia was a thief and liar at that moment.

EMILIA: I am glad I have found this napkin:
    This was her first remembrance from the Moor:
    My wayward husband hath a hundred times
    Woo'd me to steal it; but she so loves the token,
    For he conjured her she should ever keep it,
    That she reserves it evermore about her
    To kiss and talk to. I'll have the work ta'en out,
    And give't Iago: what he will do with it
    Heaven knows, not I;
    I nothing but to please his fantasy.

                 (Act Ⅲ, Scene Three, *Othello*)

DESDEMONA: Where should I lose that handkerchief, Emilia?
EMILIA: I know not, madam.

                 (Act Ⅲ, Scene Four, *Othello*)

Emilia does not realize that her misconduct will lead to the disaster to Othello and Desdemona. Meanwhile, Emilia seems to harbor a value totally contradictory to the ethics or morality generally accepted in the society.

DESDEMONA: Wouldst thou do such a deed for all the world?
EMILIA: Why, would not you?
DESDEMONA: No, by this heavenly light!
EMILIA: Nor I neither by this heavenly light;
    I might do't as well i' the dark.
DESDEMONA: Wouldst thou do such a deed for all the world?
EMILIA: The world's a huge thing: it is a great price.

For a small vice.

DESDEMONA: In troth, I think thou wouldst not.

EMILIA: In troth, I think I should; and undo't when I had done. Marry, I would not do such a thing for a joint-ring, nor for measures of lawn, nor for gowns, petticoats, nor caps, nor any petty exhibition; but for the whole world—why, who would not make her husband a cuckold to make him a monarch? I should venture purgatory for't.

(Act IV, Scene Three, *Othello*)

She seems to crave for fame and wealth at any price. Her words sound dangerous too. Thanks to the absence of opportunities, otherwise she would have made desperate efforts to achieve her objectives.

However, Emilia has another side that overwhelms the flawed aspects of her nature. Her conscience helps her stand up to evil, uncovering the truth and denouncing the crimes.

EMILIA: I durst, my lord, to wager she is honest,
Lay down my soul at stake: if you think other,
Remove your thought; it doth abuse your bosom.
If any wretch have put this in your head,
Let heaven requite it with the serpent's curse!
For, if she be not honest, chaste, and true,
There's no man happy; the purest of their wives
Is foul as slander.

(Act IV, Scene Two, *Othello*)

EMILIA: A halter pardon him! and hell gnaw his bones!
Why should he call her whore? who keeps her company?
What place? what time? what form? what likelihood?
The Moor's abused by some most villanous knave,
Some base notorious knave, some scurvy fellow.
O heaven, that such companions thou'ldst unfold,
And put in every honest hand a whip
To lash the rascals naked through the world
Even from the east to the west!

(Act IV, Scene Two, *Othello*)

Emilia shouts to Othello, condemning his wrong-doings and defending Desdemona.

EMILIA: Thou dost belie her, and thou art a devil.
…

EMILIA: Thou art rash as fire, to say
That she was false: O, she was heavenly true!
…

EMILIA: Do thy worst:
This deed of thine is no more worthy heaven

Than thou wast worthy her.

(Act V, Scene Two, Othello)

Emilia is killed by Iago who tries to prevent her from telling his secrets. Emilia finally sacrifices her life in her defense of the truth. She becomes a warrior.

Considering the characterization of the play, Emilia, despite being a minor figure, is also a round character because she has more than one dimension in *Othello*.

On the whole, the plot design (the description of different conflicts) and characterization (the depiction of major and minor characters) correspond well to the themes of the play.

Questions for Reflection

1. Find the entire script of *A Doll's House* and read it carefully. Identify the major conflicts in the play and decide how these conflicts reveal the play's themes.

2. Find the entire script of *Death of a Salesman* and read it carefully. Identify some examples of dialogue that reveal the play's themes regarding the validity of American Dream.

3. Review some of your favorite dramatic works and find examples to illustrate how the development of the central characters convey the themes of the works.

References

Ahearn, Barry. *William Carlos Williams and Alterity: The Early Poetry* [M]. Cambridge: Cambridge University Press, 1988.

Bate, Jonathan & Rasmussen, Eric. *William Shakespeare: Complete Works* [M]. Beijing: Foreign Language Teaching and Research Press, 2008.

Charters, Ann. *The Short Story and Its Writer—An Introduction to Short Fiction* [M]. 5th ed. Boston: Bedford/St. Martin's, USA, 1999.

DiYanni, Robert. *Literature: Reading Fiction, Poetry, and Drama* [M]. Boston: McGraw-Hill Companies, Inc., 2000.

Hansberry, Lorraine. *A Raisin in the Sun* [M]. New York: Knopf Publishing Group, 1994.

Hartnoll, Phyllis & Found, Peter. *Oxford Dictionary of Theatre* [M]. Shanghai: Shanghai Foreign Language Education Press, 2000.

Holman, C. Hugh & Harmon, William. *A Handbook to Literature* [M]. 5th ed. New York: Macmillan Publishing Company, 1986.

Hurston, Zora Neale. *Their Eyes Were Watching God* [M]. New York: Harper Perennial: a Division of Harper Collins Publishers, Inc., 1990.

Kirszner, Laurie G. & Mandell, Stephen R. *Literature: Reading, Reaction, Writing* [M]. 3rd ed. Florida: Harcourt Brace College Publishers, 1997.

Kirszner, Laurie & Mandell, Stephen R. *Literature: Reading, Reacting, Writing (Fiction)* [M]. 5th ed. Beijing: Beijing University Press, 2006.

Kirszner, Laurie & Mandell, Stephen R. *Literature: Reading, Reacting, Writing (Poetry)* [M]. 5th ed. Beijing: Beijing University Press, July, 2006.

Kirszner, Laurie & Mandell, Stephen R. *Literature: Reading, Reacting, Writing (Drama & Writing about Literature)* [M]. 5th ed. Beijing: Beijing University Press, 2006.

Kusch, Celena. *Literary Analysis: The Basics* [M]. London and New York: Routledge Taylor & Francis Group, 2016.

Last, Brian W. *York Notes on Arthur Miller's Death of a Salesman* [M]. Beijing: Longman York Press, World Publishing Corporation, 1991.

Liu, Jianbo. *An Introduction to Literature* [M]. Beijing: Higher Education Press, 2009.

Mason, Bobbie Ann. "On Tim O'Brien's 'The Things They Carried'" // Charters, Ann. *The Short Story and Its Writer —An Introduction to Short Fiction* [M]. 5th ed. Boston: Bedford/St. Martin's, USA, 1994:826-831.

Merriam-Webster's Collegiate Dictionary [CD]. Massachusetts: Merriam-Webster, Incorporated, 2000.

Morrison, Toni. *The Bluest Eye* [M]. New York: Penguin Books USA Inc., 1994.

OED (Oxford English Dictionary) [CD]. 2nd ed. Oxford: Oxford University Press, 2009.

Stecker, Robert. *Revue Internationale de Philosophie* [J]. L'ESTHÉTIQUE /AESTHETICS, 1996, 198 (4):681−694.

Strachan, John & Terry, Richard. *Poetry* [M]. Shanghai: Shanghai Foreign Language Education Press, 2000.

Walker, Alice. "Everyday Use for Your Grandmamma". //*In Love & Trouble* [M]. Florida: Harcourt Brace & Company, 1973:47−59.

Zhang, Hanxi. *Advanced English* (Ⅰ) [M]. Beijing: Beijing Foreign Language Teaching and Research Press, 1995.

刘守兰(Liu, Shoulan).英美名诗解读[M].上海:上海外语教育出版社,2003.

后　记

　　目前，国内已出版不少关于英美文学研究或作品选读的著作和教材，但专门系统介绍研究方法的并不多见。本教材旨在为初涉文学研究的学习者介绍一些基本的研究方法，为其更深入的分析研究奠定良好的基础。

　　解读文学作品的方法很多，学者们曾从不同层面、不用角度对文学阅读的方法进行了归纳、分析和概括。但对于初涉文学研究的学习者来说，最根本的方法还应该建立在对文本的阅读之上，即所谓的文本细读方法。研读时的所感、所思均应从文本中找到佐证。任何不以文本为中心的解读只能成为"关于作品的解读"而不是"作品（本身）的解读"。本教材提倡在文本细读的基础上，尝试对作品进行"体验""阐释"和"评价"，结合文学的基本要素对作品进行研究分析。

　　鉴于本教材以"方法"为主，在选用文学作品之时仍然以英美文学名篇为主，所选作品的语言和内容较具代表性，有的还具有较强的时代感，且难易适中。书中所选作品主要出自柯斯兹纳和芒代尔编写的著作《文学：阅读、反应、写作》（小说卷）、（诗歌卷）和（戏剧卷）（第五版）［Kirszner, Laurie & Stephen Mandell. *Literature*：*Reading*, *Reacting*, *Writing*（Fiction），（Poetry）and（Drama）［M］. 5th ed. Beijing：Beijing University Press, 2006.］和罗伯特·狄亚尼的《文学：小说、诗歌、剧本的研读》（缩印本）［DiYanni, Robert. *Literature*：*Reading Fiction*, *Poetry*, *and Drama*［M］. Compact Edition. Boston：McGraw-Hill Companies, Inc., 2000.］一书，同时，这些著作中的思考练习题也为本教材编写各部分的练习题提供了较好的参考和思路。

　　本教材的编写参考并引用了不同作者的文献或作品，在此谨向原作者表示感谢。成稿之余，还要特别感谢重庆大学出版社领导的鼓励和支持！感谢云南大学外籍教师 Samuel Jacobson，Christa Lee 和 Taylor Martin Carlson 对书稿的审阅！

骆　洪

2017 年 10 月 21 日